The Mechanic Gets His Girl

JANE POLLER

This book is dedicated to John and Julie. You welcomed us into your home for months without batting an eye. Without that space and time spent with you, this book wouldn't have happened. Words can never express how grateful we are for your friendship.

Vinci Books

vinci-books.com

Published by Vinci Books Ltd in 2026

Copyright © Jane Poller 2023

The author has asserted their moral right to be identified as the author of this work in accordance with the Copyright, Designs and Patents Act 1988. This work is a work of fiction. Names, characters, places and incidents are the product of the author's imagination or are used fictitiously. Any resemblance to actual persons, living or dead, places and incidents is entirely coincidental.

All rights reserved. No part of this publication may be copied, reproduced, distributed, stored in any retrieval system, or transmitted in any form or by any means, including photocopying, recording, or other electronic or mechanical methods, nor used as a source for any form of machine learning including AI datasets, without the prior written permission of the publisher.

The publisher and the author have made every effort to obtain permissions for any third party material used in this book and to comply with copyright law. Any queries in this respect should be brought to the attention of the publisher and any omissions will be corrected in future editions.

A CIP catalogue record for this book is available from the British Library.

Paperback ISBN: 9781036707972

By Jane Poller

Crimson Creek

The Soldier Gets His Girl
The Sheriff Gets His Girl
The Songwriter Gets His Girl
The Surgeon Gets His Girl
The Mechanic Gets His Girl
The Ranger Gets His Girl
The Cowboy Gets His Girl
The Convict Gets His Girl

Chapter One

"I don't care what you say. He's my other half, Dad, and I love him." Wendy crossed her arms and cocked a hip.

"No, he's not. He's an Army grunt. A private. You're both too young and naive."

She felt her cheeks burn. "No, we're not. I'm nearly thirty, or have you forgotten?"

"And he's what, twenty?"

She rolled her eyes and flipped her thick auburn curls over her shoulder. "It doesn't matter, Dad. We're getting married tomorrow, whether you like it or not. We want this done before the deployment."

Her dad's stance widened, his arms crossed and eyes glaring. "Why? Why the rush? Are you pregnant? Did that jackass—"

"No!" Wendy cried, her jaw going slack. "I'm not pregnant, Dad. Ugh, can't you just trust me for once?"

"It's not you I don't trust, Tink. It's him. This *boy* that I've only met once. How long have you been dating anyway? Did you know he came up to me on base right after you brought him home for Christmas?"

She winced. "No, what did he say?"

Dad's eyes narrowed. "It was what he didn't say. He's a brown noser. He wants in with the higher ups."

She rolled her eyes. "Oh my God, he does not."

Dad held his arms out. "He was acting fishy. All I'm saying is take some more time to get to know him. How well do you actually know him, Tink?"

She shrugged and rubbed her forehead with a sigh, trying to ignore the annoying nickname. "Well, enough. Look, I stopped by as a courtesy and to invite you to the courthouse tomorrow. Whether you're there or not, I'll be getting married."

Before her dad could say anything else, she turned on her heel and slammed the front door behind her. The snow crunched beneath her boots, but the cold air felt good on her too hot cheeks.

She wrenched open the door of her little blue car and slammed it too, pushing the button to start twice before it fired to life. It would feel so nice to spin her tires and throw ice up on her dad's pristine truck in the driveway.

But she was more level-headed than that. Her car couldn't handle the snow as it was and peeling out wouldn't help anything. She slowly eased forward as the phone rang.

"Hello?"

"How'd it go?" Mike asked on the other line. She gripped the steering wheel tighter and growled.

"Ugh, he wouldn't listen. I told you he wouldn't." Tears of frustration threatened to fall, and she narrowed her eyes to deny them.

"Hey, you had to try. I appreciate it."

The silence was awkward as she debated telling him about her fears and nerves, but then he continued.

"Uh, look, I have to work late tonight, and it's bad luck to see the bride before the wedding anyway."

She bit her nail, butterflies filling her stomach about the importance of tomorrow. "Alright, I'll see you at the courthouse at ten, okay?"

"Yeah, okay. See you then."

"Love you." She rushed the words, but he'd already hung up. It certainly hadn't helped her nerves that he hadn't said it back. Ever. Was she rushing into this? They'd only been dating since Thanksgiving. He'd just met her dad at Christmas, which had been a nightmare.

But it would all work out in the end. It had to.

When she finally made it to work at the Mansion, she was only four minutes late, but the weather had steadily gotten worse. She elbowed her way through the wide front door and stomped her boots on the rug.

"You're late, and we need to talk." The owner of the up-and-coming bed and breakfast in Golden, Colorado, stood at the bottom of the grand staircase with his arms crossed.

Teeth chattering, she started to take her coat off, but Walter just sighed dramatically and waved.

"No, leave it on. It'll only drag this out. Look, remember the Sandusky wedding two weeks ago?"

She felt the color drain from her cheeks as she froze and turned her head, hands still on her zipper. The knot in her throat felt as big as a golf ball. She couldn't even swallow past it.

"Clearly you remember, or you wouldn't look like you'd seen a ghost. When were you going to tell me you assaulted the groom?"

Her mouth opened and closed, but no sound came out. Her boss sighed and shoved his hands into his slacks.

"Listen, they've agreed not to press charges in exchange for your termination. So, I'm going to have to let you go."

Her jaw dropped. "Not press charges? Not press charges!" Her voice rose and she bounded the few steps over to him, tipped her jaw up, and waved a finger under his chin.

"I should press charges against him! All I did was act in self-defense."

Walter just raised a brow and stared down at her. "What happened?"

She blushed and looked away. "He—I—well, he requested extra towels, so I brought them up like normal. Then he wouldn't let me leave and—"

Her boss' sigh brought her back into the moment. "And you didn't tell anyone? You punched the groom on the day of his wedding."

"And he deserved it."

"Definitely, but why the secrecy? None of the other staff knew of it. I didn't know. We all thought the groom just got into some trouble the night before his wedding."

Her throat started to close up, so she clenched her jaw tight as she continued. "He got married and the problem went away."

"Apparently not. They're back from their honeymoon, and the bride was upset that her groom had a black eye by the end of the wedding night. She's blaming you for almost ruining the pictures and her wedding."

She waved her arms to the roof. "He tried to kiss me! He blocked me from leaving the room. Who knows what he would've done if I hadn't kicked the shit out of him. How the hell is she blaming me?"

Walter smiled sadly. "You know how these rich guys operate. He probably told her you were coming onto him. Look, I don't pretend to know what happened, and it doesn't really matter at this point."

She grabbed her head and shrieked, "Doesn't matter? My almost rape doesn't matter?"

"You didn't file a police report, did you? You didn't even tell me about it, so we could've taken action. Listen, I'd love to tell him to shove it, but there's nothing I can do. We're backed into a financial and legal corner. We can't afford any legal fees. I'm sorry, Wendy, but what's done is done. Here."

He handed her a manila envelope, but she didn't have the strength to open it.

"It's a month's pay and a letter of recommendation. Put me down as a reference for your next job. I'm so sorry about this."

She frowned and nodded once, choking out. "Fine."

For the second time in two hours, she stormed out and slammed the door. By the time she got back into her car, the fight was gone. She'd never been fired before. Top of her class in culinary school, photography program, and college, she'd always been the best of the best.

She drove back to her little studio apartment on the edge of town in a daze. When she trudged up the stairs, all she could do was stare at the note on the door.

With a shaking hand, she tore it off, unlocked her front door, and wiped a tear away as she stepped inside. One week or eviction. She took a deep breath, kicked the front door shut, and made a beeline to the fridge.

It didn't matter now. Mike was deploying next week, but they were getting married tomorrow. He would move in with her and share rent. Then she'd find another job.

She stared at the empty refrigerator. Some chef she was.

She didn't even have groceries in her own apartment. Nothing but half a bottle of wine, almost empty sour cream, and one lone, sad egg.

A reflection of her life, really. She was just a sad egg in a sea of big, scary chickens.

She took out a bottle of red wine, started a bubble bath, and drank straight from the bottle. Twas the night before her wedding, and she was alone. No bridesmaids. No fancy wedding dress.

She snorted and shook her head. Christmas joy, peace, and good will were over. It was cold, dreary January in Colorado, and she was drinking wine in the bath.

And that was dandy. After the Sandusky affair, she didn't want anything to do with weddings, even her own, which is why she'd been overjoyed when Mike had proposed on New Year's. A quick, courthouse wedding was just what she preferred.

But it was rather lonely. She didn't have her best friend or anything with her. Maryanne lived in Texas and was living her best life while Wendy… well, she was now a jobless, almost homeless, train wreck just trying to survive until the next paycheck. What else could go wrong?

Chapter Two

As she walked past the frosted windows of her apartment building on her wedding day making a checklist in her head, ice crystals clung to the glass like delicate lace.

Her friend, Maryanne, had entrusted her dress to Wendy almost two years ago, making it her precious 'something borrowed' for this special day. Her mother's pearl necklace glimmered with old-world elegance around her neck, reminding her that even though none of her friends were coming and not even her dad, she wasn't alone. Her mom's presence was comforting, even if today made her miss her more.

Her new snow boots kept her feet warm in the frigid weather, their deep blue color a pop of vibrancy against the white snow outside and matching her fleece-lined tights under the dress.

The world was still and hushed as she got into her car, as if holding its breath in anticipation of her walk down the aisle. Even the snow had stopped falling, frozen in time as a backdrop for this momentous occasion. With a deep breath, she set off towards her future, ready to embrace all that lay ahead, no matter how scary it was.

As she drove to the courthouse, she chewed a nail, her stomach in knots. No matter how nervous she was to start this new life with someone she barely knew, it was going to be fine. A whirlwind romance is what her parents had had, and they'd been married for thirty years before her mom had died.

This was going to work. It was a new day, a new start, a new love, and exactly what her soul needed. Tomorrow Mike would move out of the barracks and in with her. They'd be in a honeymoon cocoon for the weekend, then she'd find a new job next week when he deployed.

All of that was just background noise to the big freak out in her mind though, because tonight was her wedding night. It was finally going to happen. Honestly, that was the part that had her the most nervous.

She parked the car and picked up the hem of her dress, hoping to not get it wet with the snow. It was a slippery walk, but she finally made it inside with fifteen minutes to spare.

Mike would appreciate that. Like her dad and all Army guys, being early meant you were actually on time and being on time meant you were late.

She waited in the foyer on a bench and texted Mike. Ten minutes later, she had almost bitten off all her nails and her leg bounced from nerves. Where was he?

At exactly ten o'clock, boots stopped in front of her, and she looked up.

"Dad? You made it." Relief flooded her body, and her shoulders sank as she stood to face him, throwing her arms around him. He hugged her tighter than normal and when she pulled back, his frown was different too.

He was worried.

The smile slowly slid off her face, her anxiety growing. He shook his head and gingerly held her shoulders. "Wen, he's not going to make it."

She frowned. "What do you mean?"

Her dad ran his hand through his hair and glanced away. "I—I might have gone to the barracks to talk some sense into him this morning. But their unit deployed at midnight. He's halfway across the world now. I'm sorry, Wen."

She frowned and shook her head, glancing at her phone.

"His phone is probably disabled by now. Data roaming overseas. Also…"

She looked at him, but he wouldn't meet her eyes. "There was a note for you. I didn't read it."

With a shaky hand, she reached out and took it, saying softly, "Thanks, Dad."

They'd gotten into a big fight a few years ago about him reading her mail, which is why she'd moved out and into her own place. She opened the letter.

Wendy,
This isn't going to work out. The timing of our deployment is a sign. It's not meant to be. I thought your dad could get me out of it. He could pull some strings for his new son-in-law. But we ran out of time. I should've told you yesterday when they moved the date up, but I didn't know how to face you.
It's too late now. Too late for us. Too late for me. But you're free now to find someone who can love you the way you love me. You dodged a bullet with me. Now I'm going to go do the same.
Mike

Her vision swam, and she jerked her head up, her eyes narrowing. "You didn't read this?"

He shook his head, so she just shoved the note in his face. "Did he talk to you? Did you talk to him?"

Dad just shook his head again and frowned. "No, he was already gone. I thought they were leaving next week. But they don't just decide these things. It takes time to plan troop movements, you know that."

"I know." She looked down at the note, now crumpled in her hand.

Dad's voice softened. "He should have told you when he found out about the deployment date change."

"I *know*, Dad. I just don't understand—"

Dad snorted. "He's a grunt without a lick of sense. This is why you should never date a military man. They're not worthy—"

She laughed bitterly. "Worthy? Dad."

He pulled her into a hug, and she snuggled into his chest with a sniffle. The pine aftershave nearly smothered her, but for just this moment, she felt like he could fix everything.

He was Dad. He was her hero and could fix all of it. She had no idea how—she knew he had no control over deployments—but she also knew she couldn't tell him any of the rest.

He couldn't read the note that Mike was using her to get to her dad. He couldn't know about being fired, about the eviction. He would insist she move in with him, and she just couldn't do that anymore. Not after losing Mom.

Plus, he'd be so disappointed. No, he could never know.

"Come on, Lovie, just a little farther. You can do it." Wendy leaned forward in her seat and gripped the steering wheel, willing her car to keep going. She was literally half an hour away from Maryanne's little hometown in Crimson Creek, Texas.

She'd packed up her apartment the day of the failed wedding. The next day, she'd dropped most of her furniture and things off in her dad's garage while he was at work, then took him to dinner.

"You're not going to Texas. What the hell, Wendy?" He'd nearly shouted in the restaurant.

This was exactly why she'd chosen the restaurant to have this conversation. She'd leaned forward and raised her brows. "Dad, we're in public. Remember the rule."

He'd nearly snapped his jaw closed while she'd continued. "Look, I just need a breather, and my lease was up anyway, since I was getting married. I've already moved my stuff out. I'll go visit Maryanne and if I decide to stay, cool. If not, I'll be back in a month."

"Wendy." He'd tried using the dad voice on her, but she'd just frowned and narrowed her eyes right back.

"Dad."

It was an epic staring contest, but of course she won. She'd stayed the night at her dad's house, unable to sleep with all the memories of her mom pressing in on her. So here she was on the tail end of her twelve-hour drive, tired, cranky, and hungry. It was a dark, freezing drizzle of rain, and her car had been making a weird noise since Amarillo.

The clunking finally stopped. Unfortunately, so did her car. The whole thing just lost power. She put it in neutral and rolled to a stop on the little four lane highway's wide shoulder.

She pulled out her phone and called the only person she knew could help.

"Maryanne?"

"Hey girl, where ya at? I expected you to be here by now."

Wendy sighed and leaned back in the seat. "I know, but I've hit a problem."

"Another one?"

"Yeah, yeah. I know my life is a shit show. Why don't we add broken down on the side of the road to the list that is the crap shoot of my life?"

Maryanne gasped. "What? No way."

"I swear, I couldn't make this stuff up if I tried. Do you know any tow trucks? GPS shows I'm twenty-three miles from your house."

"Yeah, of course. Where are you? Send me a dropped pin of your location, and I'll send someone to get you. The tow truck can drop you off at my house on the way back to the shop."

Wendy flicked on the hazard lights and waited, singing songs to distract herself from the epic failure of her life. Slowly, the heat began to dissipate as the rain began to beat down more heavily.

She pulled out her phone, thankful for the full battery, and opened her email. If she couldn't reach Mike by phone, she'd find his email. It wasn't hard. Army email addresses were all the same, like her dad's.

Mike,

You jackass. You didn't have the courage to break my heart in person? Instead, you leave me at the altar with nothing more than a note. You knew my dad would find it, right? You better be glad he didn't read it, or your ass would be in some heavy trouble over there. He might not

have gotten you out of deployment, but he sure as hell can make your life miserable even in the sand box.
Just tell me the truth. Did you ever love me or was all that bullshit just because you wanted to get close to my dad? Just because you're an ass who joined the military, knowing they deployed, and then regretted it and tried to get out of it? For fuck's sake, just tell me the truth.
Mac

When she hit send, her fingers were shaking. She'd thought the nickname adorable, but she should've realized it wasn't. No, he probably did it for the same reason all the kids in high school had done it; to poke fun of her being Macdonald's daughter.

She'd never been able to get out from under her dad's shadow.

Until now. Until Texas. No one knew her here. She could be whoever she wanted to be. Hell, she could even flirt and maybe finally get laid.

The bitter taste of betrayal on her tongue was salty. But if she was simply a means to an end for Mike, she was damn glad she'd never given it up for him. The most they'd ever done was kiss and some fondling.

She'd wanted more. But just like her previous, all too brief, relationships, it'd just been awkward. She still didn't know what to say or how to tell a guy what she wanted.

She punched the steering wheel. If only she knew how to flirt. That had to be the key to it all. It was like making a cake. If you didn't whip the eggs just right, then the whole thing fell flat.

She googled, yet again, how to flirt. Halfway through the article, the tow truck pulled up in front of her. She slipped her phone in her purse and shoved it into her jacket before zipping it up. Now she was ready to face the world.

Chapter Three

Jake finished the dishes at his mom's house while she chatted about some church event or another, but he only listened with half an ear. He was bone tired from the twenty-four hours of travel time to get stateside. His bed was calling his name.

"I just can't believe you surprised me this time. I thought you weren't coming home for another two weeks!"

Mom was sitting at the kitchen table, nursing a decaf coffee, while Dad watched Thursday night football in the living room. It was good to be home, to see the normalness of it all.

He wiped his hands on the towel and closed the dishwasher. "I wanted to surprise you, and I didn't want some kind of big welcome home party either. It's just R and R, Mom."

"But we need to celebrate your return."

"I'll only be here two weeks, then I'm going back for the last four months. You can plan something when I get home." He walked to the kitchen table and sat beside her.

"That's not much time. I need to shift the schedule up two weeks so we can—"

"Mom, can't we just wing it for once? This isn't my first deployment, and it won't be my last."

"We didn't know Andy's last would be his *last* either, now did we. Anything can happen while you're over there. Is it too much to ask to spend time with you, celebrate what a hero you are with our friends, the church, the community?"

He snorted. He wasn't some hero. He was just doing his job, and an Army mechanic wasn't that glorious. Of course, Mom still refused to see that, even after all these years.

"It's not too much to ask, Mom, but right now, I just want to sleep. I don't want to deal with people or parties. Just sleep. Maybe see my nieces and nephews, work at the shop and feel normal. Once I catch up on sleep, maybe we can have a family bonfire or something, okay?"

"Suzie, let the boy get some rest. He'll be a new man after a good night's sleep." Dad's gruff voice echoed over the TV, making Jake grin.

Mom smiled and shook her head, her blue eyes almost the same as his own. The tiny crow's feet near her eyes were new. She looked more tired than before he'd left.

"Fine, but this isn't over. Now, are you going to see Patty while you're here?"

His phone buzzed in his pocket. The group WhatsApp for the shop had a tow request. "Oh, look at that. Saved by the bell. A poor, old woman is stranded out near Decatur. I'm going to go tow her back to town then get some sleep."

"Jake! You can't run out into the rain, in the dark, on the night you get back! You *just said* you were tired."

He grinned as he stood and grabbed his Carhartt jacket from the peg by the door. "I also said I wanted to get back to work at the shop. And I'd rather tow some woman into town than think about all the paperwork I have to go through from the past few months. I love you, Mama. I'll see you tomorrow, okay?"

He leaned down and kissed her cheek, but she jumped up and raced for the door. He was afraid she was going to block him, but instead she just shoved his dad's gloves and toboggan at him.

"If you're going to be bullheaded about it, at least stay warm and dry. You can return them tomorrow."

"Thanks, Mom." He slipped the hat on, then patted his dad's shoulder on his way out the door.

"Bye, son," his dad said. The best thing about his dad? He was the exact opposite of his mom. He was laid back and just let him live his life. He'd never tried to interfere or anything.

It'd only been a few hours, and Mom was already suffocating him. Patty? Really? Hadn't he made it clear before he left that they were through?

He started up his truck and drove the five minutes to the shop. Then he jumped into the tow truck and waited for it to warm. He sent some texts to the group, reassuring them he could handle it—they knew how exhausting traveling was—but he insisted.

He needed to feel normal right now. To slip back into real life and try to forget the past eight months.

Even the dark and dreary night was a welcome reprieve from the cold, arid mountains of Afghanistan. Plus, he was too antsy to go to sleep right now, regardless of how tired he was. Memories of every storm, every wrecked or blown-up vehicle that came into the shop on base flew through his head as he drove.

The hazard lights of the broken-down car came into

The Mechanic Gets His Girl

view, and he slowed before pulling over and backing up. He parked, flipped the switch to lower the bed of the truck, and hopped out, leaving the truck running.

A woman stepped out of the driver's side of the car and waved. Her thick, black jacket with the hood up obstructed her face. She was a tiny thing, her jacket falling to her knees and her blue boots almost that high.

"Hello! Thank God you're here. Did Maryanne send you?"

Jake hooked up the chains without looking at her. "I don't know who called it in. I just know you need to be towed back to Crimson Creek. Are you talking about Maryanne Williams?"

"Yes, she said you could drop me off there on our way back into town?"

"Yes, ma'am, I can do that. Hop into the truck before you get too wet. It's starting to come down harder."

"Oh, thank you!"

The old woman was spry on her feet, he'd give her that. She practically bolted for the truck's passenger side. He got the chains hooked up and hit the button to retract the car onto the flatbed.

The tow truck lurched forward, the wheels slowly spinning on the wet ground, and a high-pitched squeal pierced the air. Jake dropped the controls and bolted toward the front of the truck. He reached out and grabbed the open driver's door, desperately reaching for the parking brake.

Rain poured down the neck of his jacket, soaking his back. With one hand still gripping the door, he reached in with the other and pulled up the parking brake. The woman scrambled over the bench seat to the passenger side, her muddy boots leaving a mess.

"What the hell?" he cursed under his breath as he took a

moment to process as she turned to sit on the seat, but he paid her no attention. He quickly scanned the interior of the truck, making sure nothing else was out of place and searching for any other damage or malfunction.

"Oh, I'm so sorry. I think I kicked the parking brake," the woman said, sitting on the passenger seat and turning to face him. The interior lights cast a warm glow against the pouring rain outside.

He opened his mouth to give her a piece of his mind, but the words died on his tongue. Instead, what came out was a garbled mess of disbelief.

"You're not an old lady," he finally managed to say, his eyes widening in surprise at the young, gorgeous woman sitting before him.

Her hood was thrown back, revealing dark, curly, wet hair plastered to her cheeks. Freckles stood out against pale skin. Deep, big green eyes stared at him owlishly, blinking as she settled her legs away from the stick shift and back to the passenger side floorboard where it belonged.

"I'm so sorry! I don't know what happened. I climbed in on the driver's side, thinking it'd be quicker. Then I reached for the heater as I was climbing over to the passenger side and slipped on the leather seats. I was so cold and—did you say I wasn't old? Um, thank you? I think? I'm going to be thirty in March. I might not be pretty, but at least I'm not old yet."

She gave a nervous little laugh, then bit her thumb. She seemed to realize they were still cold because she then raised them to the heater and watched him warily. Was she waiting for him to pounce? To yell?

Oh yeah, he *was* going to yell. "I—it's okay. The parking brake should've been on the whole time, but maybe you kicked it, or I simply forgot. As for the heater, it's as hot as it'll go. Combined with your hotness, it should be hot as lava in just a minute."

What the hell was he doing? He felt heat rise from his toes, and he forgot the wet, cold water rolling down the nape of his neck.

"Oh! Um, thanks again?" Her pale cheeks turned pink, and she turned to fiddle with the heat vents.

"Don't touch anything else, though, okay?"

"Yeah, okay, I'll be good."

He sucked in a breath of cold, rainy air at the comment. Was she—no, surely not. He shut the door and grabbed the controls to start pulling the car onto the truck's bed again. He didn't move, just stared into space as he waited for it to finish, waited to get back into the truck so he could be near her.

Chapter Four

What was happening? Let's see. There was an exquisite woman sitting in his truck. She'd literally stopped his heart with those big, green eyes. Yet he got the impression she wasn't used to someone flirting with her. That was a puzzle, but did he really want to put it together?

The car clicked into place, and he secured it down. By the time he was done, his fingers were wet even through the gloves. Water soaked his jeans from the splashing of passing cars.

He got in the truck, trying and failing not to glance at the woman. He sat there, holding his hands to the heater and glancing at her out of the corner of his eye.

"Colorado plates?" he asked.

She said, "How do you—oh, yes. I live in Colorado. Well, I might live in Colorado."

"Might?" He released the parking brake and shifted onto the highway.

"Yeah, I might move to Crimson Creek. Not sure yet.

I'll stay with Maryanne for a few weeks while I figure out my life."

She laughed nervously again, and it made him want to put her at ease. His fingers itched to hold her hand, so he gripped the steering wheel harder.

"How do you know Maryanne?" he asked.

She turned to face him with the widest smile he'd ever seen. Her whole face practically lit up. "That's what I was going to ask you! Ha! Well, we went to middle school and culinary arts school together."

"Ah, so you're a baker too?"

The woman shook her head. "Not nearly as good as Maryanne. No, I'm a chef. I ran the kitchens for a bed and breakfast until recently. I also was their event photographer, but cooking almost always came first there."

"Sounds fun."

"Oh, it was. I loved it. But then I got fired, which was totally unfair, and—" She frowned and turned to face the front while she bit her nail. "Um, actually I haven't told anyone but Maryanne that part. Can you keep that part a secret?"

He liked the idea of keeping her secrets, but this wasn't what he had in mind. "If it was unfair, why does it have to be a secret?"

She shrugged. "It's just embarrassing. I've never been fired before."

"Did they let you go because you're too beautiful?"

She burst out laughing. A real laugh, not one of the nervous ones like before. This one was rich and full-bodied like her. It warmed him like the smoothest whiskey.

"Don't be absurd. I'm not beautiful, not even close. But I guess since I've already told you I was fired, I can tell you the whole story. There was this groom who requested room service. When I delivered it, on his wedding day no less, he cornered me. Can you believe it? The nerve of that guy."

His hands gripped the steering wheel as he tapped the brakes at the stop light. "What do you mean he cornered you?"

"The guy tried to kiss me! When he was getting married in less than four hours, and I'd only met him like five times before that day. I told him no, of course, but he wouldn't let go of my arm and kept moving to keep himself between me and the door."

"What the hell?" Anger coursed through him, and his nostrils flared.

"Right? That's what I said… right before I punched him in the face."

She mimicked punching the air, a quick glance at her fierce, indignant face making him burst into laughter. "You did not."

She turned to him, beaming. "I so did. You should have seen the look on his face. It was priceless. Almost made getting fired worth it."

He grinned back at her as he drove down the two-lane highway to Crimson Creek. "That's awesome. I'm glad you stuck up for yourself."

She gasped, her eyes going wide once again. "You— really? You don't think I should've screamed or something else?"

He shook his head. "No, punching him was definitely the right move."

She breathed a sigh of relief and seemed to melt into the seat. "Thanks. I didn't tell anyone, though. Not any coworkers. Not my boss. The guy must've told his wife some twisted version because she demanded my termination when they got back from their honeymoon."

She put air quotes around the word termination and said it in the cutest little girl voice he'd ever heard.

"I'm trying really hard not to call her names but let me just say I think she and her husband are made for each other. I wish them many years of happiness in hell together. But now that I'm out of a job, I figured it was the perfect time to visit Maryanne. Oh! Is that the town? I've never actually been here before."

"Yeah, we'll drive right down Main Street. That's the church Maryanne grew up in. That's the town square where we do town picnics and fundraisers. That's the sheriff's office. You know she's married to the sheriff, right? And her bakery is right there across the street."

It was the most he'd spoken since she'd gotten in the truck, but she let him ramble and point things out. It was good that she could listen as well as she talked. Man, was she a talker.

They came up to Maryanne's house, and he pulled to a stop, deliberately engaging the parking brake.

"This is Maryanne's house. Let me walk you inside."

"Oh, but I need to get a bag out of my car."

"Well, then I'll need to take you to the shop first. It's difficult to get into the car while it's on the truck bed. Is that okay?"

The woman nodded. "Yeah, that's alright. You seem like a good guy. Are you?"

The question threw him off, so he turned to face her as he released the parking brake. The seriousness on her face made him pause. She was vulnerable and weary to trust. He could see that clear as day on her face. Poor thing was still traumatized from that groom.

"I am. You're safe with me, don't worry. I won't hold you against your will like that dirt bag if that's what you're asking."

She breathed a sigh of relief and seemed to relax, so he put the truck into gear and continued down the street.

"That's good. Not that I'd mind if it was you. I mean, you're not getting married, are you? Or are you already married? Oh god, forget I said that. I'll just ask Maryanne. Oh *god*. Forget I said that too!"

He chuckled. "No worries. I'm not engaged or married, nor do I have a girlfriend. I'm not really looking for commitment at the moment."

He didn't miss her wince. There was a story there too, but she apparently didn't want to talk about it.

"Good for you, knowing what you want. Seems a waste, though. Such a big, handsome guy like you. Oh *god*, not again."

This time, she buried her face in her hands, and seemed to collapse into herself with embarrassment. He chuckled as he pulled into the parking lot of the shop and backed into the garage bay.

He put it in park and turned to face her. "Hey, it's okay. I know what I look like. You're not saying anything I haven't already heard."

"It's just embarrassing. And I've about had it with being embarrassed. It's not—"

She sucked in a deep breath and just held it. He reached out and pulled her hand away from her face, and she turned to look at him, releasing her breath slowly.

It felt like her gloves were on fire. Both their gloves, everywhere they touched, were burning.

"It's not what?" he croaked out, trying to ignore the sensation.

She shrugged sheepishly. "I just get so tongue tied around hot guys. It's like there's no filter at all. Whatever I'm thinking just spills out."

He grinned and squeezed her hand before letting go. The heat creeping up his arm at her touch made him want to rip his jacket and gloves off just to touch her skin to skin.

"I think it's adorable. Who cares if you talk too much? That's their problem, not yours. As a guy who's sick of women who say one thing and mean another, it's refreshing. Don't stop being you, Peaches. You're a gorgeous badass who beat up a mother fucker who deserved it. Now, I'm going to hop out and get your car into the bay. Can you take this key and go start that Ford pickup over there?"

"The jacked up one that's higher than a mountain?"

He laughed. "Yeah, that one. That's mine. Go turn the heater on and wait for me, but make sure you don't kick the parking brake."

He winked at her and opened the door as her cheeks flushed that beautiful peachy pink. "I'll honk when your car is ready to get your bag out."

She smiled, her mouth almost too wide and making her somehow more approachable. Like a goddess with this one little piece of humanity that made her attainable. She grabbed the keys out of his hand, and he could've sworn he felt tingles in his palm where they touched.

Then she was jumping down and almost racing for the truck. He got to work unloading her car, his mind running a million miles a minute. Who was this woman? He didn't even know her name.

He had so many questions, and suddenly he realized he wasn't tired at all. He was bouncing around like he'd gotten his second wind or had downed three Red Bulls back-to-back.

Why did it feel so comfortable to talk with her? It was so natural, like they'd been best friends for years instead of just meeting half an hour ago.

He had no idea what it meant, but he knew one thing. He had to get to know her more.

Chapter Five

"What the hell are you doing? Why can't you just shut up, Wendy? Come on, get it together. He's just the tow truck guy. It doesn't matter that he's sin on a stick. Let it go."

She muttered to herself as she watched him through the windshield while he worked. It was like the rain didn't touch him at all. He just kept his head down and did the job.

She lifted her camera out of her purse and snapped a few pictures. Him bent over her car, torquing a wrench and making his biceps bulge, the look of concentration on his face. Then he turned and the interior lights of the shop landed just right on his face.

He was a man's man. No complaining or whining. She could count on one hand the number of men she'd been around in the last ten or fifteen years who'd not said one word of complaint in weather like this.

He was different. What was it he'd said? "A gorgeous badass. Me! A gorgeous badass!" She burst into laughter, but a honk made her jump in her seat. Then she laughed again as she put her camera into her bag, set it on the seat, jumped out, and ran back through the rain to the now open garage bay of the mechanic shop.

He was as tall as her dad, probably around six feet. She couldn't tell what color his hair was, but the man looked sexy as hell in that orange toboggan. He wasn't some millennial in skinny jeans trying to appear rugged and outdoorsy. No, this guy was the real deal, from his scuffed-up boots to his Carhart jacket to his slightly dirty hat.

Her boots hit a puddle, and she was too distracted to realize it in time. *Thud*. Her head hit pavement, cushioned by her big, poofy jacket. Rain hit her face, and she closed her eyes.

"Shit. Shit. Shit." She'd been watching him too closely and hadn't paid attention to where she was going. She pushed herself up onto her elbows but, suddenly, he was there.

"I've got you," he murmured, his hand helping her up. "Careful. Can you stand?"

She nodded, suddenly mute with his hand on her. She got to her feet and somehow, she was facing him, staring up into his baby blue eyes, her hands on his forearms with his on her elbows.

"I'm fine. Just embarrassed, yet again." She gave a soft, forced laugh and licked her lips.

His eyes widened as he watched her mouth. His hands squeezed her elbows softly, and his nostrils flared as he said, "I know I said I wouldn't man handle you, but your lips are irresistible. I'd really like to kiss you."

A thrill went through her, warming her from the inside out, and her smile widened.

"Okay," her voice was barely a whisper. What was she doing? Her heart was racing, and she couldn't think.

"Okay?" His brows raised in surprise, and his eyes met

hers again, seeming to pry into her soul. She didn't want him to see the other secrets, the list of her failures. For now, for tonight, for him, she was just some mysterious stranger. Maybe she could be sexy?

She tipped her chin up and pushed up on her toes a little to claim his lips. Was that too forward? Oh god.

Her mind stuttered to a stop. Oh, this was good.

It was beyond good. It was the best first kiss she'd ever had.

His lips were soft as he angled his head, and their mouths both opened at the same time. His tongue swept in like lightning, dueling with hers and making her head tip back.

Then his hands were around her waist and pressing her closer to him. Their jackets and layers prevented any real feeling of how they'd fit together, but she had a damn good imagination. She'd been imagining for years and years a kiss like this.

Mike had never kissed her like this. His had been—oh no, Mike!

She pulled away and stepped back, his hands sliding once more to her elbows to hold her steady. The rain had lightened to barely a sprinkle, just enough for small droplets to pool on his long eyelashes.

"Your eye lashes are too long. Well, too long for a guy anyway. Women pay good money for lashes like that. Are those natural? You're not one of those men who wear makeup are you, because I did not have you pegged as that kind of guy."

Mouth! Shut up! For once in her life, it listened, but probably because she was distracted by his sudden laugh. He tipped his head back, his eyes crinkling at the corners. Some of her nerves settled at the sound, and she smiled.

He grinned and shook his head. "No, I'm all natural, the whole package." Then he winked.

Her stomach flipped inside out. "Oh." *Good god, woman, you go from saying everything to oh? What the hell's wrong with you?*

She blinked, trying to find something to say or do. "The bag," she finally blurted out.

He turned and waved one hand to the open garage bay.

"After you. Would you like a hand? You have a lot of bags, but I don't recommend you bring them all. We'd have to put them in the back of the truck, and I'm not sure you'd like them to get wet."

She shook her head. "No, I just need like two."

She opened the passenger seat and grabbed her carry-on and her laptop backpack. Those were the only two she'd taken into her dad's house, so it was fine for tonight. She set the carry-on down and grabbed the backpack, but he just took them both from her hands with a grin.

"By the way, I'm Jake. What's your name?"

She felt a wave of heat flood her cheeks as she met his smiling face. "Wendy. Nice to meet you. God, you must think I'm a total spaz, kissing you when I didn't even know your name."

He chuckled as he pushed a button, and the garage door began to close. "Not at all. Just impulsive." One hand on her back, he guided her out and across the parking lot.

She sighed. "Yeah, that's what my dad says too. I prefer to think of it as seizing every moment in life."

He nodded and frowned as he opened the passenger door for her. His voice was softer now. "That's a good way to look at it. We should all seize more of life."

"Exactly. We never know when it'll end, and I'd rather regret the things I do than think of all the things I didn't do."

He shut the door and went around to the driver's seat, putting her carry-on between them. It was another bucket seat type with a moveable big armrest for both driver and passenger.

He began to back up, and she got nervous again.

She bit her nail and blurted out, "I mean, I don't have a lot of regrets yet. My teenage years and twenties have been pretty tame compared to most of my friends. I mean, I've never done drugs other than pot, but it's Colorado. That doesn't count. I don't drink a lot, just once or twice a month with friends. I've only had three serious boyfriends in my life, and none of them were worth losing my virginity to, not even my ex-fiancée."

The truck jerked to a halt at a stop sign, her seatbelt catching as she was jerked forward.

He turned to look at her, and she winced, glancing away, and biting her nail again.

"Oh *god*, forget I said that too! In fact, if you could just forget the whole night, I'd really appreciate it."

She saw his eyes narrow in the reflection in the window, the streetlamp illuminating his face. Then he frowned.

"Are you fucking kidding me? You're joking, right?" His tone of voice was piercing and hurt.

She crossed her arms and slunk into the seat. "Why would I lie about something like that? It's too embarrassing to makeup."

He rolled his eyes and turned back to the front of the truck. "Oh, I don't know. To get me into bed, maybe? I swear, I thought you were different."

"What are you talking about?"

He pulled up to Maryanne's house and parked. His eyes were like glaciers now, and she shivered as he stared at her. "I mean, I thought you were honest, no filters. But now you've concocted some lie about being a virgin? Only three boyfriends? What do you take me for, an idiot?"

He threw open the door and wrenched her carry-on out behind him. She opened her own door as he rounded the truck, her anger and frustration growing. She didn't need this attitude from some stranger, judging her life. The rain started again as she reached out and grabbed the handle of her bag.

"I'll take that, thank you very much. As for the idiot comment, no, I didn't think you were. I do now though. Thanks for the ride, Jake. As for everything else I said, I suggest you forget it."

She turned and started to walk down the sidewalk. But he said behind her just loud enough for her to hear.

"Oh, trust me, I plan on it. I'm not going to fall for this shit again."

The front door opened, and Maryanne stepped onto the porch with a bright smile.

She squealed, "You made it! I was starting to worry."

Wendy smiled and went up the steps, a glance over her shoulder showing the truck pulling away from the curb. She huffed out a breath and brushed the whole encounter off as the end of a bad week.

"Yep, I finally made it. Please tell me this is the end of the rotten streak of luck, because I'm not sure how much more I can take."

Maryanne shut the door behind her. "I know you've left out a lot of details on why you're here, so start at the beginning."

Wendy took a deep breath and began to remove her coat, launching into her story.

Chapter Six

The next day, Maryanne dropped her toddler off with the sitter, then took Wendy to the Clip-N-Curl on Main Street. The rain had finally stopped in the night, and now there was just a lot of ice. They slipped and held hands as they finally made it to the door laughing.

"Well, look what the cat dragged in. Afternoon, ladies." The woman at the counter had a pile of blond hair pulled up on one side in a Viking braid look. She was gorgeous and a younger version of a woman sitting in one of the salon chairs, flipping through a magazine.

Maryanne chuckled and flipped her long, black hair over her shoulder. "You're telling me. My hair has been needing an update for weeks now. I want pink this time in honor of Valentine's Day coming up. Katie, Kate, this is my friend from Colorado, Wendy. Is Lucy here?"

A brunette came out of the back and waved. "Yep, right here. How's baby Connie?"

Maryanne launched into a story about her baby's newest achievement—learning how to throw things in the trash, including Gunner's wallet and keys—but Wendy felt left out. Would she ever have a family of her own? Know what it felt like to have that unconditional love and trust of a child? Her friends from college had all married and moved away one by one.

It was just her now, lonely and trying to move forward only to be shot down at every turn. Exhibit A: Jake and last night. Exhibit B: Six weeks of dating Mike and a failed engagement.

She sighed, but when the others turned to look at her, she pasted on a smile and said, "Nice to meet you."

The next few hours flew by, and Wendy was amazed at how much she learned of the town and the people there in such a short amount of time. Katie, the young woman with the Viking braids, apparently owned the local bar outside town, The Electric Cowboy. Kate was her aunt and owned the salon, but Katie did hair in the afternoons before the bar opened up.

Lucy gave them both manicures and pedicures while they got their hair done too. The best part was the scalp massage as Katie washed her thick curls.

"God, that feels so good," Wendy moaned.

Katie chuckled, but Wendy didn't open her eyes. She was too focused on enjoying the moment.

"You need a man who'll give you a head massage regularly."

Wendy sighed. "From your lips to God's ears." Her phone rang, and she pulled it out of her pocket. She frowned, not recognizing the number, and ignored it.

A few minutes later, Katie left her with her head leaned back on the wash basin. Then Maryanne walked over.

"Yeah, she's right here. Hold on." She held out her cell phone to Wendy. "It's the auto shop."

Wendy sighed and took the phone.

"Hello?"

"Wendy? Why didn't you answer your phone?" Jake's voice was rough, but it sent a shiver up her spine.

"I didn't recognize the number, sorry. Is this about my car? Did you figure out what's wrong with it?"

He sighed. "Yeah, a fuse fractured in the battery. I can order a new fuse or a new battery. It's your call."

She rubbed her forehead. "I don't know. You're the expert, right? What do you think?"

"New battery. I think there's something wrong with the ABS too. How was it breaking when you drove from Colorado?"

She snorted. "It's a PrIus, Jake. It wasn't made to go up the mountains, but it does decent at city driving. I thought you were a car guy. Or is this another idiot moment of yours?"

A moment of silence stretched, and it made her squirm in her seat.

Shit, now she'd stepped in it. He was going to start yelling any minute now.

"Perhaps it is, but I hate to assume. You know what they say about those who assume."

She snorted. "Yeah, it makes an ass out of you and me, but I'm pretty sure it's just you who's an ass."

He sighed. "Look, do you want me to check out the ABS or not?"

"Yes, for the love of God. But—" How did she word this? She couldn't just come right out and say she was broke, could she?

"Um what, Wendy? It's not like you to not spit it out. Say what you're gonna say and be done with it." The frustration in his voice was clear now.

"It's just, um, I need the quote to fix it before you actually do anything to it, okay? I'm not sitting on a pile of cash at the moment, being jobless and all."

"Right, I'll get the quote today or tomorrow since it's already getting late. Might not hear on the parts until tomorrow. Do you want me to email it?"

"No, text is fine. I'll program the number in."

"Sure, have a nice day."

"You too. Bye." She hung up and sighed, opening her eyes to hand Maryanne the phone back. All four women were staring at her with wide eyes. "What?"

Maryanne tilted her head. "Did you say Jake?"

Wendy nodded. Maryanne and Katie glanced at each other before Katie asked, "Have you heard anything today?"

Maryanne shook her head. "No, and I'd assumed Suzie would let the whole county know when he returned."

Returned? Where had he been? And who was Suzie? A stab of jealousy turned her stomach, but she just bit her lip.

Katie nodded and whipped out her phone, stepping to the front of the store to talk.

Maryanne walked closer to Wendy and took her phone back. "It sounds like y'all are pretty chummy, arguing like that."

Wendy shrugged, feeling heat on her cheeks as she glanced away. "I don't know him well enough to argue. It was just an hour last night when he picked me and the car up. Why? What's the big deal?"

"The big deal is you just met but you basically called him an idiot and an ass." Maryanne grinned, crossing her arms over the apron, her hair wrapped up in foil.

Wendy pursed her lips. "Hey, I just call 'em like I see 'em."

The Mechanic Gets His Girl

Maryanne burst out laughing, and Lucy giggled.

Kate snorted. "Girl, Jake's not an ass. He's one of the good ones. Not too loud or flashy. Not too self-absorbed. Loves his mama."

Wendy rolled her eyes. "Yeah, he said he was the whole package. But seriously, who does that? Guys who need to prove it, that's who."

Katie joined them again. "I wouldn't mind having a chance at his package, that's for sure."

"Katie!" her aunt scolded before she smiled slowly and shrugged. "You'll have to get in line after me, girl!"

They all laughed, all except Wendy who just gave a tight smile.

Kate tapped the salon chair and waved for Maryanne to sit back down.

Maryanne said, "You know, I thought he'd move away for good after that huge ruckus last year with his ex. Do you remember?"

Katie nodded as she turned on the water near Wendy's head and tested the temperature. "Yeah, Patty has always been bad news, though. Two years she'd been in town, and in that time, she'd probably slept with anyone with balls who'd jump her."

Wendy closed her eyes and strained to hear Kate's reply to her niece.

"That's no one's concern, as long as she keeps away from the married men. No, the problem was what she did to Jake when he returned from deployment."

Wendy sucked in a breath. He was in the military. Of course he was. She had an eye for guys in uniform, didn't she?

Maryanne's voice floated to her. "He came home, and Patty saw fresh meat. Gave him some sob story about needing a big, strong man in her life and next thing you know, they're dating. But I gotta say, it was the longest I'd seen her with only one man, you know? They made it almost seven months."

Katie said, "She tried to trap him with that baby, you know. That's the part that doesn't make sense. How long did she think she could keep that ruse up? As if you can stop someone from deploying by getting pregnant or having a baby."

"If all the military did *that*, then no one would deploy ever again," Maryanne laughed.

Lucy asked, "What happened then?"

Thank God, Wendy didn't want to be the one to ask.

Katie answered. "He broke up with her after she had someone else's baby. He was scheduled to leave again in like a week. But she went nuts. Valve stems on his truck were missing one morning, so his tires went flat. Then there was the time she broke into his house to stock his fridge with his favorite meals, which isn't so bad."

Maryanne said, "Yeah, but she took all the shampoo, toothpaste, and toilet paper with her, which forced him to go to the grocery store. Where she was waiting."

Katie pointed her brush at Maryanne. "Then he refused to talk to her and threatened to go to the police for breaking and entering. I was there. He was so mad he was shaking as he walked into the store. I left then, but I heard she slashed his tires while he was in there."

"That's when Gunner got the call. I heard all about *that* when he got home," Maryanne said. "Restraining order and she had to pay for the damages. He hired Goldie as his lawyer, and she was working on it before he deployed. I'm not sure if it can be resolved while he's gone or if it's still an open case or not. Do y'all know?"

The others all shook their heads, then the conversation turned to Goldie and some of her other cases from last year.

Wendy's mind wandered as Katie finished her hair. Was the drama with Patty why Jake had reacted like that last night when she'd told him about being a virgin? If Patty had said something similar, it was no wonder he'd reacted the way he had. Poor man was gun-shy, and she didn't blame him at all. Maybe she owed him an apology for calling him an ass and an idiot? If these girls vouched for him, maybe he was just cautious of getting hurt again.

"Okay, all set. You're gorgeous, hun! You're going to knock 'em dead at the Cowboy tonight. You'll be there, right? I want to show you my bar," Katie said as she swept the floor.

Wendy flipped her hair this way and that, feeling the clean curls. "If Maryanne says we're going, then we're going."

Maryanne grinned as she paid her bill. "Why else would we be here? Just need to pick up Connie, go home and whip up dinner, then drop her off at my mom's. Then we'll be ready to party."

"Do you mind if I cook?"

Maryanne wiggled her eyebrows. "I was hoping you would."

She laughed and went to pay, but Kate just waved her hands and smiled. "Already taken care of. Y'all have fun tonight! And anytime you have leftovers, bring 'em on by. I accept tips in baked goods and treats."

Maryanne and Wendy both laughed, although she knew her own cheeks were also heated in a blush. They left and made their way slowly to Maryanne's car. When they were buckled and on their way back to the house, Wendy turned to her friend.

"You didn't have to pay, you know."

Maryanne shrugged. "I remember what being jobless felt like, so don't worry about it. Although, if you want to help at the bakery, you're more than welcome to."

Wendy sighed. "I appreciate that. I'm game for helping, you know that. And thanks for letting me cook tonight. It's been a few days, and I'm already needing the outlet."

"Stressed? I can't imagine why." Maryanne's mock innocent tone made Wendy laugh.

"You know me. I get stressed, and I cook. Haven't had a chance to do that in a few days now. Oh! I forgot to show you the pictures I took of your house this morning while you were at the bakery. Remind me when we get home."

This morning she'd woken up to some pastries on the counter and an empty house. She'd explored the nooks and crannies and most importantly, the pantry and fridge. She had a list of meals ready to go with what was on hand and was already itching to dive into dinner.

This is why she'd become a chef. She wanted to make people happy and show how much she appreciated them. She might not share with a lot of people at the moment, but she could still help Maryanne and Gunner while she stayed with them.

"We're home. You can get started on dinner. I'm going to go pick up Connie from my mom's. Then when I get back, we'll go through my closet for something to wear tonight."

Oh god, she'd almost forgotten about the bar tonight. What would she wear? And more importantly, would Jake be there?

Chapter Seven

"What the hell is *she* doing here?" Jake muttered, crossing his arms and leaning against the bar.

His cousin, Andy, turned with drinks in hand and asked, "Who? Patty?"

Jake shook his head. "Hell no. Not her. Never her."

Andy peered at him, and Jake could practically see the questions in his mind. The bartender handed over his beer, and Jake grabbed it before leading Andy through the crowd to the quieter side room. Wendy's auburn hair was a riot of color. She was too short to see now with all the people by the door, but he knew it was her.

He pushed through the saloon doors and into the quieter side room. The pool tables were in the center of the room and booths lined one wall. Halfway down, their group spilled out of two booths and around the center pool table.

Cindy, Andy's wife, and Landry, one of his best friends growing up, held up a banner that said, "Welcome Home."

Then the whole group turned and yelled, "Surprise!"

Jake winced as Andy slapped him on the back. "Sorry,

man. I know you wanted some peace, but they couldn't help themselves. Just go with it."

Jake nodded and gave a tight smile. "And here I thought I just had to keep Mom from planning something. Didn't realize I had to worry about y'all too."

The group laughed, then Landry and some others came around for handshakes or hugs. Everyone was talking and smiling at once as music spilled into the room from the stage in the main bar area.

You'd think they'd all be tired of these little welcome home parties. He'd been deployed when Andy had gotten married over two years ago. They'd had a huge welcome home party when he got home. It had been a fun spring. But that was before Patty had ruined it. He took a drink of his beer and turned to greet the next person.

He froze. There stood Wendy with a hesitant smile on her face, her cheeks a deeper red that just made all her freckles pop. Her green eyes appeared larger with the extra makeup, and her wild mane of auburn curls now had some strawberry blond streaks through it. It was the first time he'd seen her hair dry, and good god, it was glorious. He wanted to shove his hands in and fist it. Maybe see her face tipped back as he slammed into her.

Shit. No. Not again.

"Hey, Jake. How's it going?" Her voice was barely heard over the music.

He nodded his head once. "Hey. It's good."

She waved a hand at his friends and said, "I didn't realize you're returning from a deployment. Thank you for your service."

He hunched his shoulders and shifted on his feet. "No thanks necessary. I'm just home for a few weeks on R and R. That means—"

"I know what it means. Rest and relaxation. I'm not an idiot."

His gaze snapped up, but the twinkle in her eyes made him pause. She arched an eyebrow and smiled. "Sorry, I couldn't resist. Also—about earlier—I'm sorry I called you an ass and an idiot. You're not. Well, except for when you got all pissy last night."

"I didn't get pissy."

She lifted a delicate shoulder, causing the fabric of her off-the-shoulder white shirt to slide down slightly. The long-sleeved shirt hugged her tightly, only revealing a small sliver of her stomach. Her form-fitting jeans seemed to mold perfectly to her curves, accentuating every inch of her petite figure. He ached for her, and it was unacceptable. He was barely going to be here for two weeks, then it was back to the sand pit.

His gaze raked down to her fuck me black heeled boots that reached almost to her knees. With those on, she was now the perfect kissing height. It'd be so easy for him to lean forward and kiss her, barely bending. Then he could lift her by that tight ass, and she'd wrap those legs around him.

"Earth to Jake. Hello?" Wendy waved a hand in front of his face, and he took a deep breath. The damn woman had put a spell on him, and he wouldn't be trapped into that again.

Their conversation came back to him, and he scowled, but she just smiled, lighting up the room.

"You were definitely pissy last night. I understand now why you chickened out though. I don't blame you, after what happened last year with your ex."

His brows rose in surprise. "How did you—"

"I got my hair done today with Maryanne. It was very

informative on all the things happening in town. They might have mentioned it after we spoke on the phone."

He groaned. Shit. He drank the rest of his beer and glanced around. Was everyone talking about Patty?

Wendy's delicate freckled hand settled on his forearm. Even through the thin fabric of his plaid pearl-snap shirt, he felt the heat of her touch.

He glanced at it, then at her. Her brows were pulled together as she said, "Look, I don't know her, but I am definitely *not* her. I'm just me, whom you don't really know at all. But just so you do know, I wasn't lying about what I said last night."

He leaned forward and lowered his voice. "You mean about being a virgin?"

She blushed again and nodded, her facial expression not changing. "Exactly, but please don't advertise that, okay? My goal for the next few weeks is to finally let it go, if you know what I mean? I don't want to be thirty and still waiting."

He nodded, unable to say anything over the knot in his throat.

She gave a soft smile and nodded. "Thanks. I think if I can figure out how to flirt, I can get it done. You feel like giving me lessons?"

He choked out, "God, you make it sound like such a chore."

She shrugged, and her hair fell behind her. He wanted to lick every freckle on her exposed shoulder. There must be hundreds, so it would take a while. It would be time well spent.

She said, "It could be, I'm sure. Depending on the guy. Actually, it probably will be. I've heard so many horror stories about the first time, but I'm trying to be optimistic, trying not to think about it because that just makes me even more nervous. And if I'm thinking about it when I'm trying to flirt, then I just turn into this chatterbox who won't shut up, which then scares them off and—"

He saw a finger press to her lips. His finger. It was touching her lips. It shot heat down his arm. She gasped, her mouth forming an *o*. He groaned and then let his finger circle her rosy lips softly, barely touching.

His voice was rough when he said, "Stop thinking about it. Stop talking about it. Just—just stop."

Her eyes widened, and she nodded. Her tongue slid out to lick her lips, but she licked his finger too, causing him to groan. She froze, then nipped at the tip of his finger. He jerked his finger away as if scalded.

He might as well have been. He could still feel the hesitant touch of her tongue on it. Her face was almost beet red now.

She stammered as she looked around. "I—I'm sorry. I don't know what came over me. I'll just—I'll just go now. Need a drink. Yes, a drink sounds lovely. I'll just—bye now."

She turned on her heel and practically ran from the room, the saloon shutters slapping back and forth behind her.

An elbow caught him in the ribs, making him grunt. He turned to see Maryanne and Gunner. Gunner's arms were crossed and his stance widened while Maryanne had a hand on her hip and her brows raised.

"What?"

Maryanne rolled her eyes. "You know what. That's my friend you're toying with."

"Me toying with her? Oh, hell no, she's toying with me! Not the other way around."

Maryanne stepped up and tried to stick her nose in his

face. She was almost as short as Wendy though, so it was comical. Her finger in his face was decidedly not.

"Don't toy with her, Jake. She's not used to this kind of thing."

He narrowed his eyes. "What kind of thing?"

Maryanne waved her hand. "This. Flirting. It's been the bane of her existence since middle school, trust me. You'll easily crush her if you're not careful."

"Crush her? No, she's badass. Unbreakable. No, it'll be me crushed—again—but I swore I'd learned my lesson after what happened last year. I'm not going to go through that shit again."

Gunner put his hands on Maryanne's shoulders and pulled her back to his chest. His caught Jake's gaze, and he said, "She was there when we got married in Colorado. She arranged the whole thing. I only knew her for a few days, but I know how to judge people. She's good people, Jake. Don't hurt her."

Jake set his empty beer on the side of the pool table and put his hands in his pockets. "Y'all are missing the bigger picture here."

"Oh? And what's that?" Maryanne asked.

Jake felt his jaw clench, and he swallowed hard. "She's bound and determined to hook up with someone, whether tonight or while she's in Crimson Creek. I won't hurt her, but someone else might."

"Which is exactly why we're warning you. You were the first one in her sights. Now I'm going to go find her on the dance floor and do what I did throughout culinary school. Protect her from real ass idiots."

Jake felt his ears grow hot at the smirk on Maryanne's face. Shit, she'd heard her side of the conversation at the salon.

"I'm not an ass or an idiot."

Maryanne rolled her eyes. "If you think she's anything like Patty, you definitely are both, don't you think, G?"

Gunner nodded solemnly.

Jake scoffed. "Whatever. I need another beer."

"All jokes aside, if you see her, will you look out for her?" Maryanne asked.

Jake grabbed his empty bottle and nodded. "Why wouldn't I? Like I said, I'm not an ass."

And with that, he walked back to the bar.

Chapter Eight

"Can I have a fuzzy navel, please?" Wendy asked the bartender. The man nodded and turned to mix the drink.

"Put it on my tab," a deep voice said from beside her. She turned with a smile and blinked.

A burly man was leaning on the bar, his green t-shirt stretched tight over his bulging biceps. His beard was trimmed but he had almost a buzz cut that reminded her of the Army. She tilted her head and glanced down. Jeans and boots. But not just any boots. Boots that shined, but were scuffed up from use.

She smirked. "Thank you, sir. I appreciate it, being new in town and all. I'm Wendy." She held out her hand to shake, facing him fully. The man almost snapped to attention and shook her hand in both of his, his hands warm and welcoming.

He grinned. "I'm Nick. Nice to meet you."

She arched a brow and asked. "Army?"

He blinked and frowned. "No, Marines. Why? Is it that obvious?"

She shrugged. "Probably only to me. My dad's still in the Army up in Fort Carson. You still have the look."

He grinned again and seemed to relax against the bar. "You never quite lose it, do you?"

She shook her head. "Not that I'm aware of, no."

The bartender passed her drink over and slid Nick a beer. She thanked him and turned to watch the band.

"So, what brings you to Crimson Creek? It's not exactly the most happening place, barely on the map."

"Do you know Maryanne Williams?" She smiled when he nodded. "She's my best friend. We were both stationed at Fort Hood together in middle school. We moved away during our first year of high school, but then met up again for college. All the major milestones in a girl's life, we shared. I'm at a crossroads and wanted to clear my head. So, here I am, visiting the bestie."

Nick nodded, suddenly serious. "I can understand that. I lost one of my best military friends last year. It's been a struggle without him."

She laid a hand on his arm and leaned in. "Oh, I'm so sorry for your loss."

He leaned closer and said softly, "Thanks. Me too."

A throat cleared as a hand shot between them to grab a beer on the counter. Wendy leaned back and glared.

"Excuse me. Just getting my beer. Hey, Nick. How's it going?"

Nick straightened up again and shook Jake's hand. "Hey, welcome back."

"Thanks. It'll just be for a few weeks, then I'm heading back."

Nick grinned. "Just long enough for your mom to spoil you to death."

Jake snorted. "More like smother me."

Nick put a hand on her lower back and smiled at her. "Jake, have you met Wendy? She's just arrived from Colorado."

Wendy blushed and looked at Jake, who arched a brow. His brown hair shone in the dim light of the bar, clean cut in a high and tight but longer on top. It made her want to mess it up. She glanced down, taking in his plaid, pearl-snap shirt and pressed jeans. They made his muscles stand out, and it occurred to her this was the first time she'd seen him without the added layers of a coat and hat.

And damn if he didn't look delicious. Delicious? Good god, she'd never called a man that before, even in her thoughts.

Jake simply said, "We've met."

His words snapped her out of her fantasies. Nick put his empty beer behind them and leaned closer. His aftershave was almost cloying.

"Care to dance?"

She reminded herself of the goal. She needed to practice flirting, and if Jake wasn't going to do it, then maybe Nick would help.

She nodded and handed her drink to Jake. "Can you watch my drink? Thanks, Jake."

Then they stepped into the crowd and onto the dance floor. What did Jake think he was doing? He knew she was here to find someone.

The song was almost over but it was a fast-paced one. Soon, Nick had her laughing as she was trying to keep up. It was that or cry at her clumsy attempt at dancing.

The next song was a slow one, and he just barely paused before pulling her close. She gasped and looked up at him.

"Is this okay?" he asked. The wrinkle on his forehead

showed his vulnerability, and it was adorable. This big, burly Marine was such a gentleman.

She nodded. "Yeah, it's okay. Sorry I'm such a klutz. I've always been this way, really. School dances were a nightmare, then in my twenties all my friends wanted to go clubbing. I was always the girl who stayed at the table and watched the drinks."

"But not anymore?"

She grinned slowly. "Not anymore. I've missed out on too much in life already."

"Oh yeah? What have you missed out on? Maybe I can help you seize life by the horns."

She blushed and opened her mouth to reply, but a hand was clapping onto Nick's shoulder.

"My turn. Mind if I cut in?" Jake asked. He shoved her drink at Nick and swept her into a spin. His hand in hers and the other on her hip were heavier than Nick's had been, hotter. Yet she had goosebumps.

"Jake! What are you doing? I was about to—"

"Proposition him for a night of hot sex? Yeah, I know," he said with a glare.

They spun around the room in silence, the music echoing between them.

She frowned. "I don't understand. Why did you interfere? It could've been a done deal tonight."

His hand squeezed her hip, making her stumble once more. He just yanked her closer, their bodies pressed together from hip to chest.

She gasped, but before she could say anything, his head tilted. His mouth met hers and his tongue swept in and devoured her. The music faded into the background. She didn't even know if they were still dancing or if they were now standing still.

All she knew was the feel of his hand on her hip, his tongue dueling with hers, and the rapid beat of her pulse in her ears. The kiss deepened but then it was over. He broke away, and her vision spun.

They had come to a stop in a darker corner of the room on the edge of the dance floor. Her back was to the wall, but he wasn't pressing her into it. No, he just stood there, solid and sturdy, staring at her with those baby blue eyes that saw too much.

She opened her mouth and closed it, swallowed and licked her lips. "Why?"

He blinked. "I don't know. I just know you can't sleep with him."

She frowned. "But why not? No one else is going to—"

"Oh hell no. This is not gonna happen, Jakey. Get your hands off that hussy." A shrill voice interrupted.

Jake jerked at the sound and looked behind him. Then he turned and partially hid her from the woman who'd interrupted them. Wendy peeked around his back. The woman was wearing a purple dress that flared at the hips, showing off her generous curves. She had black hair pulled back in a smooth ponytail and heavy makeup to match her dress.

But it was her eyes that sent a chill down Wendy's spine. They were cold, hollow, and nearly black in the dim light of the bar. Narrowed on Jake, the woman didn't even spare a glance at her.

"What are you doing here, Patty? You know the restraining order says—"

"I don't give a shit about the restraining order. You think I knew you'd be here?"

Jake snorted. "Yeah, I *do* think you knew I'd be here. The question is why."

The Mechanic Gets His Girl

The woman smirked and cocked a hip to the side. "I'm just here at the only bar for miles to relax on a Friday night. That's all. If I see the love of my life, then all the better. But to see you cheating on me with that—"

"We're not together anymore, Patty. You know this. We broke up months ago."

She waved a hand. "That's just temporary. We both know you'll be back after the deployment. Then we'll be a big, happy family."

Jake's spine straightened to attention, and Wendy placed her hand on it, running her hand slowly up and down his back to comfort him.

"We won't ever be a big, happy family. We won't ever be together ever again. Now leave, before I call the cops."

The woman wrinkled her forehead in a ploy for sympathy. "But Jakey, what about the baby?"

"That baby's not mine. You were pregnant when we got together and tried to pin it on me. Tried to tell me you were innocent. Ha! Do you know how many guys tried to warn me about you?"

The woman had tears in her eyes, but Jake just shook his head. "Save the dramatics, Patty. It's over. In fact, you'll be hearing from my lawyer any day now, requesting a paternity test. Then we'll settle this once and for all."

Patty's jaw clenched in fury. Jake grabbed Wendy's hand and dragged her around the dance floor and through the saloon doors to their friends.

"So that was Patty, huh?"

Jake just squeezed her hand and stopped next to Gunner. He leaned forward and said something into his ear, then Gunner frowned and stepped out of the room.

Jake turned to her and ran a hand through his hair with a sigh. As he glanced around the room, he pulled her to a corner and leaned against the wall. The whole time, he hadn't let go of her hand. What did that mean?

Together they stared and people watched. But she couldn't wait forever.

She asked, "Did Gunner go make sure she left?"

Jake nodded. "He'll be a witness and talk to my lawyer, confirming that she broke the restraining order. Good news for me, actually. Strengthens my case."

"What exactly happened? The girls at the salon might not have had the whole story."

His shoulders tensed, and he finally let go of her hand. Her fingers flexed, suddenly cold without his warmth.

"I came back from deployment in the summer. She was new in town. We met, and I thought she was just needing a hand landing on her feet. But instead, I'm the sucker who fell for the town floozy."

Wendy's brow rose. "Um, no slut shaming. You don't know what she was going through, Jake."

He sighed and rubbed his forehead. "Okay, okay, you're right. That might not be fair. I don't know how many guys she's slept with, and it doesn't matter. I don't even care."

"It sounds like you care."

"I don't." His voice was hard, just like his gaze when he pinned it on her. She couldn't look away. "It's not about who she slept with or how many. It's the fact that she told me she was a virgin."

Wendy's finger shot up, and she waved it in his face. "I knew it! I knew that was why you freaked out after our kiss last night!"

He grabbed her finger and pulled it to his chest, holding it there as he shook his head in self-recrimination. She could feel his heartbeat through his shirt, his chest muscles, and the heat.

She felt her cheeks begin to blush as he chuckled.

"Sorry about freaking out. But yeah, I don't like being lied to."

She lifted her free hand and cupped his face. She said softly, "I'm not lying."

His jaw tightened as he searched her face, looking for the lie. But she knew the truth and had nothing to hide.

"Jake? Jake!" Gunner burst through the saloon doors and quickly searched the room. Jake stepped around her and to the door, a frown on his face.

"Yeah? Did you make sure she was gone?"

Gunner frowned. "Yeah, but you need to come see this. Grab your coat."

"See what?" Jake grabbed his jacket from the coat rack by the saloon style doors and followed him out. Wendy stood for half a second, but then jumped into motion, grabbing her own coat. There was no way she was missing this, whatever it was.

Chapter Nine

Jake zipped up his jacket as he walked through the crowd at the bar. The music was still thumping, but the sense of dread running through him kept tempo with the beat. Gunner opened the door to the brisk, January air.

Once outside, they walked side by side to the parking lot. Jake looked around. "What's happened? Is she still out here?"

Gunner shook his head, and they turned the corner of the row of cars. A few rows in, and Jake came to a stunned stop.

His truck. His jacked up, souped up Ford F-150 Raptor. The one he'd spent hours and hours into customizing.

It was... it was...

"Oh my God, is that bologna? And—and what the hell *is* that?" Wendy's voice behind him made him suck a breath and jerk out of his stupor.

He walked forward and swiped a finger along the tailgate. Then he smelled it. "It's oatmeal and syrup."

"Oh my God. It was Patty, wasn't it?" She just kept talking.

He wiped his finger off on the truck and nodded. "Probably."

Gunner sighed. "Look, I'll go try to find some witnesses. Maybe someone saw her do this, get a copy of the cameras from Katie. Let me call the station and see who can come and take pictures and gather evidence."

"Hurry. The longer this shit stays on here, the more it strips the paint." Jake's voice was wooden and hollow. He felt Wendy's hand slip into his, their fingers interlocking.

Some of the tension seemed to seep out from between his shoulder blades. She started telling a story about a girl in high school who pulled a trick like this on her ex-boyfriend, but he just tuned it out. The tone of her voice was soothing, but it wasn't really about what she was saying. It was the fact that she was here, comforting him in her own way.

Soon, the police cruiser arrived, and the deputy began taking pictures and gathering statements. By then, a crowd had gathered around his truck, and they'd gotten the vehicles on either side moved by their owners.

It was seventeen degrees outside, but he couldn't feel it. He was numb all over. He turned from the deputy and glanced at his friends. Wendy stood front and center, stomping her feet and blowing into her hands for warmth.

He frowned and stepped toward them.

"Sorry this happened on your first night in town, Jake," his cousin, Andy, said with a frown.

Jake shrugged. "I was going to run into her again eventually. I just thought she'd have given up by now. It's been almost a year, you know?"

Maryanne shook her head. "If it helps, she was seeing some other guys while you were gone."

Jake put his hands in his pocket and glanced at his truck. "Yet she's apparently still not over it."

Andy nodded. "Yeah, better fill in your lawyer."

Jake sighed. "I will, but y'all can go home now. The deputy is almost done, then I'm going to go to the car wash to clean this off. Won't know the extent of the damage until tomorrow."

They all murmured to make sure he meant it, but ultimately, they all hugged, shook his hand or waved, and were on their way. All except Wendy.

Her forehead was wrinkled in concern. "Are you sure you'll be alright?"

"Yeah, I just need to take care of her now."

"Her? You mean Patty? God, Jake, don't go do something stupid now. Not after I *just* said you weren't an idiot ass."

He chuckled and stepped closer, pulling her flush against him. "I don't mean Patty. I mean my truck."

Her face cleared in realization, and her eyes widened. "Oh, your truck is a girl? Does she have a name? My car's name is Lovie, but—"

He kissed her. This time it wasn't deep and devouring. It was slow and satisfied him down to his soul. The frustration of the night, the worry about Patty and his truck, it all just seemed to melt away.

When he pulled back, he gave small, soft kisses to her lips. They were like pillows or clouds, so soft and supple.

"Go home, Peaches. I gotta take care of my other girl. Her name's Cassy, by the way." Her eyes were dazed when he released her, but she nodded and stepped away without another word. Interesting. A kiss had made her stop talking. Not a bad strategy, if he did say so himself.

He chuckled and spun on his heel only to see Landry

leaning against his truck nearby. His brows were arched, and it made Jake scowl.

"What's with that shit-eating grin on your face?"

Landry waved his hands up in an innocent gesture that didn't fool him one bit. "Hey, don't go poking at me. Have you looked at your own face?"

Jake scowled. "There's nothing wrong with my face."

Landry pushed off his truck and pulled his hands up to his chin, cupping his own cheeks and fluttering his eyelashes. In an overly shrill fake voice, he said, "Oh Jake, you're such a hottie. Kiss me, Jake. Oh yes, just like that."

"Hey, knock it off. She's not like that at all." Jake stepped toward Landry, fists ready, but he just side-stepped out of the way and laughed.

Landry tilted his head and grinned wider. "Oh? And you know what she's like, do you?"

Jake shoved him and spun on his heel, looking for the deputy. "Shut up."

Landry called after him. "One of these days, Jake, you're going to fall, and when you do, it's going to be harder than anything you could've imagined."

Jake didn't answer, just kept walking to the deputy so he could get permission to leave. He refused to argue with Landry again. They'd already gotten into it when he'd returned from the last deployment.

His cousin and best friend, Andy, had gotten married and ended up with four kids while he'd been gone. And his best friend, Landry, had gotten engaged and his fiancée had been pregnant with their twins when he'd returned.

He'd missed both Landry and Andy's weddings, but that was part of life in the military. You couldn't always be where you wanted to be. Like right now, for instance. He wanted to bury his face in Wendy's hair.

Wait, did he? Hadn't he just said that he wouldn't fall for shit like that again?

Yeah, but does that mean you have to be celibate for the rest of your life just because some sneaky woman made you miserable for a while? Come on. You want her. She wants to get laid. You can help her out with that.

He pushed the thoughts down and drove to the car wash.

Chapter Ten

Mac,
I think you have the wrong email address. I don't know anyone by your name, and your email isn't in my contacts.
As for whoever you're trying to reach, he does sound like a jackass. Anyone who leaves someone at the altar meets that definition, but what does your dad have to do with it? Anyone who wants to get out of deployment is the scum of the earth. You're better off without him. He's regular Army, isn't he? I'm in the Army Reserve, which is a little different. I chose to go active duty because—to be perfectly honest with you—I wanted to get away from memories back home.
All that to say, please don't sic your dad on me to make my life miserable while deployed. I'm just doing my job and am glad to be here, regardless of the hell we go through. I hope you find the person you're looking for, but I assure you, it's not me.
J. Smith

Wendy frowned and read the email again. This wasn't right. She bit her lip and decided to look for a different email address to confront Mike. Maybe his best friend would have his information or…

Shit. She closed her eyes and sighed. She didn't even know his family situation. He'd mentioned a sister, but he'd never introduced them. And she had no idea where his parents were or if they were even still alive.

She was such a fool. She knew more about Jake in two days than she did about Mike in six weeks of dating. She fired off a reply to the stranger.

J.
Oh, I'm so sorry to bother you in combat! I won't send my dad after you, but then again, he does what he wants. He's probably already found the Mike I'm looking for and trying to get answers for me. He may be overbearing and strict, but he loves me.
I'm sorry your memories of home aren't as good. I try to block out memories of home too, but mostly because they're too painful. My mom got cancer while I was in high school and passed away while I was in college. She fought hard for ten years. Now when I walk through the house, I keep expecting her to round the corner, a big smile on her face and arms open for the warmest hug you can imagine on earth. I moved out a few years after she died because I just couldn't take it anymore. Again, sorry to bother you.
W (Mac is a horrible nickname, and I hate it. It's short for Macdonald, but Mike said he called me that to remind me to eat more. He never understood being an ectomorphic body type. I'll probably always be rail thin, no matter how many Big Macs I eat.)

Emailing about the Army made her think of the local hero who was taking up way too much of her head space.

Jake was a mama's boy, worked as a tow truck driver and at the auto mechanic shop, and could kiss like a dream. He wasn't looking for a relationship or commitment, mostly because his ex-girlfriend was bat-shit crazy. He was also in the military, which she wasn't sure if she liked or not.

She'd gone back and forth on it over the years. Sometimes she'd swear off military guys, then she'd want one of her own just because her dad said to stay away from them. She winced, thinking of her dad. He'd been right about Mike.

What did she really know about him anyway, if she couldn't even contact him by email? She could try social media, but he'd said he wasn't on any of the platforms. That should've been her first clue, but he'd said it was to keep the enemy from finding his family.

Now that she was thinking about it clearly, she was pretty sure that it was from a movie. The bad guys wouldn't care two cents about some random Army MP or his family.

She looked back down at her email and frowned, firing off a reply. Then she finished cleaning the bakery.

"I'm so glad you came in with me today! Saturdays are always a rush." Maryanne smiled as she put some dough into the walk-in fridge.

A knock sounded on the back door before it opened. "Maryanne? You still here?"

Maryanne came out of the fridge and shut the door, a smile on her face. "Hey, Parker. What are you doing here?"

"Landry wanted me to drop this off with you. Something about the Valentine's speed dating thing Holly does?" Parker set a box on the counter by the door and scanned the room.

Wendy wiped down the counters and stared at him. The man was a hottie in his leather jacket, jeans, and boots. There was something about him that screamed preppy boy, though. Maybe it was the cut of his hair. It reminded her of Italian soccer players.

He saw her and waved. "Oh hey. You're the new girl who was at the Electric Cowboy last night, right? I'm Parker."

He stepped forward to shake her hand, but she smiled and held up the rag and cleaner. He pulled his hand back and glanced at Maryanne, who nodded at him.

He took a deep breath and smiled at Wendy. "Maryanne was telling me you used to run a bed and breakfast in Colorado?"

Wendy winced and shrugged, continuing her wipe down. "Yeah, I ran the kitchens and did photography for some events. I didn't manage it or anything, although I wouldn't have minded."

His phone rang, and he glanced down before silencing it. "Wendy, can I take you to dinner tonight? I'd love to talk more about this and get to know you."

Her heart raced. "A date?" Why was her voice so squeaky?

He grinned and winked. "Absolutely. Would seven o'clock be okay?"

She nodded dumbly, and he waved to them both and walked out, his phone already to his ear. She looked at Maryanne in surprise.

"What was that all about?"

Maryanne shrugged and grinned. "I might have planted a bug in his ear last night. And that's all I'm going to say about that until after your date. My lips are sealed. But don't worry. Parker's a gentleman, even if he is the more outgoing of the Williams' brood. He's Gunner's brother, you know."

Wendy's eyebrows raised. "Oh, that explains the resemblance. How many brothers does he have again?"

Maryanne launched into an explanation, and by the

The Mechanic Gets His Girl

time she was done, the bakery was clean. They slipped on their coats and hopped into Maryanne's car.

"Would you mind swinging by the auto shop? I'd like to get a few more of my bags out of the car." She bit her lip, but Maryanne just nodded and turned onto the street.

"You wouldn't be hoping to catch sight of a certain war hero, would you? Don't think I didn't see you two smooching in the corner last night."

Wendy groaned and slid into the seat. "You saw? Oh god, did everybody? They don't think I'm a hussy like Patty, do they?"

Maryanne laughed and shook her head as she pulled into the parking lot. "Not at all. I was rather surprised, though. There are definitely things you didn't tell me about him towing you back into town. And you *will* spill them later. Do you need a hand with your bags?"

Wendy shook her head. "Nope. I'll just be a minute."

Then she walked to the front door of the shop. The bell dinged overhead, and the front desk worker—a pimply teenage boy—glanced up. He stood up and smiled.

"Yes, how may I help you?"

"I'm looking for Jake. Is he working today?"

The boy frowned and his eyes narrowed. "No, miss. He's not in today. Is there something else I can help you with?"

She looked through the glass window at the shop. It had five bays, and she pointed to her car. "I need to get a few more bags out of my car."

"Oh, customers aren't really allowed on the floor. But if you'll tell me which ones, I'll be happy to get them for you."

She bit her lip and frowned. "There's a big pink one in the back seat, and a purple striped one on the floorboard behind the driver's seat. But not the purple and black striped one. That one can wait. And the pink cheetah print one and the green Army duffle bag. I can wait on the stuff in the trunk, I suppose."

The boy blinked and looked at the car then back at her. "Okay," he said slowly and hesitantly.

She arched her brow. "It'd be faster if we both went, you know. We can each grab two." She let the words hang in the air, but eventually the boy sighed and nodded.

"Okay, but let's be quick. I don't want to get in trouble."

She grinned and followed him through the glass door and into the mechanic area. The smell of oil, dirt, and sweaty men permeated the cool air. Several guys were working on the other cars, but no one was working on hers. The boy opened the back passenger side door as she went around to the driver's side, carefully avoiding black spots on the concrete.

She opened the door and pulled the purple and white striped one out. Then she grabbed the big pink roller and tugged. It was slow and difficult to maneuver the big, checked bag.

One more tug should do it. She took a deep breath and pulled. It fell free of the car, but it was too heavy, and she was already off balance from the purple bag. She stumbled back and hit a computer and printer on a cart, sending it rolling.

She dropped her bag and lurched for it, but strong arms stopped it before it hit anything else. She glanced up and found Jake's piercing blue eyes, one brow arched in reproach.

"Oh no," she groaned.

"Oh yes. What are you doing, other than getting into trouble?"

She waved to her bags on the ground. "I came for a few more of my bags."

He glanced at the boy and narrowed his eyes. "I can see that. Josh, take those bags to Mrs. Williams' red car out there. I'll grab these."

"Yes, sir," the boy mumbled, clearly nervous at being caught by Jake.

Jake grabbed her purple bag and pulled the handle of her big pink one up to roll through the garage.

"Sorry about the computer. I didn't realize it was—"

He stopped and looked at her, his eyes pale in the weak winter sun. "You didn't realize what? That turning you loose in here was an accident waiting to happen?" He snorted and turned back to walk through the open garage doors.

She followed at his heels. "I know I'm a klutz, but I'm not that bad."

He chuckled and put her bags in the trunk next to the other two the boy had delivered. "I'll believe it when I see it."

"I'm sorry, okay? How many times do you want me to say it?" She frowned and started to cross her arms. But he grabbed her hands and tugged her close.

Pressed against him, she couldn't breathe. The air wasn't cold anymore but steamy hot. He tipped her chin up with a finger, making her gasp.

"I'm just giving you a hard time, Peaches. Although, I'd like to give you a hard something else."

Her mouth slid open in surprise, but his finger on her chin pushed it closed as he chuckled.

Cheeks burning, she stepped back and stuttered, "Um, really? Me too. I mean otherwise I wouldn't have told you all that personal stuff. Shit. I'm rambling again. Um, hey, how's your truck? Is that it on the far side? Did the bologna strip the paint?"

He nodded and stepped away, glancing at his truck. "Yeah, I'll need to order a paint job for it. Luckily, they'll have a few months to get it done and delivered before I finish the tour."

Oh yeah. The deployment wasn't over. He was just here for a few weeks. Did she really want to lose her virginity to someone she knew was going to leave?

Yeah, she did. At least knowing he'd leave wouldn't hurt as much as Mike just up and leaving without warning. This would be better. Like knowing the band-aid was ready to come off, counting down, and then just going for it.

He tilted his head, his blue eyes curious. What were they talking about again? Oh yeah. She cleared her throat. "And my car? Were you able to get the quote for it?"

He nodded and shoved his hands in his pocket with a frown. "Yeah, I'll text it to you. But it's around $700 for the ABS sensor and $100 for the fuse for the battery."

She groaned and rubbed her temples, the movement making him blur. He shifted from foot to foot and looked down. Then his blue eyes looked up and captured hers.

"I'm concerned that the fuse won't fix the problem, though. I did some research, and it's a known problem with PrIus batteries. Once it starts happening, you could be replacing the fuses every few months. Which would also mean being stranded on the side of the road again."

She felt tears threaten but she just crossed her arms and nodded. "Is there anything else that can be done to keep the fuse from blowing?"

He paused but didn't break eye contact. He just sighed and nodded. "Yeah, a new battery. But that would cost an additional grand at least. Is that something you want me to look into?"

She swallowed and shook her head. She opened and closed her mouth, ashamed to say it but knowing it had to be said. "No, I can't afford that. I can't even afford the sensor and fuse. I went through most of my savings traveling to Texas."

"Do you have a credit card? You can't be carless forever, especially if you're going to stay around here."

"Yeah, but I don't like using it." She rubbed her temples again and closed her eyes. "You're right, though. Just order the stupid sensor and fuse, and I'll put it on the credit card. Why does adulting suck so much?"

She felt fingers cover her own hands on her head, and she froze. Slowly, his hands massaged her scalp. It felt so good, but she didn't know whether she wanted to cry or melt into a puddle at his feet.

Chapter Eleven

Her hair was soft as silk and smelled like roses. It reminded him of warm summer days playing hide and seek with Andy and Landry in his mom's garden.

Then she moaned. Oh god, that sound was the best thing he'd heard all year. It went straight to his gut like a knock-out punch.

He kissed her softly on one corner of the lushest lips he'd ever kissed. Today she tasted like cinnamon rolls. It made him want to devour her in front of a fire on a cold winter's day. After making love, they could snack on cinnamon rolls and hot chocolate.

He teased her lower lip, but it just drove the need higher. It became a sharp, stabbing need of desire that he wasn't sure would ever be put out, like a raging inferno that never died. Where they touched, his body felt alive.

The fog of the past few years lifted. He wasn't just going through the motions, not with her. This kiss was a revelation, a glimpse into the man he wanted to be, the man he used to be.

He cradled her head in his hands and kissed her slowly, with an intensity that was dreamlike. Because surely nothing that felt this good could be real. It had to only exist in his dreams.

He slowly broke the kiss and pulled back, staring down into her cute little face. Their breathing was ragged, but her eyes were still closed, her lips slightly parted. Her nose was turned up, the faint winter light making her freckles stand out. They were scattered across her nose and cheeks, even her forehead, like diamonds scattered on the sand.

Her eyes opened and blinked up at him. If her freckles were like diamonds, then her eyes were emeralds. They were deep, fathomless, and always open and clear. He loved that he could read her every thought and feeling on her face. There was no guile, no secrecy, no hidden agenda.

Right now, they screamed of surprise, joy, and desire. This woman was bringing him alive in ways he didn't even know he needed.

He caressed her cheek with a thumb and asked, "Go on a date with me tonight?"

Her eyes widened and she grinned, nodding. Then she scrunched up her face and frowned, backing away. "Actually, I can't. I already have a date tonight."

His breath rushed out and pressure increased on his chest before he sucked in a deep, calming breath. After a few seconds of breathing, he nodded, his jaw clenched.

"I see. Who with?"

She tilted her head and watched him curiously. "Parker, Gunner's brother. He stopped by the bakery today while I was helping Maryanne. I'm going to work for Maryanne while I'm here, so hopefully I won't go completely broke."

She watched him carefully, but he didn't move. He was too frozen. She wouldn't—

"Are you going to sleep with him?" he blurted. Shit, what had come over him? Why was he just spouting off like that? He really was an ass, wasn't he.

She pursed her lips and took a step back, forcing his hands to fall to his sides. "I wasn't planning on it, since he's a perfect stranger."

A hot rush of jealousy made him mouth off. "That wasn't going to stop you last night with Nick. I saw you flirting with him."

Her brows shot up in surprise. "I was trying to flirt, but you saw how miserable I am at it. I always say the wrong thing at the wrong time, and then I start rambling and won't shut up, like right now. But don't mistake this for flirting. This is just me—"

"Being pissy?" *Shut up, Jake! What the hell, man? Why are you antagonizing her like this?*

She scowled and flipped her gorgeous hair over her shoulder, letting it fall halfway down her back. "I'm not being pissy. I'm just wondering why you care who I go out with or sleep with?"

He opened his mouth, but nothing came out. Of course, now was when he actually minded his tongue, but did he really want to admit what he was feeling right now?

What *was* he feeling, anyway?

She slammed the trunk closed. "That's what I thought. If you can't just come right out and say it, then I think we're done here. I'll see you around." And with that, she turned on her heel and opened the car door, slamming it behind her.

Maryanne drove out of the parking lot, but Jake just stood rooted to the spot, watching them.

He was jealous of Parker. That's why he was poking her just now, pushing her away. He'd rather she leave in a huff than choose someone else over him. That's what had happened with his first girlfriend in middle school. He always mouthed off, forcing them to run away or storm off. It was what had happened with every girlfriend since, except for Patty.

With Wendy, it was more than jealousy. It was a raw, wild need to be the only one to touch her. That's why he had butted in last night with Nick, wasn't it? He'd been so distracted with his truck that he hadn't had a chance to think about it, but here he was, unable to *stop* thinking about it.

"Mr. Jake, am I in trouble?" The part-time teenager, Josh, stood wringing his hands in an open bay to the garage.

Jake sighed and shook his head. "You know customers aren't allowed in the bay area."

"I know, but she needed all those bags. I did good telling her you weren't here though, right? You said no women are supposed to know you're here, after that ex of yours went crazy."

Jake winced. He was getting a headache. He'd actually had one all day, but while Wendy had been here, he'd forgotten about it.

"Right, you did fine. If anyone else needs me, I'll be in the office trying to catch up on paperwork."

"Yes, sir."

His hand traced along the brick surface of the wall as he walked up the metal stairs. He reached the top and pushed open the heavy wooden door, revealing the sunlit room with large windows offering a bird's eye view of the bustling garage below. He could see mechanics tinkering on cars, their tools clanking against metal, and hear the low hum of engines being tested.

This was where he belonged - in this chaotic, yet

comforting space above the garage. The scent of motor oil and burnt rubber filled his nostrils, a familiar aroma that reminded him he was home.

By the time he closed the door, the smells and sounds of the shop were overwhelming, pushing emotions that he didn't want to face. He fell on the big, plush couch and leaned his head back with a sigh, his mind comparing this shop, *his* shop, with the military one.

His phone buzzed and he glanced at it.

Dinner tonight? I'll make your favorite.

He winced. Mom expected him to check-in today, but he'd come straight to the shop to work on the truck. Guilt speared him, so he fired back a reply before walking to the desk. If he was going to have a family dinner, he'd need to finish some of the paperwork first.

Lester was taking great care of the shop and handling customers while he was gone, but the man was a nightmare with organization. Everything was handwritten in chicken scratch that didn't help his headache when he tried to decipher it.

After another two hours, he just couldn't do it. He threw on his jacket and closed the office door.

"Hey Jake, come look at this catalytic converter. I haven't seen one this bad since '97," Lester called out.

Jake did a detour to check it out. "That's pretty bad. And they drove it in here?"

Lester wiped his hands on a rag and nodded. "Yep, blowing black smoke like you wouldn't believe. And the smell was even worse."

Jake just chuckled and shook his head. "Glad I wasn't here. I would've gagged."

"Nah, the smell was gone by the time that pretty little redhead walked through. The place smelled like roses for a good fifteen minutes after she left. I was surprised you walked past and up to the office instead of staying down here to sniff it."

Jake's head snapped up to see Lester grinning and wiggling his bushy gray eyebrows. Jake sighed and stood straight, wiping his own hands off on a rag.

"Not you too. Don't start."

The look of concern in Lester's eyes made him pause. He admired this man and looked up to him, and they both knew it.

Lester slapped his hand on Jake's shoulder and said, "You've been back two days? And already falling for the new girl in town. Whole garage is talking about that kiss in the parking lot."

Jake groaned and rubbed his temples, the movement reminding him of Wendy and the feel of her hair in his hands. It soothed him.

"Why was everyone watching when they were supposed to be working?" Jake pitched his voice to be heard through the garage and turned on his heel to walk to his truck.

Lester's laughter echoed behind him, but the other four guys working just kept their heads down, some smiling and some frowning.

Before he could open the door to his truck, Lester's booming voice threw one final comment loud enough for all to hear.

"Don't repeat your past mistakes, son, but don't let it stop you from finding happiness, either."

Jake shook his head. That was the crux of the matter, wasn't it? Did he open himself up to another new, so-called innocent girl in town or did he learn from the past?

The question plagued him all the way to his parents' house.

Chapter Twelve

W,
I'm actually not in combat at the moment. I'm home on R and R. And my memories of home are okay. It's just, my sister died in a car accident a few years ago, and it's hard to be home without her. Kind of like you with your mom. When I pull up to my parents' house, I keep expecting her to come bounding down the steps, begging me to save her from Mom. lol
You moved out after your mom died, and I went active so I could deploy. Two peas in a pod, aren't we? Lol Both leaving to escape the memories.
I had to look up what that word meant, ectomorphic. It just means you're a skinny little thing, right? Kind of petite like Audrey Hepburn in the old movies? You could send me a picture and show me what you mean…
J

Wendy threw open the sleek, red Corvette's door and slid inside. The interior lights lit Parker's smiling face, which helped settle some of her nerves. He looked good in his gray polo shirt, khaki slacks, and black dress shoes. His hair was slicked back, the product making it a darker color, almost brown.

"I was half worried you'd bail on me."

She grinned and slid her seatbelt on. "Nah, Maryanne wouldn't let me. Not that I wanted to. Well, I did want to, but not because of you. Shit. Um, so I talk a lot when I'm nervous."

He chuckled and put the car into gear. "I can tell, but it's okay. No need to be nervous. Although, I am curious why you wanted to cancel?"

She shrugged and looked out the window as they turned the corner. "I don't date a lot." For once, her mouth shut up, and she breathed a sigh of relief.

"Would it put you more at ease if I said it's more of a business date than a *date*-date?"

She whipped her head around to stare at him, but it was too dark to see him clearly. The knot in her stomach began to settle at his words.

"That would make me feel better, actually. But why? Where are we going? What is a business date?"

He chuckled and shifted gears. "We're going to the Old Mill. Have you been there yet?"

She shook her head and saw they were nearing the edge of town. The lots became bigger, the businesses looking less new and more mid-1950s.

"I haven't, no. Haven't even been on this side of town before."

He turned and went over an old wooden bridge. She looked out at the little river that ran along the edge of town.

"Oh, wow. You don't see a lot of historical bridges like this, especially here in this little piece of Texas. Haven't seen a lot of fancy cars like this one either."

He grinned as he drove on the road that followed the river. "The bridge was updated a few years back and is a preserved historical landmark, which is pretty cool. I teach history and coach soccer for the local middle school, and I love these little bits of history of our town."

"And the car?"

"Oh, I bought it in college right after my signing bonus for joining the Eagles soccer team."

"Wait, the Eagles? Isn't that a huge pro team?"

"Yep." He turned into the parking lot at the restaurant and killed the ignition. He slid out of the car, and she opened her own door before he could get around. She wanted to get out and ask all kinds of questions.

He offered his arm as they stopped at the fence in front of the Old Mill.

"Wow, a white picket fence? This is an old Victorian house, isn't it? Is there a history story here too? What's it attached to?"

Parker beamed down at her with the largest grin she'd seen on his face. He practically started vibrating with energy. "Exactly. That's why I brought you here, and *this* makes it a business date."

He waved his hand at the building. "I bought it right before Christmas."

She blinked and looked from the building and back to him. "What do you mean, you bought it?"

"The Old Mill and all the property attached with it. I had a good nest egg left over from my soccer contracts and wanted to preserve it. It's been sitting empty for a few months, but my brother, Landry—did you meet him at the Electric Cowboy on Friday—he's spent the past few weeks making repairs. It was in pretty good shape. Come on, just wait until you see the foyer."

Wendy felt her ears ringing as they walked up the sidewalk.

He pointed along the sidewalk. "Now, imagine flowers blooming along the walk. And over in that corner? It's the perfect spot for a vegetable garden. Very sunny. And that tree in the other corner? It used to have a swing on it when I was a kid."

"You came here as a kid? But why?"

He opened the old oak front door with a key, the stained-glass inserts shining from the porch lights. When she stepped inside, a hostess stepped out from behind a desk with a smile, an older woman with her white hair pulled back in a bun.

"There you are. I was thinking you'd gotten lost."

Parker chuckled and pulled her forward. "Agatha, this is the woman I was telling you about. Wendy, meet Agatha. She used to own and run this place until last year as the only Bed and Breakfast in town. And it was the best date place too. Sadly, all my dates lately have either been to Sonic or Pizza Barn."

Agatha chuckled as Parker clutched his chest in mock horror. But Wendy just looked from one to the other curiosity nearly eating at her. As Parker and Agatha chatted, they went into a large room to the right of the door. A giant fireplace on one of the long walls was lit, the fire crackling and welcoming them in.

There were booths along one wall and little wooden tables for two near the windows. They stopped at one of those with a quaint lace tablecloth.

Parker held her chair out, so she sat, still looking around and speechless. Parker chatted with the woman like he'd known her all his life, which he probably had.

It was a cute little place, the wood paneling and soft

candlelight making it dark and intimate. The booths were threadbare but not ripped, the tablecloths clean but well-loved.

She took the menu from the woman and gave her drink order. The menu was pretty standard for Texas, but she saw a few vegetarian options that could work.

"Do you like it?"

She glanced up at Parker and frowned. "What?"

"The Old Mill. Do you like it?"

She felt like it was a loaded question, and she looked around with hope. She was almost afraid to hope. Her nerves had skyrocketed again because this was her entire life's dream.

She looked at Parker and saw the same hope in his eyes. So, she leaned forward and took a deep breath.

"This place is homey and low-key fancy. It's good quality from the little I've seen. But you need to level with me, Parker, before I go making conjectures and getting my hopes up. Why am I here exactly?"

He launched into a history lesson of the place, explaining how it'd been here for over a hundred and fifty years, when it was converted into a restaurant, when it stopped the mill operations.

Agatha came back and laughed. "Parker, are you going through every little detail of this place? I swear, you love it more than I do."

He seemed to blush in the soft light and shrugged his shoulders. "What can I say, Agatha? This place is awesome. And it's the best field trip of the year, to come here with my classes every spring. You were a champ for putting up with all of us, and I can't stand the thought of this year's class not getting to come here."

The woman patted his shoulder and looked heavily at

Wendy with her brows raised. A bell dinged, and she spun on her heel and walked away.

Wendy sighed and leaned back on the booth seat. "Parker? Love the history, I really do. But if you don't tell me why I'm here on a *business date*, I might scream."

He burst out laughing as Agatha brought their food. It smelled heavenly, and her mouth watered.

"When Maryanne heard you were coming here, she called me. She knows I bought this place hoping to open it back up as a bed and breakfast, maybe a little town museum. Agatha was barely making a profit, but if we turned the actually mill building into an event venue, I bet we could make a steady income."

Wendy's eyes widened. "And me?"

He took a deep breath. "I want you to run it all."

Her heart soared and her leg bounced under the table. Tears pricked her eyes and threatened to fall. "It's always been my dream."

He grinned and took her hand in his. "That's what Maryanne said. Who am I to deny a beautiful woman her dream? People said I was crazy to want to go pro soccer, and yet I did exactly that. I'm proof that the impossible is possible. So, what do you say? Wait, don't say anything yet. Wait until I show you the rest of the place."

She chuckled and took a drink of her water to calm down. "Okay, but first, I'm going to eat. This smells amazing. Are you looking at changing up the menu or keeping it the same?"

Parker cut into his steak and said, "Oh, that would be up to you. I'd want to approve any changes, of course. For example, you wouldn't be able to put some hippie tofu on the menu like you'd see in some places. This is Texas, and we have a reputation to uphold."

She laughed and the conversation moved to his plans for the bed and breakfast guests, digitizing everything, and even her photography and event planning skills.

They exchanged stories of growing up too, him with his brothers and her with stories of Maryanne and her sister, Cindy. He made her laugh to hear about all the trouble he, Landry, and Maryanne would get into in the summers.

When the date was over, they walked back to his car, and he asked, "So what do you think? Could we make it work?"

She bit her lip and looked back at the big, beautiful Victorian house. She said, "Yeah, I'd love to take a chance on it. This is more than I ever dreamed. Thank you, Parker."

She threw her arms around his neck and hugged him. He stumbled back a step and chuckled, then he hugged her back with a quick squeeze.

"Hey, no problem. You're doing me a huge favor here, trust me." He broke the hug gently and smiled.

She tilted her head and let him open the passenger side door. "Can I ask you a question?"

"Absolutely."

"Was this ever a date-date?"

He grinned and moved to let her settle into the car. "Oh, I wanted it to be, but I saw you with Jake at the Electric Cowboy on Friday. No way am I stepping between you. He's a good man, and I have hella respect for him."

She nodded as he closed the door and walked around to the driver's side. Would anyone else in this town date her if they all thought she was starting something with Jake? Did she even want to date anyone? Or did she just want to get laid and forget about Mike?

Chapter Thirteen

J,
I'm not going to send you a picture! That's like a strange man giving a child candy. lol Yes, I'm almost child size. I still sometimes shop in the junior's section. They just have so many more options, you know?
I'm sorry about your sister. That must have been awful, to have her one minute and then to suddenly lose her. Sometimes I wonder if it would've been easier to have Mom suddenly go instead of dragging it out and seeing her suffer for years. Is that horrible to say?
You watch Audrey Hepburn? I thought you were a guy. I don't know any guys who know who Audrey Hepburn is. I love more Doris Day movies than Audrey Hepburn movies. There's just something about her energy that speaks to me. Maybe it's the wildness, since I look more like Merida, the Disney cartoon movie.
W

Jake opened the door to his parents' house to find way more people than he was expecting. His head was still pounding, but there was nothing he could do now.

The Mechanic Gets His Girl

His niece, Mandy, saw him first and yelled, "Uncle Jake! You're back!"

He grinned as she raced to him, and he swooped her up in his arms, spinning in a circle and making her shriek. Then he gave her a kiss on the cheek, making her giggle from his five o'clock shadow.

By the time he set her down, his nephews had all gathered round. "Cody, good God, have you grown three inches since last summer?"

The teenager grinned and nodded. "And my voice dropped too. Can you tell?"

James elbowed him and frowned. "Everyone can tell. You won't shut up about it."

Jake laughed and ruffled both their dark hair. "You've grown too, James."

Owen tugged on his pants. "What about me? I'm seven now. You missed my birthday."

Jake crouched and hugged him too. "I know, little man. I'm sorry I missed it."

"It's okay. I still love you."

Owen let him go and the kids raced back to their game. His cousin, Andy, was really blessed with all those kids.

"You want to take them home with you?" Andy asked as Jake stood to his feet. "It's guaranteed to cure that look on your face."

Jake's forehead wrinkled. "What look?"

"The look that says you want a few rug rats of your own."

Jake glanced into the kitchen and shushed him. "Are you crazy? Mom's right there. If she hears you, I'll never have a free night. She'll have dates lined up for me from now until I leave again."

Andy laughed and glanced over his shoulder. "Don't

worry. She's too busy talking with Cindy. But seriously, I thought you'd sworn off kids and women?"

Jake sighed and rubbed his forehead. "I don't want to talk about it. What I do want is a drink. Where's Dad?"

Andy jerked his head. "In the garage with the Shelby." Together, they headed through the house, both dropping a quick kiss on his mom's cheek.

Once in the garage, he slapped his dad on the back and bent his head under the hood. "What are we looking at?"

Dad pointed with the ratchet and said, "Spark plugs need changed out."

"You want a hand?" Jake asked.

Dad handed him the ratchet and smiled. "Why else would I be fiddling with it when you're expected for dinner?"

Jake laughed, but before he could get started, Andy handed over a drink. Dad grabbed his glass from the counter and raised his glass to Andy's.

"To a safe deployment," Andy said.

"To a year of blessings," Dad said.

"To more time doing what we love," Jake added.

They toasted and tossed the shot back. Then Andy filled their glasses halfway with Dad's best whiskey. This had been their tradition for all of Andy's deployments too. Drinks in the garage was something they'd kept going for years, even before Sarah had died, even before Andy had lost his foot in combat.

He stared at his drink, then tossed it back too before setting his cup down on the counter and turning to his dad's prized Shelby. They'd restored this car together when he was in middle and high school. It was what had started his love for cars and mechanic work.

"So, spill it. What was with the way you looked at the

kids tonight?" Andy asked, leaning against the counter and sipping his drink.

Jake grunted and turned the ratchet. "I don't know what you mean."

Dad chuckled. "Getting to be that age, are ya?"

Jake glanced up and scowled at them. "What is that supposed to mean?"

Dad shrugged. "They say women get baby fever, but once a man reaches a certain age, he gets to feeling the need for roots."

"I have roots."

"But not the love of a good woman," Andy pointed out.

Jake ignored them and worked on the spark plugs.

Andy asked Dad, "Why do so many men get married in their thirties?"

Dad replied, "Guys sow their wild oats in their twenties. Thirties is for settling down and building families, working on a legacy to pass down to the next generation."

A legacy. He snorted. "I'm thirty-two, Dad. Plenty of time. Did Mom put you up to this?"

"Nope. I was just going off of what Andy said. How did he look at the kids?"

Andy chuckled. "Like he wanted some of his own for sure."

"Or maybe I was just looking at them like an uncle who's missed so much already." His voice was harsh, but the words lingered in the air.

Andy asked quietly, "Are you thinking of getting out?"

Jake grunted. "Contract is up when I get back. Might transfer back to part-time instead of full-time."

They didn't say anything for a while, and he got one of the spark plugs changed out. He grabbed the torque wrench to tighten the new one.

"What's that make, twelve years so far? That's a good run. You sure you don't want to just retire?" Andy asked.

"I know you were up at twelve, but I'd prefer to go twenty or thirty if I can. I like the extra cash." Jake and Andy had always talked about being lifers, but Andy's injury had sent him to early retirement.

"What if you get married? Would you still stay in?" Dad asked.

Jake started working on another plug and grunted. "Probably."

"Ah-ha!" Andy said, "A few years ago, you said you'd never get married. Even last year, after that Patty shit, you swore you'd never even have another girlfriend. So, what's changed? Are you really thinking about settling down?"

Jake sighed and stood up to face them. "What do you want me to say? That I'd hoped to settle down with Patty? That I was excited about her pregnancy, even though I suspected it wasn't mine the whole time? That I'm still mad that he's not my boy?"

Andy's eyes softened, but Jake turned away, unable to bear looking at them. If he just kept his head down and focused, then he wouldn't have to think about all he'd missed. He wouldn't have to think about how Andy being a dad made him jealous. He wouldn't have to admit that he'd wanted Patty's baby to be his and had blindly ignored the warning signs.

He was a fool, but he'd never admit it. He switched out the spark plug and started on the next one.

"I saw them at the grocery store this week," Dad said softly. "He's a good-looking kid, but he doesn't look anything like you."

Jake snorted. "He wouldn't, since he's not mine."

"You sure?" Dad asked.

"I'm working on it. DNA test samples will be taken on Monday, so we'll know by this time next week."

The garage door opened, and Cindy popped her head around it. "Dinner's ready when y'all are."

Andy went to her like a moth to a flame, a soft smile on his face. Jake had to look away and grit his teeth. Andy left with her, but Dad leaned against the car and stared down at him.

"It's okay to want to settle down, son."

"My head agrees with you," Jake grunted.

"But your heart?"

Jake got the third one switched out and moved to the fourth. "My heart says it's not fair. Sarah didn't get to so why should I be able to?"

Dad cleared his throat, but Jake refused to look at him. He'd never been able to stomach seeing his dad get emotional.

Dad's voice was rough when he said, "Because you're still here for a reason. Because your mom wants more grandkids. Because we want to see you happy, with someone to love and take care of you."

Jake finished the last spark plug and lubed the boot with grease. It was messy, just like his life. Actually, that wasn't fair. His life was pretty straight forward. It wasn't nearly as messy as Wendy's. That girl was a hot mess.

"What about that girl from Friday night?"

Jake jerked up in surprise, then took a deep breath to calm himself. Dad couldn't read his mind and didn't know Wendy. Just relax.

"What girl?"

"Oh, come on. You know how your mom likes to gossip. She heard today that you were kissing some girl in the back room of the Electric Cowboy before Patty showed up and destroyed your truck. Who is she?"

He reinstalled the coil, the air filter, and cover. How did he answer that?

"She's Maryanne's friend from Colorado. A chef."

He wiped his hands on a rag as Dad went to fire it up and test the motor.

Dad asked, "So you just met her Friday and kissed her on the first day? I thought I raised you better than that."

The engine sounded like a dream, purring exactly as she was meant to. Visions of Wendy purring in his bed swam through his head, then Dad turned the engine off.

Jake eyed part by part and said, "No, the tow that I went to get Thursday night? That was her."

"Ahh, got to know her on the drive, is that right?"

Jake clenched his jaw as he wiped his hands on a rag. He'd gotten to know her alright. Her and those sweet lips. Damn, he just couldn't stop kissing that girl. Why did her lips have to be so kissable? And Parker was probably kissing them now.

He slammed the hood, his muscles tensing in anger.

Dad slapped him on the back. "Word of warning. Your mom is worried that she'll turn into another Patty situation. New girl in town is a wild card."

No, she wasn't like Patty at all. Wendy wasn't like anyone he'd ever known before. Jake slowly shook his head.

"She's not like Patty at all. She's open, honest, and doesn't really know how to keep anything to herself. I don't think she's the 'trick you into being a baby daddy' type."

And he believed it. She was pure and good and kind and… shit, he had it bad. He should have realized it when he'd dreamed about her the past two nights.

Dad nodded, his gaze solemn. "I believe you, but your

mom might be harder to convince. It took Cindy way too long for your mom to accept her. I just don't want you to let Patty ruin your chance at happiness."

"I won't, Dad." It was more a combination of being gun shy because of Patty and feeling guilty because of Sarah. It wasn't just one or the other.

But maybe he could work something out with Wendy that would keep her at arm's length while still seeing her in his bed? He didn't want to be the kind of guy to just sleep with someone and leave them, but he didn't want to get her hopes up for a love match, either.

She'd asked for him to tutor her in flirting. Maybe he could start there.

Chapter Fourteen

W,
I feel guilty living life when she didn't get to. Is that horrible to say? I used to watch old movies with my grandma before she passed. My favorite might be Sophia Loren. She was just so stunning and exotic. But if we're comparing ourselves to movies, I would be Kristoff in Frozen for cartoons and a mash-up of Robert Redford and Cary Grant. I'm definitely a guy. I would say I could send a picture to prove it, but I'm not the kind of guy to send dick pics. Are you even a girl?
J

Wendy babbled to Maryanne and Gunner's daughter, Connie, in the back seat on the way to morning church service. She had the cutest little dimples, just like her mama.

Her chubby little hand grabbed Wendy's fingers and tried to pull them to her mouth. Wendy started to tickle her, making her laugh. Would she ever do this with her own kid?

She snorted. She'd have to have sex first, which wasn't likely to happen. She'd thought getting married so fast would lead to a baby. Her own family to love. Her own solution to driving the loneliness away.

But that was now off the table, and she was fresh out of luck. Although… Now that Parker had offered her the job, maybe her luck was changing.

When they stopped at the church, she unbuckled Connie and stepped out of Gunner's SUV with the baby in her arms.

Maryanne smiled and grabbed the diaper bag as she said, "You don't have to carry her. I can do it."

Wendy tucked the baby to her chest and smiled back, soaking in that fresh baby hair scent. "And miss these sweet cuddles? Not on your life. You just lead the way."

Gunner brought up the rear, pointing to a shiny piece of the parking lot. "Mind the ice. Nice and easy."

Wendy smiled. It'd only been three days living with them, but she loved how protective and involved Gunner was as a dad. Her own dad had been career focused. More of her memories were of just her and her mom than of the three of them, and they were ones she'd cherish forever.

She'd not minded Mike being in the Army and deploying because that was the same family dynamic she'd known her whole life. It hadn't broken her heart that he was leaving; it was just a fact of life. It wasn't like she'd truly miss him, after all.

She paused on the front steps while Gunner opened the door, realization slamming into her. Oh god, she hadn't loved him at all, had she.

It wasn't a question. She couldn't fool herself any longer. She'd loved the idea of him, the idea of the future they were going to build, the family. But she hadn't really known him well enough to love him.

Tears threatened to fall but she followed her friend

inside the building and pasted a smile on her face. Now was not the time for an eye-opening realization. Maryanne introduced her to dozens of people on their way to the nursery to drop off baby Connie.

She kissed the baby and handed her over to the nursery worker with a sigh. Maryanne linked her arm through Wendy's, and they turned to mingle among the crowd who was slowly finding their seats.

"You're fantastic with her," Maryanne said, nodding to another little old woman.

Wendy smiled. "Thanks. I like kids."

"I know. Do you remember that project we did in culinary school for the kid's place?"

Wendy laughed as she followed Maryanne to the pew about halfway to the front. "Yeah, it was loud and chaotic and crazy, but in a fun way."

Maryanne snorted. "You say fun, I say overwhelming. I had nightmares about that for a week, you know. Three of my cupcakes were knocked over just trying to get from the door to the party room. And the professor knocked points off for that!"

Wendy laughed. "Yeah, I'm pretty sure she just wanted free birthday desserts for her twins. But didn't you have even a little fun?"

Maryanne shook her head. "Nope. Way too loud. But you were in those jump houses with the kids when I left. How long did you stay?"

"Oh, the whole party. Free entry into a jump house? I wasn't going to pass up on the fun. I needed that. Mom had taken a turn for the worse that week." Her voice trailed off, and Maryanne put her arm around her shoulders and squeezed.

"I know."

The musicians took their places at the front, and Wendy's brows shot up. Gunner was leading worship, and it looked like his brothers were the musicians. Parker was up there with a guitar and there were three others too. Damn, they were quite the good-looking group.

She felt heat on her cheeks when she realized she was cursing in church, even if it was just in her head. It didn't make it any less true. She started to clap her hands with everyone else, getting into the music and moving her hips.

But when she shifted from foot to foot, she could see Jake three rows up across the aisle. He sat between an older man and woman and Andy and Cindy, Maryanne's sister. He was singing every word of the hymns, and she could almost pick his voice out of the crowd.

The rest of the worship service flew by. Then she was sitting, trying not to stare at Jake. It was hard, though. He was just so fascinating, and she wanted to ask him question after question. He piqued her curiosity along with her lust.

Which was curious in and of itself. She hadn't even wanted to have sex in college, choosing instead of focus on helping her mom. It was only in the past few years that she'd made any real effort. It had always ended in disaster.

Yet she'd kissed him three times in three days. She'd never done that before. She definitely lusted after him, but this was more than mere lust. She wanted to *know* him, what he dreamed of, what made him tick.

Suddenly, everyone was standing and bowing their heads. She'd completely missed the preaching and prayed no one would ask her what she thought of it. They dismissed, and several people turned to shake her hand, asking her whether she was visiting or moving to town.

Maryanne's mom stopped by, and Wendy squealed.

"Mrs. Margarita!" She threw her arms around her, making Margarita laugh.

"Wendy, darling, aren't you a sight for sore eyes! Look what a beautiful woman you've grown into." Margarita pulled back and touched Wendy's curls.

Wendy smiled, remembering when she'd brush her hair after sleepovers and read Peter Pan to them before bed. It reminded her of her mom, and her chest felt heavy with the memories.

"I don't know about that, but it sure is good to see you. You haven't aged a bit, have you?" Wendy grinned.

Margarita patted her own hair in her bun and smiled. "I try not to, dear, but it's hard sometimes. How are you doing? I was so sorry to hear about your mom."

Wendy's smile wobbled. "I'm doing better now that I'm here. It's been a rough few years. And thank you for the flowers you sent to the funeral home. They were lovely."

Margarita nodded as a blond woman stepped up next to her. "Suzie, have you met Wendy? She's one of Maryanne's oldest friends. I've known her since she was in elementary school."

Wendy held out her hand. "Middle school, but who's counting anymore? It's nice to meet you."

Suzie reluctantly took her hand and shook. "I've heard a lot about you. You've made quite a splash about town in just one weekend, haven't you?"

"Uh oh, what have you heard?" Wendy laughed uncomfortably.

Maryanne joined them with baby Connie on her hip. "Oh hello, Suzie. You must be so happy to have Jake home for a few weeks."

Suzie's face lit up as she turned to Maryanne and clasped her hands together. "You have no idea, child! He surprised me by coming home early. But if he thought he could get out of all the things I have planned, he has another thing coming."

Maryanne laughed. "I wondered if you'd put him to work."

Suzie said, "I had it planned perfectly, since he was going to be home for Valentine's Day. But now I'm scrambling."

"To do what? Do you need help?" Wendy asked. She was completely lost on what they were talking about, but she wanted to help.

Suzie arched a pale brow. "Why, to set Jake up on some dates, of course. He needs to forget about that woman, and the best way to do that is to get him right back in the saddle. I didn't push before he left because he needed to focus on the deployment. But there's no harm in him dating while he's home the next few weeks."

Just then Jake came up behind his mom and put his hands on her shoulders, causing her to glance over her shoulder at him. "I'm glad you see it that way, Mom. Speaking of… Wendy, may I take you to lunch?"

Suzie's head swiveled from her son to Wendy, her eyes pinning Wendy to the spot. His mom was giving her the evil eye, which didn't make any sense.

Margarita nudged Maryanne with an elbow and said loudly, "You were right."

Maryanne shushed her and smiled.

Wendy bit her lip and nodded. "If—if that's okay with Maryanne and—and I guess your mom?"

Suzie's eyes widened in surprise, but she could see Jake's fingers squeezing her shoulders lightly.

"Oh, they don't mind. Why would they? Ladies, it was good seeing you. Shall we?" He stepped around his mom and offered his elbow. Cautiously, she took it, glancing at Suzie.

Her eyes narrowed as Jake led her to the front door, but she heard Margarita say, "Oh, this is wonderful, Suzie! Just wait until you get to know her. She's like a breath of fresh air."

Wendy winced, whether at the words or the cold winter wind, she wasn't sure. They were silent as he led her to his truck, spotted now from the damage Patty had done.

"I don't think your mom likes me."

He shrugged and opened the truck's door. "She wants to control who I see, but it's not her decision. She'll be fine."

The truck was already warm and running as he helped her climb into it.

"Your truck really does look awful. Is there any way to get Patty to pay for the repairs?"

He winced, holding the door open as she settled in the seat. "I've already sent the police report, pictures, and estimate on the truck to my lawyer. We'll see, but I doubt it."

With that, he shut the door and rounded the front to get in. She bit her nail as she waited. It didn't seem like he was holding a grudge about last night, but maybe she should just clear the air.

As soon as the door slammed shut behind him, she blurted, "Where are we going? I thought you were mad at me for going out with Parker last night. Are we okay? You're not mad?"

His hands paused on the seatbelt, then it clicked into place, and he looked up to catch her gaze. His blue eyes were turbulent, his confusion screaming at her to figure out the problem and fix it.

"I won't pretend to be okay with it. There's something about you that makes me…" He sighed and turned to grab the steering wheel. "Territorial is the right word, maybe? I couldn't stand the thought of you dancing with Nick and flirting with him. And I couldn't sleep a wink last night thinking of you with Parker."

She buckled as they pulled out of the parking lot. Her heart raced at his words. No one had ever been jealous of her before. She just wasn't the type. Guys saw her as the friend next door, the nosy, talkative neighbor who wouldn't leave them alone. No guy had ever laid awake thinking about her before, she was sure.

She cleared her throat. "Nothing happened, Jake. It wasn't a romantic date. It was apparently a business proposition."

"A what now?" His tone was confused as he glanced at her.

Her excitement began to build as she thought about her new job. She couldn't help but grin and bounce slightly on the seat. "Do you know the Old Mill on the edge of town?"

He nodded slowly.

"We went there. He owns the place, and he's offered me a job! Cooking, party planning, managing the whole thing. It's a dream come true. I even get to move in this week, can you believe it?"

She sighed and leaned back in her seat, her body humming with energy and her mind already planning the future.

"I'm happy for you, Wendy."

She sighed contentedly. "Last week was the worst week of my life, but things are finally starting to turn around."

He glanced at her and winked, his face mischievous. "Let's see if we can keep that going, shall we?"

Chapter Fifteen

Her heart raced at that look in his eyes. It was hot and heavy and made her squirm on the seat. "What do you mean? Where are we going?"

Jake turned down a long, dirt road, and she sat up straighter, finally paying attention to where they were. Fields were frozen and bare on either side, but she could see a copse of trees at the end with a two-story, white A-frame house.

"This is my house."

Her heart pounded in her chest and her mind raced. His house? Even though she'd only known him for a few days, she felt good about being with him. She wasn't afraid, just really nervous because she had a feeling... if she went into his house and he kissed her, she wasn't going to stop. Excitement raced through her, turning her stomach.

"I thought we were going to lunch." Her voice was way too breathy, belying her nerves.

As they drove down the lane, he said, "We are, but I

The Mechanic Gets His Girl

don't want to share you with anyone else. Not Nick. Not Parker. Not anyone who will judge me based on my past."

Her breathing grew shallow as her heart raced even faster. "I'm not like your ex."

His smile grew and his gaze darkened as he parked in front of the house. "I know. You're... something else entirely."

She laughed. "Is that a good something?"

He shrugged and kept the truck running, not even unbuckling as he turned to her. One hand on the steering wheel, the other took hers. "Yeah, like a breath of fresh air, but I'd like to find out more which is why I made zuppa de Toscana in the crockpot. We can hang out, get to know each other better."

She snorted, twisting at the hem of her sweater. "And have sex?"

He was a man; they all wanted sex, especially when they invited her back to their place. Not that it'd happened that often. She was a virgin, but not naïve. She couldn't start thinking this was anything but a physical means to an end.

He grinned, winking at her. "Any guy would be lucky to be with you much less be your first. I'd be honored, but there's no pressure to do anything. To be upfront though, I'm in the middle of a deployment, and with all the stuff going on with Patty, I'm not looking for a relationship."

Conflicting thoughts raced through her mind as she tried to think, so she shrugged. "I—I'm not sure if it's a good idea anyway. Even though I'm long overdue, and it's not that big a deal, I don't want to start any gossip around."

If she was going to take over the Old Mill, she'd need a good reputation in town. His thumb going back and forth on the back of her hand was highly distracting. It was like lightning running up her arm with every swipe.

"It is a big deal, and you should be with someone who can treat you right. Nick and Parker are good guys, but I haven't been able to stop thinking about you, Wendy. I've never been so jealous as I was when you were flirting with Nick or thinking about you on that date with Parker. I couldn't fucking sleep last night, I kept thinking about it."

Her heart pounded so loudly, and her hand trembled in his. She had to remind herself to breathe as he spoke words that she'd never thought she'd hear directed at her. He wanted *her*. As if sensing her inner turmoil, his thumb gently caressed the back of her hand.

Her voice was hesitant, but it wasn't a question. "You—you want me."

"I'd have to be dead not to. You're one of the most beautiful women I've ever met, but if you're not comfortable or if you'd rather try with someone like Nick or Parker, I can turn around right now, and we'll go to the pizza place in town instead. It's your decision."

She wanted him, but she was also afraid. Part of her wanted to take the risk and see where this would lead, while another part felt the need to play it safe and stick with what she was familiar with. It was a difficult choice, and she didn't know which path to choose.

His bright blue eyes held emotions that she couldn't quite decipher. This was it. The moment she had been waiting for. The chance to finally lose her virginity, and with such an attractive, good man at that. Maybe it wouldn't be as bad as some of her friends had warned.

"I do love a good soup. If I go inside, does that mean we have to have sex, or can I say no later?" Her hands turned clammy. She wanted to say yes, but it was one thing to say you were ready to lose your virginity. It was quite another to actually do it.

He shook his head. "Of course not. You can say no at any time. Mama raised a gentleman, after all."

He winked again, and she knew she was a goner. She couldn't resist him anymore than she could resist cooking. It was in her soul. She just had to get her hands dirty and dig in.

She nodded her head slowly and breathed deeply. "Okay, but first, food."

He laughed outright at that and reached for his seatbelt. "Amen to that. Come on, then."

She unbuckled too, but by the time she'd gathered her purse and opened the door, he was there. His truck was so jacked up, she had to step onto the railing first. His hands slid to her waist, and he picked her up, letting her slide down his body until her feet touched the ground.

She gasped, and his mouth brushed hers in the softest kiss, barely teasing her lips. Then he was pulling away, taking her elbow, and shutting the door.

In a daze of desire, they walked to his house. There was a large front porch, and it was well taken care of. A porch swing was on one end and two rocking chairs were on the other.

"Who takes care of your house while you're deployed?"

He unlocked the door and held it open for her as he said, "Andy and Landry. Landry checks on all the maintenance things. Makes sure the pipes don't freeze and things like that. Andy does too, but I think he stops by for an hour or two a week just for some peace."

She nodded. "I can't believe Cindy and he have five kids. Five! It seems like a dream."

"A dream? Do you want kids too?" His voice was hesitant, but she was too busy looking around his living room to wonder why.

"Of course. I wouldn't mind having a few of my own. I'm an only child and always envied Maryanne having a sister. What about you?"

She spun a slow circle, taking in the modern yet woodsy vibe. Tans and browns somehow meshed with gray and black. There was an L shaped sectional that took up much of the room and a giant screen TV on the far wall.

The other wall to the left was taken up by all windows, even up to the ceiling. "Wow, the natural lighting in here must be fantastic."

Where a third wall should've been was a kitchen island. In the kitchen, Jake pulled soup bowls from a cabinet. She saw his socks and took her boots off by the door, lining them up next to his.

To see both their shoes next to each other was surreal, and her vision swam. Her heart lurched, and she knew this was a moment she'd remember forever. She just didn't know why yet.

She couldn't get her hopes up that this was the start of something serious. She'd only gotten out of a failed engagement six days ago. What kind of woman would she be if she jumped into a relationship right after that?

No, this is what her friends called a rebound, plain and simple. It was purely physical, it had to be. But he was the sweetest, hottest rebound in the world.

She turned back to the kitchen, ready to eat and settle her nerves. He set two steaming bowls down at the island and smiled. "There's a salad to go with it if you'd like. And bread."

"Oh yes. Can't have soup without bread. This smells delicious. It's not a soup a lot of people know how to make."

He shrugged. "I might have googled you this weekend.

Saw it was one of your favorites on social media. But I have no idea if I made it correctly or not. It's the first time I've ever bought kale, to be honest."

She was stunned that he'd googled her, but she couldn't help but laugh. "That actually makes way more sense. Parker and I were talking about the menu for the Old Mill last night, and he specifically said, 'no hippie tofu dishes'."

She chuckled again and shook her head as they sat down to eat. He asked about some things he'd seen on Google, her experience in culinary arts school, her photography program, her hospitality degree. She told him a few of the funniest stories of her time in school.

Then lunch was all gone. She started to feel nervous again, and he nodded to the couch. "Do you want to talk on the couch?"

She nodded, blushing slightly. They sat, neither on the end but not next to each other, either. She liked that she could see his face this way.

"I've been talking this whole time, but tell me about you. How long have you been in the Army?"

He talked about joining with Andy, going active a few years ago, and his contract being up at the end of this tour.

"Are you going to re-up for another four years?"

He nodded and crossed his arms. "Yeah, but I'll probably move back to part-time and just go in one weekend a month. The shop needs me."

"The auto shop?"

He nodded. "Yeah, I bought it from the previous owner a few years ago. He still manages for me while I'm gone, but the paperwork is all kinds of messed up. Lester is old school. Not the best with technology, which makes it harder for me to make it a viable business during a deployment. I need to come back full-time to the shop and really take it over, you know?"

She nodded. "That's one thing that has me so excited about the B&B with Parker. It's a clean slate, a new start. I can really make it my own, even though I won't own it. I'll finally put my hospitality degree to good use."

He smiled, taking her hand again and linking their fingers. "Not going to lie. I'm happy to hear that you're officially moving to town. That means you'll still be here when I get back."

She blushed and crossed her ankles, her foot accidentally touching his leg. She was so short, her feet didn't touch the ground. He moved his foot, letting hers rest on top of his.

It was sweet and intimate and—goodness, was she really going to get even more intimate with him? She glanced at him, and his eyes captured hers in a look that excited and scared her at the same time.

Chapter Sixteen

Her cheeks heated in anticipation. Tingles raced up her legs and hand from where they touched and made her squirm on the couch.

He cleared his throat, his eyes turning heavy and dark. "I don't have a lot of time stateside, so why don't we lay all the cards on the table?"

She exhaled a shaky breath. "Okay."

"Do you still want to have sex?"

She sat up straighter and met his eyes with boldness and determination. "Yes, but I'm just so nervous. What if I mess up or—"

He grinned and squeezed her hand. "You're not going to mess up. It's like following a recipe. I can teach you the ingredients and show you how to put the whole dish together, okay?"

Her brows rose. "That's a good description. I don't want to be nervous about it. If it's like cooking, maybe I just need to practice and get some skills under my belt."

He smirked and pointedly tried to look up her skirt, even though she was wearing tights under it.

"Pun intended, but that wasn't an invitation," she grinned.

"Still funny, though. If it helps, I won't just show you how to flirt and things. I'll also show you how good it can be, so you'll have standards. Don't want you to just jump at any guy who smiles at you."

He frowned, his eyes going distant as he looked away. Maybe he was thinking about Patty? Maybe that's what happened between them.

It didn't matter right now, though. She needed to focus and stay in the moment.

"Most guys don't smile at me like they want me, so that's not a problem."

He scowled. "Then you've only met idiots."

She snorted, then laughed. He leaned forward, grabbed her hands, and pulled them both to standing. He was close, facing her, but only their hands touched. Her breath caught in her throat as she looked up at him.

His blue eyes captivated her. "I'd be honored to tutor you in all the things that matter, but I want to be clear about one thing."

"What's that?" Her voice was so breathy, and she leaned into him slightly.

"This is just for two weeks, then I'm going back for four months. This isn't the start of a relationship. I can't get into a relationship with Patty and her shit still hanging over my head. This is just me tutoring you and distracting myself for a few weeks. Is that okay?"

She leaned back and really looked into his eyes. His gaze was bold, heated with desire. He wanted her as much as she wanted him, but it was the vulnerability in his eyes that made her wrap her arms around his neck and tip her head back.

"I'm your rebound girl. I get it. Like your mom said, you need to get back on the horse." She nodded as he frowned, even as his eyes flashed with heat and desire.

For probably the first time in her life, she felt like an equal partner participating in this dance of desire. It was like he actually saw her, whereas all the guys before had only seen her flaws. Her lack of height, being thin as a board, her too-talkative nature.

But he truly saw her, flaws and all, and he wanted her anyway.

Rebound or not, this wasn't something she wanted to miss out on. She'd take this chance because she didn't have anything to lose.

His eyes narrowed. "What about contraception? I don't know how many condoms I have."

She shook her head. "I take the shot to help with cramps. We're good there. Are you clean? I don't want any diseases, if Patty was with all those guys."

She winced at the look of pain on his face, but his voice was steady when he replied. "I'm clean, tested the week that baby was born and shit hit the fan. Now that the cards are on the table, I think it's time for a royal flush. Let's turn those gorgeous cheeks of yours pink."

He kissed one cheek softly, and her core melted. With a tip of her head, she stood on her tiptoes and met his lips with her own. His mouth was tender, and she slowly felt his hands settle on her hips. Then her mouth opened, and he swept into her with an earth-shattering kiss.

It was more real, more intense than those they'd shared

before. Perhaps it was because this kiss would actually lead somewhere. Her heart raced as his hands slid into the elastic waistband of her skirt and pushed it down.

She gasped, and his tongue distracted her from his hands. She was consumed by his kisses, hot and wet with desire. She lost count of the minutes, simply soaking up the kisses and the fact that this man—this beautiful, smart, talented man—was hers.

She ignored the thought that it was just temporary. Instead, she slid her hands around to the buttons on his shirt. She poured everything she had into the kiss before she popped the buttons of his shirt open one by one.

His hands were sliding inside her tights and caressing her ass. She gasped, breaking the kiss with a jerk. Before she could tell him no one had even touched her naked ass like that before, he was dipping his head and nibbling along her jaw.

Down the side of her neck, he licked, kissed, and tasted. He found a spot on her neck that made her see stars, and she groaned. Her fingers slid inside his shirt, pushing it off his shoulders.

He let go of her ass to lean back and pull his arms out of the sleeves. She reached for the hem of her own sweater and tugged it over her head with one fell swoop. Before she could gather her courage, she pushed down her tights and kicked them away.

Goosebumps settled on her skin as she stood in her underwear in his living room. A man she'd met only four days before. She'd always been impulsive, but she'd never been *this* impulsive.

Butterflies danced in her stomach, and her mouth watered at his tattoos. A large one over his heart and up his shoulder, then another along his rib cage. They looked like the skin had been shredded.

Her fingers traced the one on his shoulder and over his heart, and his fingers paused on his belt. It looked like the American flag was under the skin. The smaller one on his ribs showed tattooed ribs with the Texas flag on it and a date.

"What's the date mean?"

He opened his mouth then closed it. She bit her lip as he slid his belt out of his jeans.

His eyes seemed to search hers, and he just shook his head helplessly. She smiled reassuringly, not quite certain what she was reassuring him of, and ran her fingers up and over his biceps.

"Your unit patch?" She noticed the ripped skin tattoo on his left bicep. He nodded, and she let her fingers trail down his arms and then drop to her sides.

He took a deep breath and blinked slowly. Then his gaze roamed up and down her body, taking her in.

All the thoughts of previous boys who'd made fun of her size, her lack of curves, her boyish looks all came rushing back. She shifted on one foot nervously and waved a hand at herself, glancing down at her small chest. "It's not much, but it should get the job done."

He shook his head and laughed, and her heart sank. Everyone had always laughed at her. Of course, he didn't like her body. Oh no, he—

"No, don't talk about yourself like that. You're gorgeous."

She took a deep breath, confusion swirling in her stomach. "I look like a teenager and have no curves to speak of. My skirt came out of the junior's section at the store."

His finger shot out and traced the base of her neck, then slid down between her breasts. It trailed the slight curve of her bra, first the left then the right.

"I don't care about the store. All I care about is you." He paused at the words, and her heart skipped a beat. Surely, he didn't mean he actually cared? They had just agreed this wasn't the start of a relationship. She tamped down the hope that tried to bloom in her heart. Maybe this was one of his lessons, to show her how someone else should treat her?

"I wouldn't say no curves." He cupped her breast softly, his touch feather light. "I'd say it's the perfect handful."

She gasped. Good god, she really was a goner. Why had she agreed to no relationship with this man? He caressed down her stomach, making it flex under his soft touch.

"Put your arms around my neck again." His voice was low, and the tone made her shiver in anticipation. She slid her hands up his biceps and raked her fingers into the short hair on the back of his head.

Then he slid his hand around her hips to her ass, making her gasp again.

His lips descended on hers once more. He'd captured more than her mouth. Not her heart, though. No, it was too soon for that. But she could see the train wreck coming her way, and it would be so easy to fall for him.

Her thong was no barrier, but she had to keep up the barrier around her heart. His tongue teased hers, cutting off the rest of her thoughts before he hooked his hands under her ass and lifted.

She squealed against his mouth, breaking the kiss and wrapping her legs around his waist.

He grinned as he walked to the back of the house. "See?

You're the perfect size to pick up and carry wherever I want."

She tilted her pelvis against his stomach, pulling him closer to the part that had ached for him. "Oh yeah? And where are you taking me?"

His eyes smoldered, literally smoldered. "To bed, Peaches. It's time to finish your first lesson."

Chapter Seventeen

Jake had been with a handful of girls over the years, but Wendy was something else. She was completely different from his normal type. She hadn't been lying about her small stature. He could probably lift her in one arm since he could curl over a hundred pounds easily.

But the feel of her body pressed against his made him groan. When she ground her hips against his stomach, it brought her breasts almost to his face. He kissed along her neck, his eyes opened as he pushed through his bedroom door.

He walked the few feet to the bed and turned to sit on the edge. The movement brought his dick up to nestle against the juncture of her thighs, in the place he was desperate to plunge into.

But if this really was her first time, he wanted to take it slow. It was why he'd deliberately left his jeans on. He needed the barrier between them.

She shifted on his lap, wiggling with a gasp that made him lean forward and capture her mouth. The savage lust that had been building in his veins ever since he'd seen her in the cab of his tow truck threatened to break free.

Their breath mingled, and he used the kiss to regain control. He couldn't stop her from grinding on him, though. He took their kiss deeper with every shift of her body on top of his. The sharp, wild need drove him higher and higher until they were both panting, their kisses wild and all-consuming.

He was about to come in his pants like a teenager, but he'd promised to take care of her, to show her how a real man should treat a woman. Quickly, he stood and turned, laying her on her back with a gasp.

His hands pulled her thong down as he dropped to his knees, his breathing ragged. He didn't even take the time to bask in her pretty pink pussy before he was burying his mouth on her.

She gasped, then moaned, and the sound was music to his ears. He shifted his hands to cup her ass. He wasn't able to resist her. She was like the ambrosia of the gods, better than Dr. Pepper and ice cream and anything else he'd ever tasted.

He flattened his tongue and lapped slowly up and circled her clit. She shuddered in his arms, gasping, "Oh god."

He released her, saying, "Not god. Jake. Say my name when I make you come on my face."

She glanced down and their eyes met as he lowered his mouth to her clit once more to tease it, barely caressing in a circle before pulling it into his mouth.

"God, yes, Jake!"

He smiled. "Good girl. That's it, say it again." He sucked gently on her clit, and her back arched off the bed, making her break eye contact.

"Jake!" Her voice flowed around him, encouraging him to keep going. He sucked once more, kneading her ass and prodding her to wrap her legs around his head. He settled on his knees and closed his eyes as he worked her over.

"Jake, oh god, yes."

The tangy smell of her filled his nose, making him crave more. He had to see her come. He slid a hand around and teased her entrance with a finger. She tensed, but he didn't stop or give her even a second to think about it. He eased the first knuckle inside, just half an inch, and paused.

She took a deep breath and glanced down at him, biting her lip. He lifted his brows in question, and she nodded. It was so easy to communicate with her, even like this without words and just body language.

It was uncanny, heady and addicting. He could get used to this, to her, to pleasing her.

He eased his finger out and then in, slowly adding a little more each time. God, she was tight. Maybe she was a virgin like she claimed.

"Jake, Jake." Her voice was searching, her head thrown back and her fingers sneaking down to grip the sides of his head. She held him closer, so he sucked harder on her little clit and eased a second finger inside.

He wasn't plunging his fingers in roughly like he would've liked. She required a delicate hand, but he could work her up to that. For now, she was so close, and he focused all his efforts on making her come.

He circled her clit and then sucked one more time, and it pushed her over the edge. She came on his tongue and thrashed on the bed, shuddering as she cried out. The guttural sound was beyond words. Simply a raw, intense, sound of pleasure ripped out of her as he felt her pussy pulsing.

She clamped down on his fingers in waves, and he licked her clit to savor the evidence of her orgasm. Every lick sent a ripple through her body, her body continuing to writhe for what felt like minutes.

Then she finally relaxed, her hands falling to the bed beside her with a sigh. Her legs slid off his shoulders, and he caught them with a grin before settling them gently to hang off the edge of the bed.

She was a goddess laying spread open on his bed. Her wild auburn hair spread around her head like a halo, her chest rising and falling rapidly, her lips open and eyes closed as she savored the afterglow.

And he was the one who'd put that look on her face. Pride surged through him, fighting with desire for dominance. Ultimately, desire won out, but he had to make sure she wanted all of him tonight.

He caressed her thighs and kissed the inside of her knee, dropping kisses up her thigh and making her twitch at the touch. Her eyes fluttered open, and then her head lifted so she could see more of him. Her gorgeous green eyes shone bright in the afternoon sunlight.

"Do you want more? Or have you had enough of a lesson today?"

She bit her lip and swallowed, then took a deep breath and sat up, hooking her hands behind her back and unclasping her bra. She let it fall down her arms and then tossed it to the floor, sitting on the edge of the bed like a queen holding court.

Her hands fell to the bedspread, and she looked up at him with a sliver of fear but a whole lot of trust and hope in her eyes. He didn't want to scare her. She was sitting on his bed gloriously naked, open and ready to move forward even if she was scared. She was so amazing.

He stood and reached out to cup her face. Her skin was so soft, he just couldn't stop touching her. "You okay?"

She nodded, nuzzling her face into his hand and closing her eyes with a soft sigh. "Yeah, it's just—I've never done that before. Or rather, no one's ever done that to me before. It's overwhelming."

He tipped her head up, and her eyes opened to stare into his own. Her eyes scared him. They were so open, trusting. It was like staring into his future and not knowing if he was going to blow it or not. That's what he felt when he stared into her eyes and what made him the most nervous.

They didn't have a future together. This was just him sharing skills she wanted.

"You don't have to keep going. We can take it slow, do one lesson a day."

Her soft hands settled on his hips, and she frowned. "I—I want to finish it. All of it, before I chicken out."

"No, I don't want you to feel pressured and—"

She grabbed the button on his jeans and flicked it open, making him stop mid-sentence. Then she said, "I'm not, I promise. Please, Jake, I need you. I feel so empty inside." Her hands pulled his zipper down while her eyes mesmerized him. Her fingers grazed his hard cock, and his control snapped.

He stepped back and took his jeans off all-in-one motion. Her eyes roamed down his body and stopped when she looked at the bulge hidden by his underwear. He paused with his thumbs hooked into the elastic of his briefs, still hesitant.

But then she reached out, moved his hands away to his sides, slid her own fingers into the waistband, and pulled down.

The Mechanic Gets His Girl

He sprang free, and she gasped, "Oh my god."

He grinned and his fingers brushed the hair out of her face and tucked it behind her ear. "Like I said, I'm Jake, not god."

She giggled, and his chest grew lighter somehow. It was such a pure sound of joy, and he wanted to keep her like this forever.

No, not forever. Just for the next two weeks. Maybe they'd not leave the house at all.

Tentatively, she reached out and traced her fingers from the base to the tip then back again along the underside. It was his turn to bite his lip and swallow hard. She tested his patience and control like none other.

He kept his fingers in her hair and watched the play of emotions on her face as she stared at his dick in her hand.

"It's hard and soft at the same time. Can I—how do I, um—"

His voice was husky and low when he said, "Next lesson? Like this." He gently guided her hand to circle the base, then he showed her how to squeeze and slide to the tip. His hips rocked toward her before he slid her hand back down to the base.

Then he released her hand and put his behind his back in parade rest. He gripped his hands together so hard the nails bit into his palm. His hands spread slightly, he looked down and let her explore and fondle to her heart's content.

It was the most glorious torture he'd ever experienced. If the Army could bottle this, every soldier would give up state secrets in less than five minutes. That was his goal. Five minutes to let her touch. Five minutes to watch the wonder in her eyes deepen to desire. He glanced at the digital clock on his dresser, then back down at the wonder on her face.

At two minutes, his hips were moving forward and backward with the movement of her hand. At three minutes, he was groaning softly. At four minutes, she licked her lips, glanced up at him, then bent and licked the tip.

She leaned back and smacked her lips. "Hm, salty. Kinda like a potato chip."

She did it again, and he was done. He reached under her arms and picked her up easily, tossing her higher on the bed and making her squeal.

He grinned and climbed up between her legs, an arm on either side of her body caging her in. "We'll finish that particular lesson another time. I need you now. If that's what you want?"

She nodded, her lips parted as he settled into the vee between her legs. She tensed up, and he pressed against her fully. Chest to pelvis, their skin meshed, hard against soft. He kissed her jaw up to her mouth, then captured her lips in a kiss that demanded surrender.

He mimicked what he wanted to do with her, plunging his tongue in and out, teasing as he started to grind against her clit. She gasped and spread her legs wider, her feet settling flat on the bed.

The tip teased at her entrance, and she whimpered. Shit, that whimper. He groaned and pressed into the tightest, wettest heaven on earth. God, she was like a vise, she was so tight. He rocked back, then went forward shallowly, in and out, slowly stretching her wider to accommodate his width.

When she started panting and rocking her hips up to meet him, he pushed all the way to the hilt. She gasped and froze beneath him. He held himself still, absorbing the finality of it, the reality of it.

There'd been no resistance, but somehow—deep down,

based on her reaction, her tightness, everything—he knew she was a virgin. Shit. She *had been* a virgin, but no longer.

He felt a pang of regret as he pulled back from her, gazing down at her with amazement and keeping himself settled deep into her welcoming warmth.

The moment was both thrilling and bittersweet, knowing that she had trusted him with something so precious, but part of him went feral at the idea that he was her one and only. In this moment, they were connected in an intimate bond that transcended any label or title. And for that, he felt grateful and content.

Chapter Eighteen

"Wendy? Are you—" he took a breath and exhaled the words. "Are you okay?"

She nodded, her eyes wide in pain or surprise, he couldn't tell, her teeth biting on her bottom lip. Her hands on his biceps bit into his flesh, but he didn't mind. He rained tiny kisses down on her jaw and neck.

This unbelievable woman was all his. No one else's, just his. It was a gift he'd never imagined.

Slowly, she relaxed in his arms and began to squirm. The feel of her wrapped around him was exquisite. He tried to remember any other time sex had felt this good, but all he could see was her. She filled his mind, body, and soul.

He had to make this good for her, had to make her come again. She shifted yet again, and he nuzzled her neck, making her gasp. "Wendy, I don't think I can hold back much longer."

She wrapped her arms around him, her nails scraping his shoulders. Then she thrust her hips up and said, "Then don't. Please, Jake. Please. I need you to *move*—I need—oh…"

The please broke him, and he pulled back before plunging inside once more. Her last words dragged out into a moan, and he set up a steady rhythm as old as time itself. He filled her, stripping away every thought, everything that worried him.

For now, it was just the two of them, lost in a cocoon of bliss. Her breathy moans and nails on his back drove him forward. She was so wet and tight, pulling on him as he thrust. She matched him measure by measure, beat by beat, until he pressed harder, deeper, filling her, needing her more than he thought possible, until he was consumed by her, mind, body, and soul.

Hard, rough strokes rocked them, and he sucked on the base of her neck, needing her to come soon. She gasped and clenched around him, squeezing like a glove and trying to trap him inside. His balls tightened in response, and he fought the sensation, struggling to hold on a little longer.

He changed the angle and reached for her clit, strumming like a guitar. Circling, he thrust, and her breath caught in her throat. That's it, that's what she liked. He gave her more, not stopping until she was a panting, writhing mess.

Finally, *finally*, she cried out, "Jake, god yes, Jake!"

Her body clenched around him, and she grabbed his hair, pulling hard as she mewled and cried out with her release. She clenched around him, and he saw stars. His body slammed into her once, twice more.

Then he unleashed inside her, exploding with a groan as she shuddered in waves around him, milking him for every drop. They were fused together in one hot, sticky release, the power of it driving them both beyond words.

As the aftershocks slowed, her hands fell from his body,

and he rolled onto his back. They both lay there, panting, and it felt like the universe shifted. He stared at the ceiling, uncertain of what had just happened.

It was unlike anything before. More powerful. More intimate somehow, more than just the motions. It was a connection on a deeper level. It was—

A snore broke through his thoughts, and he glanced over. Her eyes were closed and her mouth slightly open. She was loud even in sleep, it seemed, and he laughed softly.

No girl had ever fallen asleep on him so fast. He must've done a decent job to have her immediately pass out like that.

He snorted and gently rolled off the bed to get a wet cloth to clean up. He returned and slid the rag under her, cleaning the evidence of their arousal. She stirred softly, then turned onto her side, the cloth stuck between her legs.

With a shrug, he slid onto the bed with her. There was nothing better than a Sunday afternoon nap. It'd been a long time since he'd indulged, though. The past few months had been full of mortar attacks and barely getting a full night's sleep. They'd often have to wake up in the middle of the night and seek shelter.

As his arms settled around her to spoon, he sighed. It had definitely been too long since he'd taken a safe nap in his own bed.

Too long since he'd held a beautiful woman. Too long since he'd made love.

Made love? This wasn't a relationship. It was just sex, plain and simple. He couldn't be taken for a fool twice. He *wouldn't* be. He refused. It hurt too much otherwise.

He had to focus on their arrangement. He'd tutor her in flirting, sex, and all that came with it. Then he'd catch a plane back to the sand pit and—and try to forget her. She couldn't be different. It was just sex.

Yeah, that's it. It was just sex. He repeated it in his head like a mantra until sleep tugged him under.

Wendy stretched in the warm bed, her arms rising above her head.

A low chuckle made her freeze. Then a deep voice said, "You're like a cat when you wake up. Meowing and stretching in the sun."

She pried her eyes open. *Jake*. She blinked, remembering what they'd done, feeling the soreness between her legs. He was lying on his side, his head propped in a hand. The blankets barely covered his waist.

Correction. They barely covered their waists. She squeaked and jerked the covers up to her chin, making him chuckle. He reached out a hand and brushed her wild hair out of her face, caressing her skin and leaving goosebumps to run down her body.

She twisted her head to look at him more fully. "Good morning. Or afternoon? What time is it? What do people say after something like this happens?"

His gaze turned serious as he frowned and said, "I'm not sure that this has ever happened before."

She wiped the sleep out of her eyes, and turned onto her side, careful to take the blankets with her. "What do you mean?"

His face cleared, and he smiled. "I mean, people usually go their separate ways. If you're at your place, the guy is gone when you wake or leaves soon after. If you're at his place, you can sneak out while he's asleep or go to the bathroom and then escape."

She frowned. "That doesn't seem very nice. It's rather rude, actually."

He grinned and tapped her softly on the tip of her nose. "Exactly. Which is why I'm showing you how it *should* be done by both of us waking up in the same bed."

The words echoed in her head. It was like he was painting a picture of their future. She couldn't read into his words like that. This wasn't the start of a relationship. This was just a learning opportunity.

She nodded slowly and asked, "I like it. It's much better this way. I mean, my friends have all talked about the walk of shame, but I've never really understood it. I guess if they're sneaking out, it makes sense though."

He caressed her face and flicked her hair behind her head, tickling her neck. "It doesn't have to be something to be ashamed of. I'm certainly not. Are you?"

The flash of vulnerability flashed across his face before he schooled his features had her shaking her head.

"No, I'm not. I—I feel free. I can finally go on dates without this cloud of fear of the unknown hanging over me."

He frowned then scooted up in the bed to lean against the pillows, settling his hand back on her head to play with her hair.

"I'm happy to be of service, ma'am. Anytime you need a tune up, just holler," he said in an exaggerated drawl.

She giggled and slapped his thigh, then left her hand there. "Don't be silly."

His grin faded as he replied, "I'm not, I'm totally serious. We can do that as many times as you'd like."

"Until you leave," she corrected. She needed to remind

herself more than him. His easy, open expression shuttered as he nodded.

"Until I leave. Right. But until then, we can get you caught up on years of debauchery."

She giggled again. "Debauchery? Who talks like that?"

He shrugged. "I like to watch a lot of movies. A lot of the period pieces talk like that."

She was intrigued and asked his favorites. They talked about historical documentaries and movies, then moved on to spoofs and comedies that mocked them. They discussed everything from *Monty Python* to *Spaceballs*, then they compared movies and the book versions, like all the *Robin Hood* ones.

The cartoon version the favorite for both of them, naturally.

"Oo da lolly, is that your tummy rumbling? Ole Friar Tuck would have my head if I let a fine maiden like yerself starve. Up and at 'em. Let's get some grub," he said in a fake accent only faintly reminiscent of the movie.

She laughed so hard she almost missed him getting out of the bed. Her breath caught in her throat to see his naked ass, those bulging thighs that spoke to the workouts he must do even while deployed.

He slipped on his boxers and pulled a t-shirt from his dresser. He tossed it at her and smiled like the cat who ate the canary.

"Here you go. Something to wear while we eat dinner. I'll go warm up the soup."

She sat up, holding the sheet to her breasts as he walked out the door. It was so easy to be with him. Effortless. She felt like she'd known him her whole life, yet she knew so little.

Quickly, she slipped on the t-shirt, but felt bereft without underwear. She didn't really want to wear her thong, though. She thought about it as she used the bathroom and cleaned up.

His bathroom was immaculate, all blue and gray with a giant walk-in shower. No tub though, which was a pity. She glanced in the mirror. Her mascara was smudged, so she grabbed a washcloth and fixed it.

Finally, she stopped at his dresser and opened drawers. She found his briefs and pulled a clean pair on. They were very loose but could almost pass for biker shorts. It was weird to wear a man's clothes like this. Her eyes landed on some pictures on top of the dresser, distracting her from her awkwardness.

A family portrait from a girl's high school graduation. Jake was smaller in build with an easier smile, giving the girl bunny ears. On the other side of her stood his mom, Suzie, and what must be his dad. But who was the girl? He'd not mentioned a sister, but the resemblance was obvious.

Another picture showed him, Landry, and Andy. They were all much younger, but probably after high school. They were all holding beers with arms around each other in front of a bonfire.

A tray sat on top with random coins, paper clips, and keys. Then a small box was on the edge. She peeked inside. A rolled-up piece of paper, a few odds and ends, and a few really old pictures. The old pictures were of him and what she was sure was his sister.

She unrolled the piece of paper. It was a sonogram of a baby, dated last March.

"That's Patty's boy," his voice was harsh, making her jump. He was leaning against the door frame with arms and ankles crossed.

She glanced down at it, then rolled it back up and put it

away. "I'm sorry, I wanted some shorts or something, and got distracted. What exactly happened between you two?"

He sighed and rubbed the back of his neck. "It's a long story. Do you want to eat? It's going to get cold again, but we can talk about it over food."

She nodded and walked to him. His eyes took in the t-shirt, glancing from hard nipple to hard nipple before raking down her legs and back up again. When she reached the door, he hadn't moved.

She reached out and ran a hand up his bicep before cupping his cheek. Their eyes met, both hesitant but wanting.

His hand covered hers on his cheek, then he pressed a kiss to her palm and held her hand as they walked to the kitchen island. There wasn't a dining table, but the island was one long, solid piece and more than suitable. Five stools were along three sides, three in the center and one on either side of them.

He sat on the end, and she sat at a ninety-degree angle just like she had on the couch. She liked being able to see his face. She picked up her spoon while he started tearing his bread into pieces. His frown made her want to reach out and make it all better somehow, but she gave him time to think. She knew when to talk and when to shut up, and this was a time to wait.

Chapter Nineteen

Jake sighed and tore another piece of bread apart.

"I guess I can start from the beginning. I came home from the last deployment in November. The holidays were just around the corner, and both Landry and Andy had gotten married by then. I was left out."

Landry had gotten married in September, and Andy the previous December. He didn't blame them for seizing their happiness, but it made the loneliness bigger somehow, to come home to everything changed.

She nodded. "That's how I feel too. All my friends in Colorado have either gotten married or moved off for jobs or families or both."

He was out of bread pieces, so he picked up his spoon and stirred the soup. "Exactly. We had a bonfire as a welcome home party. Patty showed up. She was new, gorgeous, and we hit it off. We ended up getting drunk and one thing led to another. Then we ran into each other in town two days later and made plans for dinner, exchanged numbers. It was like that for a couple of weeks. We'd meet up two or three times a week for food and sex."

He gritted his teeth and took a deep breath. "I hadn't thought much of it, but right before Christmas, we had a night together, and she gave me a card. It was a Christmas card that said something cheesy about being a dad."

"Oh wow. What did you do?"

"What could I do? I just stared at it and let it all wash over me. I was shocked, excited, nervous, and scared to death."

"Scared? Why?"

He shrugged and finally took a bite of the soup. When he finally swallowed, he continued. "I was lonely but wasn't sure being a father was what I wanted. Andy has *five*. Landry and his wife were pregnant with the twins. They're constantly busy, and I just—I just wasn't sure that was for me."

"What did your mom say?"

He winced and popped a piece of crumbled bread into his mouth. "She was so excited. You know Mandy, Andy's daughter?"

Wendy nodded as she ate.

"Mandy used to live with my parents. That's a whole different story, but let's just say that since she moved in with Andy, my parents have been lonely too. So, when I told them at Christmas that Patty was pregnant, they were really excited. In fact, it was their excitement that changed the whole way I saw it."

"In what way?"

He shrugged. "I saw that baby as a gift after that. It was a way to get my life back on track."

She glanced around at his house and frowned. "If

having your life off-track looks like this, I don't know how you ever took me up on my offer."

She chuckled, wiped her mouth, and continued. "I mean, I had just been fired, kicked out of my apartment, and lots more shit when my car broke down. You have a house, own your own business. I'd say you're pretty on-track."

He chuckled and took another bite of soup, feeling her eyes searching his face, but he couldn't tell her about Sarah yet. No, it was too soon, and he was still too raw about his sister.

He wiped his own mouth and stood up. "I want to show you something."

She hopped off the stool and grabbed his hand, lacing their fingers together. His heart raced, but it felt right. He squeezed slightly as he walked back toward his bedroom.

"My bedroom takes up the entire right side of the house, with the closet and the master bath. But this—"

He stopped at the door across the hall and opened it. He didn't look inside, instead choosing to look at her face.

Her jaw dropped as she stepped past him and into the room, the smell of roses following in her wake. She turned a slow circle, and her hands came to her mouth in wonder.

"Oh, Jake, this is, oh, it's beautiful." Her voice was breathless as she took in the black crib across the room, the woodland decorations. One wall was black and white wallpaper that looked like a birch tree forest. A blue rocking chair with an orange fox pillow sat by the window. The same blue was on the other three walls, along with various artwork.

Above the crib was a sign that said, 'Not all who wander are lost', and in front of it was a faux bear rug. In one corner was a little kid's sized teepee with pillows inside, and beside it was a small bookshelf with bins of toys and books.

He walked to the crib and ran a hand over the blanket that hung over the edge, his chest tight. "My mom made this by hand for him. He never got to use it."

Her hand settled between his shoulder blades, and she rubbed circles on his back. Funny thing was, he'd imagined rubbing his son's back just like that in this very room.

"What happened?"

He took a deep breath and exhaled slowly. "I was set to deploy again in May. It was an unusual turnaround for us, but I was being sent ahead of the unit to help set things up, transition from the previous unit to our unit."

He turned and found her nodding. It was nice to talk to someone who understood the lingo and how the Army worked. He didn't have to sugar coat it.

"She went into labor the first of May. He was born at thirty-three weeks and weighed five pounds. It was too early, and he was too small, so they put him in the NICU for two weeks."

He swallowed hard, his eyes focused on a spot on the wallpaper. "The first week we were there, she was recovering from the birth, and two guys showed up. Phillip arrived on Monday, claimed he was the father, and demanded to see him."

Wendy gasped. "What? No."

He nodded, finally looking at her. "On Wednesday, Stan showed up and caused an even bigger scene. He demanded a paternity test."

Wendy ran her hands up and down his arms, and it made some of the cold dissipate.

"I didn't even ask for an explanation, I just walked out. She tried to call me, tried to explain. There were voicemails and texts. Over a hundred that first week. I started to feel bad about it, especially since they were still in the hospital."

Wendy frowned but didn't interrupt.

"She was released from the hospital, but the baby was still in the NICU. She sabotaged my truck so my tires would be flat, and I'd have nowhere to run when she showed up to talk. I just locked all the doors in the house and refused to leave. Then when I did leave, she broke into the house and stole a bunch of stuff."

He glanced around the room and shook his head. "But she didn't take any of his stuff. None of the clothes we'd picked out, none of his toys. Nothing. Just cleaned out my bathroom, so I had to go to the store and restock."

"And she showed up." Wendy didn't ask. It was a statement, but he didn't question it.

He nodded. "Yeah, she swore I was the father, that she was waiting on them to do a paternity test on the other two guys. I made the mistake of asking her how many other guys might be the father."

He gave a sharp bark of laughter. "She stuttered and couldn't answer. So, I left her in the parking lot and went inside. When I came out, she'd slashed my tires and keyed my truck. I filed a police report."

Wendy tipped her head to the side. "But that wasn't all, was it?"

He took a shaky breath. "No. I went back to the hospital to see him, to see if I could see a resemblance to any of my baby pictures, or my niece Mandy's from just a few years ago. I saw her hugging some guy outside the nursery. I stopped, my feet glued to the floor, and then she kissed him."

"Was it Phillip or Stan?"

Jake shook his head. "Someone new, so I left. I filed a

restraining order, jumped overseas a few days later, and tried to send happy thoughts for them to be one big, happy family."

"Based on her reaction at the bar on Friday, I'd say whoever he was didn't stick around."

Jake nodded, his eyes meeting hers. "Or that guy wasn't the father, either. I don't know how many guys she was with, but the DNA test that we send off tomorrow might actually say he's mine."

He began to pace, her hands falling away. "What if he is mine, and I've missed the past eight months of his life? What if—"

She stopped in front of him before he'd even made a lap to the door and back. She grabbed his biceps and shook him slightly. He didn't budge, but she tried, which was cute.

"Will you listen to yourself? You can't play the what if game, or you'll drive yourself crazy. You need a distraction. Do you have *Robin Hood*? I've got that song stuck in my head and want to watch it."

He grinned and felt his shoulders relax slightly. "On one condition."

She arched her brows, "Oh?"

"Stay the night? We can give you another lesson." He pulled her closer, wrapping his arms around her waist.

She gasped, and he dipped his head to kiss her. But she placed a hand on his chest, and he hesitated. She bit her lip and looked up at him.

"I'm a little sore, and I have some medication I need to take that I left at Maryanne's. Can we take a rain check on that? What about tomorrow night?"

He eased back and smiled. "Tomorrow it is. I have to say, I like that you're up front and honest with me, that you spoke up about what you need. That's a very good thing."

She beamed up at him and hugged him. "See? I told you I'd be a good girl. Now for that movie."

She released him and sashayed out the door. He was left speechless. Did she even know what that phrase did to him? Maybe he could teach her a little more than just the basics of sex.

Chapter Twenty

The next day, Monday, Wendy woke up after only a few hours of sleep and went with Maryanne to the bakery. She yawned all morning, but three cups of coffee was the wrong move. Now she was bouncing around the bakery, making a mess and cleaning as she went. Stupid caffeine and her highly sensitive metabolism.

Jake hadn't dropped her off at Maryanne's until after they'd watched *Robin Hood* and *Peter Pan*. He'd said it was in honor of her name, which had made her giggle. She wasn't exactly the Wendy Darling type but had argued against another cartoon. They'd compromised with Hook instead.

"Girl, what time did you get home? You're dead on your feet but hyped up on caffeine like a rocket," Maryanne smirked as she came into the back for another tray of pastries.

Wendy shrugged. "Midnight, I think. We got caught up watching movies. But honestly, I'm afraid if I stop moving right now, I'll fall asleep."

Maryanne sighed. "Aw, that's so sweet. It's also the longest lunch date I've ever heard."

"I know. Twelve hours for a date, and then only three hours of sleep. But it was so worth it!"

"Oh really? You sure you were just *watching movies*?" Maryanne gave two finger air quotes.

Wendy's cheeks heated, and she fanned her face. Maryanne leaned her elbows on the counter and propped her face in her hands.

"I'm on a break so spill the tea already. I'm dying to know everything."

Wendy laughed and leaned back against the other counter. "Where do I start? Oh, I know. He googled me."

Maryanne's brows arched, and she sat up. "He what?"

Wendy beamed and reached for the dough she'd been working on. "Yep, he googled me and found my favorite meal on one of my Instagram posts. And he made it for me."

"He *cooked* for you?"

Wendy waved her hands, spreading flour across the surface by accident. "He cooked *kale* for me in zuppa de Toscana."

Maryanne's jaw dropped, and Wendy burst out laughing at the look of surprise on her face.

"I know, right? How crazy is that? So, we ate—it was delicious but heavy on the salt—then sat on the couch and talked. And you know how I was still a virgin? Well, I'm not anymore. Then we took a nap, ate more soup, and watched movies in t-shirts and briefs until midnight. Isn't that amazing? I mean, me! When I can't even get through a whole date without running a guy off screaming into the night."

Maryanne barked a laugh, and Wendy waved her hands. "What? It's true. There was this one guy a few months ago, who went to the bathroom, but then I saw him running across the street yelling. No clue why, since he never returned my texts or phone calls."

Maryanne shook her head. "No, I was just surprised you were still a virgin. Why didn't you ever say anything? I could've been your wing girl."

Wendy shook her shoulders and kneaded the dough, her cheeks flushing. "It was embarrassing. When you and the others were going out on the town in college, I was taking care of Mom. Didn't really have much of a chance until the past few years. By then, you'd moved back here."

Maryanne crossed her arms and her face softened. "I'm sorry, Wendy. I had no idea. I've been a terrible friend."

Wendy chuckled. "Are you kidding? You're the best. Who let me stay with her for free and offered me a job when I was broke and homeless?"

Maryanne rolled her eyes. "You weren't homeless. Broke, maybe."

Wendy separated the dough into balls. "Definitely broke since my car still isn't fixed. On the bright side, I can move into B&B anytime this week. Isn't that great? Parker said it's ready for me, but we'll have a business meeting later today. Can you drop me off at the Old Mill once we're done here?"

Maryanne nodded. "Sure, what time do you want me to pick you up?"

Wendy blushed. "Actually, Jake's picking me up when he gets off work at the auto shop today."

Maryanne wiggled her brows. "In that case, why don't I take you home first and you can pack an overnight bag. Then you can stay the night."

"But the bakery—"

"Will be fine without you." Maryanne chuckled. "Zarrel is itching to come back in. Although—"

She tapped a finger against her chin in thought. Then she pulled out her cell phone and typed.

"Although, what?" Wendy asked as she dropped the balls into the cupcake pan to rise. The yeast in the fresh dinner rolls smelled divine.

"Zarrel used to cook in a restaurant. I bet he'd work out a deal to be your backup chef in case you ever need a day off or something. He's done here by two in the afternoons anyway."

Wendy nodded and moved the pans to the side. "That'd be cool. I'll mention it to Parker and see what he thinks."

The bell from the front of the store rang, and Maryanne glanced at the swinging kitchen door. "I better get back out there. Don't fall asleep back here. Or if you do, take everything out of the oven first."

Wendy chuckled and just moved to the next recipe on the list.

Parker drove down the long, dirt driveway slowly. She glanced at him out of the corner of her eye.

"I appreciate you driving me out here, but if you were worried about your Corvette getting dusty, why didn't you say so?"

Parker shrugged. "Not worried exactly. I just like to take care of her. That's all."

Wendy rolled her eyes as the car came to a complete stop. She grabbed her purse from the floorboard and opened the door. Parker popped the trunk and pulled her camera backpack from it.

"Here you go. Let me know if you need anything else. You have my number, right?"

Wendy nodded and slung the bag over her shoulder. "Right. Think about what I said, and we'll meet again once I get moved in on Thursday."

"Will do." He nodded and slid into the driver's seat again. She walked up the stone steps in the yard to the porch.

The front door opened, and Jake stood with hands on hips, glancing between her and the car. "I thought I was coming to get you in half an hour?"

He was gorgeous, and she sighed to see him again. She was just happier around him. She shrugged as his words registered and smiled as she walked up the steps. "We finished the meeting early, so I had Parker drop me off."

He was frowning as he stepped aside to let her in, still staring at the car before it disappeared onto the main highway.

"Is that okay?" She set her bag down by the door and bent to unzip her boots.

He stepped away and back to the kitchen. "Yeah, it's fine. I'd rather you didn't ride in cars with men if you can help it."

She straightened and walked into the kitchen. "You mean, until you leave, right?"

He glanced at her but quickly looked away. "Right. Exactly. You can do whatever you want after I leave."

He sounded bitter about it. He reached for the knife on the counter where he'd been chopping vegetables, but she ducked between him and the counter. She slid her hands up his arms and looped them around his neck.

Ever so gently, she pressed her lips against his. Second by second, he relaxed against her until he finally wrapped his arms around her. Then his mouth opened into a kiss that shook her to the core. His kiss was an unspoken promise of naughty things to come. And oh, did she want to come.

The phantom feel of him had plagued her all day, making her wet and wanting just thinking about it. His kiss quickly grew scorching, hungry, and passionate. He roughly claimed her mouth deeper than ever before.

She moaned. He squeezed her, then he stepped back slightly. His hands came around to tug on her leggings. She pushed them down as his hands moved to his jeans. Their mouths didn't leave each other, desperately clinging as if life depended on their bond being unbroken.

When they'd both stepped out of their pants, he grabbed her by the ass and lifted her. She wrapped her legs around his like before, but instead of taking her to his bedroom, he stepped to the edge of the counter away from the food he'd been prepping.

He set her on the counter, and the cold granite made her squeal. She was silenced when he plunged his tongue into her mouth. It should've been weird, but it wasn't. It was desperate, raw, passionate. He slid his hands down the outside of her naked thighs and then up the inside.

Her legs quaked at his touch, and she was pulsing with desire. Slowly, his hands pressed her legs apart, then he pulled her to the edge of the counter. His mouth tried to distract her, but she was oh so aware of his fingers tracing up and down the junction of her thighs.

Her opening throbbed for him, but he ignored it. Instead, he drew circles around her clit, increasing the pressure until her hips were rocking forward. Her hands gripped his arms, trying to press him closer as the scent of her arousal surrounded them.

The Mechanic Gets His Girl

His erection slid across her damp heat, making her jerk at the contact. He teased her folds, and she moaned. God, yes. This was what she'd wanted all day long. Her legs opened wide to receive him, but still he teased.

Emboldened or maybe just needy, she ran her hands around his waist to his ass, and dug her nails in. His length pressed against her, stretching her opening wide. She hooked her knees around his waist and pressed with her heels, begging him without words to put her out of her misery.

He plunged into her wet heat in one solid thrust. She screamed into his mouth. His cock seared into her, burning like a brand.

Yet she felt the ache that had plagued her all day finally float away. He was impossibly huge, and it hurt so good. He filled her completely, stretching her with every thrust.

She locked her legs around him, holding him captive as her hands slid up his back and began to claw at him. She whimpered into his mouth as his relentless thrusts rammed into her.

The coil within her tightened as he drove her too quickly to the edge. Heart pounding, body quivering, she saw stars behind her eyelids. She teetered on the brink, her whimpers going higher and higher.

Then she screamed again as the full force of her orgasm shattered. Convulsive waves gripped her, tossing her back and forth on the counter. The tension inside her exploded. Her body was shaking, and still, he pounded into her.

He broke the kiss and gripped her outer thighs as she continued to writhe against him.

"Mine. No one else's. Mine." Each word was punctuated by a thrust, and the look in his eye turned feral.

She gasped, "Jake!" His words triggered her release, and

fireworks burst behind her eyelids. Spasming around him, her vision dimmed, the edges going black as she soaked up the feeling of him plunging as deep as he could go, over and over, drawing out her orgasm until he groaned.

His eyes flashed, then his whole body tensed as he came, and she felt the rush of warmth as he pumped into her. He gasped, his mouth open and head tipped back.

The aftershocks of her own orgasm rocked through her, and she cradled him close. He moved forward until both their heads were buried in the other's neck. She savored the closeness of him. Their ragged breathing mingled, and the faint smell of fuel and oil still clung to him from the shop. That scent had never been sexy before, but it was undeniable now, clinging to his shirt.

Lying in his arms, she felt completely relaxed and content. The rhythmic rise and fall of their chests lulled her into a sleepy haze. She could have stayed there forever, basking in his touch and the feeling of safety and love he provided. No, not love. This was just physical. She had to keep reminding herself not to get attached.

As his fingers grazed her thigh, her muscles shook, and he shifted to lower her legs to the bed, chuckling, "You're my good girl."

He noticed her legs shaking and shifted to let them lower to the bed, tenderly kissing her cheek before whispering, "You like when I call you that?"

Her breath caught in her throat, and her muscles clenched around him at his words. "Ye—yes," she hissed.

He paused and kissed her again, causing another wave of pleasure to wash over her.

"What else do you like, Peaches?" His words sent shivers down her spine as she melted into him, completely lost in the moment.

Chapter Twenty-One

What the hell was he doing to her? She clung to him and gasped, "I—I don't know. What do *you* like? Show me how to please you and be good at this."

"Darlin', you're already fucking fantastic. If you get any better, I'll never let you leave the house." His voice sent vibrations through her, making her shiver.

She bit her lip, still buried in the crook of his neck as embarrassment and pride filled her. She'd made him lose control, fucking without even taking their shirts off.

"But as for your question, I like good girls, especially good girls who do dirty things."

Her breath caught. Oh god. Was she ready for this? Her heart had slowed in the aftermath, but now it was racing like a freight train. Her body hummed at his words, and her core kept clenching around him.

"Like—like what?" Her voice was breathless, but she had to know.

The warmth of his breath and the pressure of his lips on her neck made her toes curl. Had she just discovered how much she liked him kissing her neck yesterday? He teased her, making her squirm as he rocked his hips, sending a jolt of pleasure through her and making her gasp.

"Let me show you." He rocked again, pulling away from her neck. He reached for the hem of his dirty long-sleeve shirt stained with oil and tugged it over his head, tossing it to the floor. Then he reached for the hem of her sweater and did the same.

She reached behind and unsnapped her bra, and he helped toss that too. Then he put his hand on her chest and slowly eased her back until she laid flat on the counter, her legs still wrapped around his waist.

His hand trailed a lazy path down her chest, circling her breasts and tugging, pinching, and caressing.

He struck up a conversation like they were just sitting at dinner. "You know, when I activated to full-time Army Reserve, I went to Warrant Officer school. I've gotten used to people calling me sir. I like it in the bedroom too. Do you want to try it?"

She gasped, eager to experience all the things she'd only read about. "Yes, sir."

A slow grin spread across his lips, and he palmed her breasts, making her moan. "See? That's a very good girl. And good girls get rewarded. I really like rewarding my good girl."

He thrust into her one more time as he tweaked her stiff nipples like ripe berries waiting to be plucked. He rolled them between his fingers before he leaned forward, pressing his dick even deeper into her wet pussy.

Then his mouth was on her breast. She arched her back as he began to thrust again, sucking and rolling the nipple in his mouth. Then he switched, moving his mouth to her neglected one while rolling the now wet one between his fingers.

Her desire went from zero to sixty in point two seconds flat. "Oh god, Jake! Please, I need—"

"Tell me what my good girl needs."

"I need you to—to fuck me. Yes," she drew out the word as he slammed hard into her and twisted her nipple. "Like that. Please, fuck me, Jake. Jake."

Her breath hitched as he pulled out and plunged back in. She saw stars again, and all too soon her body was humming. She panted his name, her hands gripping his biceps, her nails digging into his skin.

The pace was brutal. The need, passion, and desperation for completion hadn't lessened just because they'd both come already. It was heightened, more sensitive. They drove on and on in a timeless dance, two steps toward the edge and one step back.

"Jake, please. I need more," she gasped, thrusting but unable to get the leverage she needed.

His hand left her nipple and slid down to her clit. He pressed roughly into it, and the added pressure of his thumb against it with every thrust sent her back arching. She came hard, screaming his name and spasming around his hard length.

He tensed, and with a roar, he joined her in the land of fucking heaven. He grew impossibly wider, stretching her once more as he filled her with his pulsing cock.

Her legs couldn't last much longer, wrapped around him like this. But she held on until they were both spent. He eased his hands around her back and helped her sit up.

With one hand making soothing circles on her back, he cradled her against his chest until their breathing returned to normal. It made her feel safe and cared for, like this might be more than just physical. Her breath shuddered a sigh as her chest tightened a warning to not get caught up with emotions.

He kissed the side of her head, not minding that her hair was all in his face. "Dinner can wait. Let's go shower. Think you can hold on to me, so we don't make a mess all over the kitchen floor?"

She chuckled and felt him slip a little further out. "Oh!"

"For God's sake, woman, don't laugh. Hold on, okay?" He picked her up by the ass, and her quivering legs locked at the ankles, his tone making her giggle.

He growled in response, and she wrapped her arms around him.

She grinned and sucked on his ear. "Yes, sir."

He groaned and pushed himself further inside her with every step down the hall. "That's a very good girl."

She clenched around him at the words, which made him slip out completely. He didn't let her go though, just pushed through the master bathroom door.

"Turn the knob clockwise," he demanded, pressing her up against the wall beside the shower.

She gasped at the cold tile, at feeling him so close to her core. Having sex was such an odd sensation, but it was also like a piece of her life had finally fallen into place. She reached out a hand and felt the spray of the water as he nuzzled her neck.

"Okay," she said shakily. "It's hot now."

He stepped inside, and then he let her legs drop to the tile. His arms held her stable, even if still a little wobbly. When she was able, they soaped in silence, each lost in their thoughts. Or maybe he was like her, and his brain was just completely blank after that good loving.

No, not loving. It was sex, plain and simple, and the

sooner she got that the less likely she'd be to get hurt. She winced as she washed her vagina, trying to be gentle.

"You alright? Was I too rough?" His concern made her smile, and she wrapped her arms around him. Slowly, he hugged her back, and she sighed, content to just be here with him.

"No, it was perfect. It's everything I'd ever hoped it'd be. The good girl, yes sir thing? Do people really talk like that?"

He squeezed her, and she felt his head nod against hers. "Yeah, they do. It can be really fun, but if I ever ask you to do something you're not comfortable with, you need to speak up, okay? Don't just do something because you want to be a good girl and obey."

She nodded into his chest. "Why is this a thing? Is it because I crave the approval of my dad?"

He pulled back, and they finished rinsing off. "I don't know. *Do* you crave his approval? What's he like?" He stepped out and dried off while she turned the water off. Then he handed her a clean towel.

"Typical Army dad. He was super strict, especially since I was a girl and an only child. My friends had to be approved by him before I could go to their house or vice versa. I never went to parties in high school either, which is probably why I didn't try much to lose my virginity then."

"And after high school?" he asked as he tossed his towel into the dirty clothes hamper and walked naked into his bedroom. She wrapped the towel around her body and followed him.

He was pulling on a fresh pair of briefs from his drawer, and he tossed her a pair before walking into his closet. She giggled and called out, "I brought an overnight bag. I hope that's okay."

"Hell, yeah, it is," came his muffled response from the closet.

She grinned and walked to his bedroom door still in the towel. She padded to the front of the house where she'd dropped her bag and bent to pick it up.

A creak behind her made her glance back. The front door was opening! She jumped behind it and glanced at Jake's bedroom door down the hall. Her heart was racing. It was too far to make it. Whoever it was would see her.

"Jake, you home? I brought din—oh. Oh my." His mom stepped inside and shut the door, eyes widening as she stared at Wendy standing in a towel and wet hair. Mrs. Suzie's thick coat swished against her thighs. Her sturdy boots were muddy as she stomped them on the mat, a container of food in her arms.

Wendy felt her cheeks burning to come face to face with his mother. She could still see their clothes tossed all over the kitchen. She opened her mouth, her cheeks already flaming as her body grew hot with embarrassment.

"Mrs. Suzie, what a surprise. I didn't expect you. I mean, obviously I didn't, otherwise I wouldn't be standing here in a towel. But that's life. Expect the unexpected, am I right? They also say when life gives you lemons to make lemonade, but I've never been a fan of lemonade, have you? I—"

"Mom?" Jake came out of his bedroom door shirtless, wearing only a pair of soft flannel pajama pants. Wendy blinked, distracted by his broad shoulders.

Then she bit her lip and glanced at his mom, who was now glaring at her for looking at him like that. Wendy shrugged, feeling that bubble of need to talk in her chest.

"What? I can't help it. Look at him. I bet if he wasn't

your son, you'd look at him like that too. I mean, he could be the model for the Army or something. Hats off to you and your husband for making him. I very much appreciate it. I—"

Jake burst out laughing as he came up beside her and wrapped a hand behind her waist. He gave her a side-hug, which calmed her racing heart enough for her to whisper.

"Oh my god, this is the most embarrassing thing that's ever happened to me." She looked around the room, and he squeezed her gently.

"It's alright. What are you looking for? Do you want the clothes from the kitchen?"

She shook her head and held up the duffle bag. "No, I have clothes here. I just expected a hole to open up and swallow me, since I'm obviously dying from embarrassment."

Jake chuckled and kissed the side of her head. "No dying on my watch. You get dressed, and I'll handle Mom."

He led her down the hall to his door, his arm still around her waist reassuringly.

"Oh, good idea. Nice seeing you again, Mrs. Suzie!" She smiled and waved, then disappeared into his room. The murmur of their voices was barely drowned by the closed door.

She leaned against the wood and felt her face. Yep, still hot and blushing. That must've shocked his poor mom. Although, she wasn't sure why the woman was glaring at her. Wendy hadn't done anything wrong, other than sleep with her son, and hadn't she wanted him to get back in the saddle?

Maybe that was it. Maybe his mom was just really traditional and wanted to pick a nice hometown girl for him.

Nothing wrong with that, but did Wendy need to apologize? She frowned and tossed her bag on the bed to get dressed, confusion and embarrassment warring within her.

Chapter Twenty-Two

"Mom, what are you doing here?" Jake's smile faded slightly as he turned to gather their clothes, pulling her bra out of the sink where it had landed. He walked down the hall to find his bedroom door closed, so he dropped them in a pile in front of it before going back to the kitchen.

She tapped her foot and crossed her arms. "What's gotten into you, Jake?"

He snorted. "I've been surrounded by soldiers for eight months. What do you think's gotten into me?"

She narrowed her eyes and flipped her ponytail behind her. "Did you not learn anything from what happened with Patty?"

He went to the vegetables that were slightly scattered on the counter and stepped on a piece of onion. He kneeled and picked up the veggies from the floor.

"I learned plenty, Mom, but you're the one who told me to get back on the horse with dating." He put the dirty ones in a bowl to wash.

"Not with a complete stranger! Patty was a stranger, remember?"

"I remember." He barely listened to his mom, not wanting her to ruin his good mood.

His mom began to pace in front of the island. "And she put on a good show. Those guys were all from out of town, mostly. Except for one of them, I think. She played the innocent really well."

He scowled, feeling some of the post-sex high pass with every word out of her mouth. "I know, Mom, I got played for a fool. Do you have to keep reminding me?"

"I didn't think I needed to, but here you are doing the same thing all over again. Why can't you just learn from your mistakes the first time? You've always been like this. I swear, you get your stubbornness from your father."

Jake snorted and crossed his arms, but refused to point out that it was her who was the most stubborn.

She waved her hands as she spun on her heel. "Did you get the DNA test sent off today?"

"Yes, Mom."

"Good. Hopefully, we can get some answers soon. But in the meantime, you have to stop messing around with that woman." She pointed down the hall.

Jake raised a brow. "And why exactly would I do that? You're judging her based on the actions of a completely different woman."

"Jake, that's not the point."

Jake sighed, rubbing the back of his neck. "What is the point, Mom?"

She stopped and faced him, waving her hands. "We don't know anything about this girl. She could be crazy like Patty, or a serial killer, or a con artist, or a clown."

Jake chuckled and began to cut up the veggies again. "She's not any of those things, Mom, and I know enough about her for now. Look, if it makes you feel any better, she and I have an arrangement. We're just going to hang out while I'm home on deployment, no strings attached, okay? You don't need to worry."

"Don't need to worry, he says," she muttered as she turned to pace again. "I brought chicken and dumplings. Why are you still cutting vegetables? I—"

She froze as Wendy came into view and slid onto a bar stool. She was wearing a fresh pair of black leggings and an oversized blue sweater with a pair of giant red lips on the front. Her smile lit up the room, and he had a hard time looking away. Her blush, her freckles, her wild auburn curls, those gorgeous emerald eyes—they all competed for his attention.

The knife slipped, and he hissed in a breath. He glanced down, dropped the knife, and turned the water on to run his finger under the faucet.

Wendy was suddenly beside him, pulling his hand to inspect. Her dainty fingers sent a jolt through his body, but her hair no longer smelled like roses. No, it was his shampoo now, and he couldn't decide on if that was worse or not. He still wanted to just bury his nose in her hair.

"Here, wrap it up. It's not too bad. Do you have a first aid kit?" she asked, looking up into his face.

He swallowed hard and nodded. "Under the sink."

She pushed him out of the way and kneeled to get the bandages out of the kit. He glanced up at his mom to find her arms crossed and her sternest frown on her face. He rolled his eyes and gave her a pointed look.

She pursed her lips and sat at the counter. Wendy held

up a Band-Aid and stood with a grin. "Found it! Here." She bandaged his finger, then gave him the trash.

"Throw this away, please? Now, what were we making? Mrs. Suzie, are you hungry? You have to stay for dinner. His soup yesterday was delicious, so I'm sure whatever we're making here will be too."

He returned from the trash to see the look of confusion on his mom's face, and it made him grin.

"I was making a chicken pot pie, before we got distracted earlier. Was going to put it in the oven to cook before going to pick you up from the Old Mill. Mom brought dinner though."

Wendy peeked in his mom's casserole dish then at the covered pan on the stove. "Oh, chicken and dumplings! It smells divine, Mrs. Suzie. But Jake's gone to all the trouble of cooking the chicken already, and the veggies are half chopped. We might as well make the pot pie too. We can eat both and freeze the rest. What do y'all think?"

Wendy began opening drawers and pulling out a pot. "Did you say you'd stay, Mrs. Suzie? I sure hope you do. There's no way we can eat a whole pot pie by ourselves. I think it'll need to go on the seasonal menu for the Old Mill."

"The seasonal menu? What are you talking about?" his mom asked.

Wendy bustled about the kitchen, and he couldn't take his eyes off her. There was something so... right, about seeing her here. She was in her element, and he loved having her in his space. Normally he was so uptight about people in his home. He didn't even let people into his room overseas.

Wendy carried the conversation, explaining Parker's

plan and her involvement with it, and he was content to just listen to her plans for the Old Mill.

"So you're staying in town?" his mom asked.

Wendy nodded with a smile. "Yep, I had hoped to make a fresh start here, and it looks like things are finally looking up. Not only do I have my dream job at the B&B, but I get to move in this week too."

Mom almost fell off the bar stool. "Move in? What—"

Jake interrupted. "Not here, Mom."

Wendy chuckled and winked at him. "I don't know. You're quite the catch, and this house is beautiful. If you needed someone to stay here full-time to take care of the place while you're gone, I could probably be convinced to try it."

Jake grinned and glanced at Mom. "What do you think, Mom? Then Dad, Landry, and Andy wouldn't have to stop by once a week and check on things. I think that's a great idea."

"Jake!" Suzie hissed. The horror in her voice made both Jake and Wendy burst into laughter. It'd been a long time since he'd laughed like that. A long time since he'd teased his mom like that too. It'd been since before Sarah.

The laughter died slowly, but Wendy's eyes still sparkled. "Jake, will you help me move? Into the Old Mill, that is?"

He grinned. "Absolutely. What day?"

"Wednesday. Thanks. I really just need the rest of my stuff out of my car. Any update on the parts?"

He held his hands on the counter. "Yeah, you should be all set by next week. I'll make sure it's done before I leave."

Wendy nodded. "Great, I appreciate that. Not that I don't trust the other guys at your shop, but I don't know them, you know?"

The conversation flowed as he and his mom talked

about the different people who lived in town. Wendy asked questions and kept up a steady flow of chatter, and it was relaxing and fun.

This type of chill night at home was exactly what he'd been craving for the past few months of deployment. If he were honest with himself, he'd admit he'd craved it since his world turned upside down, and Sarah died.

Chapter Twenty-Three

Wendy bustled around the kitchen, chatting about Maryanne and Cindy and growing up with them on base. Her nerves were making her too talkative, but she couldn't seem to stop it. In a desperate attempt to shut up, she turned the conversation to his mom.

"What do you do, Mrs. Suzie?"

Suzie's eyebrows rose, then she said, "I'm retired. I used to work at the music store in town, but then it closed. I garden a lot, spend time with the grand babies."

Wendy frowned and added the veggies to the potatoes to boil. "But Jake doesn't have kids."

Suzie looked at him with an arched brow and said, "Oh, I'm very aware. The whole town is aware. But I meant Andy and Cindy's kids."

Wendy blinked, then brightened as she remembered.

"Oh! I didn't realize you called them your grand babies too, but I guess that makes sense. Cindy said you were like the mom Andy never had, which is great. Everyone should be so lucky to have someone step in and be a mom when the situation arises, you know? I can't imagine how I'd have turned out if my mom hadn't been there for me. Did you have a good mom, Mrs. Suzie?"

His mom's eyes turned misty as she smiled softly. "Yes, yes I did, actually. She used to babysit Jake too, back when I worked and before he went to school. Do you remember that, Jake?"

Wendy turned the burner to low and began to make the crust. Jake hadn't taken his eyes off her, and it made tingles go down her spine. When he looked at her like that, she felt beautiful and sexy. Which wasn't exactly how she wanted to feel around his mom.

She stopped and looked at him, raising her brows.

He frowned. "What?"

She rolled her eyes. "Do you remember your grandma?"

Jake cleared his throat and nodded, finally looking away. "I do. We watched all kinds of movies."

Suzie chuckled. "She did love TV, didn't she? That was when she got older and didn't move as well."

Wendy drained the now soft veggies, and then set the pot back on the stove, adding the chicken and broth. It suddenly occurred to her that the awkwardness had faded completely. It seemed perfectly natural to be sitting here with his mom and the guy she'd just had sex with an hour before.

He shifted on the seat and adjusted himself. She tried to stop smiling but couldn't, so she turned away from them. If he could get a hard-on sitting next to his mom, then maybe she wasn't so helpless at this flirting stuff after all.

She shook her head, her hands busy as her mind turned back to the conversation.

"I didn't know my grandparents. All but one had died by the time I was born, and then she died before I got to know her too. You're very blessed to still remember yours, Jake, to have had that time with them." Wendy nodded, but her chest ached for what she'd never had.

She wanted a family of her own someday. Lots of kids and maybe even someone who'd have a family she could fit into. When she'd gone to Maryanne's house as a kid, it was always loud and boisterous, even if it had only been her, her sister, and their parents.

"What does your family do, dear?" Suzie asked.

Wendy poured the mixture into the crust and added the top layer, making the edges look fancy. "My dad is in the Army. He's coming up on thirty-two years, but he's supposed to retire soon."

"Oh, that must be nice, to not have to worry about him anymore."

Wendy nodded. "I know. I've lost track of how many times he's deployed. I would always worry when we'd have soldiers come through the school to visit their kids for lunch or pickup kids for an appointment. I always thought they were coming to tell me Dad wasn't coming home."

Suzie frowned. "Oh sweetie, that sounds like a stressful childhood."

Wendy shrugged. "It was, but I wouldn't have changed it for anything. High school was better. He stayed home for almost five years solid, I think. What does Mr. Suzie do?"

She didn't want to get into why her dad had stayed home during that time. She didn't want to think about when he'd deployed, and it had all been on her to take her mom to chemo and take care of her.

Suzie barked a laugh, the sound surprising her back to the moment.

"Mr. Suzie? Oh no, never say that to his face. That's

funny though. I might call him that just to see what he says."

Jake snorted. "Mom."

Suzie looked at him mischievously, looking so much like the girl in the picture on his dresser. Why hadn't he mentioned her?

Suzie shrugged. "What? It'd be fun. No, his name is Mike, and he's a welder in Denton. Well, he was. He's retired now too."

Wendy put the pan in the oven and set the timer. "That must be so nice for y'all to be retired and get to spend all the time together that you want."

Suzie chuckled and shook her head. "Yeah, you'd think so, but if we spend too much time together, we'll drive each other crazy."

Wendy smiled and began to clean the mess she'd made. They chatted some more, moving into hobbies and how they liked to keep busy. She asked about quilting and told of her serious scrapbooking fascination.

By the time dinner was over, Suzie hugged Wendy. A thrill went through her at the woman's gesture, but she nearly cried when she invited her to a quilting bee the older ladies in the church were hosting in February. Wendy jumped at the opportunity.

"Count me in. I'd love to learn and have something handmade for my bed. Maybe we can make handmade quilts for all rooms at the Old Mill. It would be perfect. Now, don't forget to take this to Mr. Suzie."

Wendy handed over the container of almost half the pot pie while Suzie laughed.

"Thank you, dear. It was delicious. I'll see you both later this week, yes?"

Jake kissed his mom on the cheek, then the door closed

behind her, and he leaned against it. Wendy grabbed her hot chocolate and took it to the couch, feeling his eyes on her the entire time.

"How'd you do that?" he asked as he settled in his corner of the couch and pulled the lever to make it recline.

"Do what?" she replied, sitting with her legs tucked under her, facing him.

"Put her at ease. You could have hidden in the bedroom until she left, but you didn't. You came out and made her laugh, and it was…"

She glanced up, curious but strangely, not nervous about his answer.

"With the deployment, it was exactly the kind of night I've been needing," he finally said with a shrug.

She set her cup on the coffee table, her chest going tight at the mention of his deployment. She understood the need for normalcy more than most civilians, and his need to not focus on the emotions.

She smiled and shifted the topic slightly. "I don't like uncomfortable situations. Confrontation isn't really my thing either, so I almost *did* just hide out in your room. But I figured if I was going to live in this town, I'd have to face her eventually. Might as well get it over with."

He nodded and reached for the remote. "I appreciate it. You're a pretty special woman, Wendy."

Her eyes met his, her lips parting slightly as a blush stole its way across her cheeks. She didn't think she was anything special—all the guys had mostly ignored her for years, after all—but for him to recognize her and truly see her?

She felt like all the pain and loneliness of the past was worth it, if it was what had brought her to this place, this moment with him. She cleared her throat, trying to push past the emotions.

He flipped to the streaming app. "Do you want to watch a movie?"

She nodded, unable to talk past the knot in her throat, and he lifted his arm to rest on the back of the couch. She snuggled into his side like she was born to it, like she'd been doing it for years. How odd that they just seemed to fit together.

What had she and her ex ever done? She'd certainly never snuggled up to him at his place, since he was still in the barracks. She'd cooked for him just once, and then he had split right after dinner, claiming to have CQ night desk duty.

Jake flipped through the streaming app until they settled on a movie, but her mind was only partly on it. There was too much going on in her head as she tried to figure out why she fit so seamlessly into his life like this.

She ended up falling asleep on the couch, and he carried her to bed. When he lifted her, she woken up. But she kept her eyes closed, wanting to prolong the feel of him carrying her so effortlessly.

He kissed her as he laid her on the bed and crawled in next to her. She quickly fell back to sleep with his warmth wrapped around her. It was honestly the best sleep she'd had in a while.

Well, Jake woke her up with kisses and a hard dick the next morning. After a lazy, slow sexcapade, she decided it was the best way to wake up, even better than coffee. She definitely wanted to do *that* as often as possible from here on out.

As they got ready for the day, it felt a little surreal to be eating breakfast with him like they'd been doing it for years. Even brushing their teeth together side by side in the bathroom was strangely domesticated and just so natural. In the course of two days, she'd learned little things, like how he took his coffee and that he was a morning person because of the Army. Such little things that added up to big because it was more than she'd ever experienced with anyone else.

They went to the Old Mill for a few hours. He helped her do inventory, writing the items as she walked through the house and pointed out things to change or update. She took pictures to update the website too.

Then they picked up a pizza before going back to his house for lunch. Naturally, they ended up in bed for most of the afternoon.

The more they talked and spent time together, the more she fell under his spell. Inside, she was still conflicted, constantly comparing him to Mike and wondering what she'd ever seen in the jerk. Jake was more than eye candy, more than just a soldier, more than just a mechanic.

He might have said she was pretty special last night, but he was the one who had captured her—no, not her heart. It was too soon.

But he certainly had her fascinated.

Chapter Twenty-Four

J,
Yes, I'm a girl. What kind of question is that? And ew, please no dick pics. I tried online dating and that seemed to be all the guys wanted to do, was send me dick pics. I've seen enough of those, thank you very much.
Have you seen Robin Hood? *The cartoon version. I watched it the other day and the songs are stuck in my head. Not that I'm complaining, they're quite catchy tunes. Who's your favorite hero who might have been real? Like, Robin Hood might've been. King Arthur? Paul Bunyan?*
W

Jake rinsed out the dishes while Wendy went to the bathroom. They'd stayed home almost all day, except for their jaunt to the Old Mill this morning. It was one of the best days he could ever remember having. Just sex, food, movies, and hanging out.

It was every red-blooded male's best dream, and he never wanted to wake. They'd talked a lot, about her life in

Colorado and how lonely it was the past few years, about his deployments and some of the funnier things that had happened while there.

They were just wrapping up dinner when she excused herself to go to the bathroom. His phone dinged, and he looked at it. Another email from that woman who'd been jilted came through on his Army account.

He read it and froze. It was Wendy. It had to be. She signed her letters as W and the dumbass who'd left her called her Mac. Her last name was Macdonald; he'd looked at her full name on the registration of her car when he'd checked her into the system at the shop. It was how he'd known what to Google on Sunday morning when he'd found her bio on her old job's website and her Instagram.

The mention of being too skinny—she'd talked about that earlier. She was very self-conscious about her petite stature.

And now *Robin Hood*? It was her. This whole time, he'd been talking to *her*. He reread all of her emails.

His fingers felt cold as he stared at the very first email... she'd been left at the altar by a guy in the Army. How could she have been engaged and still a virgin? Had she been saving herself for marriage?

He felt like a sleaze, sleeping with her when she'd been engaged to another man less than two weeks ago. Good Lord, he'd not even known her for a week!

Did she still love that jackass? Did she think about him when they were kissing or in the middle of—

His stomach churned with unasked questions, but he didn't want to burst their happy little bubble. He set the phone down when he heard the toilet flush.

She walked down the hall barefoot and glanced at the clock. "Thanks for letting me cook dinner. I love your kitchen, although I am looking forward to having a big, professional kitchen at the Old Mill. Did you see the size of their ovens? Ah, I can't wait to test them out. Did you want to watch a movie or take me back to Maryanne's?"

He opened his mouth, but then closed it. He didn't want to talk about the emails right now. It was too raw, and his mind was spinning too much. He didn't want to talk about Sarah either—and he knew she'd ask—so he didn't mention the emails or ask about her mom.

He didn't want her to leave yet, though, and that's ultimately what it all came down to. Regardless of what happened with her ex or in her past, he still wanted her. He was getting too close with her, wanting to spend every waking moment with her.

He should have known better by now. Attachments only lead to heartache and disappointment. He had lost countless exes before Patty, then had lost her and her baby. That pain tore at his soul, much like losing Sarah. Was getting close to someone worth the risk of losing them?

But Wendy's face was turned up to his, her smile easy and her eyes open. She was guileless. Just like how she'd interacted with his mom yesterday, it was better to just get it all out in the open.

He couldn't do it, though. He couldn't mention the emails or dig deeper into whatever this between them was turning into. He was leaving in a week. It was time to step back mentally, emotionally.

Although the movie did sound good. Maybe cuddling her on the couch would soothe this confusion within him. He just nodded as she kept talking.

"I was thinking of something old school. Do you think the streaming service has *Houseboat* with Cary Grant and Sophia Loren?"

A pang went through his chest, and his gaze sharpened. Did she know the emails were to him? Had she figured it out too?

He narrowed his eyes and nodded, pulling up the movie in his favorite list. She flopped onto the couch and turned to snuggle into his chest. She seemed so innocent, like she couldn't hide a thing.

Yet she was. Why did that guy leave her at the altar? What had his note said? What had her dad said? He thought about their conversations about her dad and the whole situation throughout the entire movie.

When it was over, she sighed and tipped her head back, placing a kiss on his jaw.

"Thanks. That was better than I remember. I haven't watched that in a long time. Are you ready to take me back to Maryanne's?"

She hopped up and stretched. Her ass in those leggings was perfect. He didn't know why she said she didn't have curves because she obviously did.

His hand reached out and caressed the soft slope of it, making her pause. She looked behind her with a smile and cocked an eyebrow.

"You still have energy for more? We've done it three times today already."

He smiled and tried to push down the thoughts of the emails. The guy must've been an idiot to leave her. His fingers wrapped around her hips, and he tugged.

She fell into his lap with a squeal, and when he ran his hands under her shirt to her breasts, she squirmed and began to giggle.

"No, stop, I'm ticklish," she laughed.

He grinned behind her and ran his fingers over her ribs again.

"What? I'm barely touching you." He rubbed back and forth, making her tuck her knees up and turn in his lap, trying to get away. She squealed again, and he began nuzzling her neck.

She gasped, "Stop. I can't—no more." She twisted and turned, laughing and trying to capture his hands.

He grinned, his heart lighter. She wasn't hiding things from him. She was open, honest, and cared about everyone. If she was anything like him, she probably just didn't want to talk about sad stuff all the time.

He wrapped his hands behind her and turned her in his lap until her legs fell over the armrest of the couch and her back was leaning on his arm. He breathed in the scent that was all her, roses now mixed with his woodsy shampoo.

He captured her mouth, trying to kiss away all doubt and fear. Fear of how much she meant to him already. Fear of the future. Doubt of who she was. Worry that she was more like Patty than what his instincts told him.

Her lips parted, her tongue darting to play with his. The kiss was deep, exploring every part of her like he was searching for the truth. His body hummed with anticipation, and she wiggled her perky ass on his now hard cock.

It turned brazen, needy, holding nothing back. Passion rose like the tide, inevitable and leading to only one conclusion. He'd thought the perfect day with her would have sated his appetite, but it hadn't.

He wanted her more, emails be damned. The kiss turned possessive, savage, crushing her lips and making her whimper.

The hand not bracing her back slid down her stomach and under the waistband of her leggings. She shivered and arched her hips to his hand, seeking relief already.

But he just passed over her core and kept pushing the

leggings down. When they were at her knees, he stopped and trailed a soft touch up the inside of her thigh, making her quiver.

"Oh Jake," she whispered against his lips. A thrill shot through him. It was his name on her mouth, not some jackass who didn't appreciate her. He wanted to hear her scream his name. He wanted her at his mercy, begging for him and only him. He wanted to brand himself on her soul, so she'd never look or talk to any other man ever again.

The thought scared him, and he took a mental step back. He lowered his other arm until she was lying on the couch beside him. Her eyes shone with need, and she bit her lip. God, when she did that, he wanted to fuck her mouth.

But not tonight. Right now, he wanted more.

Chapter Twenty-Five

He eased her sweater up over her breasts. She reached for the hem, but he shook his head, burning for her.

"No, let me. Raise your arms."

She slowly raised them, and he had to turn slightly to push it up. He arched his brow and met her gaze.

"You forgot, 'yes, sir.'"

Her eyes widened before she mouthed off with a grin, her eyes twinkling with mischievous delight. "Maybe I forgot on purpose."

He grinned slowly, his body going from bonfire to an inferno of need at the smart-ass remark. His pulse quickened as he caressed the soft skin under her breasts.

"Is that so? Well, then." He pushed the shirt over her head, the collar catching on her nose. He pulled it up so she could breathe, but left it covering her eyes, trapping her arms in the sleeves, half on and half off.

He pressed a hand to her chest. "If you're going to be a brat about it, then don't move. If you move, I'll spank you."

Her bottom lip pursed. "That's ridiculous. I haven't been spanked since I was a toddler."

He lifted her legs off his and stood, setting them back down to dangle on top of the arm rest. He moved the coffee table slightly, and her head tilted at the sound as she bit her lip.

"Jake?"

He quickly removed his clothes as he explained. "You wanted lessons? Here's another one. Sometimes a man gets to feeling possessive. It makes him want to hear you beg and moan until you scream his name over and over so there's no doubt in either of our minds that you belong to me. Do you understand?"

She paused, then nodded.

He tried to keep his words impersonal, but the possessive growl gave him away. "Say, yes sir," he said as he lightly traced her ankle.

Her whole body twitched at the touch, and she sucked in a breath and arched her back. "Yes, sir."

He grinned at the movement and pulled her foot to rest on the coffee table. He planted it flat and reminded her, "Didn't I say not to move?"

She nodded. "Yes, but I couldn't help it. I need you so much."

Her words pierced his heart, making him pause. He needed her too, and that's what scared him.

"As much as I love to see your luscious breasts bouncing up to greet me, when I say don't move, I mean it. Yes, sir?"

She sighed dramatically. "Yes, sir."

His lips twitched, then he kneeled in front of her. With one foot on the couch and the other on the coffee table, he could smell her heat. It called to him like a strawberry tart, tangy and making his mouth water.

He shoved his hands under her ass and wrapped them around her hips, holding her in place. He dropped his head until he could almost kiss her pink, wet lips.

"If you have a problem with listening, I can always hold you down." When he spoke, he let his mouth barely move over her clit, barely peeking out from her folds.

She moaned, and he grinned. "Would you like that?"

She squirmed, trying to move, gasping, "Maybe. I don't know. That's why you're here, right? To teach me what I like and what I don't?"

He paused, the pressure on his chest increasing. That *was* why he was here. That's all he was to her. The thought hurt, and he punished her with his mouth.

He devoured her clit, sucking hard and making her cry out as her legs shook around his head. Then he eased off, barely lapping it with his flat tongue before swirling it in a circle around the nub.

Gentle and rough, back and forth he teased her, bringing her to the brink and then slowing so she never crested into an orgasm. Her legs began to shake, and then her moans turned into more.

"Jake, please. I need—"

He broke away completely, making her moan in frustration. "What do you need, Peaches? Do you need this?"

He sucked gently and flicked her clit with his tongue. Her arms went to pull out of the shirt, and he pulled back abruptly. "Uh oh, didn't I tell you not to move?"

She jerked the shirt off and glared down at him with a frown. "But I need—"

He stood and her eyes dropped to his cock standing straight out in front of him. She licked her lips, and he wrapped his hand around it and began to stroke in front of her. She sat up on her elbows, eyes glued to his dick.

"Is this what you need?"

She nodded and bit her lip, her eyes begging. But not her mouth. She wasn't there yet, and he needed her to admit more than just needing him.

"Get on your knees on the couch. Lean against the back," he ordered.

She paused, her eyes meeting his first. Then she scrambled to obey. It sent a thrill along his spine. He moved her knees to the edge of the couch, making her lay her chest on the back of the couch.

Then he ran his hands over her glorious ass before pulling back and smacking her with an open palm.

She jerked, thrusting her ass back at him as he rubbed the spot, "Oh! Jake, what—"

"It's time you learned your lesson, Peaches."

"What lesson?" she asked before he spanked her again, just a little harder. Her legs shook as she gasped.

"That you're mine. No one else's. Say it." He pressed two fingers inside her and felt her clench. She gasped again before he spanked her one more time.

She clamped down on his fingers, and he almost lost it. He wanted to plunge into her right now. But he couldn't. Just a few more minutes…

"But you're only here for another week."

His jaw clenched. "Does that matter? You need me, Peaches. Say it."

He spanked her again a little harder, loving the way her pale ass turned red so easily. He aimed for the cluster of freckles.

She moaned, clenching around him. Fuck it, he had to have her. He withdrew his fingers, and she wiggled her ass at him.

"Please, Jake."

"Please what? Say it, Peaches."

She moaned into the couch, and he teased her entrance with his dick. She was so wet and ready.

"Please, Jake. Fuck me already. I'm yours, okay? For as long as you'll be here, I'm yours. Now, please, fuck me." She drew out the sound as he plunged inside. It turned to a moan.

He saw stars and closed his eyes. Fuck, she was so tight even with their marathon sessions today.

He pulled back and spanked her, feeling her nearly clamp his dick off as she squealed.

"That's it. Scream for me, Peaches. You're mine, and no one else's. Say it."

"Yes, yours. Fuck, Jake, that feels—oh." She drew the sound out again as he spanked her. Over and over, thrust for thrust, until he was bucking into her. Bent over the couch like this, she had nowhere to move.

He reached down and hooked her thigh over his forearm, so she stood on one leg, allowing him to go deeper.

He thrust hard, and she finally screamed, throwing her head back and making her wild mane of hair fly.

"Jake! Jake, yes, oh god, Jake!"

He couldn't hold out any longer. He needed to feel her. His free hand slid from her ass to her hair, fisting it and pulling so she arched her back.

"Jake!" she gasped.

"Come on my dick, Peaches. Right fucking now." The hand holding her leg up snuck down to her clit and he pressed hard. One more thrust, and she broke apart, screaming his name and convulsing.

He bucked against her, holding her to the couch as his balls tightened. He moaned and closed his eyes. The roar of satisfaction fell from his lips as every muscle tightened. His release was hot and violent, savage like him as he poured himself into her.

Both of them were panting and spasming in shuddering waves. Together in mutual surrender, it was a balm to his soul. She was his, and no one else's.

Whatever this was between them had just been taken to the next level. He didn't want to think about what it meant. His mind was blissfully blank right now, but he knew something between them had shifted.

Chapter Twenty-Six

Wendy lived in a haze of passionate happiness. She'd never felt so loved and cherished as she did when she hung out with Jake. Tuesday had been a revelation. To spend all day with the man and still want to be around him? She hadn't thought that was possible.

If all women felt like this with their men, she wasn't sure how they got anything done. No one would go to work. They'd just want to be together all the time.

She snorted as she drove his truck from the Old Mill to the auto shop.

After their movie and spanking session yesterday, he'd dropped her off at Maryanne's house with a breath-stealing kiss. Today, he'd picked her up from the bakery around three, and they'd stopped at his auto shop.

They'd unloaded her things from her car into his truck. But she'd been as shocked as everyone else in the garage when he'd tossed her the keys.

He'd jerked a thumb to the oldest guy at the garage.

The Mechanic Gets His Girl

"Lester needs me to stay and work on a radiator. Can you handle a truck that big?" he'd asked.

She'd grinned and stepped close, pressing her body against his. Even through the layers of clothes and coats, she could feel his body heat like a furnace.

"It sure is big, but I've been able to handle it so far," she'd said.

He'd grinned, dipping his head to kiss her in front of all his co-workers. She'd been left breathless as he'd turned to walk back into the shop.

It had taken all her energy to focus on driving his precious truck as carefully as possible. Patty might have destroyed the paint job, but the interior was still in pristine condition, all black leather and wood trim.

She'd gotten her boxes of scrapbooking materials moved inside, then her Cricut. She'd gone back to Maryanne's house to get her bags and the rest of her things, making Maryanne speechless at the sight of her driving his truck.

"Girl, this is serious." Maryanne had whispered, bouncing a sleeping Connie on her chest.

Wendy had shrugged, trying to shake off the uneasiness that came with those thoughts. It couldn't be serious. He was leaving in less than two weeks.

It reminded her of her dad, so she called him, but it went to voicemail. She left a text then got back to work.

Finally, all moved in—really, it was sad how quickly it went, since almost her entire life was wrapped up in her car—she drove back to the auto shop and parked carefully.

Wendy walked up to the open garage doors and pulled her jacket closer. When she finally spied Jake, he was standing under a truck on a lift, talking and pointing to some part while a younger guy nodded.

He handed over the tool and stepped aside so the younger guy could reach whatever he'd been pointing to. He was a good teacher, a good leader, pointing out one more thing, nodding, and smiling as he clapped the young man on the back.

Lord knows she'd picked the perfect guy to tutor her, and that was the problem. He was too perfect. She kept waiting for the other shoe to drop, for this happy little bubble to burst.

She'd felt tingles of excitement and anticipation with Mike, sure, but nothing like what she felt when she was with Jake. Hell, even just thinking about him made her feel things she'd thought other women had just made up.

With Mike, it'd been nice, like a hot shower. But with Jake, it was like a tsunami of emotions threatened to overwhelm her. Sometimes it was just pure joy, and it almost brought her to tears a time or two.

She stood on the side of the garage, and two guys working on a car glanced at her. The teenager from the other day came bouncing over to her and waved to the front office where he worked.

"We have chairs in here, if you'd like to sit down, miss?"

One of the guys working near her jerked his head to the stairs that led to a glass room above the shop.

"You can wait in his office. Just up the stairs there," he said.

Wendy smiled and glanced at the name stitched onto his uniform shirt. "Thank you, Juan. I appreciate it, but did Jake say I could be in there? He's picky about his space."

The other guy, Mel, wiped his hands and shrugged. "Oh, we know. Trust me. But you're not like the last girl." The guys all chuckled and nodded.

She tilted her head. "In what way?"

Mel said, "That truck is his baby. She knew how to hurt him most, that's for sure. The tires then the paint job? He loves Cassy like she is a living thing."

Juan turned the wrench on something. "Was mighty surprised he let you borrow his baby to drive around today, but that just shows how much he trusts you."

Mel nodded and turned to get some part off the counter. "Exactly, so if you can drive his truck, he'll be okay with you being in his office. Go on. It's warmer up there than it is down here. A little thing like you might freeze to death if you don't stay warm."

She closed her mouth and smiled tightly, waving to them before walking up the stairs. She had wanted to stay down there and talk with them, ask them questions about Jake, but when guys started commenting on her body, she was out.

Not that big a deal, but there was just no arguing with people like that. Reminded her of Mike and how he'd always try to force her to eat more than made her comfortable. She pushed the door to the office open and looked around.

A couch was along the wall to the right, the lower half wood, and the upper half of the wall glass windowpanes. She stepped over to it and looked down. It was a good view of the entire garage.

The wall directly opposite of the door held an oversized desk. A desktop and papers littered the top. The wall to the left held filing cabinets, bookshelves, and a little kitchenette. Just a sink and a coffee pot, mini fridge, and microwave.

She wondered where the employees took breaks. Did they use this little space? She snorted and sat on the couch.

Not likely. Jake would've made sure they had a space of their own, just so they wouldn't mess up his stuff.

He'd made a point of turning the handles on the pots and pans she'd cleaned and put up at his house. He'd explained that they all had to face the same way. He hadn't said anything about the toilet paper—apparently, she'd put a new roll on backward because he'd changed it at some point—or the towels. She'd accidentally pulled a few out of the drawer when she'd gone to get one for a shower, so she'd had to refold them. But they weren't Jake approved, because he'd gone back and refolded them.

She took off her jacket because the guy had been right. It was really warm here. She wondered how the heat stayed in with the half-wall of glass.

She scrolled through her phone, looking for decor for the Old Mill. Honestly, that was Jake's only flaw. Everything else he did or said didn't annoy her, like some of Mike's foibles. They were kind of cute, like the way he liked BBQ sauce on his mashed potatoes.

Her phone rang, and she smiled as she answered it.

"Hi, Dad! How are ya?"

"Ya? You've really taken to Texas, haven't you?" he chuckled.

She smiled and laid down on the couch, phone pressed to her ear. "I have. Did you get my text about the job? Isn't it amazing?"

He sighed. "I suppose it is. But does it have to be in Texas? Why can't you come home and find a job here?"

She closed her eyes and smiled. "I just need a fresh start, Dad, and it's been wonderful here so far. I moved all my stuff to the B&B today. Already settled in my room. Next step is to start playing with the kitchen so I can learn all the tricks."

"Kitchens aren't tricky, Wen."

She rolled her eyes at his attitude and relaxed into the couch.

"They are too. Sometimes the ovens run hot, and I don't want to burn something with my first customers. I met with my new boss, Parker. We reviewed the website, and he's given me admin rights on it, so I can tweak some stuff and start the blog. But there's a place where it shows a calendar and guess what? Our first guests arrive in three weeks, just in time for Valentine's weekend. There's so much to do before then!"

Another sigh through the phone. "So I guess you're not going to come see me then? I don't know about this, Wen. I'm going to have to come see you because I'm already missing you."

She felt her lip wobble. Her dad didn't talk like that often, and it made her so happy. "I miss you too, Dad. Just tell me when you want to come down, and I'll book you a room myself. I'll cook all your favorite foods, and we'll watch all our favorite old movies. When can you get away?"

"Not until March, probably. I'll have a week off after all the Spring Breakers get back, so maybe Easter. I'll send you the dates once I know."

Her stomach dropped, and she frowned. "A week off?" she asked softly. She knew what that meant.

"Yeah, I got pegged for deployment after all."

"But you're supposed to retire in six months!"

"I know." The frustration was clear in her dad's tone. She imagined him pacing and running his hands through his hair. "But there's nothing I can do. This is the last one, I swear to God."

"But what if they pull the same stunt again? How long's it for?" Her stomach didn't feel good about this.

"Through the end of the year. I'm lucky it's not a full year cycle and only six months. You know the Army never does less than a year. I'm not going to fight it, I'm just going to go with it and get out. If I try to fight it, they might extend it to a full year deployment."

She sighed and propped her arm over her eyes. "Fine but try to get two weeks and use all the days you've built up when you come down."

"Good idea. I won't be able to use them in theater, and I'll go on permanent leave two weeks after I return." He paused, then his voice grew softer. "It's going to be okay, Tink."

She swallowed hard, pushing back the emotions threatening to choke her. "I know, Dad. But if anything were to happen to you—"

"It won't."

"I know, but if it did… I'd be all alone. Please don't leave me alone, Dad. Promise you'll take care of yourself and stay out of trouble."

A pause on the other line left her holding her breath. Then he sighed. "You know I always do, Tink. I'll be back around Christmas. But first, I'll be down there to see your new place. I'll text you the dates in a few days when they're approved, okay?"

"Okay. Love you, Dad."

"Love you too, Tink."

The line went dead, and she hung up before covering her eyes with her arm once again. The tears came like normal, along with the thoughts of what would happen if her dad died in combat.

She reminded herself of the plans she'd put into place, on what to do if he died, on what to do if he was injured.

She and Mom had always gone over the plans in the weeks leading up to a deployment and those first few months during. Those were always the hardest.

She took a deep breath, choking on a sob and curling into the couch.

Chapter Twenty-Seven

Wendy woke to something tickling her stomach. It wasn't a hard tickle, but just a feather stroking from side to side, hip to hip just above her leggings.

"There's my beautiful peach. You gonna wake up?"

The smell of grease and pine filled her nostrils. She moaned and stretched, then felt his lips on hers. Soft and gentle, she felt like Sleeping Beauty waking up to the handsome prince's kiss.

"Hmm, what time is it?" she groaned. He peppered soft, slow kisses across her cheek to her ear.

She sighed and turned her head.

"Almost six. You've been asleep for over an hour." He sucked and nipped and kissed, finding the spot on her neck that made her squirm and gasp.

"Come on, beautiful. I have another lesson for you."

Her eyes opened as he leaned over her with a soft smile. His blue eyes were darker in the faint light of the office.

She wanted to take a picture of him just like this, in this moment when she could see the love shining in his eyes. She blinked, her chest growing tight. No, it couldn't be love. She was obviously dreaming because she loved him.

Oh god, she was so stupid. She'd fallen in love with him in exactly one week to the day when she'd been engaged to someone else just two weeks before!

Her eyes widened as she stiffened on the couch. He pulled back slightly, frowning, "Hey, we don't have to do anything if you're too sore. We can just go grab dinner together. Whatever you're comfortable with."

He was everything she'd always wanted. Was it any wonder that she'd fallen for him?

She relaxed at his words. He cared enough to pick up on her silent freak out. Maybe that's all this was on her end too.

Maybe it wasn't love, just normal caring for another human being. Maybe once he left, she'd fall out of it just like she had with Mike. It hadn't been that hard to get over him, after all.

It would be okay. This was just infatuation, puppy love. She cupped his face in her palm, the five o'clock stubble scratching her skin.

The emotions bubbled up. She wanted to show him how she felt, even if she couldn't say the words that might or might not be the real deal.

She sat up and stood, pulling him to his feet to wrap her arms around his neck. "I'm comfortable with whatever you can dish out. About this lesson… what did you have in mind?"

She kissed his jaw, and his arms tightened around her. She could feel his erection through his dirty jeans as he rocked his hips.

He kissed her, tugging on her bottom lip and making her core tighten. "I really was hoping you'd want to go on a real date. I promised I'd show you how a man should treat a woman, and that includes public appearances."

She sucked on his lower lip, returning the gesture. He groaned as she reached for his belt and unbuckled it.

"Sure, we can do that. But first, I have something I've always wanted to try."

When she tugged his pants down his hips and pushed him a few steps back to his desk, his brows rose as he grinned. He half sat on the edge, and she freed his dick. His grin turned into a groan when her hand wrapped around him.

It was the first time she'd touched him like this. Every other time up to now had been him taking charge, him calling the shots, him touching and teasing her.

Now it was her turn. She kissed him deeply, taking his tongue and circling it until she made herself dizzy. The passion sent her body into overdrive. The now familiar ache settled between her legs, and his hand slipped down her back to palm her ass.

She began to stroke her hand to the tip, and he gasped into her mouth. She rubbed her thumb in circles around the tip, spreading the sticky liquid around. Her mouth watered.

Her knees hit the hard floor, and she looked up at him. His eyes blazed with heat, blue flames that set her body raging with passion. He clenched his jaw, his hands plunging into her hair. She closed her eyes, nudging his hands to massage her head.

"You sure you want to do this?" His voice was as rough as gravel.

She nodded, then glanced down to finally stare her nemesis in the eye. She would conquer this one-eyed snake, come hell or high water. She wouldn't just let life happen to her anymore. This was her taking charge.

She opened her mouth and licked the tip. His fingers gripped her hair tight in response. She felt him hold his breath, then she glanced up to meet his eyes and stretched her mouth wide to take the head.

She eased him in, just the tip, and swirled her tongue around it like he did with her clit. His fingers clenched, but his eyes were wide and dark. They pleaded with her for more, even if he didn't say anything.

She eased down slowly, trying to take him as far as she could. She got more than three-fourths in, but he was too wide. She felt her gag reflex start and pulled back quickly.

He hissed a breath, his fingers tightening, but she wasn't done yet. She was just getting started.

She repeated the motion, one hand helping as it was wrapped around the base. Her head and her hand moved up and down. She challenged herself to take him deeper. His fingers pulled her wild curls back, then he began to guide her head in the rhythm he wanted.

"Peaches, that's—that's perfect. You feel so good, so wet, and fuck. I'm not going to last long if you keep—"

He broke off on a groan as she cradled his balls in the other hand. They were hot and heavy, but she didn't know what to do with them. She just held them.

He gasped, "Squeeze them. Same motion. Squeeze and tug. Oh god, yes. Peaches."

He pressed on the back of her head faster, in and out. She rocked on her knees, relishing in the taste, the sounds he made. She was driving him to the brink. Her! She felt powerful, sexy, and for once, she felt like she was enough.

Then his balls began to tighten. Did that mean he was—

Oh god. His hands shoved her down on his cock, but before she could gag, she felt his warmth shoot down her throat. He held her still, and she rubbed his balls until she ran out of air.

Elation flowed through her as she swallowed. She did it. She must've done it right too, based on his reaction.

She pulled back softly, easing into a slow rhythm as she sucked. It was like trying to suck a thick, salty milkshake through an oversized straw. Each swallow was liquid gold, bringing her to pure satisfaction. She'd done this, brought him to his knees, making his legs quiver with each suck as he looked down at her with wild need shining on his face. His eyes were languid and soft, but she couldn't read his expression.

She released him and sat back on her haunches, licking her lips. "Not bad. Salty yet satisfying. How did I do?"

She bit her lip and stood, shifting from foot to foot. He seemed to jerk out of a trance and bent to pull up his underwear and pants.

He cleared his throat and walked to the kitchenette as he zipped himself up. He turned with two bottles of water and handed her one.

She drank, swishing it in her mouth first. He downed his entire bottle in one chug session, then crumpled the plastic in his hand. He tossed it in the trash and then stepped toward her.

A hand on her back, he leaned in and kissed her forehead. When he pulled back, he was smiling but there was something hidden in his eyes. A hesitancy, a vulnerability, a wall that hadn't been there before.

"That was fucking perfect, Peaches. You're a natural."

She wrapped her hands around his waist and tilted her head. "Why do you call me that?"

"What, Peaches?" He smiled softly and tapped her on

The Mechanic Gets His Girl

the nose with one finger. "Your blush is the color of peaches. It matches your hair."

Her heart melted at the words. She'd been called carrot top, red, ginger, and every offensive nickname in the book. But never peaches.

And the way he said it, like a term of endearment. Was he starting to care for her too?

She grinned. "I like it. Maybe I need a nickname for you too. Hmm, let's see. Can't call you Jakey, since that's what Patty called you."

He scowled and walked around the desk to grab his jacket. "Definitely not Jakey."

She grabbed her own jacket and followed him to the door. "What's your call sign for the Army?"

He groaned as he locked up behind her. "I'm not a pilot. I don't have a call sign."

"Oh, come on. You're telling me—in how many years of service—that no one ever gave you a nickname?"

"Fourteen so far, and no. It's always been Smith or Smitty."

She rolled her eyes as she went down the stairs. "Smitty is a nickname, Jake. Although I'm not sure I could call you that. It just doesn't seem very you."

His lips twisted as he put a hand on her back and escorted her out the last remaining open garage door. "Not very me?" He pushed the button to roll it down.

She shook her head. "Nope. You're more of a—"

She bit her nail and narrowed her eyes at him. "Maybe an Axe. Or Masher."

He burst out laughing as they walked to his truck. He opened the passenger door and helped her climb inside. "Please do not call me either of those. Those are terrible."

She grinned as he shut the door. It was fun to tease him.

It was usually the other way around, him teasing her with his dick. Maybe she could drag it out over their date. There was something heady and addicting about making him laugh, but she had to remember he was leaving in just a few weeks.

This was nothing but a fling. She looked out the passenger window as they drove. It was peaceful, quiet music singing softly through the radio as he hummed along, but inside, her emotions warred: give in to the love or hold herself aloof to keep from being hurt when he left? That was the ultimate question, wasn't it.

Chapter Twenty-Eight

On Thursday afternoon, Wendy was engrossed in editing photos on her laptop. She had found a cozy spot on the bay window seat in the front parlor of the Old Mill, basking in the feeble winter sun.

She still had a few hours to kill before yoga with Maryanne. The photo edits didn't take long. Before she knew it, she was posting pictures to her social media and the Old Mill's website. Parker was due to stop by after school to go over the proposed budget for February.

She moved on to making the list of items to purchase that he'd need to approve. When her phone dinged again, she smiled, eagerly reaching for it. Jake had been texting her all day.

Do you want to Netflix and chill later?

Typical guy text, and it shouldn't have made her so giddy to see it, but she couldn't deny how she felt. She smiled and texted back.

I'd love to. Want me to cook dinner?

Three dots appeared, and she pushed the laptop onto the cushion and leaned back, knees drawn up as she waited. This was ridiculous. Waiting with bated breath for him to text back? What was she, twelve?

Always. You know I love anything you make. It's not good for my waistline though. I'm going to have to work out more.

She chuckled and shook her head as she replied.

You don't have to work out more. I'm more than satisfied with your physique atm. lol

She bit her nail. Was that too forward? Like their relationship, their texts had steadily increased in both number and dirtiness.

He sent a selfie of his head bent under an engine. He was twisting something, smiling into the camera, and showing off his bulging biceps. Then a message followed.

This physique? I aim to please.

She felt a blush rise, and her heart raced.

You please every time. It is much appreciated.

She groaned. God, who talked like that? She was such a dork. This was why she needed lessons.

He replied.

Likewise, Peaches.

A knock sounded on the door, and she jumped in surprise, nearly dropping her phone. With a deep breath, she walked in her thick, fuzzy socks to answer it. When she opened the door, she frowned, head tilted in confusion.

"Delivery for Wendy Macdonald?"

She smiled as the huge bouquet of orange, pink, and red roses moved to reveal a teenager holding the vase in both hands.

"That's me. Thank you so much." Her voice was breathless as she gently took the vase and turned to place it on the little lobby clerk's desk.

She turned to tip him, but he was already walking down the walkway, so she closed the door and searched for a card.

Peaches, I promised to show you how a real man should treat a woman. That includes flowers. I tried to find peach-colored ones, but these were the closest they had. I bet they don't smell as nice as you, though. —J

Her eyes began to mist over, and she fingered one of the soft petals. Her heart was bursting with love for this man who had completely tossed her life upside down.

Okay, so that was dramatic, but he was pretty amazing. Her phone buzzed again, and she pulled it out of her pocket. It was just Maryanne confirming the time to pick up some snacks tonight.

She took a selfie with her roses, but no matter how she tried to rein in her smile to a normal one, she couldn't. It was one of her widest smiles, and she didn't like posting those on social media or taking pictures of it. But the joy in her heart and pure happiness even drove away those negative thoughts.

She sent it to Maryanne by accident. Then shrugged

and sent it to Jake like she'd intended. He replied almost immediately.

Ah, the mission was a success. Your smile outshines every rose.

She felt her eyes mist again, her smile growing impossibly wider as she replied.

You are the absolute BEST thing that has happened all week.

Her hands were shaky as she pressed send. She'd typed I love you and deleted it almost as fast, but her whole body was about to burst. She stepped away from the flowers and spun in a circle, doing a little dance to expel some of the energy.

She paused when she felt her phone buzz again.

You're the best part of mine too. ;)

She was too excited to sit at the laptop again, so she took it upstairs and plugged it up. Then she went to the kitchen to experiment with some strawberry chocolate muffins.

It was a big kitchen and had been updated recently. There was a sink that looked over the backyard next to a door that went outside. One wall held the walk-in pantry and the refrigerator. The opposite wall held the stove, ovens, and a microwave. The fourth wall had a swinging kitchen door that led to the dining room. The dishwasher was there, along with all the dining sets for guests.

The island was a large butcher block table. Open shelves were underneath, some with pots and pans, some with recipe books left over from the previous owner.

The Mechanic Gets His Girl

It had an old-world charm, reminding her of an old French chalet with exposed brick along the outside wall. The big double ovens kept it nice and toasty, though.

She turned up the tunes and rocked out, singing at the top of her lungs because why not? She was just so happy. Could life get any better? She cut up the strawberries into hearts while the muffins baked. When she turned to grab her oven mitts, her eyes landed on a figure standing in the doorway.

"Parker! What are you doing here? It's not even four yet," she asked, opening the oven, and setting the muffins onto a cooling rack.

He leaned against the door jamb of the kitchen with a goofy grin, his hands in his slacks. "Just enjoying the show, that's all."

She felt her cheeks flush, and she wiped her hands on her apron before sliding the last muffin tray out of the oven.

"I'll be done in ten or fifteen minutes. Do you have time to wait?"

He nodded and moved to one of the stools at the island to sit. "Only if I get to taste test the product. They smell divine."

She took one of the cooled ones and set it on a small plate, then set a strawberry heart on top of it before presenting it to him.

"Maryanne is picking these up for yoga tonight. Think they'll like them?"

He moaned and nodded, taking a bigger bite. She went to the fridge and grabbed a jug of milk, pouring him a glass. She picked up her phone to turn down the music, noticing a few missed messages from Jake.

On my way to the lawyer's office. Wish me luck.

Jake put his phone in his pocket and walked down the sidewalk to the lawyer's office. He ran a hand through his hair. It was getting a little longer on top, and he'd need a haircut before he left next week.

But he liked when Wendy pulled on it, so maybe he'd wait a little longer. Last night, their date had left him shaken. They'd gone to a steakhouse in Denton.

When she'd taken her jacket off at the restaurant to reveal a sparkly green skirt, knee high black boots, and a black sweater that hung off one shoulder, he'd been speechless. Hard as a rock too, but around her that was normal.

It seems like everything about her left him wanting even more. He'd begun to sweat in the restaurant in his pearl-snap shirt, waiting for the other shoe to drop in their relationship. There was no denying that it was a relationship, but he couldn't define it.

If he defined it, it would hurt worse when she left. And she would leave him. They all did. He kept reassuring himself during dinner that this time, he would leave first and protect his heart.

But then she'd laugh, and he'd lose his train of thought and focus. Her eyes had sparkled like emeralds, and he'd stopped breathing. Then his thoughts would swing the other way, reminding him that she was his, and he needed to enjoy her while it lasted.

So that's what he'd done. He'd taken her to a popular make-out spot and given her a lesson in a quickie in the truck. She'd giggled about finally getting the high school experience, and it had soothed part of his roiling emotions as he'd dropped her off at the Old Mill.

While his arms were around hers kissing her good night

on the front step, his mind was clear. He didn't have to worry about their relationship, what she was hiding, or worry about her leaving. He just enjoyed her, soaking up her sunshine like a flower after a hard rain.

The door dinged as he walked into the lawyer's office, and he shook off thoughts of Wendy.

"Jake, I'm so glad you could stop by. The results just came back. Why don't you have a seat?" Goldie smiled tightly and pushed up the glasses on the bridge of her nose.

She was a knockout blond that all the guys in high school had lusted after. She was also a few years ahead of him, so he'd not known her then. They'd never been more than acquaintances who'd grown up around each other.

He'd gotten to know her a bit better through emails the past few months of dealing with Patty.

She slid a packet of papers across her desk and sat back in her seat. He picked them up and began to read. The first two pages were nothing but numbers and doctor jargon. He flipped to the last page and found the conclusion.

Based on our analysis, it is practically proven that Mr. Michael Jacob Smith III is the biological father of the child, Patrick Jacob Smith.

His fingers turned cold as he froze in his chair. He blinked. This couldn't be right.

He looked up with a frown, "What the hell does this mean?"

Goldie waved her hand, her watch sparkling in the office lights. "It means you're the father, and our entire case has to change."

"I just—I don't understand. The other three guys? She admitted to sleeping with them, with all of us, during the same three-month window, during her whole pregnancy really. And he was born so early."

Goldie sighed, her eyes softening. "Look, you need to think about this and what you want to do."

He was drawing a complete blank. "What I want to do?"

She nodded. "He's your son. She'll need back child-support, medical bills—"

He ran a hand through his hair. "No, he's already registered in DEERS. There are no medical bills for him."

Goldie narrowed her eyes. "What's DEERS?"

He blinked. "The Army's system to get him insurance. When he was born so early, I knew he'd be in the hospital a while. The fourth day, I rushed his paperwork down to Fort Worth to get him registered in the system. He's been on my insurance ever since."

"Even though we've been fighting to prove he wasn't yours?" she asked incredulously.

He shrugged. "The kid still needed care, and I knew Patty wasn't going to be able to pay for it on her secretary's salary."

Goldie rubbed her forehead. "Okay, so did you register Patty into the system too?"

He shook his head. "No, we weren't married, and that was more complicated."

"You might need to pay for her medical bills for the birth then. I'll need a copy of any medical bills you were sent through your insurance or any records of what you've paid for his care. I'll meet with her lawyer tomorrow in Denton to go over the results of this and see if we can come to some kind of settlement. But before I go, I need to know exactly what you want. Visitation? Sign your rights away?"

He drew a ragged breath and shook his head, no doubt in his mind. "I want custody."

Goldie snorted a laugh. "Not gonna happen, buddy. This is Texas, and the judge's side with the mom almost always. Even though you had grounds to leave based on infidelity, a judge isn't going to give you custody, especially not while you're deployed or able to be deployed. Maybe if she terminated her rights, but I don't see that happening, do you?"

He sighed and sank into the chair further. "No, she's more likely to draw this out and take me for every penny she can get just to spite me. She's very angry."

Goldie nodded. "Can you blame her?"

"For cheating, yes, yes, I can. I can blame her for ruining my truck too. If they won't give me custody, I want visitation rights or joint custody. See what you can get. Oh, I want her to pay for the damages to my truck too. Or better yet, take the cost of my truck out of the back child support amount. You have all the receipts I emailed you?"

She nodded again and leaned forward to type on her computer. "Yes, I have them right here. I'll draw up a list of what you want and send it to you digitally to sign tonight. Then I'll take it to her lawyer tomorrow. In the meantime, stay out of trouble, alright?"

He stood and shook her hand before leaving, taking a copy of the last page of the DNA report with him. He sat in his truck and stared at it again.

Shit. *He* was a dad. He *was* a dad. This whole time, he'd been mad about not being that little boy's dad, and here it was in black and white.

A knock sounded on his truck window, and he glanced over. Landry waved, and he rolled the window down.

"Hey man, what are you doing on this side of town?" Landry asked with an easy-going smile.

Jake nodded to the office in front of him. "Met with Goldie about Patty."

Landry's eyes widened. "Oh, and how'd it go?"

Jake looked down at the paper and back to Landry. "He's mine."

Landry frowned. "Say what now?"

Jake sighed, his eyes burning as he raked a hand through his hair. "He's mine. The baby. He's mine. And I'm a dad. And he's mine. And—"

"Hey now, breathe. Stop, just breathe in with me a little longer, and now exhale—slowly now. Let's do it again, inhale two three, exhale two three. There you go. Keep breathing like that."

Jake nodded, feeling his throat close up with emotions as the panic faded. "Where'd you learn that?"

Landry grinned. "My wife. It's going to be okay, you know. Being a dad is great. You're going to love it."

Jake gave a small smile and nodded.

"Hey, let's celebrate. The girls all have yoga tonight, so why don't you stop by the house? I'll get some guys to come over for an impromptu poker night. We missed you on Tuesday. What held you up?"

Jake chuckled and shook his head. "Had a date."

Landry wagged his brows. "Nice. Was it with the same girl from the bar last Friday? Maryanne's friend?"

Jake nodded. "Yeah, I've gotta go, but text me if enough guys can join tonight, and I'll swing by. Same time?"

Landry nodded and stepped back with a wave, walking to his own truck. Jake had helped restore that truck of his grandpa's. His fingers itched to work on something. It was the only way he could process through all this.

He texted Wendy.

Hey, change of plans. I'm going out with the guys tonight, so I won't get to see you today.

Then he backed up and drove to his parents. He didn't go through the house, though. Just went to the barn and flipped the light.

His dad's retirement project was sitting there, covered in a tarp jacked up on all fours so the tires wouldn't wear down while they worked on it. He pulled the tarp off the hood and propped it open. His phone vibrated.

Sounds good. I'll join Maryanne at yoga then. See you tomorrow?

He didn't reply but started diagnosing the list of what needed to happen with this little '63 Thunderbird. These were problems he could fix. There was a clear answer here.

He sat on the shop creeper, then laid back and pushed under the car. Shit, there must've been a mouse in here at some point, or wherever Dad had bought it from.

The creak of the door opened, but Jake ignored it.

"Son? Are you here?"

"Down here, Dad."

Footsteps shuffled closer, then he saw them stop by the tires. Mike sat on the cold concrete and laid down beside the car to peer at Jake underneath.

"What are you doing out here? I thought we weren't going to work on the bird until you came back for good. It's too cold here to work on it now."

"I'm not cold," Jake said curtly and ripped some rotten and frayed wiring out. It didn't matter where it came from; he was going to rebuild the whole thing, anyway.

Out with the old, as they say. Just like his whole life was being ripped out. He tugged harder.

"Son? What's going on?" It was the tone of voice that got him. It made him close his eyes against the feelings.

He shook his head, trying to push them aside.

"Son."

He tossed the wires to the other side of the car and stared up at the mess. He couldn't escape it or hide any of it. There was nothing Jake could do but tell the truth of his failures.

Chapter Twenty-Nine

"The DNA results came back." His voice was gravely with emotion.

His dad didn't say anything, and the silence stretched. He'd been hanging out with Wendy too long because he wasn't happy about the quiet. There was an itch in the back of his brain, and he needed to figure out why.

He rolled out from under the car and sat up. His dad was in front of him and held out a hand. Jake took it and let his dad pull him up, out of the darkness of his thoughts, his failures.

He pushed his chin up and met his dad's eyes. "He's mine."

Mike's eyes widened, but he didn't say anything. Jake gripped his head at the temples and closed his eyes.

"I didn't think he could be. There was a one in four chance, you know? She was sleeping with at least three other guys, Dad. But he's mine. Can you believe it? I'm a dad."

Mike tipped his head to the side. "And?"

Jake spread his hands wide. "And what? I'm a fucking dad. Maybe the worst dad in town."

"Jake," his dad chided.

He began to pace. "No, it's true. I failed him. I walked out when he was barely a week old. Still in the hospital and hooked up to tubes. I only held him three times, did you know that? Three times of him being just barely bigger than my hand…"

He held out his hand in a cupping motion, then spun on his heels. "And now that I know, I don't get to make up for that lost time. Isn't that just too perfect? I told Goldie I wanted custody, but this damn deployment won't let me. How can I be the dad I want to be if I can't ever see him? How can I share him with her when I have the restraining order? Dad, I don't—I can't—"

He took a deep breath and held his head again, his shoulders bowing in as he choked back a sob. His dad's arms circled his shoulders, and Jake buried his head. The familiar smells of Old Spice aftershave calmed him, reminding him of all the times when he was a kid and his dad had done just this same thing.

"Sh, it's okay now. We'll figure this out together."

"I don't know how, Dad. That's the problem. What if I mess it all up even more?"

Dad pulled back and held both his shoulders. They were of similar height and build, but Dad's eyes and hair were brown. Both he and Sarah had inherited their mom's blue eyes.

But at this moment, staring into an older version of himself, he was glad that it was Dad and not Mom out here.

"You're not going to mess up, Jake, because you're not going to give up. The only way you can fail is if you don't show up at all."

Jake's vision swam as he frowned and tried to hold back the emotions. "That's what I've done. I've been gone and not been there for him."

Mike nodded. "Yes, but that wasn't your fault. Any judge will know you don't get a say in deployment schedules. While you're here, you can try to get visitation, then when you're back for good, we can work out a schedule with her, right?"

Jake swallowed and wiped his eyes. "That's what I told Goldie. If I can't get custody, then I want joint custody or visitation."

Mike smiled and then cupped his hands on either side of his face. "And that's why you'll be a great dad. Did you think I just woke up when you were born and was this amazing?"

Jake chuckled, holding Mike's hands on his cheeks. The coldness of them helped clear his mind.

"Exactly. It took a long time before I even felt worthy of you calling me that. You'll get there, son, simply because you want to be there. Ever since you were a kid, if you'd put your mind to something, it'd get done. You're stubborn just like your mama, but don't tell her I said so."

Jake smiled, and Mike dropped his hands. "Speaking of, she's run off to town for some meeting or another. Do you want some stew? She left it on the stove, so it's still warm."

He followed his dad outside and then up to the house. They'd just made it to the front porch when Landry's truck turned onto the driveway.

They waited for him to park, then both he and Andy got out, each holding a brown paper bag.

Landry held his up. "The guys were all busy, but we wanted to either celebrate with you or help you drink your miseries away. Um, if your mom's not here, that is?"

Mike laughed and waved them inside. "Don't worry. She's gone into town for a church thing or something. I don't even try to keep up with her anymore. Come on inside. I guess you heard the news?"

Andy frowned as he came inside, his eyes searching Jake's. "You alright, man? What exactly happened?"

Landry poured them all drinks while Mike set out bowls and spoons for the soup.

Jake sighed and sank into a kitchen chair, propping his head into his hands. "I don't know. All I know is out of all the guys she was sleeping with, I'm the one who's the dad."

"Do you want to be involved?" Landry asked.

Jake sat up straight and frowned. "How can you even say that? Of course, I do."

Andy passed him a bowl of soup and asked, "Then why are you so upset about it."

Jake stirred his soup. "I walked out on him. I could've visited him more in the hospital, tried more, I don't know."

Andy sat next to him and met his gaze. "Look, I, of all people, know how you're feeling."

Jake snorted and leaned back, but Andy kept going.

"I'm serious, Jake. For three years, I had no idea Mandy was my daughter. All the guilt you're feeling right now about missing the past eight months of his life? I felt the same thing."

Jake frowned, remembering when his parents had finally told them the truth. He took a bite of the soup and nodded. "I guess you're right. It just sucks, you know? But with Mandy, she at least knew you. This kid has no idea who I am."

"What's his name?" Mike asked. "You've never once mentioned him by name. Just kid or boy."

Jake nodded and pulled the paper from his pocket,

tossing it to the middle of the table. Dad reached for it and read it.

Landry looked over his shoulder and snorted. "She named him Patrick? She's such a narcissist she named him after herself? Patricia. Patrick. God, she drives me crazy. Tried to hit on me once when I came to her apartment to fix her pipe."

Jake took a deep breath as his fists clenched. It shouldn't have surprised him, but it still hurt.

Mike pointed to the paper. "At least his middle name is Jacob. Do you think she really thought you were the dad and that's why she gave him your middle name? Or do you think she just hoped you were?"

Jake shrugged. "She probably just hoped so. I'm on the birth certificate as his father."

He tossed back his whiskey and pushed it to Landry, who topped him up before setting the bottle in the middle of the table. The soup was almost gone, so he got up to get more.

"Do you think she calls him Patty too?" Landry asked.

Jake shook his head. The futility of it all threatened to overwhelm him. He sat down wearily and sighed.

"I don't care what she calls him. I can't call him Pat or Patty because the name makes me so mad. I can't call him Jake for the same reason you couldn't call me Mike. It's just too weird."

Mike nodded. "You'll have to call him Rick. It's a good, strong name."

Jake nodded and sipped more of his drink. His stomach churned, and he pushed away the second bowl of stew. Memories came unbidden.

Patty bringing him the card and pregnancy test. Her look of relief when he'd picked her up and swung her around should have been his first clue, but he'd assumed it was a natural reaction any woman would have.

The look on her face when he'd shown her his house and surprised her with the bedroom he'd decorated for the boy. He forced air into his lungs in a shuddering breath. No, not the boy. *Rick*.

He wasn't a thing anymore, but a living, breathing person. He remembered when Patty had screamed him out of the delivery room, pacing in front of her door and worrying about the sounds coming from inside.

Then he remembered returning to the hospital with a pizza and walking in on her and the first guy. He'd almost punched him, angry, betrayed, and hurt. Patty had been crying, wringing her hands and unable to leave the hospital bed.

He'd left, cooled off, and came back the next day to *another guy*. A heavy, dull pain spread through his chest. His breath became ragged, and the sounds of their conversation flowed over him. His vision narrowed.

Then a hand was pulling his chair out while another pushed his head down between his legs. He didn't resist. He just moaned.

"Breathe, Jake. Come on. We've been through this. In one two three. Out one two three." Landry crooned.

They had been through this. He could sit here and relive all the mistakes of the past year, or he could let go of the torment of her betrayal and focus on the problem at hand. He mentally pulled up his boots and focused on his breathing.

He had to stop looking back and focus on the here and now. Then he had to plan for the future. He tried to picture it, and he saw a fuzzy image of his son at baseball practice as a kid, then learning to drive, then graduating from

Crimson Creek High. The face was out of focus, but in those few seconds, something shifted in his chest.

He sat up with new resolve.

"This is bullshit," he said, leaning back in the chair and crossing his arms. "I can't be some deadbeat dad. I have to be in my son's life."

The others nodded.

Landry shrugged. "Yeah, but what can you do? It's out of your hands."

"For now, anyway. But I'm going to find a way for her to sign over custody. Somehow. I've got four months to convince her before I get back home. It could work, right?" He leaned forward, elbows on the table, as he searched their faces.

Andy rubbed his neck. "I don't know. What woman would willingly give up a cute kid like him? They're a tough breed, mothers."

Landry hummed, then said, "Yeah, but she still goes out on the weekend. Ask Katie or anyone in town. She goes to the bar any chance she gets."

Jake nodded and downed his drink once more. His body was heated, and his head was growing fuzzy.

"I can use that. And that she's still sabotaging my truck."

Patty was probably a good mom, but the way they fought... they wouldn't be able to share the little guy. He needed custody. This was like the Army all over again. He had originally just worked one weekend a month, but then he'd begun craving the structure and rigidity of it. He'd needed that control when his life had turned upside down, and Sarah had died.

He might start out as a weekend dad, but he had every intention of going full-time. He wanted this little guy. *Rick*. He'd be the best dad around. He owed it to Sarah.

She'd wanted a big family, not him. But she couldn't have one. She'd run out of time, but he could still make her dream come true. It started right now with his son.

His son. He chuckled and shook his head, a spark of joy mingling with all the other emotions inside him. He reached for his glass to dislodge the cotton ball in his mouth and found it empty. He filled it up again.

With a raise of his hand shaky, he said, "To getting custody of *my son*."

His dad raised his. "To a year of changes and blessings."

Andy followed. "To being a family and a dad."

Landry grinned. "To your mom not throwing a fit."

They all burst out laughing and clinked glasses before downing them. Lights flashed outside as someone pulled up.

Mike glanced out the window. "Speak of the devil, she's home."

Landry and Andy stood, but Jake stumbled to his feet. "Do y'all have to go home yet? There's a stack of wood outside. It's the perfect night to sit and stare at the stars."

Landry grinned and nodded as Suzie came through the door. Andy threw Jake's arm over his shoulder and nodded at her.

"Hey, Aunt Suzie. We're going to head outside for a bit. Uncle Mike? Can you fill her in?"

Jake looked at his mom, but there were two of her. He frowned and pointed an unsteady hand. "Mom, you're a good mom. The finest. I love you so much, and I'm so sorry."

Landry grabbed the bottle off the table and shooed them down the hall. "Alright, that's enough of that. Let's go get this thing lit up."

Andy drawled, "I think he's already lit up."

Landry sighed. "Can't say I blame him."

Jake had no idea who they were talking about, and he didn't care. They were going outside to burn shit. It was going to be fun, just like they used to do when they were younger. It would drive away the past, the memories, and all the reminders from his mind. Yes, it was going to be a great night.

Chapter Thirty

Wendy glanced at her phone that afternoon.

Hey, change of plans. I'm going out with the guys tonight, so I won't get to see you today.

She frowned, then replied.

Sounds good. I'll join Maryanne at yoga then. See you tomorrow?

"Something wrong?" Parker asked.

She shook her head, but her gut told her otherwise. She bit her lip, debating how much to say as she cleaned the kitchen and turned off the oven. She didn't really know him well enough. Would he go blabbing around town?

"How much can I trust you?" she asked, leaning back against the counter.

His brows rose, and he downed the milk. "Ah, if you want something kept in confidence, then you need to specifically tell me to keep it to myself. Otherwise, it's a small town. I might not say something, but chances are someone has heard something." He shrugged his shoulders.

She chuckled. "Fair enough. News travels fast in this town, doesn't it?"

He nodded. "Yep. Take those flowers out there, for instance. Dale, the delivery guy? He hadn't even left the shop yet when I'd already heard about them at the high school."

She snorted. "I don't even know how that works."

He shook his head. "Hey, your guess is as good as mine. That's just how it is around here."

She sighed. "That's what I thought. About our finance meeting, I'm ready when you are. I have some things to show you."

They poured over the computer, then she pointed out some of the little things she wanted to change, explaining why. He left twenty minutes before Maryanne was due to pick her up, so she scrambled to package the muffins and find her shoes and coat.

The car horn beeped, and she locked the front door before racing down the steps. It seemed colder, but perhaps that was because she hadn't had Jake's body heat today to warm her up. The man was like lava.

She settled into the seat and shut the door. "Thanks for letting me tag along."

Maryanne smiled. "I'm glad you can join us. Girls' night here is a little more settled than back in Colorado. I think you'll find it's much more to your liking."

Wendy laughed. "You mean Thursday night yoga isn't code for a wild night of drunk karaoke?"

Maryanne grinned. "Afraid not. Just two hours of stretching, gossiping, and movement."

They parked and walked inside. It was a cute little studio with mirrors along the right wall. Stairs went up on the left side, and a construction zone appeared between the stairs and the check-out counter near the front door. They might be knocking out a wall or adding a doorway.

The far wall had a hallway, breaking it in half. The signs hanging from the ceiling read office to the left and bathrooms and lockers to the right.

There were more women here than she'd expected. They'd naturally split into a few different cliques. The older ladies were by the bathrooms, and Wendy winced to see Mrs. Margarita talking animatedly with a certain woman with a blond ponytail.

Of course she'd run into Jake's mom here. In front of a whole room of women. She felt her cheeks heat but lifted her head and followed Maryanne. Time to face the music.

Maryanne waved to the check-out counter. "You can put the muffins there, then I'll introduce you to my friends."

She shook hands and tried to remember names. The only ones she caught were Lola, another redhead which made her immediately like her, and Holly, another petite woman with a similar build to her own.

They set up their mats as she looked around. Two more groups of women had formed semi-circles, one to the right and one to the left. Then a group of teenage and college girls stood posing—aka stretching—in front of the glass front windows. That explained why so many boys had been walking Main Street at this time of night.

Holly, the owner, had them all spread out into rows. Wendy found herself between Maryanne and Mrs. Suzie. Holly had them stretch and began to lead them through an easy yet rigorous session of yoga. They chatted all throughout it, each group whispering in low voices. After a few minutes into the warm-up, Wendy glanced at Maryanne.

Maryanne whispered, "That's Jake's mom."

Wendy felt heat rise to her cheeks. "I know. We met at church, remember?"

Suzie leaned forward and whispered loudly, "And we met again on Monday night. Wendy, it's nice to see you wearing clothes for a change."

Maryanne gasped along with several of the ladies around them, but Wendy just burst out laughing. This was like high school all over again. And if she couldn't beat them, she'd learned long ago to join them. The best way to overcome embarrassment is to take charge of the story.

"That had to be the single most embarrassing moment of my life." She turned back to Maryanne and took a deep breath. She had to nip this in the bud. She couldn't live in this town with Mrs. Suzie and let her have the power.

Wendy tipped her chin up and completely gave up on whispering. She ignored her burning cheeks and the embarrassment that made her want to crawl under a blanket and hide. Her mama hadn't raised her to shy away from hard things.

She made eye contact with Maryanne and focused on just talking to her bestie. She'd already told her everything, of course, but this was for the benefit of those gossips who were eavesdropping.

"I had just lost my virginity, you see. I know, right? Kind of pathetic to be a thirty-year-old virgin, but there you have it." She paused as the other groups quieted. They didn't need to know that it had been a day or two before. She narrowed her eyes at the teenagers to her left, then pointed a finger, reminding herself of her dad.

"It's a good thing to wait, let me tell you. It was *so* worth the wait. First times don't have to be awful, girls, when you wait for the right guy. Remember that. Anyway, we'd just showered, and I'd left my bag by the door. And then Mrs. Suzie walked in!"

Holly gasped, and Lola's jaw dropped. Wendy grinned even as she ignored her burning cheeks.

"I know! I wanted to melt into the floor, especially when she saw the clothes strewn all over the kitchen."

"What did you do?" someone asked, as Holly moved them into another pose.

Wendy sighed dramatically. "What could I do? I went to put my clothes on, pulled up my big girl panties, and came back to the kitchen to face her."

One of the women snorted and another whispered loudly, "That's like a knight facing a dragon."

Wendy glanced at Mrs. Suzie, the woman's eyes now wide with shock. Wendy's cheeks burned, and she turned away to focus on Maryanne, Holly, and Lola again.

"But don't worry. We talked while I made dinner. We're good now, right, Mrs. Suzie?"

All eyes turned to Suzie, whose mouth was opening and closing like a fish out of water. Then she snapped it shut and nodded curtly. Wendy caught her glare and shrugged sheepishly.

"She mentioned a quilting bee in a few weeks. Who's going to that? What other events are going on around town?" Wendy asked, now easily turning the conversation. She breathed a sigh of relief as the rest of the group took the bait on the distraction.

Chapter Thirty-One

The rest of the session, most of the women were now talking as one big group, no longer whispering. They shared congratulations for milestones crossed—first baby steps, first date, first lost tooth for their kids.

When the session was over, Holly dismissed them and let them know about the snacks in the back.

Wendy spoke up. "Don't let the chocolate fool you. They're healthy double-chocolate muffins with fresh strawberries. Heart healthy whole grains, fewer fats, and nutrient rich. I know how January goes, ladies."

Many chuckled and started talking about how their diets had already crashed. A throat cleared behind her as she was rolling up her mat.

Mrs. Suzie had her mat slung over her shoulder and a frown on her face. "Why'd you do that?"

Wendy winced. "I'm sorry about dragging you into all that, but you're the one who brought it up and got everyone's attention."

Suzie's frown deepened. "I know, but I never expected

you to just put it all out there for everyone. Why'd you do it? You could've ignored my comments."

Wendy shrugged. "I don't have anything to hide. I'm new here, and I don't want to be on the wrong side of gossip starting off. Besides, I didn't want you to keep making snide comments to embarrass me. Bullies taught me long ago that it's better to laugh at yourself and take the power out of their hands completely."

"I'm not bullying you," Suzie's eyes shifted. "Wait, you were bullied? Why?"

Wendy rolled her eyes. "Why? Have you looked at me? Look at this hair; it's a wild mess. You should have seen me as a kid. Plus, I've always been the runt of the litter. Well, if my classmates were my litter."

"I'm sorry." Suzie actually did sound sorry too, but Wendy wasn't sure if she was sorry about her childhood trauma or about trying to embarrass her tonight. She wasn't about to look a gift horse in the mouth and ask her to clarify, though.

Wendy looked back at her. Her blue eyes reminded her so much of Jake, it made her relax.

"It is what it is. I've come to terms with it. For what it's worth, I'm sorry you were put on the spot tonight. I'm sorry we both were. But hopefully it's all behind us now, and we can both move forward with a clean slate. Friends?"

Wendy held out her hand, and Suzie glanced at it then to the rest of the women, most of whom were congregating by the door as they ate or left.

Suzie's voice was low when she asked, "Was it true? The part about being a virgin?"

Wendy nodded slowly, her cheeks heating. "Yes, but if we're being completely honest, I didn't lose my virginity on

Monday." She paused and waited while Suzie's eyes narrowed and her hand bit into her arm.

Wendy leaned in and grinned, patting Suzie's hand on her arm. "I lost it on Sunday after church."

Suzie barked a laugh, then she raised her hand to cover her mouth. Her eyes widened, then she laughed outright, unable to contain it any longer.

"Oh my, I'm so sorry I barged in on you two. That must've been quite a lot to take in."

Wendy wiggled her eyebrows. "You have no idea. It *was* a lot to take in, I assure you."

Wendy slapped her hand over her mouth. Her big mouth always ran away with her. Oh god, she couldn't believe she'd just said that. To his mom!

Suzie laughed again, this time both their faces turning red. She waved a hand in front of her with a gasp while she used the other hand to wipe her eyes. "No more, please. I don't want to hear or see anything like that again."

Wendy smiled sheepishly and nodded. "Deal. Trust me, I'd rather keep that kind of thing private. Well, as private as I can, considering I just told the whole town your son took my virginity. No telling what will happen once word of *that* spreads."

Suzie smiled. "You leave that to me. No one will make any snide comments or bully you again. Now you have a dragon in your corner."

Wendy winced. "Oh yeah, sorry about that. You're not—"

Suzie laughed softly. "Oh, I am. Just ask Jake or Andy or anyone. Like you said, the bullies in this town will say what they're going to say. It's better to own it. It was good seeing you tonight, Wendy."

Wendy bit her lip then burst out, "Mrs. Suzie, have you heard from Jake tonight?"

Suzie frowned. "What do you mean?"

Wendy shook her head. "We had made plans, but then he canceled to go hang with the guys. Not a big deal, I just want to make sure he's okay. I know he was meeting with the lawyer today, but he hasn't said how it went or responded to my messages."

Suzie's eyes widened as she nodded. "I'm sure it's fine, but if I see him, I'll have him text you, okay?"

Wendy nodded, and Suzie turned and took a few steps toward the door, then she glanced over her shoulder.

"Oh, and Wendy? If you ever hurt Jake, I will unleash all the power a dragoness holds to make you regret it. Am I clear?"

Wendy grinned. "I respect you more for saying it to my face, and I would expect nothing less, Mrs. Suzie. But I don't intend to hurt him. It'll be me breaking into pieces when he leaves. Oh god, forget I said that, okay? I'm going to run to the bathroom. You have a good night now, you hear?"

She turned and strode to the bathroom with her head high. She wasn't running away from the dragon. She was *not*.

But oh my god, that was the most embarrassing conversation and evening of her entire life. Second only to his mom finding her in the kitchen the other day.

Chapter Thirty-Two

The next morning, Jake's head was pounding before he even opened his eyes. He turned, trying to block out the light. The pounding continued, then stopped. The smell of sausage filled the air, and he groaned.

Voices echoed to him from the kitchen. He opened one eye and saw that he was lying on the couch at his parents' house. Landry leaned back in the recliner, and Andy was on the floor with a pillow.

"Doesn't it remind you of their high school days, Mike?" his mom said in a very loud stage whisper.

Mike chuckled. "Yeah, but it's Friday morning. If this was during their high school days, you'd be banging on a pot to get them up and out the door for school. No, this reminds me more of when they started going to the Electric Cowboy right after they turned legal."

"I miss this."

"The snoring that shook the whole house? I thought you got enough of that from me."

His mom giggled. Giggled? When had she last done

that? He frowned and shifted on the couch, closing his eyes once more.

"No, I miss having a house full of people. It's only when Andy brings the family over once a month for Sunday dinner that it's like this."

A pang of regret turned his stomach. He never wanted to see his mom sad, especially when there was something he could do to fix it. They'd all been sad since Sarah died.

Dad sighed, and Jake strained to hear. "I know, but maybe Jake will settle down now that he's a dad."

The memory of yesterday slammed into him, making him queasy. The DNA test. The determination to get custody of his son.

He rolled off the couch and stumbled down the hall, waving to his mom as she said a perky good morning. Then he promptly dropped to his knees and threw up in the toilet. He tried to purge all the regret and bad decisions from his body, because it was time to face the music.

He had things to do and shit to get done. For starters, he had to see his son, which meant talking to Patty. The thought made him heave once more. He heard the shuffling of feet behind him, then the sink turned on before a cold, wet rag was laid on the nape of his neck.

He grunted his thanks and heaved once more. Eventually, he flushed the toilet and closed the lid. Thankfully, she just turned and softly shut the door behind her. There was only so much his body could handle, and he didn't need coddled right now.

No, he needed to man up and figure out how to get Patty to let him see his son. He cleaned up and washed his face. Then he found the spare toothbrush they always kept under the sink and washed his mouth out.

Finally feeling human, he went into the kitchen and fell

into a chair at the table. His dad looked over the newspaper at the opposite end of the table and smiled over his reading glasses.

"Morning, son. Are ya feeling better?"

He grunted as his mom set a cup of coffee in front of him along with two painkillers. He winced, not looking forward to mixing toothpaste and coffee.

"Can I have a bottle of water first?" he asked, looking up to see her at the fridge filling a glass with water.

She lifted her brows and smiled. "Already one step ahead of you. Breakfast will be ready soon."

He glanced at the clock and winced. "It's nine already? Goldie should be meeting the other lawyer. Maybe she'll have good news to report by lunch."

Suzie set the water down and turned back to the stove. "I heard a lot about you last night at yoga."

Mike's newspaper wavered. "You went to yoga? Whatever for?"

Suzie shrugged. "It helps keep me limber. Plus, they talk a lot while they do those fancy stretches. It was very insightful."

Jake frowned as he finished the water. He didn't care about any town gossip right now. He only cared about his son.

Mike sighed, taking the bait. "Why were they talking about Jake?"

Suzie glanced over at them and smiled. "Because your girlfriend was there."

He jerked in his seat and held his head. "She's not my girlfriend, Mom. I told you. We have an arrangement."

Suzie nodded. "Yes, I know. Two weeks and then you're done. But that's a shame. She's such a lovely woman."

Andy sat up from the floor and wiped his eyes, and

Landry spun in the chair with eyes wide open. Jake just gaped at her.

She laughed. "What?"

Landry wiggled a finger in his ear. "Did I hear that right? You *like* Jake's girlfriend?"

Andy stood and stretched. "No way. She's been against every girl any of us have ever dated. There's no way she actually approves of one."

Jake took a drink of coffee to dispel the cotton mouth. Landry pushed down the footrest and stood, rubbing his chest while Andy went to the bathroom.

Suzie chuckled and shook her head. "I do not *dis*approve of all of them. Just the ones that might hurt my babies. Wendy's like a bright ray of sunshine, that girl. She's brave too."

Jake felt light-headed and spots appeared in his vision. He closed his eyes and swallowed. What was happening with his life right now? Had he woken up in an upside-down world?

He opened his eyes as Landry patted him on the back and said, "You need to go marry that girl right now."

Andy came out of the bathroom and chuckled, one hand full of an ointment they kept under the sink. "It took her months to warm up to Cindy."

Landry nodded. "Holly too, but it wasn't as bad as what Cindy got."

Suzie scowled and shook a wooden spoon at each of them. "I'll have you know, I was just looking out for you two."

Andy pushed the spoon away and kissed her on the cheek. "And we appreciated it, trust me, but you need to let Jake make these decisions on his own. He's a big boy now, a dad. He'll make the right ones, don't worry."

Andy sat down and rolled up his jeans to the knee, revealing his prosthetic. It reminded Jake of the months he'd spent in the hospital, the countless hours of therapy just to learn to walk again. He removed the fake one and applied the ointment to his gnarled skin, wincing as he did so.

If his cousin could survive that, he could survive this drama with Patty. It might take hours of work, months of pain and heartache, but he had no other choice. He had to walk on his own two feet.

His phone rang, and Goldie's name on the screen made his heart race with anticipation. Sweat began to form on his forehead as he answered the call.

"Hello?"

"Jake? Good news! How would you like to spend the weekend with your son?"

"What?"

"We're still working out the financials, but she's agreed to let you have him for the weekend. Since there's still the restraining order to deal with, we need a mutual drop-off location. I don't know the first thing about babies, so it can't be my office. Any suggestions?"

"My parents' house?"

Goldie sighed. "I think it needs to be a neutral location. She might not feel comfortable being around your family."

He blinked and blurted out, "The Old Mill? There's a woman there named Wendy who might help. Although Patty did see her with me at the bar last Friday. That might not be a neutral third-party after all."

"Hold on." There was a shuffling on the other line, then Goldie said, "No, that's fine actually. Patty is here with her lawyer, and she's agreed to that. I'll get some documents drawn up with her lawyer that will allow you to decide on his care while he's with you. I'll let you know when he's ready for pickup."

She made him sound like a takeout order of fried rice. He wiped the sweat from his brow and thanked her.

"Oh, and Jake? Be thinking about joint custody. Patty is open to the idea, but not to you having sole custody."

Jake blinked as the phone went dead. He remembered the look on Patty's face when she'd seen the nursery he'd put together. He remembered how excited but scared about being a mom she'd been.

He sighed and rubbed his forehead. She might be crazy when it comes to messing with him, but she was probably just angry and upset at being left alone to raise the kid all by herself. He'd known the entire pregnancy that she'd be a good mom, even if she doubted herself.

Why hadn't he considered joint custody before? He'd assumed his son would be with just her or just him, as much as they fought now. But if they could move past their personal issues that caused the restraining order... if she could forgive him for leaving and if he could forgive her for cheating, maybe they *could* do joint custody.

He turned to face the kitchen table, everyone else now eating while his mom fixed her own plate. Suzie's eyes narrowed on his. "Not your girlfriend, huh? Yet she's about to meet your son before you do. Uh huh."

He blinked again. Wendy! How could he have forgotten her? He sighed and rubbed the back of his neck. What was she going to say about this? He hadn't even had a chance to tell her he was the baby's dad.

Landry asked, "Does Wendy even know what the DNA results said? Did she even know you were getting the test done?"

Jake sank into the chair again, holding his hands to his eyes. "She knows I was getting the test done."

Suzie set a plate down in front of him along with another cup of water. "You need a shower. You smell like whiskey and death warmed over."

He winced. "Thanks, Mom, I know." He pushed the food around on his plate.

Andy looked up from his plate and pointed his fork. "I recommend you go home, clean up, then go find Wendy and explain."

Landry nodded. "You definitely don't want Patty showing up unannounced at Wendy's work, now do you?"

Mike sat back in his seat and put his hands on his stomach with a sigh, his plate now empty. "I think I need to meet this woman if she's captivated both Jake and Suzie. What do you boys think of her?"

Andy brightened. "Cindy grew up with her. They went to the same schools, had sleepovers all the time. I think Wendy's dad is still in the Army too."

Jake nodded, taking a bite of his sausage and gravy.

Landry side-eyed Jake and smirked. "I know he met her on Thursday and was kissing her on Friday at the bar, so it must've been instant chemistry."

Jake pulled his collar, popping a few of his buttons. "Is it hot in here or is it just me?"

Suzie laughed, finally sitting down with her own plate to eat. "You're just in the hot seat today, Jake. Better get used to it."

His head swam as they finished breakfast, his mind thinking of all the things he had to do to prepare for his son. What was he going to tell Wendy?

Chapter Thirty-Three

Wendy woke up Friday morning to the sound of birds chirping outside her window. She sat up and immediately reached for her phone. The lack of new messages made her frown. She started to type out a message to Jake but deleted it.

She didn't want to be a nag, constantly trying to keep tabs on him. He'd mentioned Patty doing that once, and she didn't want to appear needy. Sure, she loved him, but that didn't mean she had to know his whereabouts every minute of the day.

But was it too much to ask to know that he wasn't lying in a ditch somewhere?

She shook her head and walked to the bathroom. He was a smart man. He wouldn't have done anything stupid. He had probably just needed a breather, a night to relax.

Her insecurities threatened to bubble to the surface, but she shoved them down as she got ready for the day in a baggy sweater and leggings. She felt good and was ready to tackle the Old Mill. She was going to clean it top to bottom until he texted her back.

Maryanne was at the bakery so Wendy wouldn't bother her with asking about Jake. If something had happened, she'd have heard about it by now. She put in her headphones and turned on the music, rolled up her sleeves, and got to work.

Hours passed, and she got hungry. It was too early for lunch, but a tomato bisque and grilled cheese sandwich sounded just the thing. She went into the kitchen and pulled out the soup makings, throwing it in the pot to start a low simmer.

A shadow by the back door window drew her eye. She glanced over and frowned. A woman stood on the back step with hood pulled up, peering into the window. The woman waved and knocked.

Wendy turned off her music and pulled out her headphones, then opened the door with a frown. "May I help you? Oh, um, Patty? Jake's not here."

Patty had pushed back her hood to reveal her hair pulled back into a tight braid. "I know. I'm supposed to drop off Ricky so Jake can pick him up. Can we come in?"

She carried a baby carrier over her arm, the top covered to keep out the chill. Wendy waved her inside.

"Sure, of course. It's freezing outside. Is he asleep? What do you mean drop him off? Does Jake know? I haven't heard from him today, so if this is something y'all arranged yesterday—"

Patty shook her head, and Wendy turned back to the bread on the stove while she set the carrier on the floor along with two bags.

Wendy flipped the bread to grill the other side, then

added two slices of cheese. Patty glanced down at the carrier, her face scrunching up as she sniffed.

"My lawyer and I met his lawyer early this morning. The DNA results proved what I said all along. Ricky's his. I mean, those blue eyes and that chin speak for themselves, but he never believed me." She wiped an eye, and Wendy pulled the sandwich onto a plate.

The baby was Jake's! That must have been why he'd bailed on her last night. It stung that he hadn't wanted to confide in her, but then again, his mom hadn't said anything last night. So maybe he hadn't talked to anyone. Maybe he'd stayed home and processed it all alone. Her heart ached for him, knowing how much pain he'd already gone through over this kid.

She glanced down, but there was no movement in the carrier yet. Patty's eyes were forlorn and all the fight she'd had in her last week at the bar seemed to have evaporated, whether in the light of day or because the truth was finally revealed.

The poor woman had been through a lot in the past year. She'd been with Jake, had a baby, probably looked forward to raising him together and getting married. Wendy was all too familiar with that particular dream. She couldn't imagine what Patty had felt to have it all come crashing down, while recovering from delivery no less.

Wendy slid the sandwich over as a peace offering. "Are you hungry? There's more than enough."

Patty's brows rose and her spine straightened. She blinked a few times while Wendy went to the fridge to grab two water bottles. She handed one to Patty, who looked from it back to Wendy and back to the water.

"You're—why are you doing this?"

Wendy was tired of people asking why she did things.

The Mechanic Gets His Girl

She pursed her lips and set the waters on the counter, then spooned soup into a bowl.

"You're a mom, and you look tired," Wendy said curtly.

Patty's voice was sarcastic as she said, "Gee, thanks."

Wendy rolled her eyes and set the bowl next to the sandwich, then went to fetch spoons and another bowl for herself. "Give it a rest. You're gorgeous, and you know it. That doesn't mean you're not human. We all get tired, and having a baby makes it hard to get enough sleep, so I've heard."

The words seemed to break the dam inside Patty because she finally sat on a stool and pulled off her gloves and jacket. "You have no idea," she murmured.

Wendy set two more slices of bread on the pan to toast and turned to lean against the counter. "Want to talk about it?"

"Why, so you can run and tell Jake all about it?" Patty eyed her suspiciously.

Wendy shrugged. "You don't have to. That's fine. What else would you like to talk about?"

Patty's face crumpled and tears began to fall. Wendy quickly walked around the island and slid an arm around her shoulders. "Hey, it's okay. We'll figure all this out, and it'll be fine."

Patty shook her head. "Easy for you to say. You've not even been here a week and have this beautiful house and Jake and I—I'll just warn you right now, it all falls apart. I had my dream job when I moved here. Then I had Jake, and now it's just—"

She choked on a sob, and Wendy rubbed her upper arm, giving her a little squeeze. She didn't wait for the tears to stop because she had to flip the bread, but when she turned away from the stove, Patty had started to get herself under control.

"You're not even going to ask about the other guys? I know you've heard about them."

Wendy shrugged. "Who am I to judge? Especially when no one knows what happened. You could've been forced or blackmailed or who knows what else."

Patty's tears returned, and she whispered, "No one's ever given me the benefit of the doubt. Not in all these months, it's just been people staring at me with either hatred or pity. The whole town is against me."

Wendy frowned and turned off the stove. "I'm so sorry, Patty. I don't know how I can help, but the gossip in this town is fierce. I can take countermeasures and remind people they don't know what went on between you and those other guys."

She turned with her own sandwich and dipped it in her soup. She ate across from Patty, standing at the island.

Patty laid her spoon down and asked softly, "You'd do that?"

Wendy nodded, biting into the gooey cheese. She was hungrier than she'd thought.

Patty's phone chirped, and she glanced at it with a frown. She cleared her throat and stood to put her coat back on.

"Thanks for lunch. I appreciate it. As for Ricky, he should wake from his nap in about half an hour. I've written out his schedule and instructions, and they're in the side pocket of the bag. Please tell me you have experience with children. It's okay to leave him, right?"

Patty frowned and pulled on her gloves. Wendy swallowed and nodded. "Yeah, I used to cook for a homeless shelter in Colorado a few times a week. There were lots of kids there and babies needing some love."

Patty paused, her nearly black eyes piercing Wendy's soul. "You really are that kind of girl, aren't you?"

Wendy frowned. "What kind of girl?"

"The thirty-year-old virgin all-around good girl next door type."

Wendy felt heat rush to her cheeks at the mention of good girl, as it made her think of Jake. Patty's eyes took on a mischievous twinkle, then she smirked.

"Ah, I see. No wonder Jake's fallen for you."

Wendy scoffed. "He hasn't fallen for me at all. This is just a two-week fling while he's home. Then he's leaving again."

Patty walked to the door with a grin. "I guess we'll see, won't we? But perhaps if you are who you seem, then he'll come back to you after all."

Wendy frowned. "Wait, when is Jake coming to get Ricky? When will you be back?"

Patty looked over her shoulder, her eyes hooded. "I'll be back Monday around noon. Obviously, no one asked you about drop off, but is pick up here okay?"

Wendy nodded, and then she disappeared out the door. Her mind swirled with questions, so many questions. She called Jake, but it went to voicemail. She sent a quick text, then finished her lunch and cleaned up, turning her music on to a low setting and leaving her headphones off.

By the time she was done, there were movements under the carrier cover. She wiped her hands on a towel and kneeled. When she pulled back the cover, her heart melted. There was this tiny, black-haired, blue eyed, beautiful baby boy kicking and playing happily with his toes.

She unbuckled him and pulled him out. "Hey there, gorgeous. Aren't you as cute as a button?"

She booped his nose with a finger, and he tried to grab it, pulling it to his mouth to gnaw on. She grinned, feeling his wet diaper. She took his bags to the front parlor and changed him. He squirmed the whole time, then he rolled over and began scooting across the floor.

She pulled out the directions and was reading them when there was a knock on the front door. She scooped up the baby, carrying him on her hip. He fisted her curly hair and tugged as she answered the door.

Chapter Thirty-Four

Jake's headache was now just a dull roar, but when Wendy opened the door holding his son, he almost passed out. He saw stars and his vision tunneled, focusing on her smiling face and the baby in her arms.

"Jake, you're here! I've been trying to reach you about your car's extended warranty." She laughed at her own joke and opened the door. "Come in, come in. Tell me everything that's happened. Oh wait, you probably want your son, don't you? Here you go."

She shifted the baby and held him out, then he was holding his son for the first time in months. The two stared at each other, and little hands reached up and patted his jaw.

He felt his throat start to close and his eyes water. "Hey, buddy. Long time, no see."

Ricky babbled back at him, his clear blue eyes just like his own. He was suddenly wide awake, his headache there but forgotten as he slowly followed Wendy. His thoughts were scattered, his emotions raw. This is what he'd wanted for so long, and now he was finally holding his son.

The boy started to gnaw on his fist and whimper. It made Jake's heart race, and he bounced slightly like he used to do with Mandy.

"Hey, it's okay, buddy. Daddy's here. I've got ya."

Wendy waved a handful of papers. "He's probably hungry. He just woke up from his morning nap. Patty was very helpful with leaving directions, but it's all pretty standard stuff. Kinda funny. Three pages on how to care for a baby. As if I'm incompetent or something."

Jake snorted and followed her into the kitchen. He watched in fascination as she placed the carrier on the island and folded back the handle until it was in a sitting up position. He didn't know it could do that.

She waved to it and took a bottle to the stove, pulling out a pot and filling it with water. "Strap him in. He's a wiggly thing, and we don't want him falling off the counter. You'll have to sit by him to feed him. Have you eaten? I have a tomato bisque and can whip up a grilled cheese sandwich."

He panicked as he stared at the carrier. "Yeah, sure, but um—how does this thing work?"

She stopped and looked at him with a frown, then her brows rose. "You don't know how to put him into the carrier?"

He shook his head. "I've only ever been around Mandy when she was a baby, and never in her carrier. Mom barely let me hold her. And Rick was still in the hospital when I left, so I never figured this part out."

She nodded, then took his boy and showed him how to strap him into the seat. She smiled and kissed him, making Rick laugh when her wild hair tickled his face.

The sound made some of the tension in his shoulders ease.

But when she kept smiling even as she tugged her hair out of his tiny little grasp, his legs wobbled. She stood and turned to face him, but the smell of roses swept over him. One hand on the carrier just to be safe, he pinned her to the island, making her gasp.

Then he kissed her like a desperate man on a deserted isle who sees rescue on the horizon. She was amazing. His tongue swept into her mouth to tangle with her own, and it was like a hot shower on a cold, winter's day. He felt the ache in his bones ease, his headache slowly fade, as if her kiss was the nectar of life.

Rick's tiny hand found his finger, breaking him from the spell, and he pulled back. Wendy's green eyes opened, and she smiled warmly again. Her hands crept up to either side of his face, cradling his cheeks.

Then she said, "I was really worried about you last night. I thought you'd gone out with the guys, gotten drunk, and ended up in a ditch."

He winced. "Not quite. I did end up drunk, but I was with my parents. Landry and Andy came over to help me celebrate or grieve or whatever the fuck we were doing."

She paused, then asked. "Celebrate being a father but grieve the missed time with him?"

He blinked. How had she known? It was like she could read his soul. He nodded, and she raised onto her toes and kissed him softly on the lips.

She pulled back and walked around the island to the stove. She made a sandwich and tested the temperature of the bottle on her forearm.

"How do you know what to do? Strap him in, heat a bottle."

She set the bottle on the counter and handed him a small bowl of the bisque. Then she added a scoop of some powder from a can with a baby on it and explained.

"I did some volunteer work after Mom died. The shelter had kids of all ages. Lots of new moms were there since it was right next to the pregnancy center. If the moms needed a decent nap and I wasn't cooking, then I'd watch the kids. It was a lot of fun, but often heartbreaking too. Still, those baby cuddles gave me hope when I needed it, soothed my soul."

He swallowed, not wanting to point out that this is the first time she'd mentioned her mom's death. He just nodded, and she continued.

"This is baby cereal. He's eight months, right? He's at a weird age. He's too young for a lot of solid foods, but too old for just formula. So we can mix some things with cereal—this soup for example. We can also mix his bottles with some cereal to make it more nutritious, but you can't mix too much, or he won't be able to drink it."

She handed over the bowl. "See how it's not thick like mashed potatoes? We could make it that thick, but let's see how he likes it first."

She passed him the baby spoon, and he scooped out a heaping spoonful. The boy was still very tiny, a result of being born premature most likely.

Wendy chuckled and slid a bib over Rick's head. "You might want to start small. He's going to push out most of that scoop."

Then she turned to the stove and left him to it. Nerves turned his stomach, but he could do this. It wasn't like a carburetor. Rick waved his arms, his voice babbling louder as if demanding the delicious smelling food.

Jake fixed a smaller spoonful and approached his

mouth. Rick's hand shot out and sent it flying. Jake watched it splatter on Wendy right as she'd turned back to them. The red paste coated her face and shirt.

She blinked as the spoon fell to the floor, then she looked down and picked it up with a loud sigh.

"Looks like you might need some help, huh?" she asked as she walked to the sink and washed off the spoon. She grabbed a towel to wipe her face. Then she dipped the spoon into the bowl.

"Watch. Are you watching?" she asked.

He nodded. He couldn't take his eyes off her if he wanted to. Even with red sauce in her hair and rumpled clothes, she was gorgeous, kind, and so patient with him. He reached out a hand and caressed her ass when she stepped closer.

Her cheeks flushed, but she simply turned to Rick with a smile. "Hey, buttons. Let's eat some yummy food, yeah? Open wide. There ya go! Yum, yum, yum. That's it, chomp away."

She mimicked opening her mouth when she wanted him to open his. She waited for him to spit out half of the spoonful, then she wiped his face with the spoon to scoop it back up. She showed the baby how to chew it up with exaggerated movements. The entire time, she talked and smiled, dodging his little hand or holding one of his arms with hers while she fed him with the other.

She was in her element in this kitchen with a baby and him. She glowed, and he was like a moth to her flame. He needed to touch her, to see her happy and content like this always.

With her, he felt like he could be exactly who he was, no more and no less. She hadn't harped at him about last night like Patty or his exes would've done. No guilt trip or snide comments or pouts. No, she'd just clearly stated her worry for him, then moved on.

After a few bites, she handed over the spoon. "There, you see? Nothing to it. Now you finish feeding him while I finish making your sandwich."

She walked away, and his hand felt cold, but she only walked to the sink and took off her shirt.

"What are you doing?" his voice was raspy. Could they have sex with the baby in the room? Surely they could. How else had people with one room houses back in the day done it?

She shoved her cream-colored sweater under the sink. "I don't want the tomato to ruin this shirt. It's one of my favorites. I should've known better than to wear it when eating soup, but then again, I didn't think I'd be dealing with a baby today, either."

She pulled out some kind of cleaning agent from under the sink and scrubbed. He wanted to run his hands down her freckled spine and unhook the lacy pink bra. She rang out her shirt and went to the laundry room behind the kitchen.

She returned, still wearing nothing but her bra and leggings. Was she wearing underwear? He hadn't felt a panty line when he grabbed her ass.

He couldn't take much more of this. With Rick demanding his attention on his left and Wendy capturing him on his right, he felt like he was going to explode. Perhaps it was his headache back in full force.

A little hand shot out and tried to swipe the spoon again, but Jake recovered. He had to focus on being a father, not on Wendy. This was what he'd wanted, right?

Wendy slid a sandwich and bowl of soup over to him and walked to the door of the kitchen. "I'm going to go grab a clean shirt. Think you can handle him for a few minutes?"

Jake shook his head. "Nope."

She just laughed and walked on out. She'd probably thought he was joking, but he wasn't. Now that he was staring at his son face to face, it was rather overwhelming.

Chapter Thirty-Five

A loud pounding downstairs woke her up with a start. Wendy sat up and blinked, her heart racing. What was that? She glanced at the clock. Just after midnight.

She slipped her feet into the slippers by her bed and grabbed a throw blanket from the foot of the bed on her way to the bedroom door. The banging continued below, and she hurried down the stairs. A peek out showed Jake, standing there with fist raised.

She threw open the door. "Jake? What are you doing? Where's Rick? What's wrong?" Her heart wouldn't slow down, and she felt a knot form in her throat. Oh god, if something had happened to that baby after she'd assured Jake he could handle it, she'd never forgive herself.

Jake jerked a thumb to the truck still running in the driveway. She could hear the screaming from here.

"He won't stop crying. I don't know what I'm doing, Wendy. You have to help me, please."

She ran down the front steps in her flannel pajamas, poor choice since it was just above freezing. But she climbed

The Mechanic Gets His Girl

up into the truck and tried to soothe the baby. His cheeks were red, and she felt around for his bottle or pacifier or something to help.

Jake was behind her and for once left her ass alone, even though it was right in his face. He sounded worried.

"I tried everything and followed the instructions. I heated the bottle like you showed me and rocked him to sleep. Then when I tried to put him in the crib, he woke up and started crying. I did the same thing, but he refused the bottle. And now he's pissin' mad, and I can't fix it."

She felt his diaper and found the pacifier in the diaper bag. He was too mad to take it, instead grabbing it and throwing it across the cab. She picked it up with a sigh, the cold from the open door starting to make her shiver despite the truck's heater.

She grabbed the pacifier and diaper bag and wiggled back to the ground. "Unbuckle him and bring him inside. I'll turn off the truck."

They worked in sync, and finally they were inside the house, the door closing soundly behind them. She'd found the bottle and shook it, then tested it on her arm. "This is cold now. I'll heat it up, and you change his diaper."

She didn't even wait for his reply. The swinging kitchen door barely muffled his cry, and she knew he wouldn't wait for her to warm it the preferred way. She took the lid and nipple off, then shoved it in the microwave.

She bit her nail as she waited, then reassembled it and tested the temperature. She walked back into the front parlor to see Jake kneeling on the ground. Ricky was squirming and waving his arms as he took the diaper off.

But Jake looked up at her at the wrong moment, because when he looked back down, he got a face full of pee. She chuckled, and Jake cursed as he scrambled to cover him with the top of the dirty diaper.

She kneeled beside him and offered him a wet wipe. "Here, for your face."

She couldn't help the laughter in her voice, she really couldn't. Jake just glared, reminding her of his mom. But he took the wipe and cleaned his face. She peeked in the diaper and lowered her voice to a soft croon.

"Hello there, buttons. What's got you so mad tonight, huh? Is it this dirty diaper? I bet that doesn't feel good at all, does it. Come on, let's get you cleaned up. But you need to stop peeing on Daddy. It may be funny, but he doesn't like it."

The softer her voice went, the lower his cries came as he tried to listen to her. The whole time, she showed Jake how to clean him and keep him covered so he didn't pee on them both. When the change was done, she picked him up and put him on her shoulder. She rocked back and forth, rubbing his back and talking softly.

"I thought you were going to your Mom's this afternoon?"

Jake disposed of the trash and grumbled, "I did, but he didn't have a poopy diaper then, just pee, which she took care of it."

Wendy grinned to hear him say the word poopy. It seemed so foreign on his lips. He'd gone from her place to his mom's.

"She did show me how to bathe him though," he conceded, sitting on the couch under the window. Ricky seemed to be calming down at the movement, and she shifted him to hold like a football and popped the pacifier into his mouth. Still, she continued to shift from foot to foot, rocking him.

He whimpered and his movements turned sporadic as he turned his head to snuggle to her breast. She felt an ache in her heart, wishing that this precious boy was hers, wondering if she'd ever have this for herself.

"What would I do without you?" Jake murmured. She glanced up to find his eyes hooded, the dark circles under them now prominent.

She smiled and shook her head. "I've been asking myself the same question about you all week."

He frowned and then nodded to the now sleeping baby. "You know how I'm teaching you certain skills?" He wiggled his eyebrows, and she chuckled low.

"Will you show me how to do this? How to take care of him?"

His voice was vulnerable, his eyes hesitant and hopeful. She nodded and smiled. How could she say no to this man? How could she not help a child in need?

"First lesson," she said, winking at him. "Did you follow Patty's schedule on her instructions?"

Jake frowned and shook his head. "Mom and I gave him a bath and lotioned him up around eight. Then I drove back home, and he fell asleep in the truck. By the time I got into the house, he was agitated. So I played with him, made him laugh, then made the bottle and tried to rock him."

She rolled her eyes. "There's your problem right there. If he has a routine, you have to try to maintain it. Didn't her paper say he goes to sleep by eight?"

Jake nodded but crossed his arms.

"Well, there ya go. Tomorrow, just follow the instructions."

He stood and walked to her, stopping a foot away. Ricky held her hand with both of his in a hug, while her fingers were pressed to his pacifier to keep it from pushing out.

"Easier said than done. I don't think I can do this without you, Wendy. It's too new, too—I don't know. Will you just help me? Please?"

She felt a grin spread her mouth wide as she looked up into his baby blue eyes. "I kind of like you begging. I can see the charm of it."

His face went from worried to a predatory grin in an instant. His shoulders relaxed at her teasing too.

"Come home with me," he whispered, his eyes blazing with desire.

She shook her head and stepped back. "No, you can't get him out in the cold again. He might catch a chill. Come on. Let's see if we can fashion some kind of sleeping arrangements here."

He followed her up the stairs and cupped her ass, making her smile. "Will you at least come home with me tomorrow?"

She nodded, the knot in her throat leaving her unable to answer. Home. Was his house home for her? Or was the Old Mill? Or her dad's house? She wasn't sure what she wanted.

But she knew he was leaving in just over a week. His house wouldn't be home without him, she knew that down in her soul. She walked to the room at the end of the hall and nudged it open.

It was smaller than the other guest rooms, but it was her favorite for its view of the rose garden out back. The closet floor was empty, her clothes being in the dresser or hanging up. She frowned and looked around.

"Can we make him a space in the closet?"

Jake looked inside and frowned. "I don't think that's very safe. He might not be fully crawling yet, but he's definitely scooting. What if he wakes up and scoots around the room? This place isn't baby proof, not that my place is, but still."

Wendy sighed. "I thought you might say that. Okay, here's a lesson for you. If you rock him to sleep, there's a moment where his whole body goes limp. Pick his hand up and let it drop. There, see? That's how you know he's ready to be laid down in the crib. If you try to lay him down before that, he'll just startle awake again."

She pulled her blankets back with one hand and laid him down in the middle of the queen bed. Then she kicked off her slippers and crawled in behind him. Jake shifted on one foot, looking unsure of himself.

She waved to the open bathroom door. "Bathroom's in there if you need it. If you sleep on the other side, we'll both feel him if he starts to scoot or roll around."

She yawned. Jake went to the bathroom but didn't turn on the light. She pulled the blankets up and gently laid her hand on the baby, feeling the slight rise and fall of his breathing. His hand twitched, and she grabbed it. His little fingers wrapped around one of hers, and she smiled as she drifted off.

The bed dipped when Jake settled on the other side of Ricky. Something settled in her chest. She was afraid to hope for something more with Jake. Even though it'd been a really strange day, she felt at peace. Settled in a way that she'd never been before. Jake and Ricky were a ready-made family, and she wouldn't mind being part of it.

When she woke, the sun was already up. The clock showed barely seven, but Ricky was kicking. Jake was sprawled on his back, Ricky practically huddled up to his armpit. She pulled out her phone and snapped a picture. Then she walked around the bed and took another from a different angle. Ricky pressed a foot into Jake's rib, but still the man didn't wake up.

She ran to the bathroom and quickly got ready for the day, knowing it was only a matter of time before he started to whimper or cry. The baby, hopefully not Jake. She nearly laughed out loud at her own joke as she circled the bed and gently picked Ricky up.

Then she walked out the room and shut the door softly behind her. She changed him, then found the bottle from last night in the fridge. Jake must've gone back downstairs and put it up.

It was almost noon before Jake came down the stairs and found her working on her laptop at the bay window seat with Ricky fast asleep on some pillows on the floor, worn out from playing with his wooden spoons and throwing the couch pillows around.

She smiled as he tip-toed over and sat beside her. "Morning," she said softly.

He winced. "Sorry I slept so long. You should've woken me up."

She shrugged. "We were fine, and you needed the sleep."

"Yeah, but I'm his dad. I want to spend as much time with him as possible before I go back."

She tapped her chin thoughtfully. "Well, with that in mind, what do you say we go to the park after he wakes up from his nap? He won't remember it, but you'll make some good memories."

He looked so vulnerable but agreed anyway. She was glad because a plan had started to form in her mind of a present for him.

Chapter Thirty-Six

On Sunday morning, Jake woke up at home to the sound of Ricky playing in his crib. He stretched, thinking about the day before. It had been a rare sunny day for January, so they'd taken him to the park between naps.

Jake hadn't thought Ricky was old enough for the playground, but Wendy had shown him otherwise. She scooped up Ricky in her arms and carried him up to the top of the smallest slide. With a careful hand on his back, she positioned him on her lap and down they went together. The sound of Ricky's infectious laughter echoed throughout the park, filling the air with pure joy.

A lump formed in his throat as he watched the two of them bond in such a simple yet beautiful moment. The bright colors of the playground equipment and the warm sun shining down added to the scene, creating a snapshot of happiness that would stay with Jake forever, sustaining him through the rest of his deployment.

She looked at Ricky with such love, but she wasn't smothering or coddling like his own mother had been.

Mom had practically tried to wrap him and Sarah in bubble wrap. She'd done the same thing with Mandy too, when she'd gotten custody.

Wendy had taken Ricky to the baby swing too, and after a few minutes of pushing him had convinced Jake to take over. She'd eventually talked him into going down the slide with Ricky too. With her megawatt smile, she could convince him of anything, and wasn't that the problem?

As she took pictures, he contemplated how his life was changing so fast. It'd been barely a week since he'd met her and less than twenty-four hours as a father. His well-ordered world was tilted sideways, and he wasn't sure if it was a good thing or not.

They'd gone to the Diner to warm up, ordering soup and hot chocolate. It had seemed like everyone had been there, but then again it was a Saturday on payday weekend. Wendy had chatted with everyone who had stopped by their booth to talk, even calling some of them by name and asking about specific situations: an upcoming birthday party, a surgery, the results of a date.

He'd been shocked but he shouldn't have been. She might have only been in town a week, but she was a vivacious woman with a heart bigger than Texas. She'd been focused on every single person and truly cared. He'd never met anyone who cared so much.

But did she care for him? She laughed and talked equally with men and women, but had her smile been brighter for Nick? And then she'd seen Parker grabbing an order for pickup and had left him and Ricky to go talk to him. Was that just business or was there more going on there?

He watched them closely but wasn't sure. They'd left when Ricky had gotten cranky. He'd fallen asleep on the way home, then they'd watched a movie. He was tired of watching movies, of sitting still and thinking, but not tired of holding her close to his chest while they sat on the couch.

Ricky let out a squeal, reminding him it was Sunday and time to get up and go to church. Jake eased out of bed as Wendy began to stir and pulled on his old basketball shorts. If he looked at her, he might not get to Ricky anytime soon.

He stepped across the hall and pushed open Ricky's door. A whiff of something terrible hit his nose immediately. Ricky sat up in the crib waving his hands in runny green poop. He looked up at Jake and smiled, raising his hands and babbling.

Jake stumbled out of the door and into the hall. "Shit. Fucking shit everywhere."

Wendy appeared in the door of his bedroom wearing one of his t-shirts, frowning. "What?" She glanced past him, and her eyes widened.

Then she burst out laughing.

Jake frowned and walked back inside. "It's not funny. It's everywhere! What are we supposed to—"

Click.

He spun his head to find her lowering the camera with a wide grin on her face. He shook his finger at her.

"Put that down and help me."

She took another picture and then shook her head, almost dancing back when he tried to grab for her. "Nu uh, you're on your own, buddy. You wanted to learn, right? Well, consider this trial by fire."

She burst out laughing again, and he just turned to the crib, afraid to get too close.

"What exactly am I supposed to do first? Oh god, look. It's on the wall."

Her voice still echoed with laughter as more clicks sounded, and she said, "First, pick him up and take him to the bathtub. You need to scrub him clean. It's not good for it to get in his eyes, as that's how they get pink eye."

Jake sucked in a breath. If Ricky ended up with pink eye, Patty wouldn't ever let him come back. He picked him up under the arms and held him straight out. More clicks and laughter sounded as he stalked out the room and down the hall to the guest bathroom where they'd bathed him last night. His lips twitched at the sound of her joy.

He gave Ricky a bath while she took a few pictures and then disappeared. When he was done, he wrapped the squirming boy in a towel and carried him back into the bedroom to dress him for church.

The crib had been stripped, and Wendy was scrubbing the wall, the crib moved into the middle of the room. He breathed a sigh of relief. He'd been afraid she'd turn up her nose and say it was his kid, he should deal with it. But she'd just seen a way to help and jumped in.

He shook his head at Ricky as he sat him down in the little tent in the corner to play. Wendy stood up with a twinkle still in her eye and threw the disinfectant wipes in the trash can.

As she moved the bed back against the wall, she said, "Well, that should be it. Do you see any on the floor? I checked the bear rug, and I think it's clear, but I don't know." She bit her lip as she bent to peer at the floor.

He gently placed his hands on her waist, feeling the warmth of her skin seeping through his fingertips. When he pulled her closer, she spun in his arms, her eyes sparkling with joy as she tilted her chin up to meet his gaze. Her smile lit up the room, bringing joy, laughter, and peace to the darkness of his heart.

"Thank you," he said simply. It wasn't enough; it would never be enough.

With her here, he'd felt like he could conquer the world and actually learn how to be a dad. She somehow got him out of his head, out of thinking of his sister and how guilty he felt to be alive. Somehow, she made him want to *live*. She made him look forward to tomorrow.

It scared the shit out of him.

She went up on tiptoe and gave him a chaste kiss on the lips. "You're welcome. Why don't you jump in the shower right quick, and I'll get breakfast ready. We'll be cutting it close for church, but we have to be there."

He sighed and went to shower. She was right. They had to go to church. It was important to him that he carry Ricky inside, important to his mom. It was the fastest way to spread the word that he had a son, that he was going to do right by his son, that he hadn't just abandoned him.

Although he had. His stomach twisted again as he scrubbed and let the hot water wash the last of the poop smell away.

An hour later, he took a deep breath as they were almost the last ones through the door. Wendy turned toward the nursery, but Jake shook his head.

"No, I want him with me."

Wendy's face softened, then they walked down the center of the aisle side by side. It was surreal to walk with any woman down the aisle. He felt himself start to sweat, as it seemed like everyone watched them. Were they planning a wedding? Talking about what a bad dad he'd been so far?

He reached his parents, and his mom reached out to take Ricky. Jake didn't say anything, his stomach just churning as he sat. Wendy shifted on her feet and bit her lip.

She looked back a few rows, then Jake shoved the diaper bag under the seat in front of them and frowned.

"What are you doing? Sit down. They're about to start."

She took a breath and stepped past him to sit between him and Mom. Ricky kept lunging for Wendy's wild hair, and she just leaned toward him, whispering with his mom and both of them laughing softly.

When worship started, Ricky clapped along with everyone else. He was happy, and Jake began to relax.

When the preacher spoke, Ricky chewed on his fist and drooled. Wendy gave him the pacifier, but he kept just spitting it out. Jake pulled out the bottle, and Wendy reached for it, but he shook his head and gently took a wiggling Ricky from Mom.

Somehow, he fed him until he fell asleep. He waited for his little body to go limp, then he removed the bottle and put him on his shoulder. He rubbed soft circles on his son's back and tried to focus on the tail end of the message.

But all he could think about was how to make this a permanent reality. He wanted to do this every Sunday. Maybe not the poopy morning, although he could smile about it now.

But a family? Yes, he wanted that. This. Ricky. Her. Could they turn this into something that'd last? Maybe they could keep emailing for the next four months.

The fear of the future, the survivor's guilt, it all diminished in the soft light through the church windows, his sleeping son in his arms and a good, strong, beautiful woman at his side. He glanced over, and the light hit her upturned face as she listened to the preacher. She was an angel, a godsend that he never expected and didn't deserve.

His throat closed with emotion as they bowed their head in prayer. A sliver of fear crept back in that he wouldn't be able to capture this moment and make it a permanent reality, that he would fail the memory of his sister yet again.

The congregation stood as the preacher dismissed them, and Wendy gathered the diaper bag. Ricky startled awake and began to cry.

Needing an escape, Jake slung the diaper bag over his shoulder and held his son tight to his chest. "He's wet. I'll go change him," he said, walking away.

Chapter Thirty-Seven

"Would you look at that? He's even doing diaper duty?" Suzie asked as Jake wove his way through the throng of people milling about in the aisle.

Wendy turned and grinned. "And voluntarily too. As for that, funny story this morning." She giggled her way through the poopy tale. By the time she was done showing Suzie the pictures, more of her friends had joined them until they were all laughing.

Maryanne, her sister Cindy, her mom Margarita, and one or two other girls from yoga gathered around them.

Margarita wiped the tears from her eyes and asked, "Do y'all have somewhere to go for lunch? I made a big pot roast, and you're welcome to join us."

Suzie shook her head and put her arm around Wendy's shoulder. "They're already coming to our house."

Wendy smiled. Jake must've forgotten to mention it. She hugged Maryanne and her crew, then turned to walk with Suzie to the entrance.

"I didn't know we were coming over. I've got BBQ pulled pork in the crock pot at Jake's."

Suzie said, "Well, go grab it and change. I've got beans in the crock pot and cornbread already done. That'll pair nicely together."

They found Jake standing by the doors, smiling and showing Ricky off to anyone who'd stop to say hello. He didn't say much, but his face was beaming with pride.

An hour later, Jake carried Ricky and the diaper bag into his parents' house while she carried the crock pot behind him.

"Mom, we're here," he called, holding the door open for her.

Wendy looked around. It was an older home with wood paneling. There was a wall separating the galley style kitchen and the living room, but the dining table was open to both rooms.

She walked to the kitchen. "Where should I put this, Mrs. Suzie?"

Suzie waved to the counter. "Oh, right there. And please, just call me Suzie, dear. You've met Mike?"

Jake's dad waved from the recliner in the living room and called out, "Nice to meet you, Wendy. Heard a lot about ya."

Wendy chuckled and stepped back into the dining area so she could talk to both him and Suzie at the same time. "All good, I hope?"

Mike grinned and winked, and Wendy had to do a double take. Except for the eyes, he looked just like an older version of Jake.

"Of course."

Jake sat on the couch with Ricky, and asked Mike, "What's the score?"

It was apparently football Sunday. She went back to the kitchen and asked, "What can I help you with, Mrs. Suzie?"

Suzie frowned and pointed her finger. "Suzie, I said. And you can set the table if you'd like."

"I'd love to. How was your weekend?" They chatted while Wendy set the table and mashed some beans and cornbread to mix for Ricky. When they all sat down to dinner, Jake held Ricky while Wendy fed him even though there was a highchair already there.

The conversation flowed easily from Jake's deployment to Andy and Cindy and their kids to Wendy's favorite recipes and the plans for the Old Mill. After they finished, Jake changed Ricky again, then got Ricky down for a nap, holding him tight and bouncing him softly as he shifted from foot to foot watching the game.

Wendy stopped cleaning up the kitchen long enough to pull her camera out and take a few pictures.

"You like photography, don't you? My daughter didn't like to take pictures, but she sure loved to have her picture taken." Suzie laughed and waved her down the hall.

They entered a musty bedroom that appeared to hold mostly boxes on one wall and a twin bed on the other. Suzie sat on the edge of the bed and pulled out a photo album from the bookshelf that served as a nightstand.

Together they flipped through the albums. Suzie was quiet at first, then Wendy started asking questions about pictures that included Jake. A few times, Wendy put her arm around Suzie's shoulders as she sniffled.

They heard the TV turn off, then Jake appeared in the doorway. He looked around the room, but simply said, "Ricky's awake now and changed. Game's over. Are you ready to go home?"

Wendy nodded, her own throat thick with emotions. She

hugged Suzie a little longer than normal, then with a rough voice thanked her for lunch.

By the time they got settled into the truck, she didn't feel like she was going to cry anymore. But she was curious about what had happened to his sister. She knew she'd died, but how?

She bit a nail, her thoughts easily moving from his sister to her mom. The pain of it never really went away. She thought it would, but it didn't.

Would Jake deploying be a similar pain? When her dad was gone, it was bad the first few months, then they'd gotten used to the rhythm of life without him. She expected a few miserable months as she got used to being alone once more. She didn't mind being alone. It was the loneliness that she despised.

The pain of his deployment probably depended on if they kept talking or not, though. They'd said this was just a two-week fling, but this felt like so much more. Going to church together this morning, being seen at the Diner by everyone yesterday... It felt like the start of a real relationship.

She didn't want all the pitying glances once Jake left and they broke up. Could they even label it a break-up if they weren't officially dating? She snorted as he parked the truck. The church thing today had practically screamed *we're serious about each other*. They'd walked down the aisle and sat together as a family for crying out loud.

Maybe she was reading too much into it. When they got to his house, she put on a cheery smile and reached for Ricky in his car seat.

"Da da da da," he said. She paused, glancing at Jake as he stood behind her with the open truck door in his hand.

He opened his mouth like a fish out of water. His blue eyes met hers, bewildering. "He's saying dada?"

She smiled, nodding as she handed Ricky to Jake. He squeezed Ricky and spun in a circle, repeating it with him. "Da da da da."

Wendy laughed and gathered the diaper bag and crock pot. She followed Jake inside, and he held the door open for her. He immediately put Ricky down on the floor in the living room, and Ricky took off scooting across the floor. He looked like he was swimming, as he wasn't fully crawling yet.

"We have to celebrate. We haven't heard anything but baby talk all weekend. Maybe that's his first real word?"

Jake beamed at her. "You bet your ass that's his first word. I don't care if Patty says it's not. You heard it. I heard it. Where's my phone? I want to record it."

She laughed again and went to run water in the crock pot. "We need to celebrate."

"Can you do a photo shoot? I mean, a professional one. I want lots of pictures for the deployment." Jake's voice was subdued, but she kept up the now brittle smile. Her heart ached, but he didn't need to see it right now.

They laughed and dressed Ricky up in cute clothes. Jake wasn't happy with some of them, but she posed them in every way she could imagine.

Jake changing his diaper, putting clothes on him, Ricky grinning and laughing as he kicked and tried to roll away. She took pictures of him in his tent, playing with the bear rug, and sitting in his now clean crib. They ate leftovers for dinner, and she took pictures of Jake feeding him, then bathing him, and finally rocking Ricky to sleep.

Jake fell asleep in the rocking chair too, so she took pictures of that. Then she gently moved Ricky to the crib

The Mechanic Gets His Girl

and laid him down. She pulled a blanket over Jake and closed the door softly.

She was restless and knew she wouldn't be able to sleep. So she set to work on editing what she could, flipping through pictures and trying to find the best shot. There was one big thing missing from all of this.

The next morning over breakfast, she convinced Jake to take them to the auto shop. There, they staged Ricky all over the shop. On the creeper looking up at an engine, then with Jake on another one pointing up at something. They put Ricky into a tire and some dirt got on his cheeks.

It was perfectly adorable, especially when Jake handed him a wrench, and he immediately threw it. Thankfully, he didn't have enough thrust to break a window. The entire photo shoot ate up their morning, and then they were racing back to the Old Mill for lunch... to say goodbye.

Her throat began to close, and she took a shuddering breath. She pushed the thought of not seeing Ricky again to the back of her mind. She was going to be busy next weekend with the grand re-opening of the Old Mill. She wouldn't have time for him or Jake anyway.

Jake would be on his own with Ricky next weekend. Then Jake would head to the Dallas airport, and that would be the end of this little found family that she'd come to love so deeply so fast.

The fragile ice wall around her heart cracked as she imagined the loneliness creeping back in.

Chapter Thirty-Eight

Jake saw Patty's sports car pull up to the Old Mill and squeezed Ricky in a hug. His chest felt tight. It'd only been a few days, but he was already aching at the thought of letting him go.

Ricky squirmed in his arms and shoved a hand into his mouth. Jake kissed him under the ear, making him squeal and shout, "Da da da da."

The babbling words made it even harder to let him go. Wendy laid a hand on his back and another on Ricky's full head of hair.

"Don't worry, Jake. You'll get to see him next weekend, right? This is just for a few days," she said as she took him and bounced him on one hip.

He shook his head. "I don't know, actually. I'll have to ask my lawyer if she can arrange it."

She grabbed one of Ricky's hands and said, "You're going to miss your Daddy, but you'll see him again soon. Now kiss him one more time. Go like this."

She turned her face and puckered up. Jake grinned and

The Mechanic Gets His Girl

gave her a loud smack on the lips. Then he leaned down as Ricky tipped his head up just like Wendy.

They both laughed as the boy tried to give a kiss but couldn't do anything but open his mouth.

Then Wendy was walking to the front door, her face animated as she kept talking to him. On silent feet, Jake took the stairs two at a time. It felt like his heart was twisting with each step.

The doorbell rang, then the sound of voices echoed up the stairs. He kept just out of sight, not wanting to deal with any of Patty's drama.

"There's my big boy! Mama's missed you so much. Did you have a good time at Aunt Wendy's?"

He frowned at Patty's voice. And he didn't think of Wendy as Ricky's aunt at all. She was a natural mother to him.

He shook his head, dispelling the fantasy. Ricky had a mother, and that wasn't something Jake could do anything about.

"How was your weekend? I just made some hot chocolate if you'd like some." Wendy's voice was polite and open, just like her.

"I'd love some. Thanks. It was such a good weekend, you have no idea. I went to Dallas for a job interview on Friday. Then I just stayed in the city all weekend."

He peeked around the corner. If he laid on the floor, he could see into the parlor through a mirror. Wendy had sat Ricky down in his makeshift playpen and was pouring hot chocolate from a porcelain tea set. She and Patty sat next to each other, each turned to the other as they talked.

If he didn't know better, he'd say that they'd known each other their whole lives. Wendy was just being her friendly, open, and welcoming self. She was like that with everyone. He'd seen it all week, but especially this weekend.

"It was probably my first decent night's sleep in months too. How did y'all make it with Ricky? Not too much trouble?"

Wendy smiled, her face lighting up. "None. Well, except for Jake having a hard time getting him to sleep. But he's getting the hang of it, and he loves him so much, you know?"

Patty nodded, her face falling. "I know. The look on his face in the hospital when he realized that Ricky might not be his? Oh, it just gutted me."

Wendy just sipped her hot chocolate and nodded. Patty continued, her voice thoughtful. "He's a good man, isn't he?"

Wendy's brows rose. "The best I've ever met, certainly. Why?"

Patty shrugged. "I've been so angry with him for so long, I just kind of forgot how much I loved him. I did, you know. Love him."

Wendy nodded and bit her lip. "Can't say I blame you there. It's all too easy with him."

Patty laughed, her black hair thrown back. She was gorgeous in a Morticia Addams kind of way, but he felt nothing for her. She was just someone he needed to get along with now. For the sake of their son.

"You've got it bad, don't ya, girl?" Patty asked.

Wendy's cheeks turned pink, but she just shrugged and smiled. "You know Jake's last weekend in town is next weekend. Do you think he could have Ricky for it?"

Patty frowned, her eyes locked on Wendy. "Maybe. I'll talk to my lawyer and see what we can do."

The Mechanic Gets His Girl

Wendy shifted nervously on the couch. "Do you still love him?"

Patty smiled then patted Wendy's knee. "No, that ship has sailed. Don't worry."

Wendy smiled in relief, her face brightening. "Oh, I almost forgot! I did a baby photo shoot with him. I hope you don't mind, but you have to see this."

She hopped up and grabbed her laptop from the bay window. Then she plopped down with a beaming grin. They oohed and awed over the pictures for what felt like forever, but he was lost in his own thoughts.

He propped his head up on his folded arms and just watched them.

This weekend had gone better than he'd expected. He'd learned a lot about himself, but also about Wendy. A week ago, she'd been a drowned rat on the side of the road who wouldn't stop talking.

But she was so much more than that. She was strong despite her size. Beautiful, of course. But it was that twinkle in her eye, the way she laughed so easily, the way she handled people—

The way her hips swayed as she walked up the stairs to him. His focus narrowed on her, and he slowly stood up, never taking his eyes off her. He had a week left with her. He needed to make his time count.

He needed to show her how much he appreciated her, make some sort of attempt to repay her kindness and support. They said actions spoke louder than words.

She reached the top of the stairs and smiled. Her shirt was stained at the shoulder where Ricky had been gnawing on it. Her wild hair was piled up high on her head in a big bun. He wanted to drink in the moment, to remember this feeling and the way she looked right now.

That must be why she was always taking pictures. He saw that now. It wasn't a way to separate her from what was happening in real life; it was a way to preserve it.

She stopped at the top of the stairs and tugged on her shirt. "I'm going to take a shower and change. Did you want to do anything this afternoon?"

She walked by him and down the hall, and like a lamb to slaughter, he followed at her heel. He slid his hands to her hips and pulled her back against his groin, making her stumble and gasp. But he held her safe and together they walked the last few steps into her bedroom.

"I can think of a few things to do this afternoon. Namely show you how much I lo—appreciated all your help this weekend."

She gasped, "It was no problem at all."

He walked them to her bed and kicked her feet to stand wider. His heart raced. He'd almost said those three little words, but he couldn't. He didn't. It was pointless, since he was leaving. They were just two ships in the night, docking in the same harbor before going their separate ways.

The thought made heat radiate through his chest, and he pushed down on her back until she was face first on the bed. Delicate hands fisted the blankets as he ran his hands down her spine and under the hem of her shirt.

He pulled her shirt up, caging in her arms and eyes. Then he unhooked her bra and slid it down her arms too. He traced patterns on her back like connect the dots from freckle to freckle. She gasped, wiggling that perky ass at him.

He grinned and slid his hands inside her leggings before lowering them inch by delectable inch. He kissed the small of her back, then went down her ass as each piece of skin was revealed, licking and kissing down to her ankle. The pants and underwear were tossed to the side, and he kissed his way up the other leg.

She giggled when he breathed on the back of her knee, but he didn't want her laughter right now. No, he needed to hear her moan and come. Slowly, he helped her settle each knee on the edge of the bed.

With him kneeling, he could stare straight at her pretty pink pussy. The intoxicating scent surrounded him, igniting the wildfire within him to a blaze of need. He nuzzled closer, raining kisses around the places she needed him most. Her ass wiggled against him, chasing his mouth.

"Please, Jake."

He crushed his mouth around her clit, and she screamed into the bed. Then he moved back and let his fingers play her like a guitar. His tongue dove into her wet center. He flexed it like a spear, penetrating her deeper than he thought possible.

She moaned, and the sound drove him on. He was so hard he hurt, but he wanted her to come before he took her. His nose pressed against her ass, and in his lusty daze, a terrible hunger crawled through him.

He shifted, moving two fingers to give her the friction she needed in that sweet pussy, his thumb still moving on her clit. He watched her clenching, felt her muscles around his fingers.

"You like that, don't you, Peaches?"

"Yes, sir. God, yes, Jake, I need to come. Please."

She was getting so good at saying the words his soul craved, but he wanted to please her just as much as she pleased him. He leaned forward and licked around her last remaining hole. It puckered and flexed, but the squeal she gave made him press on.

"Jake! What are you—oh god," she groaned into the bed.

He licked and teased until she was rocking her hips back on his face. Then he leaned back and teased a finger inside. He barely got in the first knuckle before she froze, clenching around him.

He groaned, his vision tunneling to her orgasm, and he felt phantom pussy around his dick as he remembered what she felt like. They'd only made love once this weekend, in the dark of night as Ricky had slept in the other room, and it hadn't been enough to quench the thirst for this woman.

But he had to make her crave him, need him as much as he needed her. To do that, he'd use every tool at his disposal. He reached into her bedside table and found the tiny toy he'd discovered when he'd snooped through her room last weekend.

Chapter Thirty-Nine

He brought the lipstick shaped vibrator up to his mouth and coated it heavily as he worked his other hand on her. Then he replaced his finger with the dildo. She paused when he'd gotten just the tip in her ass.

"Jake?" Her voice was throaty, nervous, and needy. He stood and removed his fingers from her dripping pussy. He teased her hot sheath with his dick, setting up a gentle rocking motion with both the tip of the vibrator in her ass and the tip of his cock in her pussy.

"Are you ready for this lesson, Peaches? Do you trust me?" he asked, praying for her to say yes. He was seeing spots now with his need for her. He imagined plunging into her, each shared pleasure making them moan.

He felt her take a deep breath and nod, then he slowly pressed both himself and the vibrator inside. She was clenched tight, and he ground out, "Take a deep breath and relax."

Her breath was shuddering, but as she inhaled it became easier to slide both himself and the vibrator inside her. He bottomed out, barely seeing the end of the vibrator and the little white button. He turned it on. She threw her head back with a squeal, clenching tight on his dick.

He roared, unable to wait anymore. He was hard and hungry with need. He pulled himself out almost to the hilt, but left the vibrator deep in her ass, the humming sound filling the air. The feel of it vibrating against his dick, separated only by a thin layer of skin, drove him wild.

Her thighs shifted wider to take him deeper, and he obliged, going so deep he began to sweat as he held himself back. His plan to make her come first had been successful, but he refused to come inside her alone. He needed to feel her clench and lose control like he did. One hand on the vibrator to keep it steady, the other hand slid around her hip to her clit, he pounded into her like he was digging for treasure.

She was the treasure here though, and he wanted to fulfill all of her fantasies. If he pleased her enough, maybe she'd fall in love with him too.

He rubbed furiously, and she bucked against him. He bent over her back, biting and kissing her skin as he set up a bruising rhythm. She stretched and melted around him, and he rode her with the passion of a wild beast.

It wasn't pretty. It wasn't soft and loving like he'd wanted. It was wild, feral, and savage. She was deliciously tight, squeezing him every time he rammed himself home. His body was hard and primal in her soft heat, and she welcomed him with mewls of ecstasy.

They were beyond words now, each trying to outlast the other. Everything else was stripped away until it was just this raw mating, hips bucking, shaft throbbing. He plundered her, not backing down.

Together they flew to the top. He felt her tense up

beneath him, and then she was coming with a scream that could be heard through the whole house. His balls tightened in response to her writhing, frantic orgasm. She shook beneath him, and he bit her shoulder as he flooded into her. Body tensing, he unleashed his love into her in lava-like spurts.

They gasped and groaned as they came hard, each fueling the other's climax. They were pure, white-hot heat and together, they could rival the sun.

When he finally caught his breath, he moved to standing. She still twitched under him, her flexing muscles threatening to push him out. He turned off the vibrator, and she sank to the bed as her knees gave out.

"That was—that was unexpected," she panted.

He kissed her ass and grabbed a tissue by the bed to clean her up. "Happy to serve, my lady."

She chuckled, and the sound drew him closer. He wanted to gather her in his arms and never let go. Instead, he turned to the bathroom and the shower. The hot water helped bring him out of the fog of emotions, the longing to make this thing between them something real, something permanent.

The weekend had flown by, but he needed it to slow down so he could figure out what this was between them. She made his chest lighter, his body warmer. He was tired, but not exhausted. More like a fulfilling way, like he was exactly where he wanted to be.

Was this how his dad felt with his mom? Andy with Cindy? Landry with Holly?

He frowned. Had his sister ever felt like this? Pain lanced through him with lightning speed. He put a hand on the shower wall and leaned forward, letting the spray soak him. Everything hurt now, even his throat. He couldn't swallow.

He saw the steam rising, but he still felt cold as he pictured his sister's face in the hospital. By the time he'd made it to her from overseas, she'd already slipped into a coma. She'd been battered and bruised, and he hadn't been able to fix it.

He gasped at the hand on the small of his back. He didn't want to face her like this, so he spun to put his back to the wall and pulled her into his chest. He held her in a fierce hug, his chin on her head.

Her hands settled on his hips, and she sighed. He'd heard that talking about these things helped, but he didn't see the point. Wendy pulled back, a content smile on her face until she looked into his eyes.

Slowly, her smile turned into a worried frown. "What's wrong?"

Two simple words. That's all it took for his universe to crumple. He took a shuddering breath and pursed his lips. He'd said it before. He could say it again.

"I had a sister."

Her eyes widened, and she nodded. "I gathered that much from the pictures on your dresser and at your parents' house. What happened?"

He swallowed past the knot in his throat. "Car accident. She was in the ICU a few days, awake. Then she slipped into a coma and was gone. The tattoo with the date is the day she died."

She cupped his cheek with her dainty palm. "I'm so sorry, Jake."

He closed his eyes, soaking up her support and love. No, not love. He couldn't have that. That wouldn't be fair to Sarah.

"She wanted a big family. She would've loved Ricky."

Wendy nodded and reached for the soap and loofah. "Was she like your mom?"

Jake smiled and nodded, unable to force his hand away from her body. It wasn't a sexual need, but a need for something deeper.

"She was like Mom, but more sarcastic. Her wit was killer. She never put up with shit and could hold her own in any fight. Not that I let her, of course. I was a year older, you know, so I got into a lot of fights in high school."

Wendy giggled. "And how did she like you trying to protect her?"

He grinned, finally feeling the weight on his chest loosen. "She wasn't a fan. She punched me in the face once, right after I'd just beat up the guy who'd kissed her outside of school that afternoon."

He paused, one hand in his hair full of soap as he realized. That first night he'd met Wendy. She'd talked about punching a guy in the face too. Maybe that's what had drawn him to her, the fact that she was a little like his sister, a little like his mom, and a lot of unique Wendyness.

Wendy laughed as she rinsed her hair, her breasts pressing up and distracting him. "What'd your mom say about it?"

He finished his hair. "I told Mom it was the guy who'd punched me, but overall, Mom approved. She didn't like any of Sarah's boyfriends or my girlfriends. Not until now, anyway."

Their eyes met, her lips parting in surprise. Neither had defined their relationship. If anyone had asked him a week ago, he would've said it was just a fling.

But he couldn't ignore the pull of her any longer. This

was real. It was scary and unlike anything he'd ever known before, but it was very real.

He just didn't know what *it* was yet.

Wendy switched places with him so he could rinse as she said, "It must've been nice."

"To be punched in the face? Not really."

She chuckled and playfully slapped his chest before running her hands up and down his torso.

"No, silly. It must've been nice to have someone in her corner like that. I bet she loved and appreciated you more than you can ever know."

He was curious and couldn't resist prying into her background, knowing full well the answer already. "You don't have any siblings, right?"

She shook her head, still staring at his chest and running her hands over him. "No, just me, Mom, and Dad, when he wasn't deployed."

"What did your mom do?"

"She was the school's secretary. It was cool having her there. I got to eat lunch with her every day and didn't have to ride the bus with the other kids."

He waited, hoping she'd tell him the rest. The water turned cold, and he sighed as he turned it off. She stepped out first and pointed back at him.

"Don't move. Freeze right there."

He froze but called after her. "I *am* freezing. That's why I turned the water off. What are you—"

"Say cheese," she said in a sing-song voice. He blinked at the flash and swiftly covered his junk.

"Hey, no nudes," he whined.

She grinned and wiggled her brows. "That you know of."

He grinned back and began to prowl after her, dripping

all over the tile. He lunged for her and the big camera, but she shrieked and hopped out of reach, pulling the camera up and snapping another picture.

He growled, and her laugh spurred him to action. He was faster this time and threw her damp body over his shoulder. He heard another click and giggle as he walked to the bed. But the smack to her ass made her gasp and jump.

He rubbed the spot before tossing her on the bed. She landed with a bounce, her hair spreading wildly. He fisted his cock and put his knee on the bed, opened his mouth to say something—

And she snapped another picture. It surprised him enough to laugh, but when he heard another click, he grabbed the camera strap and jerked it out of her hands, setting it gently on the side table while holding her back from it with the other hand.

"Think you can get away with being a little brat?"

She smirked and stretched provocatively on the bed, purring, "Yes, sir, I do."

The fire in his veins ignited into an inferno, and he trapped her head between his hands. He leaned close and breathed into her ear a low growl. "Oh, then this is going to be a very interesting lesson indeed."

Chapter Forty

The first week of February flew by for Wendy. She had beefed up the marketing for the Old Mill and grew busier and busier as the grand re-opening grew closer. Suzie had shown the photos of Ricky to all her friends, and she had several appointments lined up for photo shoots too.

Her car was all fixed up now, which was good. Every night, she either went to Jake's house like after Thursday night yoga, or he came to the Old Mill like on Tuesday after his poker night.

The weekend was much the same, but with the addition of Ricky's bubbly little laugh. They had originally planned a 'see ya later' bonfire over the weekend, but since they had Ricky, it was postponed to Monday night.

Jake was slowly getting the hang of diapering, feeding, and bathing. But it was the little moments that melted her heart. Ricky asleep on his chest as they reclined on the couch, which she took a picture of. She took more and more pictures of Jake as the weekend went on, but he never said a word.

Not even when she took pictures at church. She tried to ignore the questions that were getting louder in her head. But sitting next to him for a second time on the pew, holding Ricky and singing with his mom... it had to mean something, right? One time could be a mistake, but twice?

After church, they'd invited his friends to his house for a Superbowl football party. She'd cooked too much but had so much fun playing hostess. Inside, she was in turmoil, though. What did it all mean? All his friends—now her friends—saw them as a packaged deal now.

And through it all, her heart grew heavier and heavier. He was leaving. It wasn't some far away thing, but just two days away. Since last weekend when he'd gotten emotional talking abut his sister, he'd steered their conversations to more light-hearted topics. They laughed a lot, watched movies, and talked about every inconsequential thing imaginable.

Everything except their feelings for each other. The closer he came to leaving, the further away she felt from him. The emotions built throughout the week until her chest was tight and her shoulders drooped.

And now it was Monday, and Patty had just walked down the steps with Ricky. She'd had another few good talks with Patty at drop off and pick up, but Wendy felt her heart breaking as she buckled him inside.

When Patty backed out of the drive with that precious boy, Wendy couldn't take it anymore. She stood on the front porch and cried. She hadn't hidden her emotions from Patty very well, either.

Not only was Jake leaving, but Ricky was too. Strong arms wrapped around her from behind, and she turned and cried into his chest. She didn't even try to hide her pain from him. She loved him. She couldn't hide anything from him any longer either.

He scooped her into his arms and kicked the door shut behind him, then headed up the stairs.

She didn't care. It didn't matter where they went. She was hurting, but it was selfish of her. He wasn't her son, just like Jake wasn't hers, either. They'd agreed to go their separate ways when the two weeks were up. He sat on the bed and scooted to lean back against the headboard.

His hands rubbed her arm. "Sh, it's okay. You'll see him again, don't worry."

She sniffled and shook her head, the scent of pine radiating from him. "Not likely. Didn't you hear her? She got the job in Dallas and is moving in a few weeks."

His chin nodded against her head, and his voice hardened. "I know, but when I get back, we'll figure out how to share custody. At least until he's ready for school, I know it's possible. It has to be."

It was her turn to soothe him. She sat up, hearing the vulnerability in his voice, and straddled him. She cupped his face in her hands.

"If anyone can make it happen, it's you. You're all that's good in the world, Jake." She kissed his lips softly, just a peck. She loved him so much more than she ever thought possible. It was almost painful to hold it in.

He snorted. "Doubtful, but I'm trying to be a better man."

"You're the most amazing man. You're strong and resilient." She kissed him again.

"Steadfast and loyal." Another kiss.

"So gentle and patient with Ricky." This kiss was a second longer than the one before.

"Kind to your mama." She tried to kiss him again, but he put a finger on her lips to stop her.

His brows were raised but there was a twinkle in his eye. "If you're going to kiss me, do not talk about my mama. I can't think about her and kiss you at the same time."

Wendy giggled and sat up, wiping her tears. She could feel his erection through his jeans, and she rocked her hips. She bit her lip as his hands began to caress her body.

"Jake?"

"Hm?" came his distracted reply as he thumbed her hard nipples through her shirt.

"Will you make love to me and make me forget?"

His blue eyes pierced hers. "Forget what, Peaches?"

Pain shot through her chest as she whispered, "That you're leaving too."

His eyes softened, then he reached forward and claimed her lips. The kiss was deep and echoed of promises he'd never keep. A promise to return to her, to love her and cherish her always. A promise to hold her when she cried and take care of her when she needed someone in her corner.

Tears leaked out of her eyes, and he cupped her face, wiping them away. He broke the kiss and frowned. "I don't think I can keep going if you're going to cry, Peaches. It makes me hurt to see you hurting. Please."

She ground onto his groin and thrust her chest in his face, holding onto his shoulders. "Please what, Jake?"

Swiftly, she pulled her shirt over her head and tossed it aside.

His mouth dropped. "You're not wearing a bra."

She smiled slowly, even as a tear rolled down her cheek. "Not wearing underwear either. Wanna see?"

She raised up on her knees to shove her pants down,

which shoved her breasts into his face. They were small, but he loved them. He worshiped them, latching on to one hard nipple and sucking, nipping, and kissing.

She twisted and fell onto the bed on her back, kicking the pants away. He followed, running his hands and lips over both breasts now. She sighed and tipped her head back, then reached under her pillow for her eye mask.

She slipped it on and smiled. "There. Now you can't see whether I cry or not. Now will you make love to me, Jake?"

His mouth stilled on her stomach, then he sat up. She felt the bed shift as he stood and assumed he was getting undressed.

"Touch yourself, Peaches. Show me where you want me." His voice sent a shiver up her spine, and she trailed her fingers down to her nipples. She circled them, then pinched and pulled.

It made her back arch off the bed, and she gasped, "Jake."

"That's it, Peaches. Where else?" She heard a drawer open, and her heart raced.

Her hand slid down over her short hair. She planted her feet and spread them wide. With just a few fingers, she circled her clit and hoped he was watching. Something cold touched her clit, and her hand pressed on the inside of her thigh to spread her leg wider.

It moved against her, and her hips lifted. "Is this where you ache, Peaches?"

She nodded, and the bed dipped. Then she felt the tip of his thick cock pressing at her entrance.

"Is this what you want?"

She nodded again. The cold little vibrator on her clit turned on, and she bucked. He plunged in almost simultaneously.

She gasped at the feel of him stretching her wider than she thought possible. Every time, he amazed her with his size, but he didn't give her time to adjust. He just eased out, groaning a little, then drove back in.

Hard, steady, painfully slow strokes made her shake. He penetrated deeply, burrowing in her wet heat. Her hips rose to meet him, seeking more of the vibrations, more of his dick. She was trapped between torment and ecstasy.

Then he leaned forward, and she felt his hands on either side of her head, trapping her in a safe cocoon of warmth. When he plunged inside, her shoulders hit his wrists, and he went deeper. She gasped, and his mouth claimed her.

Her toes curled and her back arched as she came. Every cell of her body vibrated and sizzled through her. It was soul-wrenching as she moaned into his mouth. He fucked her through it, not stopping his rhythm, not slowing down.

Then the wave was building even higher. She chased another orgasm, and only then did his speed shift. Her muscles gripped him tighter, and he pistoned harder, his shaft slicking in and out.

When she saw white spots explode behind her closed eyelids, fueled to new heights, they came as one. His body crushed her, but she gripped his back and held him close as she spasmed uncontrollably.

They gasped, each fueling the other. Heat spread through her womb as he poured inside her, pulse after pulse of the proof of his love.

Not love. Lust. Mind spinning with aftershocks, she somehow reminded herself that this wasn't real. It wouldn't last. It was puppy love.

It would hurt like hell when he left. Her tears flowed once more, and she thanked God that she'd put the mask on. It soaked up the proof of her heartache.

He shifted, kissing her jaw with soft, slow kisses. He nuzzled her neck and whispered, "What are you doing to me, Wendy?"

He held himself still until their breathing calmed, and she was barely twitching. He pulled out, leaving her lying on the bed blindfolded. Alone.

She pushed the mask off and rolled off the bed, following him into the bathroom and avoiding his eyes. What was she doing to him? No. The real question was, what was he doing to her? And more importantly, would she really get over him as easily as she hoped?

Chapter Forty-One

She'd had a fragile, forced smile about her all day. That morning, she'd driven him crazy from her furious cleaning of the B&B. He'd sent her to town to get a massage after lunch, hoping to calm her down. He'd run to the auto shop for a few hours to finish some paperwork. When he'd gone home to clean up for the bonfire that night, she'd been there cleaning his house.

All he'd wanted was a nice, quiet afternoon. Maybe watch some movies. Work on a car or two. But her chaotic, worried energy had driven up the tension between his shoulders. His parents came over, and Wendy and Mom had talked so much, it'd driven him outside to the barn.

He'd organized his tools even, for crying out loud.

An hour later, more people started to arrive. For the second time in two days, they held a party. Only this one wasn't a football party, but a bon voyage bonfire. Wendy was busy getting the lettuce separated and slicing vegetables for burgers while Jake started the grill outside.

Landry and his brothers showed up, then Andy and

Cindy. Landry handed him a beer, which he nursed while flipping burgers.

"Can't believe you're heading back already. I didn't get to take you down nearly enough in our poker matches the past few weeks." Landry's grin was infectious.

Jake began to relax as the guys all ribbed him about not even showing up that first week he was back.

Andy leaned against the back porch rail and crossed his arms. "Come on, guys. We all bled him dry on Tuesday. Once was enough misery for him, don't you think?"

Landry's grin widened. "I think he must not be too hung up about it, what with his new girlfriend consoling him at the end of the night. Is she a firecracker with that red hair?"

Jake felt his heart race in frustration. "Kiss my ass, Lan."

"Ooh, hit a nerve, did I?" Lan practically sang out.

Jake saw his knuckles whiten on the spatula as he pulled the burgers off.

Andy slapped him on the back, then squeezed his shoulders tight. The pinch forcibly reminded him to relax his shoulders, as they were almost up by his ears.

"Lay off him, Lan. You know how touchy he gets the day before he leaves. Between coming to terms with fatherhood and growing that new relationship with Wendy, the man's strung tighter than a rubber band."

Landry nodded and handed him another beer. "Well, put it all out of your mind tonight. Tonight, we party like there's no tomorrow."

Andy frowned. "But don't go over there thinking that. There *is* a tomorrow, and you better come back in one piece. You have a son to think about now."

The sorrow of leaving rose, the guilt of not being here for Ricky's first birthday or to make sure his mom and dad weren't lonely... it all started pressing into him. His throat felt like he'd swallowed an apple. He downed the beer, then grabbed the last of the burgers and went inside.

It was even more overwhelming inside, more full of more people than he'd ever seen in his house. One of his poker buddies raised a beer in salute when he walked in, saying as he passed, "Thanks for the invite, Jake. Love the house."

Jake nodded and smiled tightly, a headache already forming behind one eye. Wendy's hands on the small of his back made him almost jump as he set the tray of burgers down on the table. He turned and wrapped his arms around her for a quick hug.

But he couldn't breathe, couldn't swallow. The heat of her arms and all the people in the house was too much. He went to the fridge and opened both it and the freezer. He grabbed another beer, not really wanting it but needing an excuse to get in there.

"Jake? Are you okay?" Wendy asked softly behind him.

He took a shuddering breath. It was his time to paste on a fragile smile. He turned and kissed her cheek as he went to the food. "I'm fine," he said quietly, barely heard over his mom banging a spoon on a pan to get everyone's attention.

Oh no, all eyes were going to be on him. This might be the worst part about deploying. All the fanfare around it. If he could've snuck out in the middle of the night last night, he would've. Then he could've avoided this whole fucking day.

His mom smiled at the crowd. "Thank you all for coming tonight. But this is just a see ya later party, a bon voyage and come home soon. Four months will come and go, much like the past two weeks have. We'll miss you, Jake, and can't wait to see you again."

Her voice choked as she met his gaze with eyes so like his own. Then she lifted her glass of wine. Everyone else followed suit, then his dad was praying over the food.

When he opened his eyes, the crowd swarmed the table and kitchen. Wendy was smiling and helping scoop ice out of the cooler for people's solo cups, talking the whole time and laughing. He backed up with a shuffling step, then fled out the back door.

His mind was a jumble of thoughts, but some sense of dread settled in his stomach like a stone. He walked to the bonfire and began to toss fluid on the wood. The cold February air helped clear his head.

The whole thing was soon ablaze, and people began to pull up their camping chairs and sit down to eat. The chatter was softer out here, and not so demanding. His panic abated, and then Wendy was there.

She was more beautiful by the firelight, and he suddenly realized that they'd never made love in front of the fireplace. He'd wanted to spoil her, savor her. But their time was up.

It had to be up.

Just then, she turned and caught his eye, her face open and softening as she smiled a secretive smile that was just for him. Maryanne said something, and then Wendy laughed as Parker walked up to them from the house.

Wendy's face lit up when she saw him, and then she was practically launching herself into Parker's arms. The raw wound in his soul split open and grew in dismay. How could she possibly hug another guy like that and feel anything for him?

It just wasn't possible. Others tried to talk to him, but he just smiled tightly, nodding and not even pretending to listen. He watched as Wendy walked around the bonfire, talking with just about everyone.

She put her hand on some guy's arm. He'd seen the same thing with Patty. The signs were there with Wendy too. When he came back from deployment, she'd be shacked up with some other guy like Nick or Parker.

Wendy laughed and turned to the next person, but Jake felt like he was going to snap his jaw in half, as hard as he was clenching it. She was almost to him when she stumbled and practically fell into Nick's arms.

Jake's eyes narrowed. He'd seen that move dozens of times at the bar. It was a practiced move that all girls must've been taught from infancy. How had he never noticed before?

She was easily talking with everyone, and what exactly was flirting if not talking? She talked with ease. There was no way she could've needed flirting lessons. Hadn't he said from the beginning that everything was just so easy with her?

It was easy to talk with her. Open up with her.

Resentment stirred in his chest because that was obviously a ploy, and not a two-way street with her since she had never opened up about so much in her past, about her mom. She finally reached his side, and he tipped his chin up.

"What's that all about?" He jerked his chin to the fire.

Her expression was so open and honest, but he saw that as a lie. She hid too much from him. He could feel it, knew it to be true, and her face just twisted that knife in his gut more.

Wendy touched him on the arm and leaned in as she asked. "What do you mean? Did you eat? I lost you in there. Let me go get you a plate."

He shook his head and grabbed her hand before she'd stepped too far away. "No, let's take a walk. I need some space."

She nodded, and after they'd stepped three steps away from the fire toward the field, he dropped her hand. It was too much of a reminder of her trickery. He'd had enough.

All the day's emotions bubbled over as he swung to face her with a clenched jaw.

Chapter Forty-Two

"Were you faking the flirting thing this whole time?"

"What are you talking about?" Confusion warred with the chill in the air. His icy demeanor was one she'd not seen from him since that first night they'd met.

"You're flirting just fine out there with those guys." Scorn dripped from his voice. It was the same tone of voice he'd used on Patty at the Electric Cowboy. The chill seeped into her bones.

Wendy's eyes widened. "I was not. They were just saying how much they liked the s'mores dip."

"I bet they were. I saw the way you touched Nick's arm."

He'd misinterpreted her clumsiness as flirting. She breathed a sigh of relief. That was easily cleared up. Then they could go back to the party and the warm fire. He had to see how she felt, but if he was so blinded by the past that he couldn't see the future, she'd tell him to his face how much she loved him, even if the thought of admitting it scared her.

She tried to wrap her arms around his waist and smiled. "That's ridiculous. My boot was caught. I used his arm so I didn't fall when I pulled it free. How could I—"

He pulled away and began to pace, leaving her cold and bereft. "And when you hugged Parker? He's your boss, Wendy."

Surprise made her cheeks flush as she gaped at him. "I know he is, that's why I hugged him. I'm a huggy person, Jake. You saw me at church the past few services. And they're all practically strangers!"

"Did your previous boss really fire you for punching a groom? Or were you hugging up on the boss too? What about the groom? Did he think you were open to it because you hugged him too?"

She gasped as a pall of dread chilled her body. She crossed her arms and rubbed them even as her body stiffened in outrage. "Of course not. Why are you being so obtuse?"

"Obtuse? Obtuse? Who says that? This must be why your fiancée left you at the altar. You're so damn—"

"What did you just say?" her voice was low, and he froze. But it was her heart that had begun to ice over. She tried to build a wall and protect herself, but it was like ice and easily cracked. This was so much worse than when Mike left her in that courthouse.

Jake ran a hand through his hair. "I mean, uh—"

"How did you hear about *that*? Was it Maryanne?" Her voice was sharp.

He shook his head and shoved his hands into his pockets as he glared at the ground. "Emails."

"What email—oh. Ooh," her eyes widened as she covered her mouth with her shaking fingers. What were the odds that *he* was the one she'd been emailing? Oh no, what had she emailed? Panic raced along her spine and her voice wavered.

"You're MichaelJSmith, aren't you? I thought I was emailing my ex, but it was you. You're the third, your dad is Mike Smith the second. Your mom said yesterday, but I never—"

"Yeah, you never even realized that the guy you were pouring your heart out to was the same one who was trying to get you to open up here." His hands fisted at his sides.

But she saw red as her surprise gave way to anger. Her cheeks heated despite the cold air around them. Why didn't he say anything? "You knew? This whole time, and you didn't say anything? Why the fuck didn't you just ask me about it? Is that why you stopped replying?"

He waved his hands wide, his beautiful blue eyes cold as ice. "I stopped responding because I didn't need to. I was right here, ready for you to talk to in person. But you never did, did you?"

She frowned and pulled back. Her stomach knotted at the yelling, the anger, the heightened emotions threatening to pull her under. Her heart raced, making her light-headed as he spun on his heel and kept chewing her out.

"You chose to keep that little secret failed engagement to yourself. Why is that? Why are you so upfront about everything else but that?"

The emotions bubbled up, and her rapid breathing became shallower. She didn't want to think about it, about her many failures. She wanted to move forward with a new, better life. But here he was, reminding her of all she'd done wrong, all she'd tried to escape.

"Maybe it's because you weren't really a virgin after all.

Well, let me tell you something. If you're pregnant with that jackass' baby, don't you dare try to pawn it off on me. Fool me once, shame on me. Fool me twice? Not gonna happen."

His words snapped her out of her shocked stupor. She opened and closed her mouth, feeling her heart break into a million pieces. Anger burned hotly and her hands fisted at her side. "The only jackass around here is *you*. Maybe your nickname will be Jakeass."

She turned on her heel to walk to her car. She didn't need this shit. She needed to get her panic attack under control, and he needed to sleep it off.

Jake pointed at her and followed hot on her heels. "Don't you try to turn this around on me. This is about you not being who you say you are."

Her body began to shake, but not from the cold. It was a white-hot fury that pumped through her veins. How dare he stand there and judge her? Especially for lies with no grain of truth. Jake's eyes were so hard and cold, the light of the distant bonfire not warming them at all.

She turned to face her car, ignoring him and clenching her teeth.

He stalked beside her. "You didn't even have the decency to be all of you. Just showed me bits and pieces. Do you know how long it took me to get you to even talk to me about your mom's death? Yet in that email to a stranger, you were perfectly fine talking about it almost immediately. Why don't you trust me? Why didn't you let me in? It's because of this isn't it?"

He waved his hand back to the bonfire and the cluster of people around it. She frowned, not following his logic.

"What the fuck are you talking about?" Frustration raced through her, warming her up with adrenaline. Onward she trekked through the frozen grass.

"That shit right there, with your hands all over those other guys. I was just a two-week fling, wasn't I? Practice for when you made your move on whoever was next in line."

She stumbled to a halt and put her hands on her hips. She glared at him. "We both agreed it was a two-week fling, but—"

His finger came up and pointed in her face. "Exactly. And now it's done. Over. We've both had our fun and can move on."

Pain rocketed through her, piercing her heart and making her grind her teeth together before almost growling, "You're picking this fight on purpose, aren't you? Making it easier on you when you leave tomorrow. I thought you were above that bullshit, but apparently not. Well, thanks for all the fun, Jakeass. I'll put all your lessons to good use while you're gone."

She pushed past him, but he grabbed her arm and tugged her to his chest. Nose to nose, he whispered furiously, "That was always the plan, wasn't it? Love me and leave me. It's a good thing you brought your car tonight. I'm going to go back to that bonfire to enjoy a nice evening with my *real* friends, not some chick who flirts with every guy in a five-foot radius."

She jerked at his words, pulling herself out of an embrace that normally brought her so much comfort. She made a beeline for the parking area, trying to make it to the safety of the shadows of her car before the tears spilled over.

She wouldn't let him see how much it hurt. His words echoed in her mind. She'd been called names before, but he'd made her feel so much worse. The bullies, the jealous classmates, all of that had rolled off her back.

But his words landed in a bullseye.

The cold wind stung on her wet cheeks. She wiped them with her jacket, not even knowing when she'd started crying. She thought about letting the cold seep into her bones and just lay down and stare up at the stars until the cold swept her under.

But that wasn't going to solve anything. It'd just prolong the pain. She walked slowly over to her car and left. Her body was numb, and next thing she knew, she was walking into the B&B.

She took a hot shower to warm up, but it didn't work. She knew she wouldn't be able to sleep; it was too early, and her mind was spinning too much. The should'ves, would'ves, could'ves had started rotations in her brain.

She walked downstairs and made some hot cocoa, then turned on the oven. There were cookies to make for Valentine's weekend coming up. If she still wasn't tired, then she'd move on to candies.

She should've talked about her mom more when he talked about his sister. Why hadn't she? It wasn't a secret. Surely, she'd mentioned her mom a few times before.

If she'd known he felt that way, she would've talked for hours about her mom. About how she'd gotten sick, watching her waste away. Angry tears fell onto the counter, and she used her apron to wipe them away.

She could've been more open with him about Mike. But honestly, who wanted to relive a failed engagement? Even if it had been a quick, impulsive one like theirs had been.

The candy and cookies turned out great. They'd be a nice welcome for their first guests on Thursday. She wrapped them all up and put them in the giant freezer so they'd stay fresh.

It was barely eleven, and still her blood was boiling in

her veins. Who did he think he was? A knock sounded on the door, and she went to see who it was at this time of night.

She sighed and opened it. "Maryanne, what are you doing here?"

Maryanne swept inside and held up a bottle of wine. "We got to the bonfire bon voyage party late. There were whispers. I got to the bottom of it and came as soon as I could. Are you alright?"

Wendy shrugged and shut the door. "I've made cookies and candy already. I was about to start on a different project, but I don't know what yet. Was Jake still there? Of course he was. It was his party."

Wendy shook her head and went back to the kitchen, Maryanne hot on her heels.

"Yeah, and he was drunk off his ass, complaining loudly about crazy chicks who couldn't keep it in their pants."

Wendy gasped and spun around. "He said that?"

Maryanne nodded. "Yeah, but to be fair, he was throwing Patty's name for most of it. I'm not sure he was talking about you specifically. Why? What *did* he say to you?"

Wendy brushed away the angry tears and reached for the rag to clean the island. Then she relayed their fight tonight while Maryanne poured them large glasses of wine.

"The thing is, I don't know why I didn't tell him about Mom or Mike. I mean, it's not like they're big secrets or anything."

Maryanne nodded. "Yeah, but like you said. It was supposed to be just a two-week fling. Why would you open up an artery for a two-week fling? That's more of a serious relationship sharing moment."

Wendy bit her lip and paused, her mind whirling. "Yeah, maybe that's why he was so mad. The past two weeks certainly haven't felt like a fling. We went to church together, twice. His mom likes me. We just... fit together, ya know? Like it was meant to be. But then he just threw it all away." She shook her head. "I don't know. It's all so confusing."

They took a sip of their wine, then Maryanne asked softly, "Do you love him?"

Wendy sighed and nodded. "Yeah, but it has to be puppy love. With Mike, I was over him so fast. I fell for Jake just as fast, so that means it's puppy love, right? It can't be the real kind, like you and Gunner. That takes more than just two weeks to build."

"I don't know," Maryanne sounded doubtful.

Wendy shook her head, taking a larger gulp of her wine. Then she said, "It doesn't matter now. I've officially renamed him in my head. From henceforth, he shall be known as Jakeass. Oh, and did I mention what he said about not really being a virgin?"

"What?"

Wendy nodded, her cheeks flushing. "Yeah, he said I better not try to pass off a kid of Mike's as Jake's because he's already gone through that shit once. Stupid Jakeass. As if I would ever lie about being a virgin."

Maryanne gaped and nodded. "Definitely. Jakeass is perfect."

Despair twisted in her gut and turned inside her. "I thought he was perfect," she whispered forlornly. She gulped her wine and then set it down hard on the counter.

Maryanne filled her glass up. "No one's perfect, not even Gunner."

"I know," Wendy said as she dragged her feet to the pantry and pulled out a bag of flour and sugar. "But he was perfect for me. It doesn't matter now though. How about heart shaped brownies? I think I need chocolate."

Maryanne nodded, hopping up to get the rest of the ingredients. All she needed was some binge worthy food, a good wine, and a great friend. Soon she felt floaty and could mostly ignore the ache that kept pressing on her chest.

Chapter Forty-Three

Jake drove his truck the next morning to his parents, his mind foggy from the alcohol and effects of the party. He'd stayed up way too late, trying to erase the look of pain on Wendy's face… and the pain in his own body. It felt like he'd been chewed up and spit out by a bear.

His mom was on a rocking chair on the porch when he arrived, sipping coffee. He glanced at his watch as he walked up to her.

"Why are you drinking coffee? It's almost lunchtime."

She shrugged, her eyes hooded. "Couldn't sleep much last night. You know how it is. My baby is about to leave, possibly for the last time."

He felt a jolt to his chest, the pressure increasing again, and he couldn't say anything even if he wanted to. Jakeass was the word of the day, running on repeat in his head since last night. He kept putting his mom through these deployments when he could just as easily get out and retire. He was a selfish Jakeass. He sank onto the other chair, and together they just rocked in silence.

Finally, she said, "Do you remember when you and Sarah used to run off to the creek and pretend to save all the animals?"

Jake smiled and nodded. Those had been good days. Sarah had always had an affinity for animals, and they'd set up a pretend vet practice under an old oak tree on the creek bank.

"Sometimes I think she goes with you, still looking to save the little lost lamb that is my son."

He pursed his lips and rubbed his forehead, his eyes burning. "I'm not a lost lamb, Mom, and I'm certainly not little."

She smiled, her face pinched and tight. She'd seemed to age overnight, but then again, these goodbyes were always the hardest. This is exactly why he tried to avoid them at all costs.

She waved a hand. "Then perhaps just a blind, deaf, and dumb one. After all, you pushed Wendy away last night."

He cleared his throat and leaned his head back as he rocked. "Ah, who told you about that?"

"Oh please, it was hard to miss. Your dad and I went out to tell you we were heading home, but you were already tipsy. Gave me a big hug and told everyone that I was the best woman in your life and the only one you ever needed."

He groaned, then felt bitterness and regret well up inside. "So what? It's true, isn't it?"

Suzie's rocking stopped, and he opened his eyes to look at her. She was frowning, then sipped her coffee and looked at him.

"I used to think so. Lord knows everyone in town called you a mama's boy when you were growing up. But now I'm not so sure." She seemed to peer into his soul.

"Only time will tell if you've made the biggest mistake of your life letting her go or not. All I'll say for now is you've got four months to think long and hard about your actions. And hers. These past few weeks, I've seen you happier than you've been in years. That alone tells me all I need to know."

A truck rolled down the drive, and his dad came out of the house. Jake stood and turned to him, but he just said, "About that time, huh? Gonna miss you, son."

Jake hugged him tight, the simple words hitting him in the gut as much as Mom's words of wisdom. "I'll miss you too, Dad."

Then he turned and scooped his mom into a hug too. "And you, Mom. This right here, the three of us? This is all I need. Now, I'll see y'all in four months. And no welcome home parties this time, yeah?"

He forced a grin and then practically ran down the steps, stopping only to open his truck and grab his backpack. His dad would take care of his truck, making sure it was taken to the paint place in Fort Worth and came back better than new.

He opened the door to Andy's truck and jumped in, then they were backing up and rolling through town. Everywhere he looked, his eyes tried to find Wendy. But she wasn't there. She was at the Old Mill preparing for the grand re-opening this weekend.

He sighed as his phone pinged. When he glanced at it, his heart raced to see an email.

Hey Jakeass,
Maybe I deliberately didn't talk about Mom and Mike with you because I wanted to focus on the present instead of the past. Did that ever occur to you? I've spent too long living in the past already.

Too bad you're still living in the past and projecting your dumb past trauma onto me. Too bad you don't know me well enough to know I would never lie about my sexual history and never cheat or flirt with someone else.
Maybe if you'd straight up asked, I would've talked more about it, opened up more. They're no big secret, and I wasn't hiding them from you. I just wanted to enjoy our precious few weeks together, but apparently that was too much to ask.
You're right, though. It's been fun. Be careful and come home soon. However, when you do, don't look me up. Don't call. Don't text. I never want to talk to you again. Like YOU said, we're over.
Wendy

Jake swallowed hard and his vision blurred.

"Bad news?" Andy asked as they drove to the airport in Dallas.

God, had he really said those things? Jake shook his head and leaned it against the window. "Just Wendy. We broke up last night."

"Oh really? I hadn't heard." Andy's voice dripped with sarcasm, and Jake groaned.

"Has everyone in town heard? Fuck me."

"No thanks. I'm taken. As for the town, yeah. You weren't exactly being discreet last night, calling her names after she'd left and all."

Jake's head jerked up to stare at Andy. "I did no such thing."

Andy snorted. "Yeah, you did. Crazy and cheap were thrown around a lot."

Jake shook his head. "No, I must've been talking about Patty. I'd never call Wendy that."

Andy shrugged. "Stopped at the bakery for breakfast this morning, and that's all anyone is talking about.

Maryanne went to see her last night, you know. They stayed up late baking. Between the angry tears and crying tears, Wendy fell asleep on the window seat about two, so Maryanne just went straight to the bakery without going to bed. She looked about ready to drop."

Andy's voice washed over him, and he closed his eyes against the images swimming through his head. Wendy crying after Ricky left Sunday. Her tear-streaked face haunted him. It was like a vise gripping his chest, and he rubbed at it absently.

"Maybe Wendy will understand and forgive you. Eventually, anyway. I mean, she's gotta be used to the drill from her dad's deployment experience, right?"

Jake frowned, shaking himself out of his reverie. "What are you talking about?"

"Wendy. She has to know that this is just how soldiers deal with deploying, right? We push people away, somehow stupidly thinking it'll make things easier when we leave. Like some martyr, an emotional sacrifice, a clean cut through our souls."

Jake blinked. Hadn't Wendy mentioned something like that last night? It was all kind of fuzzy. He banged his head against the headrest.

"It doesn't fucking matter. What's done is done, and it's better this way. She said she never wants to hear from me again, and that's fine with me. Honestly."

Andy let a few seconds pass, then he drew out one word. "Sure."

His fingers itched to email her. He knew he owed her an apology, but how did he say it? He typed out half a dozen replies, but ultimately didn't send any of them.

It really was better this way. They could make a clean

cut. He sank into the seat as misery overwhelmed him. It was for the best, but it sure didn't feel like it. It felt like hell.

Chapter Forty-Four

Wendy dragged herself out of bed every morning that week and threw herself into preparing the Old Mill for its reopening ceremony. She pasted on a brittle smile, all while frantically going down the checklist to make sure everything was in order.

She refused to think about Jake. The pain was too raw to process, so she buried it deep inside and dug into work. She worked herself to the bone, just trying to distract herself.

If she didn't, she'd lay awake at night and wonder what she could've done differently, what was real and what was pretend. She'd chewed through all her nails and the inside of her lip was raw from constant rehashing of every single moment of the past two weeks.

Thursday finally came. At lunch, there was a big ceremony, with the mayor and Parker cutting a red ribbon on the front porch. The newspaper reporter was there along with half the town.

Wendy smiled and busily worked the kitchen. They had

opened the restaurant side of the mill early that day, just for the ceremony, and it had a steady flow of people all afternoon. She also met with the five couples who were their first Bed and Breakfast guests.

They were lovely people, and Wendy only cried at hearing their love stories twice. She was grateful for the fast pace because it meant she didn't have to go to ladies' night yoga. She wasn't sure she could face Jake's mom this week or anyone else.

Through the weekend, she trained the two teenage waitresses and worked with Zarrel and Rosita in the kitchen. They started to develop a rhythm and figure out their quirks and strengths. They laughed a lot.

By eight each night, it was just her running the kitchens, though. Zarrel was still working at the bakery with Maryanne, and Rosita was one of the cooks at the middle school where Parker worked.

The restaurant was only open from Thursday to Sunday nights, giving her time to prepare for the guests during the rest of the week. After the opening weekend, most of the guests had left, and she spent the following days cleaning the rooms before welcoming new guests on Valentine's weekend.

As Sunday afternoon arrived and the last guests drove away, temperatures dropped. Although they had a few guests stay throughout the previous week, this week there were no scheduled arrivals until Friday morning. She wrapped her sweater tighter around herself as she closed the door behind her.

For the first time in two weeks, she was alone. Alone with her thoughts and the dull ache in her chest that was every memory of Jake. That ache drove her forward, though, because without it, she was just numb.

She wasn't hungry, cold, or tired. Just numb. It was more than anything she'd felt after Mike had left.

Her phone rang, so she sank onto the window bench seat to watch the weather roll in.

"Hello?"

"Hey babe, how are you?"

Her eyes widened, but nothing more. She felt nothing when hearing his voice.

"Mike? Why are you calling?" She really didn't care. He was long gone, and she'd left him in the past. He was just a bump in the road to her being here, fulfilling her dream.

"Aw, don't be like that. You know I love you."

She snorted and ran a hand over her face, tiredness soaking into her bones.

He protested. "No, really, I do. Yes, the deployment freaked me out. But it's not so bad over here. The past month without you has been the worst part. I—I'm sorry I left the way I did. You didn't deserve that."

"No, I didn't. But you did it anyway. Do you know what it does to a girl who's left at the altar?"

He sighed, but she just leaned her head back and stared outside.

"I know, babe, and I'm sorry. Look, can we just talk? I needed to hear your voice, to be reminded of home. How's winter been? How's the snow? God, I miss the snow. Nothing but desert and sandstorms that choke the life out of me."

She laid on the bench seat and propped her head up on a pillow. "I don't know about the snow in Colorado. I moved to Texas."

"Texas! Whatever for?"

She snorted again. "Seriously? *You left me at the altar*. I was being evicted the next week, did you know that? I was counting on moving in together and sharing the rent. And I was *fired*. So yeah, I fucking moved to Texas, and I fucking moved on. Exactly like you said to do, dumbass."

"Oh God, Wendy, I'm so sorry, babe. I—"

She sighed and pulled the throw blanket up over her. "You know what? I hope you are sorry because this ship has sailed. We're never, ever, ever, getting back together."

She practically sang the last sentence, driving him crazy with her impersonation of the pop singer.

He groaned, hating when she did that. "Wendy, don't be like that. We can work this out. We can talk, and I'll be home for R and R in a few months."

She laughed. It was a cold, hollow sound, and tears pricked behind her eyes. She closed them, trying to keep them at bay, but it was no use.

"Mike," she said softly. "When I say this ship has sailed, I mean I've fallen in love with someone else. If you need a friend, I'm happy to talk to you while you're gone, but I'd prefer not to. I don't need any reminders of how I didn't meet expectations, of how I wasn't good enough for you."

She wasn't sure if she was talking to Mike or Jake in her head. She needed to give herself this talking-to.

"This needs to be a clean break. The past month has been eye opening. I don't hate you if that's what you're looking for. You're forgiven. I've moved on."

She squeezed a small pillow to her chest, hoping and praying that she could make the last part a reality. She didn't want to be a bitter old maid. She didn't want to stay hung up on any guy. No matter how much it hurt, she had to let go.

"Wendy, I—"

"Goodbye, Mike." She hung up. Yes, she'd said she was

willing to be his friend, but she just couldn't right now. It was too much.

Her chest was heavy as sobs wracked her body. Not because of Mike, but because she knew she'd never get an apology phone call from Jake. He was long gone. Soon, she cried herself to sleep.

When she woke from tumultuous dreams, it was nearly midnight. The wind howled, but she couldn't pinpoint what had woken her up. She paused, then sat up from the window seat and rubbed her eyes.

She followed the sound to the laundry room. It was the back-up generator. Why was it on? She looked at her phone and the alert. A freak snowstorm, according to the weather app. Temperatures had dropped almost twenty degrees in eight hours.

She went upstairs to add more layers, realizing that the lights upstairs were all out. The generator must only work for the kitchen to keep the fridge from going bad. She quickly bundled up, then went back downstairs.

After a snack of leftovers, she built a fire in the front parlor—the only fireplace in the house—and laid down in front of it. Sleep claimed her once more.

The next few days were covered in ice and snow. Power was out all over town, and they had no way of knowing when it'd come back up. She checked on Maryanne by phone, then bit her lip and texted Suzie to make sure they were warm.

All's well here. Mike and I are holed up in front of the fire. Are you warm and safe and okay?

Wendy felt tears prick her eyes. It was such a mom thing to say, and she missed that. She fired off a reply, then texted a quick update to her dad when her email pinged.

Wendy,
Heard about the storm. Do you have a generator? Are you safe? I can send one of the guys with a four-wheel drive vehicle to get you and take you to Mom and Dad's. Just tell me you're alive and what you need.
Jake

Her hands shook, so she set the phone down and leaned back on the couch. The ache had turned to a pounding, writhing pain to her chest that made her headache come back with a roar.

She was just settling into a new rhythm, just getting used to the loneliness, and he goes and pulls something like this?

Jake,
Don't you dare act like you care. So what if I'm safe or not? It's my business, not yours. You have no right to know whether I'm freezing or anything, just like I have no right to know whether you're alive or dead in a foreign country. Leave me alone. I can't move on if you keep doing this. Just... just go away.
Wendy

She set the phone down and drifted off to sleep again. The pain was just too much. Sleep was easier. It didn't hurt when she slept.

When she woke, it was late afternoon. She had a few missed texts from her dad and Maryanne. Then she checked her email.

Wendy,

Talked to my mom. She said you're fine.
Jake

That was it? Two fucking sentences? She tossed her phone on the couch and went to cook dinner. Her anger was back, and she needed to bake something. Plus, maybe the oven would warm her up a bit more. Even with the fire, it was so cold in the big Victorian house.

The next day the house was still without power. She stripped the blankets from upstairs and took the stapler to the wall, creating a barrier of hanging blankets to trap the warmth of the fire in the parlor.

The day after that, she was bored from reading and ventured outside. It wasn't even trying to melt yet, but the birds and animals had left tracks. She took pictures of the house with the snow for the website, then went back inside to update the blog.

Thursday, she woke up to a red nose and fuzzy head. The snow began to melt, but the power didn't come back on until Friday. The guests had all canceled for the weekend, so she spent it nursing her cold and bruised heart while scrapbooking the photos of Ricky and Jake. Seeing the pictures made her cry more, which didn't help her stuffy nose at all.

It took longer than she wanted to bounce back from the snowstorm. Her cold lingered, but the symptoms shifted. Maryanne brought her soup that first week of March, and still she walked around in layers. Zarrel and Rosita dominated in the kitchen, as none of them wanted Wendy's germs to expose the food. Parker took over some of the weekend management duties so she wouldn't get too close to the guests.

She was exhausted, dizzy, and short of breath just going

up the stairs to her room. She was napping every single day and forgot too much. It reminded her of when she was first diagnosed with vitamin deficiency and anemia. She doubled up on her medications and powered through March and the Spring Breakers who had booked reservations.

In the back of her mind, she kept comparing her symptoms now to her mom. A random memory would pop up, and she'd push it away. No, she couldn't be sick like her mom. That wasn't what this was.

But still, the niggling doubt in the back of her mind plagued her. By the end of March, she was a nervous wreck. Finally, Maryanne convinced her into going to the doctor. So she made the appointment and went to the lab to draw some blood.

Chapter Forty-Five

"Hello, Ms. Macdonald. I'm Dr. Vaughn, but most people just call me Dr. Kendall. How can I help you?"

Wendy kicked her feet nervously as she sat on the examiner's table. She hadn't liked doctors in quite some time. Her mom had been in and out of hospitals and doctors' offices for a decade, and Wendy was the one who took her to almost every single appointment.

"My mom had cancer for eleven years before she passed, and I'm worried. I have anemia and a vitamin B deficiency that I take medication for. My medication dosage changed around Christmas, and everything was fine until the snowstorm. Ever since, I've not been myself. I went to the Quest Lab and had them run every blood test they could. Did you get the results? Do you know what's wrong? Is it my mom's cancer?"

The handsome doctor listened intently as he clicked on the computer in the corner. "I see the lab results and your records from Fort Carson. I was in the military too, but never had the pleasure of being stationed there."

She smiled tightly and nodded as he made small talk.

He nodded as he continued reading and scrolling on the computer. "Your vitals look good, but your iron, B1, and B12 are definitely off. Your B9 is borderline. Did the snowstorm impact your immune system at all?"

Wendy nodded. "Yeah, I was sick for a few weeks afterward."

"And how do you feel now?"

She shrugged. "Not good, honestly. Kind of nauseous. Food tastes off. I just feel crummy all over. Weak, forgetful. Both things my mom had. I started carrying post-its in my pocket so I can write everything a guest says they need. I even write what time I start to boil water because I accidentally burned a pan. Me! A trained, professional chef! I'm telling you, Dr. Kendall, this isn't normal for me."

She blushed in embarrassment at the memory. A message box popped up on the screen, and he clicked on it. A new screen opened up, but it was too far away and turned at just the wrong angle to read over his shoulder.

"Hm, well this certainly puts another spin on things."

"What, what is it? The cancer?" Wendy bit her nail and felt tears prick behind her eyelids.

He turned on the stool, his green eyes warm and comforting as he smiled. "Not that I can see from this test. I can order a more thorough blood panel if you'd like. This particular test shows your hCG levels. You're pregnant, which would explain why your vitamin levels are all thrown off."

Her fingers froze to the edge of the table. Everything froze in time. Not even the clock moved as her mind tried to process his words.

"Pregnant?" she blurted. He nodded, and she felt a weight begin to press on her chest. "But—but I'm on the shot. It was helping manage the anemia. I was going to ask if you could give me another shot, because it's been three months now, and I'm due. I—"

She felt the room spin, and suddenly he was standing next to her, gently pressing on her shoulder to lay her down. He pulled the foot slide out so her legs would go straight.

Her chest felt too tight. She couldn't breathe. This wasn't what she needed right now. It was— "Oh god, what if I have mom's cancer gene and pass it on to the baby? Oh no, Dr. Kendall, can you test for that? Can you check?"

The doctor smiled down at her warmly and nodded. "Yes, but for now, we need to get you to breathe. Follow with me. There you go. In, two, three, four. Out, two, three, four. Again, deep breaths."

He brought out the stethoscope while coaching her to breathe. Finally, she felt her body relax.

"Was that Lamaze breathing? I've heard about that."

He shook his head. "No, my sister Holly runs the yoga studio in town. She's big into meditation, breathing, and staying calm under pressure."

Wendy's eyes shot up. "Oh, Holly's your sister? I love her! She's so fun and easy to follow in yoga."

The nurse came in with a portable computer screen and smiled. Dr. Kendall moved to the other side of the table and explained, "If you go to yoga, you probably know my wife, Lola, too."

"They're good friends of Maryanne, who is my friend and the entire reason I moved here."

He laughed and got out his stethoscope. "I moved here because of Andy, a friend from the Army. It happens a lot around here. Good people, good friends all around. You're going to be okay, you know."

She took a deep breath, reminded that she wasn't alone. "I know."

He smiled and tested her vitals while he talked. "We're going to do an ultrasound and get an idea for how far along you are, your due date, things like that. Are you ready?"

He waited, and while her heart was racing, it wasn't overwhelming anymore. She nodded and bit her lip. The nurse set the machine up while Dr. Kendall had her raise her shirt to expose just her stomach.

She gasped at the cold, but the sound made her draw in a shuddering breath. A whomping noise echoed in the room, strong and fast.

"Is that—the heartbeat?" Her voice was a whisper. Oh God. She really was pregnant. She was going to have a baby.

She laughed as the nurse and doctor nodded, pointing to the screen and showing her the little peanut shaped blob. It felt like a weight had lifted off her shoulders. Goosebumps made her shiver.

Life as she knew it was going to change yet again. At least this time, she'd have a few months to prepare for it.

Her body began to warm for the first time in months. Light-headed, she waved a hand weakly. "That's my baby. I —I'm going to be a mom."

She couldn't think of anything but this little nugget who was relying solely on her. She was lost in a daydream of what her baby would look like. In her minds' eye, she saw a little baby like Ricky waddling through the Old Mill, except instead of black hair, her baby had red curly hair. But still those same baby blues as Jake.

The thought of him jerked her back to the moment. The doctor was talking about diet and nutrition and vitamins. Now her euphoria had turned into dread, settling in her stomach like a stone.

"Doc, I can't, um—" She turned her head to the side and threw up on the floor.

The other two leaped into action, but she just closed her eyes. Someone helped her sit up and someone else pressed a waste bin into her hands.

Her whole body ached, and she lost sense of time as she tried not to think, but it was impossible. She would have to tell Jake, and the idea of facing him made her cry.

He had wanted Ricky to be his child, but he'd also said some mean things the night before he left. Things about her being pregnant by the guy who'd left her at the altar.

For the first time, she felt like a loose woman. Pregnant and alone. Tears began to roll down her cheeks as she hung her head in the kidney shaped pan. She rested her head on her forearm along the edge of it and sobbed. Someone rubbed soothing circles on her back.

"There, there. It's alright. Have you been sick the past few weeks?" the doctor asked.

Wendy kept her eyes closed but shrugged. She'd felt crummy, but she hadn't thrown up before now.

"Well, that might be your first round of morning sickness, then." He began discussing ways to manage it, but her brain was too foggy. Now her exhaustion made sense.

She finally sat up slowly and handed the pan over for the nurse to dispose of. They gave her a wet wipe and a bottle of water, so she cleaned her face and washed out her mouth.

After a few more minutes, she felt more in control of herself and knew what she had to do. She had to raise this baby on her own. Or at least get through the pregnancy on her own.

The Mechanic Gets His Girl

Yes, that was it. She would wait for Jake to come home. If he tried to reach out to her or see her when he returned, maybe they could patch things up. Enough to co-parent, at least.

But she wouldn't tell him about it while he was gone. Hadn't Maryanne told her a similar story about her sister's husband, Andy? He'd not found out he was a father until well after he returned from deployment.

She hoped it wouldn't come to that. She prayed the rest of her year wouldn't be full of drama like Patty and Jake's had been. Surely, they could work out an arrangement to co-parent peacefully, right?

If Jake treated her like he had Patty, she'd be miserable, and she couldn't be a good mom if she was angry and bitter over Jake. No, she had to let him go. She had to play nice with him, if he tried to talk to her when he returned.

But—fingers crossed—maybe he'd just ignore her and leave her to raise their child in peace. It might be better that way, if he thought the baby wasn't his?

No, no, that's what happened with Patty. He was a jealous, territorial insecure bastard because Patty had cheated on him, and Wendy wouldn't do anything that would turn him back into that person.

She cradled her head in her hands. God, this was such a mess. She couldn't decide on whether she wanted him to find out or not, whether she wanted to be with him or not.

Regardless of how she felt, her baby was relying on her. The Old Mill was relying on her. She had things to do and couldn't keep agonizing over Jake. She firmed her jaw and straightened her spine.

The doctor typed up all the notes, since she wasn't processing what he'd said at all and needed it written. He fixed her prescriptions, and she made sure he and the staff wouldn't say anything about the pregnancy to any of their mutual friends.

One thing she did know, though. She did *not* want to get back together with Jake just because of the baby. She did *not* want anyone else to tell him but her, and that meant she couldn't let anyone in town know about this.

The next few months of keeping this hidden would be challenging, but she hopped off the table on wobbly legs, determined to make it work.

Chapter Forty-Six

The following Thursday afternoon, Wendy was busy checking in two couples at once when the phone rang.

"Just a minute please," she told them both as she pulled up their reservations on the laptop and picked up the phone. "Hello, this is the Old Mill. How can I help you?"

"Wendy? This is Patty. Do you have a minute?"

Wendy looked up and covered the speaker. "My computer is frozen at the moment, but if you're hungry, you're welcome to wait in the dining hall. Tell the waitress I said your appetizers and desserts are on the house, since you're having to wait. I'm terribly sorry about this."

Thankfully, both couples just smiled and walked to the restaurant. She took a deep breath and turned back to the phone.

"Okay, yeah, what's up? How's Ricky?" Her heart raced, worried because why else would Patty be calling? Yeah, they followed each other on Instagram now, but Patty never posted any pictures of Ricky. It was all professional, work-related posts dealing with her big city job.

"I need a favor. I have a work conference this weekend and don't have anyone here that I trust with Ricky. Can I leave him with you?"

Wendy's heart pounded, and she rubbed her head, pushing her hair out of her eyes. "Yeah, I'd love to see him, you know that. When can I expect you?"

"Fifteen minutes?"

Wendy's eyes widened. "Did you just assume I'd say yes?"

Patty paused, then said curtly, "Maybe."

Wendy laughed softly and just shook her head. "Luckily for you, I'd never turn him away. We're swamped tonight, but I'm here."

"Great, I'll see you in a few." The line went dead. Wendy scrambled to finish checking in the couples before Patty arrived. She got their room keys and delivered them to their tables, took their card to have it on file, and went back and forth.

When the door opened, Ricky babbled loudly. Bright blue eyes lit up when Patty walked in, Ricky on her hip. He clapped and started saying loudly, "Da da da da."

Wendy beamed and rounded the desk to hold out her arms, ignoring the pain in her chest. "That's right. This is where Dada is, except he's not here right now, buttons."

She kissed him and held him tight. He laid his head on her shoulder, then grabbed her hair in her ponytail.

She winced and untangled him. Despite the pain, having him in her arms soothed a lonely piece of her heart.

Patty dropped off three bags by the front door and frowned. "Why did you call him buttons?"

Wendy smiled and kissed him, making him giggle and squirm. "Because he's as cute as a button."

She wondered if her own kid would have his bright blue eyes. Perhaps she'd look at her own son like this someday.

"Cool, I'll be right back with his car seat. I think the older he gets, the more stuff he has." Just as quickly as she arrived, she left. Then Wendy was left holding a squirming ten-month-old.

Melissa came down the stairs, her black boots tromping loud enough to be heard over the sound of those in the dining room. "Wendy, room three has a leak under the sink."

Wendy sighed and waved to the front desk. "I need you to man the desk for a while. I need to get this little guy settled somewhere. I'll call for the plumber while I'm at it."

She picked up her cell and glanced at the clock. Ricky was getting restless in her arms and trying to squirm away, but she called Landry to ask if he could come fix the leaky sink. Ricky babbled in her ear and tried to take the phone.

"No, Ricky, stop. Here, show me how big you've gotten. Can you crawl yet?"

She set him down in the parlor only for him to immediately go to his knees and start crawling away.

"Did you say Ricky?" Landry asked.

She sighed and rubbed her lower back. "Yeah, Patty dropped him off for the weekend."

The line was silent, then Landry asked, "Does Jake know?"

Wendy felt a sharp pain through her chest, and she moved from rubbing her back to her heart. "Since we're still not speaking, I doubt it. Um, can you swing by the store and grab some of those baby proof electrical covers? He's so fast now!"

Landry laughed. "Yeah, do you need anything else? Pack and play?"

She rubbed her forehead now and followed Ricky as he crawled down the hall. "I didn't even think of that. Yes, that would be great. Thanks."

She really needed to get one for the B&B. They'd eventually have guests who'd need it.

The house was a flurry of activity, and all the rooms were booked. Landry not only fixed the sink but also set up the pack and play in her room and moved Ricky's bags upstairs too.

Not long after that, Parker showed up. When she asked, he'd just grinned and said, "Lan called and said you needed a hand. It's good to see the Spring Breakers out in force, right?"

She chuckled and settled Ricky into a highchair in the kitchen. "Hopefully this is the last week of them."

Parker nodded and grabbed two plates that were ready to go out to the restaurant. "Yeah, but there will be some families showing up for Easter, I hope."

Wendy grinned as she crushed a biscuit for Ricky to feed himself with on the tray. "My dad's going to come down, too."

Parker nodded and took the orders out. It was her turn to take over the kitchen, as Rosita was already gone. Zarrel and Rosita each worked two nights, but only until seven.

In between flipping steaks and stirring vegetables, she fed Ricky half a biscuit with gravy while he mostly played with the food on the tray.

Just before eight, he started to get fussy, and the fog on her brain seemed to lift. Of course. How could she forget? She bit her lip, trying to figure out how to get him to sleep upstairs while still manning the kitchen down here.

Her cell buzzed in her pocket, and she answered without looking at it.

"Wendy? This is Suzie. What's this I hear about Ricky being at the Old Mill?"

She breathed a sigh of relief. "Oh, Suzie, thank God. Are you busy? I think I need some help."

"Yes, of course, dear. Give me ten minutes, and I'll be right there."

It was eight when she strode through the kitchen door in her poodle skirt and Elvis shirt. Ricky was cleaned up as best she could while still in the highchair, but at least he was happy to be banging wooden spoons and throwing them as far as he could.

Another one went flying and almost hit Suzie. Her eyes went wide as she took in the mess in the kitchen. "Oh goodness. What do you need me to do, dear?"

Wendy nodded to Ricky. "Can you give him a bath and put him to bed? My room is the last one at the end of the hall. The kitchen doesn't close until ten now, and we still have orders coming in."

Parker came in and dropped dishes in the sink. He flashed his grin at Suzie and said, "Well, Mrs. Smith, what a pleasant surprise. I see you're taking little Ricky? Wonderful. I was about to throw him into the sink with the dishes."

Suzie and Parker laughed, and Wendy felt her shoulders relax for the first time all day. She turned back to the stove while they chatted, then Suzie was bouncing a dirty boy on her hip and singing to him.

When the kitchen was finally closed and spotless, it was eleven-fifteen. Parker had locked up all the doors when he'd left, and she'd double checked that everything was clean and ready for tomorrow. She trudged wearily up the stairs to her room.

Suzie was asleep on top of her bed. Ricky was on his stomach with his pacifier, sound asleep in the pack and play.

She took a quick shower and fell into bed, not even caring that Suzie was right there with her. She was too exhausted.

The birds woke her up the next morning, but it was her damn stomach again that forced her out of bed at six-thirty on the dot. She raced for the bathroom and made it just in time. It felt as though everything she'd eaten yesterday came right back up.

A wet rag settled on the back of her neck as she dry-heaved one more time. Tears fell from her eyes and into the toilet as she sank to the floor, pulling the rag to her face. She curled into a ball but heard the toilet flush, then a soft hand pushed her hair out of her face from where it'd dislodged during sleep.

"There, there. You're okay now. Was it something you ate?" Suzie asked softly.

Wendy finally looked up at her and shook her head. She sat up and breathed the cool air of the rag, needing to feel clean again.

"No, it isn't something I ate."

The silence lasted, and Wendy couldn't stand it. She pulled the rag down and looked at this woman whose eyes were too much like Jake's.

"Well, aren't you going to say something?" Wendy demanded.

Suzie folded her hands on her lap where she knelt on the floor and said primly, "What do you want me to say? Do you want me to jump to conclusions or let you get it all out?"

Wendy took a shuddering breath and exhaled. "Fine. I'm pregnant, okay? Is that what you wanted to hear?"

Suzie's eyes flashed, and she leaned forward, "And?"

Wendy groaned and stood up, waving her hands. "And it's Jake's. *Now* are you happy?"

Suzie got to her feet, and Wendy sighed as she grabbed her elbow and helped her stand. She wasn't frustrated with Suzie. She was just tired and dizzy and mentally fuzzy.

Suzie finally faced her, almost eye to eye. "Yes, I *am* happy, actually. But more importantly, are you?"

Wendy shrugged and turned to brush her teeth. "Does it matter? Jake's still gone, and after what happened with Patty, do you really think he's going to even believe this one is his?"

"Have you given him reason to think it might not be? I mean, I saw you were pretty comfortable with Parker last night."

Wendy spun so fast her legs wobbled, and she reached for the wall to steady herself. "I haven't so much as *hugged* another guy. Not since that stupid bonfire where everything blew up in our faces."

They both heard Ricky start to fuss, and Wendy felt more tears sting her eyes.

Suzie asked, "What are you going to do?"

She brushed her teeth furiously, as if she could punish herself for being so foolish as to get pregnant.

She spat in the sink and replied, "First, get through the pregnancy until he comes home."

"And when he's here at the end of May? What then?"

Wendy shook her head, hands on the counter as she breathed deeply. Tears threatened again. "I don't know. I—I was engaged in Colorado. Left at the altar the week I came here and met Jake. He—he said the night he left that I might not have been the virgin I claimed. He—he said not to try to pass a baby off as his…"

Wendy shook her head, pain exploding behind her temples and making her nauseous again.

Suzie crossed her arms. "If my son is dumb enough to

believe his own fears over the truth, then that's on him, but you can't keep this baby from him. He's already hurting enough over losing time with Ricky."

Wendy took another drink of water and spit into the sink, keeping her head lowered as she wiped her mouth.

"I know," she said softly. "And I won't. I just can't tell him while he's gone. I'll probably tell him when he's home, safe and sound, but I have enough to worry about with the B&B, and my dad coming to visit soon, and now Ricky's here, and I don't know what to make of that, and—and will you please not tell him? Or anyone else? Please, Suzie. I know you like to gossip, but please don't tell a soul until I talk to Jake."

She pleaded with her, and finally Suzie sighed and nodded.

Then she waved a finger. "But if you think I'm not going to go all dragoness on your ass and make sure that grandbaby is safe and taken care of, you've got another thing coming. That means watching out for you, missy. Don't think I didn't notice you're off-balance. I'm going to be over here every day, and you're going to either love me or hate me by the time he gets home."

Wendy felt her eyes water, and she almost stumbled into Suzie's arms. The motherly embrace grounded her, and the tears fell freely then.

She whispered, "I already love you, silly. My mom is gone, and you don't know how much I've needed someone like you in my life. Thank you."

Suzie squeezed tighter, hugging her and patting her back with a chuckle. "Well, we'll see if you're still saying that in two months when he gets back. Have you been to the doctor yet?"

Wendy nodded and told her about the visit last week. Then they went downstairs to make the breakfast buffet and take care of Ricky together.

Chapter Forty-Seven

Jake walked through the shop and monitored the mechanics on the floor. A convoy had just come into base, and he had to make sure their Humvees and vehicles were safe and in top working order.

Sometimes that meant replacing doors pock-marked with bullet holes. Sometimes they could recover lost vehicles en-route, but the damage was often too much to fix. Still, they had to try.

It was part of the job. He had thrown himself into the job these past few months. It was now April, and he only had just over a month left in theater.

The advanced team from the unit replacing them had arrived, and he worked long hours to catch them up to speed on their inventory, vehicles, and issues.

His watch chirped at him, and he handed the wrench over. It was time to call home. He went to his room, just one storage container in a long row of "houses" that had a makeshift wall thrown up to separate it from the officer on the other side.

The Mechanic Gets His Girl

There were perks of being an officer, he supposed. A room to himself was one, along with no longer needing to go recover the vehicles himself. It was safer this way, even if more monotonous.

He opened his laptop and pulled up the video call for his mom. It rang and rang. He hung up and then checked his emails.

Jake,
Your girl's car broke down again this weekend. I already ordered the replacement fuse, but thought you'd want to know. Also figured you'd like to know that when I picked her up in the tow truck, your little boy was with her...

The rest of Juan's email detailed little things and bigger jobs they'd worked on. He was much better with technology than old Lester and was slowly working his way into more responsibility with the shop.

Jake sat back and ran a hand over his short-cropped hair. Ricky was with Wendy. Why? There were so many questions, so he tried calling his parents again. Still no answer.

He began to pace in the cramped space.

Wendy's car was going to continue to break down unless she got the new battery. Guilt clawed at him about how he'd left her in tears.

It was a daily emptiness and disappointment. Not in her, but in himself. He'd acted like a fool, pushing her away and grasping at straws for any reason to break it off with her.

The reality was much harder to face. He thought about her every day, ached for her smile, wanted to see her happy. He even missed her talking so much. The silence in his room at night pressed in on him, making it harder and harder to sleep.

He'd even bought a new pillow from the PX so he could spoon with it. It had taken weeks for a rose perfume to arrive in the mail, but he sprayed it on the pillow hoping to feel more at home.

He couldn't let her go. Two weeks of her wasn't enough. He wanted more but didn't know how to apologize. With this new information, maybe…

As he emailed Juan back with details for the shop, his video app began to ring. He answered it and smiled. His mom's face was too close to the laptop again.

"Suzie, sit back. You're too close, and I can't see him," his dad muttered, tugging her back.

"Hey Mom. Hey Dad. Good to see you," Jake said, feeling some of the tension in his shoulders relax. They looked good.

His mom's eyes were bright as she sat back in the chair at the kitchen table. She waved and smiled. "Good to see you too. How was your weekend? Are you staying safe?"

He nodded. "Always. Sometimes being an officer is boring. I just stayed at the shop all weekend."

His dad said, "Better boring than being in danger. They still think you'll come home in May?"

Jake shrugged. "Could be anywhere from the last week of May or the first two weeks of June. Haven't heard for sure yet."

Suzie said, "Well, you tell me this time when they do. No more surprising me, okay? I have to make plans."

Jake groaned, "What plans, Mom? You're not going to set me up on those dates you had lined up over Valentine's?"

Suzie waved her hand. "Not at all. Those ladies are long

The Mechanic Gets His Girl

gone. No one's going to wait around for you to get home, Jake. Haven't you realized that yet?"

Her words sank into his soul and made him stutter a breath. The pressure on his chest weighed on him. Did she mean Wendy? Was Wendy dating someone else? It felt like a spear was stabbing him in the side. It would serve him right if she *was* dating someone.

He peered at her closely, trying to read her expression. Her arms were crossed, and her lips pinched. Questions bubbled on his tongue.

"Mom, why are you so peeved? What's going on? Is it Wendy? Is she dating someone else? Why did she have Ricky this weekend?"

Suzie waved a finger at the camera. "Don't you take that tone with me, Michael Jacob Smith."

Bewildered, his eyebrows rose. She never full-named him. "What tone? I'm just trying to figure out what's going on."

Suzie lifted her nose and sniffed. "Fine, Patty had a work conference, so she dropped Ricky off while she was gone. She's due back tomorrow, so he's still over there."

Suzie's eyes brightened as she leaned forward. "In fact, I could probably take this iPad over to the Old Mill and let you talk to him, if you'd like. He's getting so big already. He's pulling himself up, did you know that? Should be walking around his first birthday, which is one of the parties I have to plan. You do want me to schedule it so you can attend, right?"

Jake's throat threatened to close up, and he opened and closed his mouth like a fish. "His birthday is the 24th. Will Patty let me have him for a party?"

Suzie waved her hand again. "Of course. Wendy's already talked to her about it."

"Really?" His throat grew tight with emotion.

"Well, she texted when I mentioned it this weekend. If she hadn't texted it immediately, she would've forgotten, poor thing."

"Wendy?" Jake's heart thumped too hard in his chest. Finally, she was getting to what he really wanted to know.

Suzie nodded, "Yeah, she's got some medical things going on. It's affecting her memory. I've been going over there every day for the past few days to help."

His dad interjected, "Your mom's practically living at the Old Mill at this point. She sleeps there and everything."

Suzie ignored him and held up a hand to tick off a finger. "Friday morning, she forgot the eggs in the waffle mix and then forgot to spray the pan. I don't think the waffle maker is salvageable, but she's determined to scrub her fingers raw trying."

She ticked off another finger. "Saturday, she forgot to take her medication and kept trailing off in the middle of her sentences because she'd forgotten what she was talking about. We went to the store together, and the number of post-it notes with grocery lists was mind-boggling. I ended up getting her a little daily pill dispenser. She certainly didn't want it, but it will hopefully help her remember to take what she needs."

She ticked off another finger. "Sunday, we went to church, but were really late because she couldn't find her keys. We ended up taking my car, but when we went back to the Old Mill for lunch, I found her keys in the refrigerator."

Another finger. "Today, the fire alarm went off early in the morning because she had somehow put a plastic lid in the oven after doing the dishes. Then forgot it was there and turned on the oven to make some muffins. That was a disaster, but we got it cleaned up. Although the smell of burning plastic did make her sick."

His mom frowned, then shook her head, looking at her watch. "It's about that time, though. I need to head back over."

"Why? Why are you going every day? I don't understand—"

Suzie gave a long-suffering sigh and twisted her hands. Then she sat on them and frowned at him. "My grandson is over there. Where else would I be? Now, do you want me to call you when I get there so you can see him or not?"

Jake reeled and nodded. Mom kissed Dad on the cheek, then he heard the door slam in the background.

Mike rolled his eyes and crossed his arms. "She forgot to take the iPad. And she thinks Wendy's memory is bad?" Dad chuckled.

Jake was worried. It didn't sound like normal Wendy behavior. And what kind of medication did she take? Guilt ate at him for not knowing.

Sure, she'd always made a point of being prepared to stay at his house with an overnight bag. The first night she'd had to go back to Maryanne's to take medication, he'd assumed it was just birth control pills or something.

"Does Wendy take medication for her memory?" Jake asked.

Mike shrugged. "How am I supposed to know? You're the one who dated her. Shouldn't you know that?"

Jake rubbed a hand over the back of his neck and groaned. "Yeah, but I was a shitty boyfriend."

Mike's brow rose. "I'm not the one who said it, but if the shoe fits."

Jake sighed and leaned forward. "Have you ever screwed up with Mom?"

Mike burst out laughing. "Where were you your entire childhood?"

Jake chuckled and shook his head. "I mean, how did you make up with her? Did you say anything in particular? The movies say to bring flowers to apologize, but does that actually work?"

Mike's face softened. "I can't tell you how to fix things with Wendy, son. You know her better than I do. With your mom, it was always something different. I once bought her a bunch of flower bushes. You know how she likes to garden. I think that's the key, though. I know what your mom likes, what she needs, what she'll appreciate the most. Do you know Wendy enough to do the same?"

The door slammed again, and his mom came back into view. "I forgot the iPad. Had to turn around at the end of the drive. I'll call you back when I get there."

Jake nodded and told his dad bye.

Chapter Forty-Eight

Jake paced his room while he waited for his mom to drive to the Old Mill. He wasn't sure he knew Wendy enough after all. How well could he know her after just two weeks?

He knew thinking of her made him ache to hold her. His fingers itched, wanting to bury into her hair and smell her essence. He picked up his new pillow and breathed deeply, trying to calm his nervousness.

It wasn't an exact match for her scent, but it did help. He could picture holding her while she cried after Ricky was picked up that second weekend. He could picture her laughing while cooking in his kitchen. He could picture her asleep on his chest, mouth open as she snored slightly through the movie.

His knees felt weak, and he sat on the edge of the twin bed. He was drawn to her more than anyone who'd come before. It was time to stop pretending otherwise.

He needed to touch her, see her, and make sure she was happy and cared for. That she was so forgetful made him worried. He wanted to wrap her in a blanket and love her until they grew old together.

His vision blurred as his heart exploded. He loved her. She was gentle and loved everyone, but he loved *her*.

He'd known it when he left, but here he was, months later, and his feelings hadn't changed at all.

She was vivacious, open, and willing to laugh at herself. She was optimistic even in the face of her life falling apart. He'd seen that the night they'd met. Then he'd seen how she put everyone's needs above her own.

She was incredibly capable, calm, cool, and collected, even when change was scary. New job, new boyfriend, new town. Yet through it all, she'd smiled, laughed, and jumped to help take care of everyone. His son, her friends, her interactions about town and at church.

Hell, even at the grocery store she helped the workers while she struck up random conversation, asking about their families.

She was a busybody who knew everyone in town already, plus all their business. It almost reminded him of his mom. But with Wendy, he knew it was because the more she knew about others, the more she'd be able to step in and help them.

This woman with the biggest heart of anyone he'd ever met had let him into her life. He'd loved her with his mouth, his body, falling more and more under her spell. Suddenly, the pain of the past few months without her all made sense.

He missed her. She was more than a true beauty with a caring heart. She was the one who made him want to wake up in the morning. She was the first thing he thought of when he opened his eyes and the last thing he thought of before he fell asleep.

He'd thought she was cut from the same cloth as Patty,

but she wasn't. She was genuine, and he never should've hurt her.

His laptop rang, and his heart raced. Maybe it wasn't too late to fix it. Maybe he'd get to see her smiling face. He sank into his chair and answered the call, his breath coming fast.

Suzie had sat the iPad on the island in the Old Mill's kitchen. She turned it so he could see Ricky in the highchair, banging on the tray littered with soft vegetables.

But he could also see Wendy in profile. She was talking while stirring something on the stove, steam rising as she leaned over to smell the aroma.

He kept quiet and just listened. His chest squeezed, and in response he squeezed the pillow still in his arms.

"So, then I told Juan to just order another fuse. I don't have the time or resources to deal with a new battery, you know?"

Suzie interjected. "I could have Mike look at it if you'd like, or we could pay for the battery. If you're going to haul around my grandson, I want you to be safe, you know."

Wendy spun and shook her head. "Oh no, absolutely not. You're not going to get me a new battery, Suzie. That's just silly. I'll keep saving up and get a new one by Christmas though, okay? I promise to be safe when the baby comes—"

"Oh, there you are, son," Mom cut Wendy off midsentence, and Wendy frowned, then noticed the iPad.

He waved as her eyes widened. She blushed, but looked pale as the spoon in her hand began to shake.

"Hey, Peaches," he said softly.

Tears pricked her eyes. He couldn't see them, but he saw her blink furiously as her mouth opened and closed quickly. Then she spun back to the dinner on the stove.

"Hey, Jake, I didn't know you were there. Um, Ricky's here. Did you see? Patty had a work conference."

"I can see. Mom told me earlier. I hope you don't mind, but I haven't gotten to see him in a while." Jake shifted on the seat and leaned forward, trying to soak up every inch of the scene unfolding on his laptop screen.

Ricky's head turned to the iPad at the sound of his voice. Then he began banging the tray with a spoon and saying, "Da da da da."

Jake chuckled, his eyes misting. "Hey, buddy. Long time, no see. How are ya doing? Are you being good for Gamma?"

"Ga ga ga ga ga," Ricky babbled.

Off-screen, his mom said, "That's right. Gamma's here. Are you ready to go up for a bath?"

Jake smiled, as Ricky took the veggies and squeezed them in a tiny hand, then ran his hand through his hair.

"No, no no no no," he said.

Wendy's laugh sent a jolt through his body. His breath caught in his throat as he soaked it up, and his eyes burned. Ricky laughed, and Jake made faces at him through the camera. His son squealed and clapped, then threw his spoon and food. Mom quickly picked Ricky up and put the highchair tray into the sink.

"Wendy, darling, you have the timer on? I don't want you to burn anything while I'm upstairs," Wendy said.

Wendy turned the stove off and removed the pan. "Yep, but it's already done. I'll eat right quick, then come up and take over so you can eat."

"Oh, I already ate with Mike, dear, but thank you. Take your time and bring the iPad up with you when you come. Jake? I'll expect you to sing the good night song to Ricky before you hang up, okay?"

Jake grinned. "Yes, ma'am."

Then she was walking through the swinging kitchen door, leaving him and Wendy alone. An uneasy silence settled as he watched Wendy move the food onto a plate for herself. She avoided his eyes and chewed.

He cleared his throat and leaned to the edge of his seat. "Um, Wendy? About what I said the day I left... I'm sorry."

She paused, her mouth full of food. Then she swallowed and took a drink. She waved her fork, still not looking at him in the camera. "It's fine."

Her tone was curt but resigned. She stabbed her fork onto the plate hard, and he winced.

"No, it's not fine. I shouldn't have said what I did. I can't exactly remember what I—"

Her green eyes flashed at him, and she pointed the fork. "You made me feel like a tramp."

He shook his head. "You're not. I know you're not. I was projecting Patty—"

"That's not an excuse to be mean, Jake, or to call me a liar."

"I called you a liar?"

She glared at him. "You said I wasn't a virgin, that I probably slept with my ex-fiancée and was trying to pass off a baby as yours like Patty had done. Well, guess what, Jake? Patty didn't lie and neither did I."

She blinked furiously, then looked down at her plate and took another bite. His chest squeezed at the look of pain on her face. He'd caused her so much heartache, and he couldn't even hold her or make it up to her. Not while he was here, anyway.

"I know you didn't, Peaches. You're not a liar."

"That's right, I'm not," she said curtly, her fork screeching on the plate and making them both wince. "I might not have wanted to talk about him or my mom, but that didn't make me a liar. I was open and honest with you, Jake, and you broke my heart, and I—"

She choked but not on the food. She wiped a finger to the corner of her eye as she turned with her plate and walked off-screen. He heard it clatter in the sink, then she was heating a bottle in the microwave before walking with the iPad.

The movement was jarring, but he had to salvage this. He couldn't lose her, not when he finally realized how much she meant to him.

"Wendy, I swear never to hurt you again. Just please forgive me. Talk to me, Peaches."

She sighed and pulled the tablet up so he could see her face. She was walking up the stairs and looked tired and defeated. Yet, even with the bags under her eyes, she was so beautiful it took his breath away.

"I forgive you, Jake, but that doesn't mean we're going to start back up where we were before. I just—I can't take the risk. Not anymore."

She walked through her bedroom door, and he heard his mom reading *Peter Pan* to Ricky. Her cryptic words forgotten, Mom closed the book and smiled as she handed Ricky to Wendy.

Wendy sank onto a rocking chair in the corner. It hadn't been there before. The pack and play in the corner was new too. Mom walked off-screen and the iPad moved to the side-table by the bed.

He watched as Wendy began to rock with Ricky, feeding him the bottle.

Mom said softly, "Jake, remember the song we'd sing to Mandy? That's the one I've been singing to Ricky. He needs to hear your voice."

Jake cleared his throat and sang the go to sleep song. Wendy's face softened as she started to hum along. Something in his chest shifted, and his voice deepened, choking with emotion.

She was everything he'd ever wanted, and he'd thrown it away. But this... this is what he wanted to come home to. Wendy and his son, happy, content, and the center of his whole universe.

He sang softly, whispering as he saw Ricky fall asleep in her arms. He wanted to be there with them like this. He wanted to be a family.

Wendy tipped her head back, rocking gently as she waited for the little hand twitching and the bottle sucking to stop. The song turned to a soft hum, and Wendy's rocking slowed to a stop. Soon, he saw his mom come back onto the screen as she picked Ricky up gently and laid him down in the pack and play.

Wendy didn't even move. Suzie covered her with a soft throw blanket, then turned and picked up the iPad, walking out of the room and closing the door softly behind her. She walked down the hall to the next room and held the iPad up as she sat on the empty bed.

Suzie frowned as she peered at him. "She needs you, Jake."

He took a deep, shuddering breath as he nodded. "I need her too, Mom," he finally admitted. It felt like something came loose in his chest. It was freeing, like a final puzzle piece sliding into place.

Suzie nodded. "Good, because it should be you here taking care of her and helping with Ricky. You need to make this right, son. Whatever it takes, you hear?"

He nodded, "Yes, ma'am."

Soon, they hung up. And though he laid down, still

holding onto the pillow, his mind whirled with thoughts and plans on how to fix things with Wendy.

Chapter Forty-Nine

A few days later, Suzie dropped her off at the auto shop and left. Even though Patty had picked up Ricky on Tuesday and Suzie wasn't staying at the Old Mill anymore, she still came by every morning to check on her.

It made her feel... wanted. Loved. Like a daughter again.

The teenager smiled when she walked into the repair shop's office to pick up her keys. He slid over the receipt for her to sign as she pulled out her debit card. But the numbers didn't make sense on the paper.

"This isn't right. It says zero balance due."

The teenager nodded and continued typing on the computer. "That's right, ma'am. You can just sign and head on through to get your keys."

"But what does it mean?" She waved the receipt in the teenager's face at the auto shop.

He frowned and shook his head. "I don't—"

"Why does the receipt show a new battery too? Who

paid for it?" She waved the paper again, but one of the workers stepped into the front office space. She glanced over, recognizing Juan and Mel as they came in.

Mel nodded, tipping a hat that wasn't there. "Ma'am, what seems to be the problem?"

She huffed and held out the receipt. "Who paid for the new battery?"

Her cheeks were flushed. Even though it was just barely April, she was hot and uncomfortable. Morning sickness was kicking her butt. She was tired, cranky, and now someone had paid her bill. She needed to pay them back, thank them, and settle the score. She wasn't a charity case.

Juan smiled and held out her keys. "Boss' orders, ma'am. Take it up with him."

Her breath hitched in her throat, and her fingers tingled. Then she took her keys and grumbled, "Oh, I will. Thanks for getting it done so quickly though. I appreciate it."

Mel held the door open for her. "Anytime, ma'am. Let us know if you need anything else."

She walked to her car, pulling out her phone as she went. It rang as she dialed Suzie.

"Hello?"

"Suzie? Did you put Jake up to buying me a new battery for the car?"

There was a pause on the line as she started the car, but she didn't back up. Not yet. She needed to sort this out.

"Of course not, dear. That was sweet of him, though, wasn't it?"

Wendy practically growled. "Yeah, sweet. Has he said anything to you? About anything? Did you tell him about the baby?"

Uneasiness raced along her spine.

"No, I told you I wouldn't. I won't go back on my word. You're still going to tell him when he comes home though, right?"

Wendy leaned her head on the steering wheel and groaned. "Probably. I'll see you at yoga tonight?"

"Yep, I'll see you there."

They hung up, so Wendy put the car into gear and drove to the bakery. She parked and went through the back door. Zarrel was busy making some delicious smelling pastry, and Wendy smiled.

"Hey, whatcha making?" she asked as she came closer.

"Apple turnovers. Want to help?" he asked, chopping apples.

She washed her hands, and Maryanne came out from the front.

"Oh, hey. I thought I heard voices. What are you doing here?"

Wendy shrugged. "Got my car back, and no one's checking in today at the B&B. Thought I'd hang out and maybe take my bestie to a late lunch."

Maryanne's face brightened. "Oh, that sounds great! I can leave in maybe an hour?"

Zarrel nodded. "Yeah, let me get these in and out of the oven, then I can man the front."

Wendy threw on an apron and started helping as they talked about the menu at the Old Mill, Zarrel's dreams, and her own visions for the place. Within an hour, Wendy was back in her car, Maryanne in the passenger seat next to her.

"Where are we going?" Maryanne asked as she turned off Main Street to head out of town.

"Sonic? I've been craving a juicy cheeseburger all day,"

Wendy said. Maryanne didn't care, so they were soon parking.

Wendy's mouth watered as she ordered a vanilla float, cheese sticks, and a double patty burger with extra mustard.

Maryanne laughed. "Have you not eaten all day? That's a lot of food."

Wendy flushed and paid for both their orders. "Couldn't really eat this morning, so kinda."

She rolled up the window to keep the cool air inside.

"You kinda didn't eat?"

Wendy shifted on the seat and kept her face staring straight ahead. Then she shrugged and leaned her head back on the seat. "Just slept in is all. Didn't wake until almost eleven."

Maryanne hummed. "Seems like you've been sleeping a lot."

Heat spread along her cheeks, and she turned the air up more, trying to ignore her friend.

Maryanne's hand settled on her arm, and she finally turned to meet Maryanne's concerned gaze. "What's wrong, hun? You're acting all fidgety."

Wendy couldn't keep it in any longer. She had to confide in someone other than his mom.

"I'm pregnant," she blurted.

Maryanne's eyes widened as she gasped. "Oh my god. Congratulations! I'm so excited for you. Does Jake know?"

Slowly, Wendy shook her head and bit her lip.

"When are you going to tell him?"

Wendy shrugged and sank into her seat. "I don't know. Probably after he gets back."

Maryanne frowned. "Are you—how do you feel? Excited, nervous, angry? When did you find out? Are you having morning sickness? Tell me everything."

The Mechanic Gets His Girl

Wendy leaned her head back and sighed, spilling everything to her friend. Their food came, and as she ate, she began to calm down and think clearer.

"The part that worries me is I don't know what he's going to say when he finds out."

Maryanne sipped her slushie, then asked, "What do you mean?"

Wendy chewed as she thought through her fears. "He wanted Ricky to be his. Then, once it was confirmed, well, he's been working with his lawyer to get joint custody. He can't do anything while deployed, but I know him. He'd prefer full custody."

Maryanne nodded. "He's a good man. He'll make a great dad. I don't see what has you chewing a hole in your lip."

Wendy swallowed her bite and glanced at her friend. "What if he tries to take my baby too? What if gets nasty like he did with Patty? I've talked with her a lot. Well, at least an hour every time she's dropped off and picked Ricky up. She's a nice woman and what happened between them was just—"

Maryanne snorted. "She cheated on him, Wendy. Repeatedly."

Wendy nodded, frowning. "I know, and that was terrible, but in getting to know her, I can see how all that happened. What if he gets mean? I mean, he already was the night of the bonfire breakup. He said some really hurtful things, and I don't know if he'll do it again. What if he has this nasty, mean side, and I just haven't seen it fully yet? What if—"

Maryanne chuckled softly, and it surprised her enough that she stopped talking and turned to her friend. Maryanne lifted a brow and gave her a droll look.

"How many years has your dad been in the military?"

Wendy shrugged. "All my life. Why?"

Maryanne rolled her eyes. "Military guys are built differently, Wendy. He lashed out when he was scared to leave. We used to talk about it all the time growing up. Our dads both got really cranky right before they left."

"Yeah, so?"

"So it's just part of being human. Jake's a great guy. I've known him all my life. He doesn't have a mean side, even after all these years in the Army, but he is human, and a male. That means he's going to fuck up. A lot." Maryanne laughed, and Wendy smiled as she sipped her milkshake.

"But there's really just one thing you need to ask yourself," Maryanne continued. She looked Wendy in the eye and her smile fell away.

"Do you love him? Not the puppy love you hoped it was the night of the bonfire, but real love. How do you feel about him after not talking or seeing him for two months?"

Silence descended as she thought about Maryanne's words. She had a point. Her body still ached for him.

When she was throwing up every morning, she just wished for him to be there to make her feel better. When she made something particularly delicious, she wanted to share it with him just to see the look on his face as he bit into it.

Mike wasn't even a thought after a week. But Jake… Jake had burrowed into her soul. The love was still there, a dull ache in her chest from missing him.

"But I'm still scared," she whispered.

Maryanne reached over and grabbed her hand. "That's human too, hun. Just like doubt, uncertainty, and nervousness. Hope, joy, and contentment. You can't have all the good emotions and no bad ones. That's just not how life works."

Maryanne squeezed her hand and then let go. "You need to decide if you're going to give love a real shot without the deadline of a deployment hanging over your heads. When he comes back, you have to tell him. That's a given."

Wendy winced. "But what if he says we need to get back together because of the baby? I want him to want me for me, not because I'm bearing his child."

Maryanne shrugged. "Maybe wait a while to tell him, then? Remember what they say about deployments? Don't make any major life changes the first three months he's back."

Maryanne chuckled again, and Wendy nodded with a sigh. That was common knowledge, but did that mean she didn't need to tell him right away about the baby? She could let him integrate back into civilian life first, give him a few weeks or months.

She didn't even know if he'd want her back. He'd apologized Monday and had bought her a new car battery, but would it last? Did he mean it or was it just because they'd seen each other for the first time in months?

She sighed. Either way, she owed him a thank you for the battery. Perhaps she could bridge the gap between them with an olive branch email. She pulled out her phone and typed the email.

Jake,
Thanks for the battery.
Wendy

She'd leave it at that. Payback for the two-sentence email. Ball was in his court now, and it would be up to him on whether he wanted to play or not. But if he did reply, maybe she could feel him out, see if he still liked her or had feelings for her at all.

She bit her nail as she backed out of the parking spot to take Maryanne back to the bakery. She needed a nap before yoga, the heavy meal made her sleepy.

She had a reply before she went to yoga.

Chapter Fifty

Wendy,
I didn't like worrying about you breaking down on the side of the road again. The new battery should fix the issue with your car. Now you're safe, and that's worth whatever the cost of the new battery is. Anything for you, Peaches.
Jake

Jake hit send on the email and went to work. He didn't know if Wendy had the video chatting app for him to call, but he would try to apologize more and win her back by email. It was worth a shot and might help ease the awkwardness that had developed between them.

She'd said they wouldn't start up where they'd left off. He could and would respect that, but he could also try to develop a new relationship with her. They said actions spoke louder than words, and he was determined to use both to win her back.

Jake,
I appreciate it. Are you being safe too?
Wendy

He winced at her short reply. But at least she was concerned about him too. That had to mean something, right? He replied, telling her about his job and the base. No details, but enough for her to know he was fine.

… I've been watching a lot of the movies we talked about and watched together. Houseboat. Robin Hood. *Just been watching them repeatedly because they remind me of you. I miss you.*
Jake

His heart raced when he sent that last one. It made him feel weak and vulnerable, but his gut told him that was the way to win her over. He went to order her another present, just a little trinket or two. Actions, not just words.

Jake,
Thanks for the flowers. They're beautiful. I've never seen roses quite that color before, but now that I have, they're my favorite. I called the florist and ordered another bouquet for the foyer too. Yours are by my bed. The smell of them is helping me relax at night.
Wendy

He frowned. She hadn't said she missed him too, but she was talking more, and that was good news. When his chatty peaches went quiet is when he had to worry most.

Wendy,
They're supposed to be the color of peaches. It's the color that reminds

me of warmth, home, and love. I miss running my fingers in your hair. I miss holding you at night.
I've not been sleeping well either, but I have a pillow I like to pretend is you. I have a rose scented perfume that I spray to make it smell a little like your shampoo. It's not the same, but it helps.
Jake

Slowly, it became easier and easier to open up to her. And when she replied, he breathed a sigh of relief. She was opening up to him too.

Jake,
I always buy the same shampoo, not because it's the best for my hair, but because it reminds me of my mom. It was the same one she used too. She was a homebody, always cooking or puttering around the house, gardening, fixing up this or that. When she wasn't working at the school, that is.
Your mom would've liked her. It might be why I like your mom so much. She makes me feel closer to my own mom somehow. I know she's gone, but with your family... it's not as lonely. Except at night, when I'm all by myself at the Old Mill. Then it doesn't matter how much I love your family, I'm still alone.
Wendy

Jake felt his heart race, and he grinned as he replied.

Wendy,
Two more months, and I'll be there to hold you if you'll let me. Then neither of us has to be alone ever again. I felt lost when Sarah died, like I was the only one who was missing her. It took me a while to realize my parents were hurting too. There's a different type of loneliness that comes with grief.

But when I was home on R and R and with you… it was like the sun started shining again. You smiled, and the brightness of it drove away the fog of loneliness.
I wish I had more pictures of you. I still stalk you on social media and love the pics you post, but I only have a limited window of time on the computer. I wish I had a picture of you for my wallet, so I could pull it out and look at it at work or before lunch. Maybe then I could remember there's more to life than this sand pit of loneliness.
Jake

PS. Thank you for sharing your memories of your mom with me. I know I lost my cool and picked a fight over it, but I know grief is very personal. I shouldn't have gotten mad about you not wanting to talk about it in person. I'm sorry I pried and pushed us apart. I regret it and the pain it caused you.

They continued exchanging emails and grew closer. A few days later, a care package arrived from his mom. In it were two scrapbooks. He knew Wendy had made the one of Ricky, but the second scrapbook was less colorful. A note fell out of it, and he smiled as he read it. Mom had made the second scrapbook with Wendy one night.

It was full of pictures of Wendy and Ricky. Wendy cooking. Wendy feeding him. Wendy asleep in the rocking chair.

He wiped tears off his cheeks as he flipped reverently. Somehow, his mom had known exactly what he needed before he'd needed it himself. That was the great thing about his mom. She truly was the best.

Jake,
I'm working on a scrapbook for Ricky for his first birthday. I have one of you too. When he came last week, I showed him pictures of you. He

would point and say "Da da da" over and over. It was adorable but broke my heart.
Wendy

PS. I don't mind sharing about my mom. She was wonderful. But I was trying to keep things between us casual because I thought that's what you wanted.

Jake took a deep breath and shook his hands to get the jitters out. This was it. He could tell her how he felt right now. Except... What if she didn't feel the same way? He frowned and typed his reply carefully.

Wendy,
I thought casual was what we both needed, but it was never what I wanted. I wanted all of you from the beginning. I still do.
Forever yours,
Jake

Now it was all out there. There was no use recalling the email. He'd taken the shot, and hopefully it'd be a bullseye.

Jake,
I've been looking for something that'd last for a long time. With my ex-fiancée, it was way too easy to get over him. Mike and I had made out a few times, but it was never more than that. I thought I was saving myself for our wedding night, but somewhere in the back of my mind, I knew he wasn't the one. What I had with him was so easily forgotten. I moved on so fast.
I haven't been able to move on from you. I haven't even thought about another guy. You take up every spare moment of thinking space in my brain... and every square inch of space in my heart.

Always here,
Wendy

Jake breathed a sigh of relief. Perhaps there was hope for them to patch things up after all. Now he just had to get through the next couple months.

Chapter Fifty-One

A week later, Wendy ate lunch in town and checked her email for the hundredth time. They'd exchanged a dozen emails in the past week, and it was almost back to a comfortable, if hesitant, relationship. She had to remind herself it wasn't a relationship at all. It was just talking, getting to know each other better.

She'd gotten flowers delivered, signed simply *Jakeass*. Then two days later, she'd found a package on her porch from Amazon. It was a bunch of totally random scrapbooking supplies: glue dots, washi tape, and vintage paper.

Then today, just before she'd left the Old Mill, she'd found another package. This one was a movie night gift box with multiple types of popcorn and candy.

The door dinged at the Diner, and Wendy looked up, breaking free of her reverie. She grinned as she leaped to her feet and ran between the chairs to throw her arms around her dad's neck.

"Dad! You made it!"

He laughed and picked her up, making her squeal as he gave his signature bear hug.

"I've missed you so much." She grinned as he set her down. They might not have been close while she was growing up, but the past few years they had grown closer. It was just the two of them now.

He wasn't one for a lot of words, especially mushy ones. The only time he'd ever broken down was when he'd been drunk after her mom's funeral. He'd told story after story, and Wendy had cried herself to sleep on the couch listening to him.

He tugged one of her curls and smiled. "You too, Tink."

She rolled her eyes and turned to lead him to her booth. "You hungry? This place has the best food in town. Well, aside from mine, of course."

She eased into the seat and pushed her sleeves up as she took another drink of water.

He said, "I sure do miss your cooking."

She laughed. "I can tell. You've lost weight, I think."

He scoffed. "Maybe you found it. You're looking good, kid. Like you've finally grown up. This is a nice place."

He looked around, ignoring the emotions that choked his voice. The white and black checkered floor was old but shined with wax. The red booths were bouncy from age, but comfortable. Pictures of old rock stars and actors and actresses, some signed, dotted the walls.

He smiled and nodded. "It's like a step back in time. I took your mother to a place like this a lot when we were stationed in Kentucky."

Wendy paused, then finished putting her water down. She wouldn't bring attention to it, she wouldn't—

"I didn't know that. I don't remember Kentucky."

He shrugged. "She was pregnant with you. We moved right after you were born."

"You don't talk about her very often."

His dark eyes met hers and softened. "No, I don't. I'm sorry about that."

The waitress walked up to them before she could respond. "Well, hello there. What can I get you folks?"

They placed their orders, and she walked away.

He tipped his head to the side. "You look different."

She arched her brows. "Different good or different bad?"

He waved a hand. "You know what I mean. You look happier. More settled."

She smiled and leaned back, thinking about the past few months. "I feel more settled. Living here suits me. After lunch, I want to take you to see the Bed and Breakfast and get you checked in."

His brows rose. "Checked in? I thought I was staying with you."

She grinned. "You are. I live at the Old Mill."

He smiled as the waitress delivered their food. The smells overwhelmed her, and her mouth salivated. She chowed down on the burger, barely washing it down with the water.

She finally paused when she saw her dad hadn't touched his food. He just stared at her, his eyes narrowed.

She swallowed and frowned. "What?"

He shook his head slowly. "Nothing. It's just, I didn't know you ate mustard, much less dipped your fries in it."

She shrugged. "I haven't been able to get enough of it lately. I've been eating it on sandwiches, fries, and mashed potatoes. Even had some on the roast I made last week."

He shifted on the seat and leaned forward, snapping his

fingers and then pointing. "That's it. That's why you look different."

"What are you talking about?" There was no way he knew the truth. He didn't pay that much attention to her. How could she look different to him when he hadn't seen her in months?

"We only kept mustard in the house for about a year, and that was when your mom was pregnant with you. She craved it and would eat it on everything."

Her cheeks heated, and she glanced down at her burger, picking it up to take another bite.

"Wendy Ann Macdonald, you better fess up now because if you're pregnant—"

She choked on her food. It burned going down, the bite too big but eventually dislodging after she drank water.

She took a deep breath and leaned forward to whisper. "Dad, can we talk about this later?"

He shook his head, his hands flat on the table. "No, we will not. We'll talk about this right now."

She glanced around, noticing a few others eating a late lunch on the opposite side of the room.

"Dad, keep it down."

"Keep it down?" He sat back with a lurch and his voice just raised as his face flushed. "Keep it down? How am I supposed to react when I find out my only daughter is pregnant? If I wasn't deploying soon, I'd be marching you right back to your place and packing up your things right this minute." His finger pointed at her and then the door.

She whispered, "Dad, now isn't the time. I'll tell you everything, but can we just eat first? I'm starving."

His eyes widened, and he shot forward to lean over the table. "Are you starving? That can't be good for the baby.

What's that little shit head Mike say about this? You need to—"

"Eat, I know, Dad. Now eat your burger before your fries get cold. You know you hate cold fries."

He begrudgingly sat back in his seat and picked up a fry. "I don't know that I can eat until I know what's going on."

She took another bite and chewed. Finally swallowing, she nodded and said softly, "Well, for starters, it's not Mike's baby."

Her dad's fry fell to his plate as his mouth opened in surprise. "You—whose is it? When—how—no, who is he?"

She smiled softly as she finished the last bite of her burger and sat back. The waitress came by to refill their drinks, and she ordered a milkshake to go. The bell above the door rang again as someone else entered.

Wendy smiled and lifted her hand in a wave. "Dad, don't say a word about it for now, okay? If you love me, just don't say anything to anyone about it."

Maryanne, her sister Cindy, and their mom Margarita all walked toward them. When they were closer, Wendy smiled.

"Dad, do you remember the Martins? Maryanne and I were best friends?"

He threw down his napkin onto his clean plate and stood. He glanced from woman to woman with a smile, then wiped his hands on his pants and shook each.

Wendy continued, "Do y'all remember my dad? He's visiting from Carson before he deploys one last time."

The ladies all said their hellos, with Margarita shaking his hand and patting her hair at the same time.

"I think the last time we saw each other was at Ft. Hood, wasn't it? That 4th of July brigade event?" her dad drawled, finally releasing Margarita's hand.

They all nodded, reminiscing on the event and the many BBQs they'd attended together. Wendy stood up as the waitress stopped by with her milkshake. They paid for their meal and left.

"You want to follow me to the B&B?" she asked.

He pulled out his keys and nodded. "I'll follow you wherever you want to go, kid."

She bit her lip as she drove, going exactly the speed limit like Dad always wanted. But she didn't take him to the B&B. Not yet.

She owed him the truth, so when she pulled up in front of the A-frame house and got out, Dad was frowning. She waited by the front porch steps for him to join her.

"Where are we?"

"You know how I said I live at the B&B? Well, when I first moved to town, I stayed a few nights at Maryanne's. But then I mostly lived here for two weeks. This is Jake's house."

She sank onto the porch swing on the front porch. They wouldn't go in, as she didn't have a key and hadn't actually come back here since he'd left. Landry and his dad must've still been taking care of the place.

He walked to the front door to try the handle. "Is he home? I have some things to say—"

She laughed and patted the seat next to her. "Nope. He's deployed, actually."

His jaw dropped. "You're shitting me."

She giggled. "Let me tell you all about it."

Half an hour later, they rocked gently on the swing. His arms were crossed. He had barely said a dozen words while she'd spilled almost everything.

She finally bit her nail and waited for him to say something. Her palms were sweating in the early April heat, but the constant Texas breeze made it bearable.

Finally, he sighed and nodded once. "Fine. I guess I'll talk to him when I come home on R and R?"

She leaned her head on his arm, then he wrapped an arm around her shoulders. Together, they swung gently on the porch swing. It was one of the most peaceful moments she'd ever had with her dad.

Tears threatened once more. "Thanks, Dad. For letting me handle this how I need to."

He kissed the top of her head, but his voice was gruff with emotion. "Anything for you, Tink."

She smiled a watery smile, not even caring about the nickname anymore. "Do you think—I mean, he said he wants to get back together when he returns."

"Do you want to?"

She shrugged. "I don't want to get hurt again, but they say true love is worth the risk. Is it?"

He froze, then squeezed her arms a little harder. His voice was rough when he finally answered.

"Yeah, it's worth it. I wouldn't have traded a moment with your mom for anything."

She listened to the grasshoppers in the field and let the peace of the moment settle her.

He cleared his throat. "There's really only one question. Do you love him, and does he love you?"

She bit her nail and thought of their emails. She definitely loved him. The pain of their fight and his absence was still as raw as it'd been when he'd left. It wasn't puppy love at all, but the real deal.

He hadn't said he loved her, but if she read between the lines of his emails, maybe... maybe he did? What did he mean when he said he wanted all of her?

She opened her mouth to ask her dad about it when her phone rang. She sat up to answer it.

"Hello, Wendy? Have another favor to ask."

Wendy's eyes widened. "Patty? Is everything okay? Ricky—"

"He's fine. Look, can I just swing by tonight and talk for a while? I have a proposal."

Wendy frowned and stood, stretching her back. "Yeah, I'll be home in a few minutes."

"Great, I'll see you then."

She hung up and turned to her dad with a smile. "So that was Patty—"

"His ex-girlfriend?" he asked as he stood and followed her down the porch steps.

Wendy nodded. "Yeah, she's coming over tonight. You'll get to meet Ricky after all and see how perfectly adorable he is. Dad, you're going to fall in love!"

He rolled his eyes, making her laugh as they got in their vehicles and drove to the Old Mill.

Chapter Fifty-Two

Jake,
So Patty's here. She's staying the night tonight, and then we're going to go talk to your lawyer in the morning. I've attached the document that she and her lawyer have drawn up. Hopefully, you get this email and will reply before we go to the lawyer in the morning.
Wendy

He opened the attachments and read. By the time he was finished, his legs felt like jelly, and he had to push air into his lungs.

Patty wanted him to have custody. Well, she wanted to move Ricky in with Wendy until he got home from the deployment. Then Ricky would be his full-time with Patty having visitation rights.

He went back to read it again. His mind shuttered to a stop. Before he could process it, he got another email.

Jake,
You and I have had our differences. I know Wendy sent you the docu-

ments, but I wanted to say a few things. I need to get them off my chest so I can move on with a clean conscience and leave the negative feelings in the past.

I'm sorry I cheated on you. It wasn't intentional. It just happened. I really thought I loved you, but I realize now I was just looking for love from everyone else because I didn't love myself.

But the love I had for you wasn't the lasting love, and I didn't really know what love was. I was still restless and had a lot of issues I never told you I was dealing with. The guys I was with… well, it wasn't healthy, what I did. I've been in counseling the past few months in Dallas, and it's helping me work through it all. I'm still working on forgiving myself and hope you can forgive me someday too.

My new job is sending me to Atlanta in a few weeks. I really love my job. I've learned a lot, grown into a better person here, but it's a big promotion that I want to take.

If I took Ricky with me, it would be really hard. That's nothing I can't handle. I handled it when we moved to Dallas, after all. I've loved him for a year and always will.

But taking him to Georgia would not be very fair to you, Wendy, or your parents. Ricky needs to stay here in Texas where he will have more than just a workaholic mom. He has a dad and grandparents who love him. That's not something I can provide for him in Atlanta.

Two weeks ago, when I had that conference, Wendy showed me some of Ricky's pictures. It really got me thinking. I keep comparing what his life would be like in Atlanta versus if he stayed with you.

So if you still want custody, I'll sign over custody tomorrow morning. My lawyer has already drawn up my portion of it. Look at the documents and let me know if this is still something you want.

If it's not, I'm perfectly happy taking him with me. I'm trying not to think of how much I'll miss him, because I would love to take him with me. But I don't want to be selfish anymore. I want to do what's best for him. And right now, that's you and Wendy.

Patty

Jake took a deep breath and rubbed the back of his neck. His heart was racing, and he was seeing spots. He glanced at the clock.

He had to go to work in twenty minutes and had only logged in to track the next little gift he'd sent Wendy. He still didn't know what to say to her, how to reply to her email. But this…

He replied to Wendy.

Wendy,
Are you up? Do you have the video chat app?
Jake

He hit send, then started pacing the room. His head was spinning, and he almost stumbled when he turned on his heel to walk back the way he came.

The video app rang, and he practically dove for it. Wendy's beautiful face came into view as the kitchen door swung shut behind her.

"Jake? What time is it there?"

He shook his head. "Almost seven. I have to go to work, but is she serious? What the hell is going on?"

Wendy's smile lit up the room as she set her laptop on the kitchen island and sank onto a stool. She was practically beaming, her cheeks pink and freckles popping. Her hair was drawn up in a big bun on her head, and he could see a pink tank top.

"Yes, it's really happening. We had a good, long talk tonight. She's been here for hours, Jake, and the documents look legit. You're finally getting custody."

Her eyes misted, and he watched her wipe them. His own teared up as his heart felt like it'd burst. He opened and closed his mouth, but no words came out.

The kitchen door opened behind her, but instead of Patty, he saw a tall stranger walk up to Wendy and put his hands on her bare shoulders.

Jake felt a punch in the gut at the sight. She had moved on. He felt like he was going to be sick as he watched her glance up and smile at the older man.

Then she turned back to the camera and said, "Jake, this is my dad, Colonel Macdonald. He's visiting for Easter before deploying one last time. It is the last time, right, Dad?"

His jealousy dissolved at her words. Her tone turned anxious, and his heart yearned to set her at ease. The man smiled down into her face and nodded.

"Yep, retirement will be completed next year when I get back. Nice to meet you, Jake. Where are you based?"

Jake told him, recognizing the authority in the man's voice. Then he said, "It's nice to meet you too, sir. I've heard a lot about you."

Her dad's brow lifted, and Jake saw the family resemblance now. "Oh, me too. Me too. I wish we could meet in person and have a nice long chat, but I'll be in theater by the time you come home. Be safe, you hear?"

Jake's spine snapped to attention, and he almost saluted. "Yes, sir. You too, sir." Her dad kissed her on the head and told her good night before he left.

The door swung closed behind him, leaving them in silence. Jake's head was reeling from information overload, and his emotions were tagging right along with it.

Wendy smiled but it was a nervous, self-conscious smile. She was hesitant as she tucked an errant hair behind her ear and glanced down.

"So, um, how are you? Are you okay if I go talk to your lawyer tomorrow?"

He took a deep breath and nodded. "Yeah, you'll need to call my parents. They have joint power of attorney over my stuff while I'm gone, so they can sign documents for me. I want to be there on video call though. Wait. Since I'm deployed, it'd be easier for my parents to take Ricky, wouldn't it?"

Wendy blushed and nodded, refusing to look at the camera. "Yeah, I asked Patty about that too, but she said it meant a lot to her that you and I are in this together, raising him as a family."

Jake frowned and leaned forward. "But we're not together. Are we?"

He kept the hope reined in tightly, but it was like a weed, blooming between the cracks in his heart. Wendy wiped a tear and looked so forlorn and lost as she nodded. It nearly broke his heart again.

He opened his mouth to ask if she wanted to get back together.

She took a shuddering breath. "No, we're not. I know we're not. Everyone in town knows we're over. But since she lives in Dallas now, no one in town has talked to her or told her that we broke up. Do you want me to tell her?"

He shook his head. "No, not if this is what it takes for her to be comfortable giving me Ricky. What time are you heading over to Goldie's office? I'll see if I can take a break at work and come back to my room to call."

She nodded, her frown smoothing into a neutral expression. "That'd be great. We're going at nine when she opens. I've already left her a voicemail, but you might want to email her too. Oh!"

Her face lit up and she leaned forward. "Did your mom tell you Ricky's cruising? He pulls himself right up and starts walking around the couch. Still holding on, of course.

He's not ready to let go yet, but it's the most adorable thing."

His heart seemed to expand as he pictured it. He wanted to be there when he took his first steps, but he didn't really have a choice in the matter. He couldn't come home for at least a month.

That was going to be a month of Ricky living with Wendy. He stared at her, her freckles showing on her shoulders, her cheeks flushed as she talked about Ricky. Finally, she slowed to a stop.

He cleared his throat and glanced at the clock. "I have to go to work, but I'll call you here at nine your time. And Wendy?"

"Yeah?" she asked.

"If he's going to stay with you, I'm going to want to call you more often. At least once a day. To see and talk to him, of course."

Her expression turned guarded as she tucked another strand of hair behind her ear. "Of course. I'll talk to you tomorrow morning," she murmured.

He nodded, wanting to end their call with a different tone. He cleared his throat, nearly whispering as he leaned in.

"And Wendy? I do want to be with you. I want you back, and I'm going to do everything in my power to convince you to forgive me. Even before this came about with Ricky. So don't tell Patty we're not together, because I'd like to be. I'd like to get back together with you if you'll have me."

She bit her lip, and he ached to tug it into his mouth. He wanted to soothe her worries and fears. Finally, she said, "I'll think about it. For now, let's just keep talking, okay?"

He nodded, swallowing the lump in his throat. He

wanted to tell her how much he loved her. How beautiful she was. How amazed he was that she was willing to do this for him, willing to raise and look after his son for at least a month all on her own.

But the line disconnected, and her shy smile disappeared. He took another deep breath, his own reflection staring back at him on the screen.

He'd spent two glorious weeks with her, so he didn't know her that well. He hadn't heard the full story about her failed engagement. He didn't know the details about her mom.

But he knew he trusted her with his son. He trusted her, loved her, and wanted to spend the rest of his life with her. They had the rest of their lives for her to tell him about her past.

What concerned him the most was their future. Perhaps the next month of constantly talking on the phone would help her see that they belonged together. Perhaps it would help convince her to forgive him for being such a Jakeass.

He went to work with a smile as he thought of his nickname. He might've been a Jakeass, but he was her Jakeass, captivated by everything that she was.

After work, he called into the video app to be present during the appointment with the lawyer. "Wendy, can I talk to Patty for a few minutes? Before all this gets started?"

Wendy nodded and handed her phone to Patty. Patty turned it so they met eye to eye for the first time in months. He took a deep breath.

"Patty, are you sure about this? I'm afraid to get my hopes up."

Patty looked tense, her jaw nearly locked in place. She nodded curtly. "Yes, I'm sure. Wendy is great with him, and your parents—I can't give him a family like this, Jake. I know you'll be good with him, for him."

Jake nodded and shifted in his chair. "I—well, I hope so. but you're his mother, Patty. It about killed me when I deployed and had to leave him. What's going to happen to you? Can you really do this?"

Patty took a shuddering breath, her eyes filling with tears. "I don't know, Jake. I just know that it's the right thing to do. If you still want him, that is?"

Jake nodded. "I do, of course I do. I swear, I'll be the best father in the world, Patty. But what kind of visitation are you going to do if you're going to Georgia?"

She rubbed her forehead. "I'm thinking at least once or twice a month. I can fly in and spend the weekend at the Old Mill?" She trailed off and glanced away.

Jake felt a knot form in his throat as he nodded. "Yeah," he said with a gravelly voice. "Of course. I think Ricky would throw a fit if you just disappeared. Once a month minimum would make him so happy."

Patty breathed a sigh of relief and nodded. "Okay, then. I'll talk with the lawyers and Wendy about visitation."

Jake nodded. "Whatever you want to do, Patty, I'm here."

She glanced away and then started to hand the phone back to Wendy. He called out, "Patty?"

She looked back at him, and he took a deep breath. "I'm sorry about how we split up. I'm sorry for leaving you like that. I—"

Her lips twisted and a brow rose. "Jake, we're two sides of the same coin, you and I. I'm sorry for cheating on you. You're sorry for leaving. Everyone's sorry. Let's just let it all go and focus on Ricky from now on, okay?"

Jake nodded. "Yeah, let's do that. And Patty? Thank

you. For sharing him with me. For having him. For everything."

She nodded, tears in her eyes as she handed the phone back to Wendy. When he saw her face, he felt the knot in his throat start to dissipate. Her bright eyes were excited and hopeful, and it made his shoulders relax.

She grinned into the camera. "Okay, Jake, are you ready for this? Your lawyer just arrived."

Jake nodded, and she flipped the camera around to face the group.

Chapter Fifty-Three

A few weeks later, Jake was in his office doing paperwork when a knock sounded on the door.

"Come in," he said, glancing up. His eyes widened, and he scrambled to his feet, coming to a full salute.

"Jake. At ease, son," Wendy's dad said with a raised brow.

Jake gaped, then finally asked, "Colonel, what are you doing here, sir?"

The Colonel sat in the chair in front of him, his eyes glancing over the desk casually. But Jake wasn't fooled. He was assessing him.

"Came to meet the man who's, well... I saw and heard how you interacted with your son and my daughter while I stayed with her over Easter week. I wanted to meet you in person."

Jake swallowed hard, twisting a pen in his hand. Then he jerked and held out a hand. "It's nice to meet you in person too, sir."

The Colonel leaned forward and shook, but his face

The Mechanic Gets His Girl

never changed from the stern assessing gaze. He asked about Jake's job, so Jake offered to give him a tour of the vehicle bay.

As they walked around, neither mentioned Wendy nor Ricky. Neither talked about Texas or brought up family. They discussed cars, vehicles, and the Army. When the tour was over, the Colonel looked at his watch and said, "Looks like lunch. Come on."

Jake looked at the shop, then called one of the others to let him know he was taking lunch. Then he jogged a few steps to catch up with the man.

"So, what's your preferred sport of choice, Jake?"

"Sir?"

"Are you a football man? Soccer? Or are you more of a musician type?"

"No sir. Football. Cowboys, of course. Hard to grow up that close to Dallas and not be a fan, right?"

The Colonel chuckled and nodded. "I suppose so. I met your parents while I was in town. Wendy took me to church. Nice folks."

Jake took a breath. "How'd they look? Did Mom seem tired? Are they—"

"They're fine, son. Your mom was over at the Old Mill almost every day I was there. She's taking good care of my Wendy darling. Makes it a little easier on me to let her stay there."

Jake snorted, but kept his mouth shut. As they approached the chow hall, the Colonel glanced at him and barked, "If you have something to say, spit it out."

It wasn't a tone to be argued with. So, Jake shrugged his shoulders and opened the door for him to proceed ahead of him.

"Nothing, sir. It's just... Wendy's going to do what she

wants, regardless of whether you want her to or not. There is no *letting her stay there*. If she wants to be there, she will be."

The Colonel paused just inside the door and eyed him. "True, she's stubborn like her mama. I tried for two days to get her to stay in Colorado, but ultimately, she flew the nest on her own."

Jake nodded and followed him to the line. "As it should be. You've raised a mighty fine woman, sir. She has the biggest heart and can take care of herself and a dozen others with one hand tied behind her back."

The Colonel chuckled, and they grabbed their food. They sat down across from each other at a long table near the corner. They were halfway through their meal when a blond man walked up to the Colonel, twisting his camo hat in his hands.

"Sir, you might not remember me, but—"

The Colonel jerked to his feet, his hands fisted at his sides. "Oh, I remember you."

Jake jumped up and stepped between them, one hand on the Colonel's chest. "Hey now, what's the problem?"

The Colonel's green eyes flashed, and his nostrils flared. "This is Mike Smith."

Jake frowned, shaking his head in confusion. That was his dad's name. "Who—"

"The jackass who left Wendy at the altar," the Colonel practically snarled.

Jake glanced behind him. His vision narrowed on the scruffy, disheveled man who turned beseeching eyes to him. Jake felt the air move like a blast of hot, desert wind, and the next thing he realized, the man was lying on the floor of the mess hall and the Colonel had his hand on Jake's uniform collar, fisting it and holding him back.

People stopped eating and stared as Jake looked down at

The Mechanic Gets His Girl

the man. His hand stung, and he looked at it in surprise. The knuckles were already red and bloody, stinging. The man on the floor whimpered as blood gushed from his nose.

A couple of MPs came running up, but the Colonel held up a hand.

"What's happened," one of them said, one hand on his holster.

The Colonel stepped around Jake and jerked the man to his feet. "Nothing's happened. Smith here stepped into the other Smith's elbow as he stood up. That's all."

One MP glanced at Mike as he stood straighter, still holding his nose. "Is that true?"

Mike glanced at the Colonel and nodded. But the other MP looked around and asked, "Anyone care to give a witness statement?"

A few hands shot up, and the MP walked to them, flipping out a notepad. Mike looked between the Colonel and Jake, but Jake felt nothing but satisfaction. He didn't even care if Mike pressed charges. It would've been worth it.

Mike whined, his voice sounding like he had a stuffy nose. "I don't understand. I wanted to apologize and—"

The Colonel held his hands behind his back and nodded. "Apology accepted. Jake here apologizes as well."

"I fucking do not," Jake said, his fists clenching in his hands. "You left her at the altar. You deserve so much more than this."

The Colonel's arm shot out, and Jake stood still, back ramrod straight. Mike's eyes narrowed on Jake. "You know Wendy?"

Jake lowered his voice and leaned in. "She's mine. You fucked up and blew it. I won't make the same mistake."

The MP's head kept swiveling back and forth, taking in

the scene. Then he asked Mike, "Sir, would you like to press charges? Clearly, something else is going on here."

Mike simply shook his head. "No, we're done here. I'll head to the infirmary now."

They both walked off, but it wasn't until the door slammed shut behind them that both eased back onto the benches at their table.

Jake glanced down at his food, not even slightly hungry, and stirred the pasta with a fork.

"Did you mean it?" the Colonel asked.

Jake looked up and took a deep breath. "What?"

He didn't even remember what he'd said in the heat of the moment. He was just trying to figure out what Wendy had seen in that guy.

"Did you mean it? When you said you weren't going to blow it with Wendy. I mean, it seems like you already *have* blown it. You broke up, yes?"

Jake's shoulders sank as he nodded. His sigh was pathetic, loud and dejected. "Yeah, I was dumb and pushed her away the night before I left. I don't even remember what I said. I just thought it'd be better this way. Clearly, I was wrong. Until Ricky stayed with her, I hadn't talked to her in almost two months."

The Colonel grunted, "If Ricky wasn't staying with her, would you still be stewing in your dumb decision and missing her?"

Jake shrugged. "Probably, but just because I couldn't figure out how to talk to her. I apologized, but it seems so— I don't know—not enough? I sent her some apology presents, and we've been emailing a lot, but I don't know if it's enough to convince her to—"

His voice trailed off as the Colonel began to chuckle. Then it turned into a full-belly laugh. Others began to stare, but Jake didn't care. The laugh reminded him of Wendy, and it made him smile.

Finally, he calmed and said, "I've done the same thing a time or two in my day. We all make dumb decisions before a deployment, but the question now is what are you going to do about it?"

Jake blinked. "What do you mean, what am I going to do about it? The past week, I've been calling her every night. Sure, it's under the guise of talking to Ricky and watching him walk. But things are getting easier now, as far as talking with her goes. It's still not as easy as it was on R and R, but we're getting there."

The Colonel raised his brows and set his napkin on his plate. "That's your plan? Talk to her?"

He shrugged. "Until I get home anyway, yeah."

"And what then?" her dad continued, crossing his arms. "What exactly are your intentions with my daughter?"

Jake sucked in a breath, his heart tripping in his chest. His palms grew sweaty, but he was frozen to his seat. What were his intentions with Wendy?

He frowned. "I don't know what will happen when I get home. I do know that I love her, sir. I want to be a family, her, me, and Ricky. I want to take care of her the way she takes care of everyone else. But whether she forgives me and lets me have a second chance at loving her? That's up to her, isn't it?"

The Colonel stood, and Jake followed. They stood nearly eye to eye, and he didn't flinch away from the piercing green eyes. Then the Colonel reached out and hugged him.

Jake gasped as he slapped his back hard and barked a laugh in surprise. When the Colonel stepped back, his green eyes twinkling, he said, "Well, in that case, call me Witty."

Then he grabbed his empty tray and headed to the return bin. He glanced behind him and said, "Let's do lunch tomorrow too. Same time, same place."

Jake's mouth opened and closed in relief. He hadn't been expecting Wendy's dad to be here, much less eat lunch with him. But it was an opportunity he wasn't going to pass up. Perhaps this was his lucky break, and he'd be able to find out all the details he hadn't learned from Wendy yet.

She'd been to his parents' house, seen his baby albums and heard so many stories. Now it was his turn.

Chapter Fifty-Four

Wendy greeted the guests in the restaurant side of the Old Mill with a grin. Her new friends were all there for Ricky's first birthday party. Patty had even flown in from Atlanta. They'd agreed that she'd spend at least one weekend a month in Texas with Ricky, and this was her first trip back.

She felt a pain of sadness spear her because Jake was missing it. But he'd be home in a few weeks, and then they'd celebrate as a family together. He'd gone on and on about how he hated parties, so she knew he was fine with her throwing the party without him. She'd seen the look of relief on his face when she'd mentioned it.

Maryanne brought out the last tray of food and set it on the side of the room. There was a buffet of chicken fingers, hamburgers, and hot dogs. Maryanne had brought cupcakes and a tiny cake just for Ricky to blow a candle and smash.

When she'd woken up this morning, a giant, wrapped box had been in the corner of the restaurant. Parker had left a note on it saying he'd brought it by early that morning, but he didn't want to wake any of them up. She'd rushed out the door for church but had left before the service was over to finish getting everything ready.

Now, almost everyone in town was here to celebrate with her, Suzie, and Mike. The paperwork had been completed that week too, awarding Jake custody. It had taken over a month to process.

Ricky began to fuss, and Patty started to get nervous. So, Wendy gently took him from her and smiled at the little old lady who'd been talking with Patty.

"Little guy saw the food and got hungry, did he?" Wendy asked, bouncing him on her hip. He seemed to melt into her arms and, as always, found a piece of her hair.

Patty smiled in relief and handed Ricky a small toy in a plot to distract him from Wendy's hair. "I can't believe how much he's grown in such a short amount of time."

"He's such an angel," the older woman said.

Wendy smiled and kissed the baby. "He is. I hope he stays this way forever. No terrible twos for you, mister," she said mockingly in a faux stern voice. The lady and Ricky both chuckled before the woman excused herself and walked away.

Wendy leaned closer to Patty. "Are you sure you're okay?"

Patty smiled, her face pinched with sadness as she nodded. "It's been hard, but we've gone over this, Wendy. I told you last night. It was the right choice to make. I stand by my decision, and my therapist is helping me work through it."

"Do you—do you think you'll want Ricky back?" Wendy felt her fingers tingle in fear. Now that he was such a daily part of her life, she couldn't imagine spending a day without him.

But Patty shook her head. "No, I think flying in once a month to see him will be fine. I need to focus on myself right now, and my career. And my therapist was right about staying away from guys for a while. It's helping me clear my head, that's for sure."

Suzie waved to Wendy. "You ready, my dear?"

Wendy nodded and stepped to the highchair they'd decorated for Ricky. She got him settled in, and Landry waved to hush everyone.

"Alright, everyone. Suzie and Mike have something to say, then Ricky's going to open this giant present. After that, we're going to bless the food, eat, have the birthday boy blow out his candles, and open the rest of his presents. Mike?"

Wendy saw Patty hanging back in the crowd, but she quickly stepped away and pulled her behind the highchair. She leaned over to whisper, "You might have signed over custody, but you're still his mom. Stay up here with us. It's where family belongs."

Patty's eyes misted, and she wrapped an arm around Wendy's waist. They stood side by side as Mike began to speak.

"It's been a long road, but I'd like to introduce y'all to my grandson, Ricky. We want to thank Patty for bringing him into our lives and putting up with Jake for as long as she did. We're all so blessed, and Ricky is one special little man to have us all here today to love on him."

The crowd clapped, then Suzie turned bright, tear-filled eyes on Wendy.

She said, "I'd also like to recognize this amazing woman. Some of y'all know Wendy, but for those who don't, she's a breath of fresh air. She swept into town like a Texas tornado and has captured our hearts. She's like a daughter to us, and after losing Sarah... well, it's nice to have another girl around."

Patty cleared her throat and tipped her head back. "I–I want to say something too." The crowd murmured, but she ignored them, turning first to Suzie then to Mike.

"I was in a dark place last year, but Jake brought me such a ray of sunshine when he gave me Ricky. I'm thankful for you all opening your arms to my son, for giving him such a loving home. But I also want to thank Wendy. Without her, I don't think I'd have had the guts to leave Ricky here where he belongs. I know he's in good hands. She's like a second mother to him. And almost equally important, she's become a good friend to me. Thank you, Wendy."

Wendy ignored the tears and wrapped her arms around Patty as the crowd cheered. The past month, she'd talked more with Jake but also with Patty. She was finally getting the help she needed and moving forward in a healthy way with her life, not spiraling out of control and ruining paint jobs on trucks.

Landry stepped forward one more time. "Uh, before we bless the food, I'd like Ricky to open his first present from the Williams' brothers. We all chipped in on this one."

He waved to the giant present, and Suzie picked up Ricky and took him to the box. Patty disappeared in the crowd, and Wendy grabbed her camera from the table where she'd set it. She started to snap pictures. Ricky was amazed by the little piece of paper he tore off the box, but then started to squeal as he realized he could rip the rest of it.

He dug in, nearly leaping out of Suzie's arms as he pulled and tugged. Suzie laughed, and Mike stepped up to help. When the top was exposed, the crowd shifted. Wendy stepped onto a chair for a better angle, just in time to pull her camera up as the top opened.

Suzie gasped, and Ricky lunged forward.

Jake stood up from the four-foot box and swept the boy into his arms. He tossed him in the air and made him squeal as the crowd cheered. She wasn't even looking through the lens of her camera, just clicking over and over.

She couldn't see through the tears. He was home. He'd made it safely home.

A weight seemed to lift from her shoulders as sobs wracked her body. He leaned forward and hugged Suzie, then Mike. Still, she clicked like a mad woman on the camera.

Landry and Parker helped with the box, and Jake stepped out. People patted him on the back, and Suzie couldn't stop touching him.

He was smiling the biggest grin she'd seen on him since before he'd left. Somehow the video calls hadn't been able to capture that smile.

His gaze found hers. Even through her tears, she saw his smile shift. Then he was walking toward her with Ricky on one hip.

He stopped in front of her, and the crowd seemed to melt away. She looked down at him from the chair, her camera lowering in a shaky hand. Someone took it from her, but she didn't pay attention.

Her entire soul was centered on one thing: Jake. His smiling blue eyes were full of warmth and love and hope.

"Wendy," he said softly, hesitantly. The flash of vulnerability made her pause, and her hands cupped her own face, cooling her heated, flushed cheeks.

"Jake," she whispered, feeling cool tears seep under her palms.

He pulled a ring out of his pocket and held it up to her. It glimmered in the light, a gorgeous emerald teardrop with diamonds around it, set into a rose gold band.

"Will you marry me?" he asked.

She looked at it, then at him, her mouth opening and closing. "I—I don't know. Why do you want to get married?"

He chuckled and shifted on a foot, propping Ricky up higher on his hip. But his eyes never broke away from hers.

"Mom was right. You've captured our hearts. I didn't think it was possible to fall in love in just two weeks, but you fascinated me from the beginning. You might have been broken down on the side of the road in the storm, but really, it was me who was broken down inside. The storm of life had beaten me down, and I was bitter, angry, and unable to see that life could be so much more."

Tears spilled down her cheeks. She licked her lips and whispered, "And now?"

He smiled as Patty took Ricky from him. Jake frowned. "Patty, I treated you like crap, and for that, I'm sorry. Yes, I was hurt, but I shouldn't have abandoned you."

A tear slid down Patty's cheek, and Ricky just patted her face. "I'm sorry too, Jake. I don't blame you for leaving, but I hope we can be civil, for Ricky's sake."

Jake nodded. "I'd like that. If all the crazy stuff that's happened in the past year has taught me anything, it's that things sometimes happen. I can only control my reaction to it, and I want to be better. For you, for Ricky, for my family. Wendy taught me that. She always has a bright smile on her face, no matter what terrible thing happens."

Jake looked up at her, his face reverent as he stared and spoke straight to her soul.

"Now I see your face, and there are no more storms. It's

The Mechanic Gets His Girl

sunshine and rainbows, not because we won't face hard times. Not gonna lie, the past four months without you sucked. But with you... the hard parts don't seem so overwhelming. You light up a room, Wendy. You light up my heart. I love you and can't imagine living another day without you by my side. Will you put me out of my misery and marry me? Will you—"

She didn't need another word. He'd said what she'd longed to hear for months. She launched herself at him, falling off the chair and into his arms. The momentum of her fall forced him to swing her around in a circle, and the crowd went wild.

But when his lips met hers, all sound vanished. Her heart thundered in her chest, and she could hardly believe it was happening. She felt safe, loved, adored, and appreciated. His mouth was tender, his embrace secure.

He set her on her feet and pressed her close, then the kiss slowly broke. He pulled back, his eyes soft. They were in their own little cocoon, locked away from the crowd.

He murmured, "I'm sorry for what I said before I left. I can't promise not to be a Jakeass ever again. But I do promise to always apologize, get better, make up for it, and try not to make as many mistakes. I know I have a lot to make up for, but if you'll let me, I'll love you until maybe one day you love me—"

She pressed a quick kiss against his lips, trying not to get lost in the heady sensation of being back in his arms.

"Jake, I already love you."

He pulled back, his eyebrows raised in surprise. "You do?"

She grinned and nodded, "Yeah, I've loved you since before you left, you Jakeass. Couldn't you tell?"

He laughed, and the sound soothed some part of her

soul, like a balm filling a crack in her heart. She'd thought it was puppy love, but it wasn't. It still burned bright within her, even after all these months of loneliness and—

She gasped and stiffened in his arms. He slid back, his hands on her upper arms and concern on his face.

"What? What is it? Are you okay? If you really don't want to—"

She shook her head swiftly and grabbed his hand, placing it on her only slightly rounded stomach. She looked up at him with wonder as another kick hit, just a flutter. Jake frowned.

"Are you that hungry? What would you like? I'll get you whatever you want to eat, you name it."

She shook her head and laughed. "No, Jake, do you feel that?"

He nodded, frowning.

She grinned. "That's our baby kicking for the first time. I think she likes your voice."

Jake's eyes rounded, then he blinked furiously. "We're—we're going to have a baby? A girl?"

She shrugged. "I don't know if it's a girl or not. I was hoping you'd go to that appointment with me in a few weeks to find out. But yes, we're definitely pregnant, and before you go off on a rant, it's definitely yours. The only guys I've hugged since you left were our dads, okay? I've shaken hands, but no more hugs, I swear. You're the only guy I've ever—"

His kiss cut her off, his mouth hungry and his hands diving into her hair to hold her head at the angle he needed. She trembled in his arms as his mouth told her without words the story of his love. His commitment. His wonder and amazement.

He broke the kiss to rain tiny kisses on her lips and face.

"My God, Wendy. You've made me the happiest man on the planet twice today. Who else knows? Landry didn't say anything when he picked me up at the airport this morning."

Wendy smiled. "Just our parents and Maryanne. I was so afraid someone would tell you and then you'd be mad at me and—"

He kissed her cheek and said softly, "I'll never be mad at you again, I swear."

She giggled and leaned back. "Don't be a Jakeass. Of course you will. We're bound to fight now and then. Just promise that we'll always make up after? That we'll talk it out?"

Jake nodded, a slow grin spreading across his face. "I like the idea of make-up sex. Maybe we can try that out?" He wiggled his brows, and she giggled again as she wrapped her arms around his waist.

"I wouldn't mind that." She tipped her head up for another kiss.

Just then, Parker walked by and said loudly, "Get a room." Laughter echoed around them, and she blushed furiously, realizing they were in the crowded dining hall surrounded by all their family and friends as they sat to eat.

She gasped, "Oh, my dad! I have to email him and tell him about the engagement and—"

Jake kissed her softly one more time, then led her to the buffet line. "Don't worry about it. I asked his permission to marry you. And I saw quite a few cameras and videos being taken, so we'll get a copy and send it to him."

She felt tears prick behind her eyes once more. "You—you asked for his permission? Oh, Jake."

The emotions threatened to choke her, but he just put his hand on the small of her back and eased her into the food line in front of him. A kiss to the side of her head, and then a nuzzle on her neck, and she was putty in his hands.

"Come on, let's get this party started. The faster we wear everyone out, the faster I can take you upstairs and wear you out."

His low voice sent vibrations of need through her, and she grinned. The party she'd been looking forward to for weeks suddenly couldn't end quick enough.

Chapter Fifty-Five

One and a half years later

Wendy fiddled with the roses and tried not to bite her lip. It'd smear her lipstick, and she didn't need that right now.

Maryanne walked over in her ice blue dress and smiled. "You ready? Everyone's lined up."

Wendy nodded and took a deep breath. They were upstairs in the new wedding and event space Parker had built near the Old Mill. It was a barndominium, with a grand set of stairs that led down to the main floor.

They'd added chairs on either side of the stairs, and this would be the first wedding held in the space. Their pictures would go on the website for the Old Mill. They were already booked months in advance now.

She walked to her dad, who stood fiddling with his tie while looking in the full-length mirror. She met his eyes, then turned and reached up to adjust it.

"There, that's better. Not that there was anything wrong

with it. I'm glad you moved down here, Dad, and that you're retired and safe and—"

He pulled her in for a hug, and she took a deep breath of that pine aftershave. It helped settle her nerves a little.

"We're making the right choice here, right?" she whispered.

He pulled back and smiled, tears in his eyes. He nodded and kissed her forehead. "You and Jake might have jumped into each other's arms, but you've slowed things down enough to know the truth. Is this the real deal? The kind of love I had for your mother?"

Wendy nodded, her eyes misting as she did so. She arched her brow. "Is this the kind of thing you're feeling for Maryanne's mom?"

Her dad's cheeks turned as peachy as her flower bouquet, and he hunched his shoulders. "Oh stop. It's too early for that kind of talk. Today is about you and Jake and finally bringing your little family together."

Wendy peered into his eyes and frowned. "And you're really okay with it? I thought you'd be kicking and screaming like with Mike."

He arched his brow and snorted. "Please. That guy wasn't worth your time. Jake's made of sterner stuff. Plus, I made him promise it would be a real wedding and not some courthouse fiasco. I've waited thirty years to give you away, Wendy. I wanted to do it right."

Wendy felt a tear fall down her cheek and her smile wobbled. "You—is that why you were so mad about me marrying Mike? Because it wasn't a full-blown wedding like this one?"

He nodded, then glanced over her shoulder and nodded again. "Besides the fact that Mike wasn't right for you, yes. I'd promised your mother I'd only give you away to

The Mechanic Gets His Girl

someone who appreciated you. Jake may not deserve you—no man does—but at least he understands how precious you are and will treat you accordingly."

He gently took her hand and set it in the crook of his arm. Together they turned to go to the top of the stairs where Maryanne waited. Cindy and Andy's kids were already walking, and she could hear oohs and awws as they threw flowers and carried the rings.

Cindy and Andy walked behind them, then Maryanne and Landry were walking down the stairs. When she stopped at the top and finally looked down at the crowd, everyone stood up and the music changed.

She spied Suzie and Mike on the front row. Suzie held a sleeping Aurora, not yet one, whom they called Ro. Across the aisle sat Patty sitting on the front row with Ricky, now two. She'd slowly started to visit less and less, but all of them were adamant about her remaining in Ricky's life. They were a mis-fit family that somehow worked. Ricky was clapping and kicking his feet, trying to climb out of Patty's arms.

But she only had eyes for Jake. He stood on the raised platform at the other end of the room. She almost tripped down the stairs, but her dad held her steady. She laughed under her breath, and he said, "Easy now. No need to race down."

She grinned and almost pulled him along behind her as she marched down the stairs and up the aisle to Jake. They were almost to the front when something caught at the corner of her vision. She turned her head to see Mike jerking forward.

Then Ricky was running down the aisle and screaming, "Mama!"

Wendy's heart almost burst. She thrust the flowers at her dad just in time to bend down and catch him. The crowd was laughing, but when she stood up to walk the last twenty feet, it was Patty who caught her eye. Patty smiled a tear-filled smile and whispered, "He has the best bonus mama."

Wendy reached out and squeezed her hand, then turned to walk the last few feet to the altar with Ricky on her hip. Jake's smiling face captured her attention.

The laughter of the crowd caused Ro to jerk awake. The startled wail got louder, and when she reached the front, Jake stepped away. He took Ro and cradled her to his chest.

Finally, they met at the front, both holding babies and grinning like fools. The crowd sat, and he leaned forward to whisper loudly, "You sure you want to sign on for this circus? It's never quiet between these two."

She grinned and leaned forward too. "I'm sure I love you and can't imagine spending the rest of my life without you. But you *are* wrong."

He frowned as they turned to face the preacher. "I am?"

She nodded, keeping her eyes glued to his face. "There's not just the two of them."

He tilted his head as he processed, then his eyes widened. "Are you—"

She nodded, her grin widening. "How do you feel about adding on to the house? We're running out of rooms."

He leaned forward and kissed her, making the preacher gasp and say into the microphone, "Um, we haven't gotten to that part. That's at the end."

The crowd laughed, but Wendy just melted into the kiss. Ricky was pulling on her fancy up-do hair, knocking it askew. Ro was still whimpering and crying, the smell confirming that she had a very stinky diaper. The pictures for the website definitely wouldn't show the perfect wedding.

But it was perfect for them because they were together, now and forever a team.

The preacher finally got the crowd to quiet, and Suzie passed the pacifier to Jake, so Ro settled down too. The preacher flipped his papers and frowned.

"This can't be right."

"Um, what's wrong, sir?" Jake asked, but Wendy narrowed her eyes at his too innocent expression and tone.

The preacher muttered, but everyone still heard it through the microphone. "Your names. What are your names, sonny?"

Jake gently swayed with Ro, but the quirk of his lip sent a thrill through her. He was up to something.

"Just read the vows, sir," Jake said gently.

The preacher frowned and nodded. "Alright then. Dearly beloved, we are gathered here today to join Peaches in holy matrimony to Jakeass."

The crowd lost it. Wendy burst into laughter, and Jake's eyes twinkled. No, it wasn't always sunshine and rainbows. It wasn't picture perfect. But together, with lots of laughter, patience, and grace, they'd make it through.

Next in the Crimson Creek Series

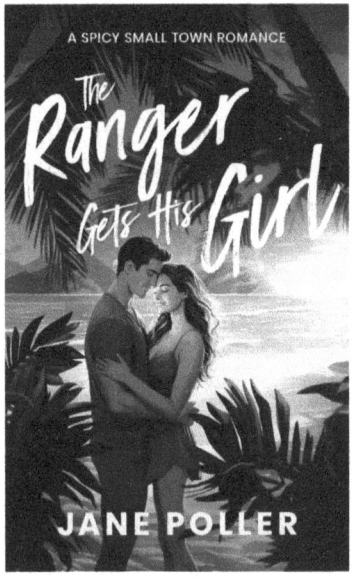

vinci-books.com/ranger-gets-his-girl

One forbidden night in paradise changes everything.

Lucy's carefree Hawaii vacation becomes scorching-hot trouble when a sizzling night with older, off-limits park ranger Mason turns into a forbidden romance. Can a fling survive reality—or will paradise burn them both?

Turn the page for a free preview…

The Ranger Gets His Girl: Chapter One

September

Lucy stopped her little beat-up sedan in a cloud of dust and grabbed her garment bag and backpack. She rushed up the steps of the white church in Crimson Creek, continuing to the left hall and ignoring the crowd in the sanctuary. A closed door had deep voices on the other side, so she strode past. Instead, she made a beeline for the last door and pushed it open.

"Lucy, thank God! I thought you weren't going to make it," Nana Helen said as she smiled and held out her hands.

Lucy grabbed them, pulling her into a hug. "I know, I'm so sorry. My professor was late, and I had to take the final today to pass the class. I got here as fast as I could."

Helen turned back to the mirror where Katie continued putting the finishing touches to her makeup. They'd met at the planning meeting Helen had arranged last month right after Ray had proposed. They had it all planned so well they hadn't even needed a dress rehearsal last night.

The Mechanic Gets His Girl

She smiled at Nana's best friends, Vonda and Margarita. They wore the same peach colored gown and glowed as they chatted about their grandkids.

Lucy hung her garment bag on the back of the door and dropped her backpack, unzipping it as Vonda said, "You've got half an hour, Lucy. Think you can make it?"

Lucy nodded. "Yeah, I did my hair early this morning, so I just need to pin the curls back."

"Does your dress need to be steamed?" Margarita asked.

Lucy shook her head as she pulled it out of the bag. "I don't think so. I think it's fine. Thank you though."

The next few minutes flew by in a flurry of activity. Lucy chatted with Katie about the town. They'd run into each other a few times over the years. Although Lucy had moved to Denton in middle school with her parents, she'd spent all her summers here.

"I can't believe you're finally done. That's so exciting," Katie said.

Helen beamed. "I'm so proud of you, sweet pea. This has been a long time coming. And your mother, bless her heart... she'd be so proud of you too."

Lucy turned and waved to the back of her dress, her throat threatening to close. Katie zipped her up but didn't say anything. Some topics didn't need words.

Lucy pulled her heels out of her backpack and slipped them on. She grabbed some pins from the small table littered with hair accessories and makeup.

"Lucy, I know this isn't the right time to ask, but now that you're graduating—"

"Assuming I pass this class and finish my dissertation," Lucy said wryly.

Helen raised her brows. "Of course you will. You're my

clever little sweet pea. You've always been an excellent student."

Katie grabbed a pin and batted Lucy's hands away. "Once you graduate, what are your plans? I know you were doing nails in Denton to help pay for tuition. Are you going to stay there or move on home?"

Lucy met Helen's gaze in the mirror. "Did you put her up to this?"

Helen lifted her hands in an overly innocent gesture. "Me? Never."

Katie grinned. "So she put a bug in my ear. No big deal. I'm just saying, we need a nail tech at the salon. Our last girl moved away this summer with her new husband. You'd be the only one in town, so the demand is there."

Lucy smiled, her cheeks heating in a blush as she worked on her hair. "I could give it a try, sure. I was hoping to move back to town this semester anyway."

"I can get you set up as early as next week with appointments," Katie said.

Lucy's brows rose. "Wow, that's so soon!" Excitement rose, making her giddy. Bouncing on her toes, she clapped her hands. "Alright, let's do it! I'll have to talk to my roommate about moving out and find a place to stay, but I'm so excited now."

Katie laughed as she cleaned up the room from the hair supplies she'd brought. "Great, I'll text you, and we can work out the details. But for now..." and jerked her chin to Helen, who was wringing her hands, staring out the window unseeingly.

Lucy took her hands so she wouldn't mess up the nail job she'd done last weekend. "You sure you want to go through with this? I can still sneak you out the back, Nana."

Helen's far away gaze cleared as she smiled. "What? No,

it's just... the last time I was in this position was so long ago. It makes me think of your grandpa, that's all."

Lucy's eyes misted. "He's looking down with Mama right now. He's probably excited to see you finally so happy again, Nana."

"You don't think it's too soon?" she asked softly.

Lucy hugged her, the familiar scent of vanilla enveloping her. "You've been dating for months, Nana. Sure, it's not that long, but you've known him your whole life, right?"

Helen nodded and turned back to the mirror with a frown, fiddling with the lacy sleeves on her v-neck dress.

"But your aunts and uncle—"

"They can shove it," Lucy said, crossing her arms.

"Lucinda!"

"What? They can. If they can't feel happy for you, they shouldn't be here, so it doesn't matter that they're not."

Helen's face fell. Lucy's mom was gone, but she had two aunts and an uncle who could've been here for their mom. Well, one aunt was deployed, but the other two could be here if they'd only made the drive.

Lucy put her chin on Nana's shoulder and stared at her in the window's reflection. "Do you need them here to marry him? Or do you love him and are ready to be with him forever?"

Helen sighed. "Of course I'm ready, but between them and your grandpa, it's just—"

Vonda interrupted. "Helen, I swear to God, if you're pussyfooting around because you're comparing Ray to Jerry, let it go. They're like night and day."

Margarita nodded and stepped closer. "She's right, Helen. Jerry would want you to be happy, wouldn't he?"

Helen nodded, her eyes bright with tears. "I just wish the kids were happy for me too."

Vonda patted Helen's forearm. "Now, now, don't mess up the makeup."

A knock on the door interrupted them, and Vonda's granddaughter, Lola, opened the door. "Ready? The guys just went into the sanctuary."

Katie left with Lola to join the guests, and Vonda and Margarita followed to line up in the foyer. Lucy watched Helen, seeing her jaw firm and chin lift.

Lucy relaxed to see that excited, determined look cross Helen's face before she turned to the door and waved. "Well, let's get this show on the road."

Lucy chuckled and followed her nana down the hall to stand in line behind Margarita. Then Vonda was walking down the aisle with Margarita a few steps behind her. Lucy took a deep breath, pasted on a smile, notched her head up, and strode down the aisle to the beat of the soft music.

As the woman glided down the aisle, Mason's heart raced, and his palms grew clammy. The sheer sight of her beauty felt like a physical blow to his chest. Her long, flowing hair cascaded down her back in perfect curls, sparkling diamonds woven throughout catching the light and emitting a radiant glow. He stared at her delicate features—the curve of her jawline, the fullness of her lips, the sparkle in her eyes. She was like a goddess floating on air, and he couldn't believe she was real. Who was this woman and why had they never met before?

Her long-sleeved peach v-neck dress was the same as the much older ladies standing across the aisle from him. But on her, it clung to every curve. Those curves trapped his mind in possibilities. No, he couldn't go there. He refused to think of her like that.

He dove into his training, trying to cut off his emotions and make a professional assessment. She was average height, probably five-seven or five-eight. She was fit and toned, an athletic type, but with curves that made him salivate.

She had an elegant, swan-like throat that sparkled with the diamonds that caressed it. She was now close enough to see freckles dotting the bridge of her nose. Maybe she liked hiking or fishing. She had a body meant to be worshiped outdoors.

No, damn it, turn it off, Mason. Get it together.

She walked past the pews, smiling at each person on her right, but when she met his eyes, she stumbled a step before catching herself.

Her expression froze like a deer in the headlights. Then she stepped beside the other two bridesmaids and the music changed to the bridal march.

Mason blinked, and it seemed like the ceremony was over. He couldn't stop staring at the Maid of Honor and lost track of time.

Professionally speaking, she should've been average in every way. Brown hair and eyes, medium height, athletic build.

But there was something about her that pulled at him. She exuded this quiet energy that seemed to brighten the room. He kept waiting for her to hop away like a bird, the way she looked at him then away like she was hoping he didn't notice.

Music pulled him to the present and Helen and his grandpa, Ray, turned to face the now cheering crowd behind them. Ray tucked Helen's hand into the crook of his arm and beamed down at her. She smiled, her cheeks flushed, as they began to walk down the aisle as husband and wife.

Mason cleared his throat and offered his elbow to the peach vision. Her cheeks flushed too as she briefly met his eyes then looked away.

Hesitantly, she took his arm. His stomach flipped, and he felt like he'd won the lottery. He dragged his eyes off her and stared after his grandpa. Together, they walked down the aisle and followed them to the foyer.

The girl let go of his arm and hugged Helen. "It was beautiful. I'm so happy for you, Nana. Congratulations."

Nana? Oh. *Oh*. Of course, she was Helen's granddaughter. He'd seen pictures in Helen's house when he'd gone for dinner a few weeks ago. They didn't do her justice at all and must've been several years old.

In person, she was a vision. A vision that he couldn't afford to get involved with. He shook his grandpa's hand and slapped him on the back.

"Congrats, Pops."

Ray just nodded, a big grin on his face as he turned back to his bride. The girl stayed beside Helen, so he fell into line beside her. She skittered around him like a little bird, careful not to venture too far from mama bird. Or in this case, grandma bird.

The receiving line would funnel the crowd into the fellowship hall. The rest of the bridesmaids and groomsmen joined them, and the entire town stopped by to shake hands on their way to the reception.

The entire time they were taking pictures, he tried to ignore her. But the nature of being Best Man meant he stood beside her most of the time. She smelled like oranges, and more than once, he breathed deeply just to capture it.

When they finally approached the main table at the reception, he pulled out her chair. He half expected her to dance and flit away from him, but she sat. She barely glanced at him through her long lashes, but he took another breath and tried to distance himself.

He sat beside her as the food was served. Avoiding eye contact during the surrounding conversations made it awkward.

He turned to her and held out his hand as a server placed their plates on the table. "I'm Mason, Ray's grandson. You're Helen's granddaughter?"

She wiped her hands on her dress and pasted an overly bright smile on her face. Finally, she looked him in the eye. "Yes, I'm Lucy. It's nice to finally meet you."

"You too," he said, enveloping her long fingers in his big hand. He felt like a bear pawing at an orange. She was a delicious delicacy, and he was a big oaf.

"I guess we're family now, huh?" he asked, cutting into his chicken. She fiddled with her fork and squirmed on the chair, then nodded.

"I guess you can call me your stepcousin?"

She laughed and nodded, the sound enchanting him. "I've never had a stepcousin before. I have a few cousins on Nana's side, but I haven't seen any of them in years."

The sadness on her face made his chest ache, and he changed the subject to try to cheer her up. "I guess you have nice, quiet holidays with her then?"

Lucy nodded, but didn't say anything, so he continued. "We don't usually get together for Thanksgiving, but we do a little small get together for Christmas. Not sure that my brother will be here this year, but what kind of Christmas present would you like?"

She glanced at him through her lashes, "Oh I couldn't possibly think of anything right now. I have everything I need."

She bit into her chicken and shook her head as she chewed. She still seemed reserved and lost in her own thoughts as she looked at the newlyweds, almost sad still.

He angled his body closer to hers. "Oh, come on. You have to have something you want. Every girl I know has a list a mile long."

She shrugged. "Sure, I have a list, but I don't even know you, and if you get me something, I'll have to get you something, and it'll turn into this big thing. How do you and Ray normally do Christmas?"

He took a drink before answering. "We normally go to dinner either before or after Christmas. I'm usually working, so I'm not guaranteed holidays, but since I'm working Thanksgiving, I should have Christmas off."

"What do you do?" The fork slid into her mouth with a grace that held him captivated before her words penetrated his brain.

"I'm a Texas Ranger." He frowned, not sure how much longer that statement would be true. "What about you?"

She took another bite, and he waited for her to chew. "I'll be graduating college in December, but I work at a nail salon in Denton and teach yoga a few times a week. I might be moving to Crimson Creek soon though."

The excitement and joy on her face made him relax, and he stopped paying attention to his words. "Ah, that makes sense. I thought you were the athletic type," he said.

She frowned and her body tensed. "What's that supposed to mean?"

He froze, fork halfway to his mouth. Shit, what had he said? "Uh, you've got muscle definition. Not a lot of women do, that's all."

She leaned forward, her frown growing deeper. "What are you trying to say? That I'm not feminine enough?"

He frowned and turned his head to face her, feeling the collar on his button-down shirt grow tighter. "What? No, not at all."

"Uh huh, sure." She stabbed her chicken with the knife and cut it so hard the knife screeched on the plate.

He winced. This was why he needed to stay away from women and relationships. He could never say the right thing, and it always ended in disaster. He shifted on the chair and rubbed his back, trying to ease the constant pain that radiated down his leg.

"I'm sorry, but that's not what I meant. You've got curves in all the right places, trust me." He felt his ears burning. Damn it, he needed to shut up already.

She shifted on her chair uncomfortably, but before he could open his mouth and shove another foot in it, his grandpa stood and tapped the knife against his glass.

The crowd hushed. "I'm not one for speeches, but I appreciate everyone comin' out today to celebrate with us. This is one of the happiest days of my life. I didn't think I'd have a second chance at love, but here we are. To Helen. May God give her patience in the years to come."

The crowd both chuckled and cheered to Helen. Then the speeches were on. A flurry of activity and a flow of wine led to more laughter. He didn't have a chance to talk to Lucy again.

Dancing was impossible because of the small fellowship hall, but everyone was elated to shower the couple with flowers at the end of the night. They drove away with coke cans tied to the tailgate of Pop's old truck.

He lost sight of Lucy as the crowd dispersed. So he told his few friends goodbye and hopped in his own truck. He wasn't too drunk to require a designated driver, and Pop's house was just a few blocks away.

A beat-up car was already parked when he arrived. He frowned, seeing movement in the lit bedroom upstairs. He pulled out his phone and checked his app, verifying that Pops wasn't home. He was at Helen's house before heading to their honeymoon in Colorado.

He got out of his truck, careful not to slam the door closed, and grabbed his duffel bag. He checked the doors of the car and found them locked. He looked inside but it was spotless other than a backpack.

He frowned. If it was some teenager hoping that the wedding would lead to an easy score in the house... Mason sighed and pulled his gun out of his back holster, then he walked up the steps on silent feet and unlocked the door.

The Ranger Gets His Girl: Chapter Two

Lucy stepped out of the shower and wrapped the towel around her body. The headache from the wine led her to the medicine cabinet, where she found some pain pills. She needed water though, so she opened the bathroom door.

Click. "Freeze, you're under arrest."

A gun was pointed at her head, and she shrieked. She threw the closed bottle of pain pills and fell to the ground, covering her head and curling into a ball.

"Lucy?"

She looked up at the behemoth and lowered her hands. "Mason?"

He lowered the gun to his side, and his brows rose as his gaze swept over her. "Uh," he stammered.

She looked down and gasped, quickly grabbing her towel and readjusting it. "What are you doing? Get out!"

He nodded, still staring, so she slammed the door with her foot. Her heart was hammering in her chest. Oh God, what had he seen? It's just her luck that the first guy to see her naked had been an accident.

"Lucy? Are you alright?" he called through the closed door.

She struggled to her feet and adjusted the towel, tucking the end into itself. She looked in the mirror and took a deep breath. Her hair hung wet and tangled around her pink face scrubbed almost clean of makeup. There was a zit on her chin and mascara leftovers smudged under her eyes.

"Lucy?"

She winced, tightening the towel as her heart still raced. "Yes, I'm fine. What are you doing here?"

"What am I doing here? This is my grandpa's house, remember? What are you doing here?"

Glancing around, she gathered her dress and underwear from the floor. "I had too much wine, so Ray offered his house for the night. They didn't say you'd be here too." She put on the dress, but damp skin made it cling to her. She reached behind her to struggle with the zipper.

"Yeah, well, they didn't tell me you'd be here either, but it's too late to drive back to Waco tonight. Look, are you sure you're okay?"

Her stomach flipped but she knew she had to face him. She couldn't stay in the bathroom all night or keep struggling with her dress. She wasn't a coward. She took a deep breath, held the towel and her underwear in front of her like a shield, and threw the door open.

He stood where she'd left him, but the gun was put away somewhere. His suit jacket was gone, and his white button-down shirt was rolled up at the sleeves with a gun harness over both shoulders. Arms crossed, his shirt looked ready to burst at the seams.

Standing face to face, he dwarfed her and filled the doorway. There was something about the way he looked at

The Mechanic Gets His Girl

her so intently, the way she could feel his presence soaking into her soul that made her mouth salivate.

His black hair was cut short on the sides, gray at the temples matching the five o'clock shadow giving him a sexy man of the world vibe. His hair looked almost long enough on top to run her fingers through, and the silkiness called to her, making her hands itch to test the texture.

She held her hands tightly to the towel and watched him warily. "See? I'm fine. Now if you'll excuse me, I'd like to get more comfortable clothes now."

He stepped back and waved a hand. She bolted down the hall and to the door at the top of the stairs, slamming it behind her. She breathed a sigh of relief as her phone dinged.

She pulled her leggings and yoga tunic on then checked her phone to see a message from her former college roommate.

Are you coming back to Denton tonight?

No, I'm staying in town, apparently with my new stepcousin. (eyes wide open emoji)

What does that mean?

Ray's grandson.

You're babysitting?

No. (laughing emoji) He's gotta be in his thirties or forties.

Oh, is he cute? Send pics.

Lucy gave a thumbs-up emoji and wanted to text Helen too but refused to intrude on her wedding night. She would just have to face Mason herself. Surely, they could share the house for the night without further incident.

She went through her memories to catalog what she knew of him. He was a Texas Ranger. Ray had two grandsons as his only family, and Mason was one of them. That was really all she knew.

She opened the door and ventured downstairs. He leaned against the counter with a glass of water in one hand, his biceps bulging, pulling his dress shirt tight.

Blue eyes captured hers as he watched her come to a stop and sit at the kitchen table.

He cleared his throat. "Sorry about earlier. I thought you were an intruder. If I'd known you were staying here tonight—"

She waved a hand and tried to relax in the chair. "Don't worry about it. Neither of us knew, so there's no use crying over spilled milk."

"Or spilled bottle of aspirin." He smirked, setting the pill bottle on the table along with a fresh glass of water. The tilt of his lips made her want to kiss him.

"Thanks," she said softly, looking away as she took the medicine. She'd never had this sort of reaction to someone this quickly before. Sure, she'd had crushes here and there over the years, but nothing this immediate or intense.

It made her stomach flip. She raised her phone and propped her elbows on the table, pretending to type as he rinsed out his glass in the sink. Then she took a picture and sent it to Taylor.

"You're welcome." He turned and leaned against the counter, staring at her with that intense gaze that sent shivers down her spine.

She smiled and tucked a wet strand of hair behind her ear. "Right, so I need to be up early tomorrow for a yoga class in Denton. I'll see you at Christmas?" She hopped up and avoided eye contact as she darted for the door.

"You never said what you wanted for Christmas," he said.

She put a hand on the door frame that separated the

kitchen from the living room and stairs. His blue eyes swirled with emotions she couldn't read.

"We might be family, but there's no telling what Nana and Ray have planned for Christmas. Don't worry about me. It was nice to finally meet you, Mason."

And with that, she darted up the stairs and shut the bedroom door behind her. It was going to take a long time to go to sleep tonight. He was going to be right across the hall.

Her phone buzzed.

(wide-eyed emoji) Fuck, you need to go play the slots. You hit the jackpot with him.

He pulled a gun on me, Tay. Thought I was an intruder.

A gun? WTF did he have a gun?? Are you safe??

Yeah, he's a TX Ranger.

(laughing emoji, wide-eyed emoji) That's the most action you've ever gotten.

Shut up.

You gonna hit that?

Hell no. I'd never!

Chicken.

If she were a bolder woman, she'd march down there and proposition him. If she were Taylor, she would've already seduced him by now. While Lucy had learned a lot from their friendship, she wouldn't ever have the courage to just ask a guy for a casual encounter.

No, she was more of a long-term relationship type of person. She'd had the same boyfriend for a year in high school, but that was the most she'd ever let herself connect. It had been a nightmare by the end. Then there was all that with her mom.

Her mind turned to the past and threatened to tug her under the tumultuous memories.

December

"Welcome back, Nana! How was your trip?" Lucy asked as she slid into the booth across from Helen and Ray. They both practically glowed with this settled, content look on their faces.

"It was great. I'm glad we timed it right for your graduation."

Lucy nodded, her leg bouncing under the table. "Me too. I know it'll probably be my last graduation, and it means a lot that you're here. Both of you," she said, nodding to Ray.

Ray grinned, his bushy white eyebrows shifting as his face widened. "Wouldn't miss it for the world, kiddo. Neither of the boys went to college, so this will be a real treat for me."

The server came and took their brunch order. Graduation was a couple of hours away, so they had time for the couple to tell her all about their adventures in Colorado. They'd loved their honeymoon so much they'd gone back for some of the Christmas markets.

"We were afraid we might not make it back, with that snowstorm that popped up," Ray said as he bit into his biscuit.

When the meal was over, Helen pulled an envelope out of her purse and slid it over the table.

"What's this?" Lucy asked as she opened it. Her eyes scanned the letter and ticket. "Oh my God, are you serious?"

Helen and Ray both beamed, but Helen leaned forward, her eyes shining. "Yes, absolutely. We won it on the cruise that brought us together this spring, and who better to use it than you? Consider it a graduation present, sweet pea."

She looked at the dates on the ticket. "This is—I mean, I don't know what to say."

"Say you'll go," Helen said softly, her eyes shining. "You deserve a break. You've worked so hard going straight from high school to college and to now get your master's. It's time to relax before starting the next chapter of your life."

Lucy felt her throat close up and tears threaten. "Thank you," she said, afraid to say anymore. She didn't get a lot of gifts but to get one as big as this was once-in-a-lifetime.

Ray rubbed the back of his neck uncomfortably. "Yes, well, that's not the end of it either. You know how you've been staying at my house since the wedding?"

Lucy nodded, "Since I started working for Katie in town, it's been much easier than driving back to Denton every day. I appreciate it so much. Have you finally decided to sell the house?"

He grinned and shook his head. "Not quite. If you want to move out to Crimson Creek permanently, the house is yours for however long you want it."

Lucy's brows rose as she glanced from him to Helen and back again. "Are you serious?"

Helen laughed, "I hope you're more eloquent in that book you're writing."

Lucy's cheeks heated as she nodded. After all her hard work, her life was finally coming together.

Ray fiddled with his drink, so Helen patted his leg and said, "You don't have to pay rent, but you'll need to cover the utilities and cable or anything else you need. Please say yes. Having you back in Crimson Creek this semester has been... more important to me than I thought it'd be. If you move into the house, it'll make me feel like it's more of a permanent thing."

Lucy's eyes stung as she held her hand out over the table. The past semester, she'd been commuting to Denton for classes, having only needed one more in-person class to go along with her dissertation. She'd quickly gotten the job with Katie at the salon and had just in the past few weeks started teaching more yoga at the yoga studio under Holly.

Now that she was graduating, she'd have more time to spend writing her novel, something she'd always talked with Helen about. Since she'd been a child and had hung out at the library after school while her grandma worked the front desk, she'd been determined to publish her own books. It was a dream that Helen had whole-heartedly supported for years.

She squeezed Helen's hand. "I don't know what to say. I think I need to talk to Taylor first about the living arrangements."

"Holly will be looking for you to take over more classes, what with her being pregnant with the twins," Helen said, her face brightening with a grin.

Lucy nodded as the server came to cash out their meal. Ray insisted on treating them in honor of her graduation.

Thankfully, the graduation ceremony was indoors because there was a frigid chill to the wind that afternoon. When all was said and done, Lucy agreed to their Christmas plans for the following weekend before kissing them both goodbye.

When they were gone, Taylor dragged her out for a late-night post-graduation party on campus. They arrived at a house on the seedier side of town and tipped their driver.

"Two drinks, Tay. That's it. It's too cold to be out all night," Lucy said, flipping the hood of her jacket up.

"Oh, come on. Don't be a spoilsport. This is your last hurrah, Luce. Live a little before you grow up and adult for real." Taylor practically skipped up the porch steps and opened the door.

Loud music assailed them, but several people turned to see who was here.

"Hooray! Taylor's here," two guys said, clinking their beers together with a grin. Taylor threw her jacket off, revealing a too short skirt and a sweater with a v-neck cut down almost to her belly button.

"That's right, bitches. I have arrived," she waltzed into the crowd with a laugh, leaving Lucy to pick up her coat and shut the door. She looked around while she laid both jackets on a dining table immediately to the left of the door.

To the right was a large living room with two couches and a loveseat. A few couples were already making out where they sat. Behind one couch in the corner was a DJ with some complicated speaker system.

Lucy snorted to see the DJ wearing sunglasses inside. At night.

She'd lost count of how many parties Taylor had dragged her to over the past six years. Inevitably, she found herself in the kitchen pouring drinks. It was easier to be the drink girl and take care of everyone else than actually interact with people.

She didn't mind people. It was good book research to come to places like this and observe the human condition. It was fascinating to see. Sometimes she would make bets with herself on which person would slap someone first.

The longer she'd been in college with Taylor, the better she'd gotten at her game. She smiled and handed over a drink to a girl who was already swaying. Another guy walked up for a drink.

She set the vodka down and glanced up, a smile on her face. "What can I—oh. Oh no."

Her smile froze on her face. It was Mason, but not the Mason she'd met a few months ago. Instead of a neatly tailored suit, he now wore hipster jeans, pristine black shoes, and a black silky polo golf shirt. Her heart skipped a beat as he crossed his arms. Holy hell, those biceps were going to be the death of her.

His brow lifted in challenge. "Oh no indeed. What do we have here? Does your grandma know you're at a place like this?"

She frowned and shook her head. "No, does your grandpa?"

There was a shout behind them, then someone started yelling, "Dance, girl, dance!"

Mason looked back at the crowd and frowned.

Lucy narrowed her eyes. "You've dyed your hair. Trying to reclaim your youth, old man?"

Disappointment shot through her like an arrow. She'd thought he was older, a real adult. Real adults didn't go to frat parties looking for young college girls to hook up with. She'd misjudged him.

She thought she'd gotten better at identifying dirt bags, but apparently not.

His head spun to face her at her words, and his eyes narrowed. Some guy bumped into him and grabbed the tequila bottle. "Hey, watch it," the guy slurred as he poured the drink mostly into his solo cup.

Mason rolled his eyes and stepped around the island toward Lucy. She backed up, but he neatly boxed her into the corner with one hand on either side of the counter. He leaned in, the manly scent of him overwhelming her with his nearness. Her hands fluttered to his biceps. She was ready to push him away but was conflicted. Her body said bring him closer, but her head said run.

Their bodies were close, and she could smell his aftershave. Something musky, woodsy. It made her brain stop resisting, and she leaned into him.

"Don't move, little bird. Yes, I dyed my hair. Yes, I'm thirty-five and at a frat party, but it's not what you think. I'm here in a professional capacity, and I need you to not blow my cover, got it?"

She sucked in a breath, making her chest graze his.

Just then, Taylor came bounding up behind him. Her eyes widened when they met Lucy's over Mason's shoulder. "Oh, thank God, I was thinking no one was going to pop that cherry. Do you need a condom? I've got a few in my bra."

She started to dig inside, but Lucy was afraid her boob would come out. "No, no, it's not like that."

"It might be like that," Mason growled into her ear. "Just play along."

He kissed the side of her neck, making her shiver and her eyes flutter. Holy mother of pearl. Mason was one hot mother fucker. She blushed as she heard her grandmother reprimanding her in her head for that language.

Taylor grinned. "Right," she drawled out. "I'll just leave this on the table, shall I? We really need to invest in a bowl of free condoms or something at these parties."

Lucy couldn't catch her breath with Mason so close. She squeezed his biceps as panic set in, but he pulled back and turned to smile at Taylor. "That's a good idea," he nodded his head.

Lucy could practically see Taylor swoon as she got a good look at him, and it was too early for her to be drunk.

She snorted and poured another drink. This time, she chugged it herself.

Taylor hooted. "Hell yeah, now it's a party! Ready to dance, Luce? Lover boy here can drag you upstairs when we're done."

Lucy didn't have time to argue. Taylor grabbed her hand and dragged her into the other room. She looked over her shoulder in time to see Mason slide the condom off the table and into his pocket.

Grab your copy…
vinci-books.com/ranger-gets-his-girl

About the Author

Jane Poller always wanted to write romance. After years of back and forth, she finally took the plunge and never looked back. She still teaches online and homeschools her teenagers full-time. But with a commercial pilot and Army veteran for a hubby, she has a lot of free time in between his trips to write whatever stories the characters demand of her. She lives in Texas in a small town on four acres with her family of four, plus their two dogs. When she's not doing all the family things, she's reading in the hammock by the pond, writing in the treehouse, quilting and crafting, or arguing with her characters who refuse to do what she wants.

Acknowledgments

Special shout out to my hubby, who pushed me to start and finish this book so I wouldn't go crazy from the deadline. I really should listen to you more often. ;)

Special thanks to Clare for pushing me and always acting interested in my plot musings. Bonnie and Annie, y'all are invaluable and I appreciate your feedback so much. And finally, thanks to the Tease Me Collection Anthology. You welcomed me into the fold and spurred me to be the best we could be. It was a fun ride, and I thoroughly enjoyed it.

www.ingramcontent.com/pod-product-compliance
Ingram Content Group UK Ltd.
Pitfield, Milton Keynes, MK11 3LW, UK
UKHW040121190326
469155UK00004B/1294